HONEYMOON WITH A PRINCE

NICOLE BURNHAM

For Geralyn Dawson, Christina Dodd, and Susan Sizemore.

Knowing you has made all the difference.

CHAPTER 1

KELLY CHASE WOKE WITH A START, nearly knocking over her daiquiri as she flung her hand to the right, in the direction from which she could've sworn she'd heard the low *whunk* of design books slamming into the floor.

She blinked when the sounds of rolling surf and distant laughter reminded her she was nowhere near the office. While her heartbeat slowed to its normal rhythm, she cursed herself for trying to ruin a perfectly good honeymoon by dreaming about work.

Then again, her friends accused her of ruining a perfectly good honeymoon by opting to take it without the groom.

Having barely rescued the daiquiri, Kelly pushed herself to a seated position, righted her sunglasses, and took a long, fortifying sip of the sweet pink drink. Before her, a cerulean sea spread out as far as the eye could see, its surface glittering in the late afternoon sunshine. Small boats bobbed along on the waves, some carrying fishermen back to shore after a day of work, while others served as floating escapes for those who wished to relax away the summer undisturbed.

Satisfied that all was as it should be, Kelly stretched back on her lounger and closed her eyes. Rays from the sun seemed to warm her from the inside out, lifting her mood, making her feel unencumbered and free.

No matter what friends and family said, this trip was absolutely the right decision.

Since her presumed groom was a first-class jerk, boarding the plane alone yesterday for the overnight flight to Europe seemed the perfectly logical thing to do and not ruinous at all. She'd wanted to visit the idyllic Mediterranean island of Sarcaccia since she'd first heard of the place. Even if none of her friends could accompany her on short notice—either that or they didn't want to, given that she'd dumped her fiancé ten days before the wedding—she wasn't about to let the airline ticket and rented villa go to waste.

Besides, not only had she paid all the deposits for the trip out of her own hard-earned cash, she'd put in countless pushups, crunches, and treadmill miles while living on salad, egg whites, and veggies over the last three months, all so she'd look good in her wedding photos and the pricey bikini she now sported. She wasn't about to let *that* go to waste.

The breeze picked up, ruffling Kelly's hair and cooling her skin just enough to make her drowsy again. She'd earned this nap, in this chair, on this beach, even if she did end up dreaming about work. And frankly, dreaming about work wouldn't be so bad—she'd never been afraid of hard work, since it gave her life a purpose—if she hadn't sold her business for the presumed groom.

The thought of oh-so-perfect Ted Robards and all his promises made her mutter aloud, "Arrogant jackass."

Woof.

The unexpected sound was so deep and close to her ear that Kelly launched from her chair, carried by the warm blast of dog breath that signaled a sizable beast. This time, she did knock over the daiquiri.

Her heart threatened to pound out of her chest as her feet hit the sand and she whirled to look behind her. A dog the color of rich, dark chocolate and with roughly the size and build of a German Shepherd sat at the head of her chair. A dark tongue hung from between pointed teeth, bouncing up and down as he panted.

"Hello," she addressed the creature, who seemed perfectly harmless aside from his massive build. His strong shoulders and lean frame didn't budge as she stared at him. It was as if he'd been trained to sit in that particular spot until commanded to do otherwise. "You surprised me. Would your bark happen to sound like a thick stack of books hitting the floor?"

The dog cocked his head as if he understood. He was gorgeous, all restrained muscle and shiny fur. Though she'd grown up with dogs and loved them to pieces, she'd never seen one quite like this. His eyes were a surprising blue and his nose long and lean, ending in a wet black snout. When she put a hand on the arm of her lounger, allowing the big boy to come close and sniff, then nuzzle, she discovered his short coat was soft as the fuzz on a newborn kitten.

"My goodness, but you're beautiful." Once he seemed comfortable enough with her, she scratched his triangular ears, which stood at attention, then moved her hand down his neck to feel for a collar. Nothing. Despite the lack of identification, the dog seemed well-loved. His weight was healthy, his eyes clear, and his coat neat, especially given that he was at the beach. She scanned the chairs nearby. Most were unoccupied, since the majority of beachgoers who'd arrived early in the morning to claim their spots had now left for the day. Of the few that remained, none appeared to be searching for a dog.

"You're welcome to stay here if you like," she said as she cautiously resumed her seat in the lounger. Hoping he knew a few basic commands, she urged him to lie down beside her. He stepped forward, so he was at her hip, then sat once more and cocked his head, as if waiting for instruction.

Testing one of the hand gestures she'd used for her own pets when she was a kid, she urged, "Down."

No dice. She tried a few different gestures. Different commands. Still no luck.

"Oh, come on. The least you can do is lie down like a good boy after causing me to lose a very expensive drink. Bar service on this beach is infrequent and not at all reasonably priced."

He scooted closer, then rested his head on her thigh. His gaze shifted to meet Kelly's in a not-so-subtle hint.

"You" —she rubbed circles behind the dog's ears— "sure know how to kiss up. Do you do this with your owner, too? I bet you do."

The dog let out a low, happy whine of satisfaction, then promptly turned around and stuck his butt in her lap.

"You've gotta be kidding me," she murmured, but since the dog seemed hungry for attention—or a good scratch—she obliged. "You'd better not have picked up any fleas in this sand."

As the dog shifted to get closer to Kelly, she discovered he was wet under the uppermost layer of his coat, close to the skin. She glanced toward the water, wondering if that's where his owner might be. A white boat, about the right size to carry four to six people for a day of fishing, approached the local marina about a hundred yards down the beach from her. From this vantage point, Kelly couldn't tell how many people might be on board or if they were looking for a dog, but she didn't pick up any unusual vibes. Another two men stood at the walk-up bar where the dock met the beach, but given that they'd passed her a few times earlier that afternoon carrying beer bottles and large bowls of appetizers with no sign of a dog at their heels, she doubted the big boy was theirs. Behind the bar, a walkway leading to a set of six boat slips stood empty. Five boats were docked and covered for the day. She assumed the vacant slot belonged to the white boat.

She glanced in the other direction, toward the parking lot and the cliffs that framed the beach, but nothing indicated the dog had come from there, either.

The dog let out another low moan and shoved its rump harder against Kelly's hand.

"You're incorrigible," she complained, though she continued to give the dog attention. After a few minutes, he let out a deep, throaty groan, then flopped in the sand beside her, turning so his head rested on the lounge chair near her hip. Though his body went lax, his eyes remained open, scanning the area as if watching over her.

Soon someone would miss this dog. Wouldn't they?

Keeping one hand tucked into his short fur, she leaned back in the lounger and waited. Soon the sun would dip low enough to cool the air and chase the last of the beachgoers home. If she couldn't find the owner by then, she supposed she'd need to call the local police. There had to be some type of animal control organization on the island. Hopefully they'd find the owner and not send the boy to the pound.

She couldn't bear that thought.

"You're fine with me," she whispered. It felt reassuring having a dog to keep her company after all the upheaval of the past few weeks. He likely needed love, just as she had. She most certainly wasn't going to let down this sweet dog the way Ted—the liar—had done to her.

As if he understood, the dog pushed himself out of the sand and climbed into the lounger beside her, shoving Kelly to the very edge as he squeezed against her with an *oomph.*

Kelly laughed, but allowed him to take over the space. "I bet your owner doesn't let you do this on the sofa at home, huh, boy?"

He let out a whiny grumble in response, then plunked his head on her shoulder.

It wasn't her idea of a honeymoon cuddle, but she had to admit it was infinitely better than sharing her chair with Ted.

With any luck, she'd never see him again.

Massimo Barrali held a hand over his eyes, shielding them against the glare of the setting sun as he walked the beach. Somewhere, likely jumping in and out of the surf, he'd eventually find his dog.

He only hoped he wouldn't find the crazy thing in trouble. Gaspare wasn't exactly a people dog. He'd been trained to protect Massimo and—though he was never aggressive—preferred not to associate with most other humans. Water, on the other hand, did strange things to Gaspare. While Sarcaccian Shepherds were bred to work with livestock and thrived on running through the rough terrain of the island's high country, Gaspare seemed more at home frolicking in any body of water to which he could gain access. The ocean, lakes, even—on one memorable occasion—the fountain behind the royal palace. It was the one situation in which Gaspare's rigorous training failed.

Massimo's gaze traveled from the surf toward the seaside bar, where two men nursed beers and chatted with the bartender, to the large storage locker beyond it. A lifeguard busied himself dragging lounge chairs from the incoming tide and stashing them in the wooden structure so they'd be protected overnight. Beyond the lifeguard, a family trudged toward the steps leading to one of the private villas that lined this section of beach. Towels were draped over their shoulders, the father carried a small cooler, and the teenaged son and daughter elbowed each other as they walked. Despite signs that the beach was emptying, the dog didn't materialize.

Since Massimo couldn't call for Gaspare without drawing attention to himself, he turned from the dock and made his way along the shore in the direction opposite the bar, toward the parking lot. Gaspare was an intelligent dog. Perhaps he'd simply gone to the car, knowing it was time to head home.

Massimo swore to himself as he strode along the beach, his mood becoming blacker by the moment. It was his own fault, of course. He should've known Gaspare would leap overboard and doggy paddle the last two hundred meters to shore. The beast itched to swim from the moment he'd realized Massimo was driving him to the boat dock for a spur-of-the-moment fishing excursion this morning. Unfortunately, Gaspare's wild jump angered a group of nearby fishermen, who'd been compelled to yank their lines as the dog approached. Massimo had to spend several minutes soothing their tempers. He couldn't have them telling their friends—or the media—that Prince Massimo and his dog ruined their afternoon catch. Unfortunately, during the time Massimo spent making nice with the fishermen, he'd lost track of Gaspare.

Next time, he'd come alone. Despite humoring his parents' suggestion that he always have Gaspare along as security when he spent time outdoors by himself, no good came of bringing the dog fishing. Then again, he'd rather have Gaspare for company than anyone else.

A wave rushed up the beach and over Massimo's feet as he made his way along the firm sand at the water's edge. A few lounge chairs remained on this section of the beach, but only one appeared occupied. A pair of long, lean legs stretched up from the lounger's footrest toward an extremely firm, round backside clad in a tiny pink bikini. The woman lay on her side, showing off a hip perfectly curved for a man's hand, seemingly oblivious to the fact she was the last remaining person on the beach. Normally pink wasn't his favorite color—he'd always had a strong preference for bright red or a sexy, not-so-innocent white when it came to bikinis—but given what this woman looked like from the waist down and the fact he had to pass her to reach the parking lot, he suspected he was about to discover the wonders of pink.

As he moved closer, what he saw from the waist up wasn't bad, either. A shoulder rounded with just enough muscle to be firm without being hard. A long, elegant neck. A tangle of shiny, reddish-brown hair exactly the color of the palace's infernal afternoon tea twisted on top of the woman's head.

Then he heard the moan.

He paused, stunned. Only one creature on Earth made that sound, and then only in one instance. Gaspare. Getting his butt scratched. Something the dog never allowed any human to do other than Massimo and—on rare occasions—Massimo's sister, Sophia.

Who in the world was this woman, and what had she done to his dog?

He covered the stretch of sand that separated them in quick steps. When he came to the base of the chair, he drank in the sight of Gaspare's large body wedged alongside the woman's. Sure enough, she had one arm stretched to rub his dog's backside. Gaspare's head was tipped back in ecstasy. And no wonder...even with her eyes covered by a pair of large sunglasses, the woman in the chair looked better from the front than from the back. She gave no indication she'd seen him approach; he got the impression her eyes were closed.

Gaspare, on the other hand, let out another moan and wiggled closer to the woman, deliberately ignoring Massimo.

"You are unbelievable, you nutty dog. Did your owner send you away for excessive cuddling?" she said just loud enough for Massimo to hear. So, an American. And the soft voice was every bit as sexy as the woman.

A slow smile spread across his face. *Good dog.*

CHAPTER 2

"Excuse me, but I believe that's my dog," a resonant, accented male voice cut into Kelly's nap.

The dog let out a rumble of protest as Kelly used one elbow to push herself to a seated position and took in the sight of a tall, athletic-looking man standing at the foot of her chair. Despite being clad in nothing but a pair of olive green swim trunks and a thin white T-shirt, he held himself with the authority of a police officer or military commander. And no wonder...the man had a body that appeared honed by years of physical training, including rock-hard abs his T-shirt did nothing to hide. He was every bit as gorgeous and intimidating as his dog.

She doubted he'd respond to gentle coaxing and a scratch of the ears. Rubbing his butt was definitely out of the question.

That thought left her fumbling for words, all too aware of the fact she wore nothing more than a miniscule bikini. All she managed was a quiet, "Oh. Sorry." Though what prompted her to say it to a man who let his dog stray—however good-looking the man might be—she had no clue.

The jet lag from yesterday's long flight to Rome and the second, shorter flight to Sarcaccia must be taking its toll on her brain. Surely she'd learned her lesson the hard way when it came to kowtowing to good-looking men.

"I would ask your forgiveness for allowing him to bother you, but you both seem quite content," the man continued. "Normally, he's not so friendly."

Kelly couldn't help but grin at the consternation seeping into the man's voice. "He seems quite friendly to me. He's been here awhile."

"My apologies for that. I was coming in on my boat and he decided to take a swim. I'm afraid he got ahead of me." The man stepped to the side of her lounge chair and extended his hand. "I'm Massimo. Your friend here is Gaspare."

The dog's head lifted at the sound of his name. He looked to Kelly with what she'd swear was an expression of regret before turning to his owner. With exaggerated effort, the dog loped from the chair to the sand, then turned to sit by the man's side, as if he knew this was his expected place.

"I'm Kelly. Kelly Chase," she replied, accepting the man's handshake. As his fingers wrapped around hers, she noticed the broad span of his palm. He seemed exactly the type of man to own a large dog.

"Thanks for watching him. He tends to stay close to my side, but water is his weakness. He can't resist."

She eyed Gaspare, who appeared every inch the vigilant protector at the moment, sitting with his ears perked and his eyes scanning the beach. "So this is what he's usually like? Is he trained as a guard dog?"

"He is."

She pushed her sunglasses atop her head and squinted, giving the man an obvious head-to-toe perusal. *Obvious* wasn't her typical approach, but it was her vacation, after all, and it wasn't as if she'd see the guy again. Besides, something in his demeanor made her want to rebel, to show him she couldn't be cowed by a domineering man.

Domineering. Yes, that definitely described the man looming over her.

His dark hair was cropped close, though not quite to military standards. Eyes somewhere between brown and green assessed her from a perfectly symmetrical face grounded by a firm jawline. Arms tanned from the sunshine rose to shoulders encased in a healthy amount of muscle and a chest that didn't need puffing to attract female attention...or dissuade an attacker.

Even his name suggested as much. *Massimo* struck her as...well, massive. She wouldn't describe him as massive, though. Authoritative and self-possessed, certainly. And yes, tall and broad-shouldered, but not to excess. He wasn't out to win bodybuilding competitions. His physical power was more graceful and efficient than forceful and ground-shaking.

She wondered what he'd been like as an infant for his parents to choose such a strong name.

"You don't seem the type to need a guard dog, Massimo."

That drew a wry smile from him. "Good thing, since the boy has an Achilles heel where water is concerned and we're surrounded by it."

Massimo's gaze moved to the small table alongside her chair. The smile disappeared. "Is Gaspare responsible for that?"

She glanced toward her spilled drink and the glass that had fallen to the sand. She retrieved it and set it on the table so the bar owner would see it. "He is. No big deal, though."

"The least I can do is buy you another."

So he went for obvious, too. "If you haven't noticed, the bar is closing."

He didn't spare it a look. His gaze remained locked with hers, almost in challenge. "I have a better place in mind. But if we go there, dinner's included. The owner will insist."

Adrenaline fueled by the unknown surged through her. It'd been ages since any man besides Ted flirted with her, and never had a guy—let alone a guy this stunning—been so direct. It was as if he assumed she'd go.

"You know the island, then? Do you live here?" From what she'd read about Sarcaccia when booking her honeymoon, most beachgoers in this area were either vacationers or day-trippers from Italy, since the ferry ride from the Italian coast to Sarcaccia's capital city of Cateri only took forty-five minutes. Locals preferred private swimming pools or driving to beaches on the far side of the island.

A quizzical look passed over his face, vanishing as quickly as it appeared. "I do. I take it you're a tourist?"

"I am. And I'm not exactly dressed for dinner." She waved a hand to indicate her skimpy swimsuit, though from the appreciative glimmer in his eyes, he'd already noticed. That look alone made notching up the treadmill incline over the last few months worthwhile.

"So is that a no?"

"No."

She hesitated, dizziness grabbing her as if she stood at the edge of a cliff and had been dared to look over the side. Never before had she gone out with a complete stranger. Even her blind dates were with friends of friends, so she'd known something about the men beforehand.

Yet that hadn't prevented her from being hurt. At least this guy was loved by his dog. And frankly, she wanted to prove to herself she could hold her own with a man like Massimo.

"It's a yes," she finished, because why the hell not? She'd planned on spending her so-called honeymoon alone, deciding how best to piece her life back together, but perhaps this was the universe's way of forcing her to face her fears. Massimo seemed the perfect challenge after her time with the suave, suited-up Ted. Or perhaps he was the antidote to Ted. "I'll need to change first."

He angled a thumb toward the parking lot. "I'm over there if you'd like a ride to your hotel. Or I could meet you if you tell me where you're staying. Your preference."

"I'm actually renting a place above the beach." She turned and indicated the small whitewashed villa she'd reserved months ago, forking over a hefty deposit to secure the premiere location. The sea views and staircase to the beach pictured on the villa's website had sold her. "If you give me ten minutes, I'll meet you—and Gaspare—at the lot. Does that work?"

"Take your time." His grin was devastating, making her wonder just how adventurous her evening might become. "Gaspare and I will wait."

A LOW *WOOF* from Gaspare signaled Kelly's approach.

"Your favorite girl is back, you traitor," Massimo said under his breath. He still couldn't believe Gaspare acted so out of character. Nor could he believe he'd actually asked the woman out. In the two weeks since he'd returned home, he'd wanted nothing more than to escape the endless stream of people wanting to know how he was, grilling him about what he'd experienced, asking when he'd appear at this or that party. All he'd wanted was to be alone.

Maybe he'd hit his head while he'd been in Africa, because nothing else could explain the urge that'd caused the word *dinner* to escape his lips. He knew nothing about her, other than the fact she was American—judging from her accent—and that his dog reacted to her as he'd never before reacted to a stranger. He supposed that alone caused the invitation to pop out of his mouth before he had a chance to reconsider it, though her incredible figure and unassuming smile hadn't hurt.

That and she apparently had no idea who he was, which was as compelling as Gaspare's interest in her. When she'd pushed herself to a seated position, there'd been no, "Oh, you're..." or "Has anyone told you that you look like...?" Not even the usual spark of recognition followed by an attempt to play it cool, as he was used to seeing whenever people connected his face with the island's famous royal family. Nor did she display the fakery he'd come to expect from tabloid reporters hoping to trick him into sharing personal information. Instead, she'd spoken to him as if he were her equal. As if she were *deigning* to consider him her equal.

However, as Massimo had waited by his Jeep, using the time to pour a bowl of water for Gaspare and to duck into one of the changing huts to don more appropriate clothing, he found he didn't regret the invitation. Spending the evening with the mysterious Kelly

Chase meant skipping his family's regular Sunday dinner, which was no great loss. A so-called family dinner was never simply family where the Barralis were concerned; rather, the tradition offered foreign dignitaries the chance to wine and dine with the royals amidst the splendor of the palace, all in the hopes that political and economic partnerships could be formed.

The last topics he cared to discuss tonight were politics or economics. When dining with dignitaries, he had to project a certain persona. He wasn't simply Massimo, but Prince Massimo Barrali, a representative of his entire country. Every word he uttered, expression on his face, or gesture he made became magnified in importance, to be dissected by the news media—and on occasion, the paparazzi—on the evening news.

Spending his Sunday night with a woman who knew nothing of his heritage, his money, or his social connections should prove refreshing. Besides, it'd been months since his libido made so much as a momentary appearance. Even if he didn't get laid tonight—and he got the impression Kelly-from-the-beach wasn't even first-date-kiss easy, despite the fact she'd agreed to a date without knowing a thing about him—it was reassuring to know his body still functioned on all cylinders. He'd been starting to wonder.

"You changed clothes," Kelly said as she approached his red Jeep. She swept a hand to indicate her own outfit. "I hope this is appropriate for whatever you have in mind? I forgot to ask before I went to change."

"Perfectly appropriate," he assured her, though the first word that came to mind was *stunning*. He'd thought the bikini suited her. The light blue sundress she now wore made her expressive, almond-shaped brown eyes stand out almost as much as it highlighted an absolutely perfect set of breasts. Never in a million years would he imagine a dress improving on what a bikini could display, but this one did. Better yet, she'd left her auburn hair twisted atop her head, which was probably for the best, given their transportation.

"Hop in," he urged, opening the passenger door of his Jeep. Gaspare leapt in ahead of her, accustomed to his spot on the passenger seat, but gamely moved to the back when Massimo shooed him. Once she was seated, he closed her door and then walked around to take his own seat. Before starting the vehicle, though, he grabbed Gaspare's collar from between the front seats and snapped it around the dog's neck.

"In case he runs away again?" she asked, eyeing the tag bearing a phone number, but no name.

"That and it's the law here. It's a good thing you found him, rather than animal control." Lucky dog. He'd taken off the collar in case Gaspare went for a swim, not imagining that a swim would take the dog out of his sight.

Wouldn't make that mistake again.

"I hope you don't mind having your hair blown in the wind," he said as he fastened his seat belt. "I didn't plan on company when I left home this morning, so I didn't bother putting on the hard top."

"I already have beach hair going. An open-air ride is more likely to improve it than not."

Once they were out of the parking lot, Kelly turned to him and asked where they were heading. "Town's back there," she said, gesturing behind them. "Even I know that much."

Her casual tone contrasted with her stiff posture in an unspoken acknowledgement of the tension sizzling between them as they roared uphill, away from the beach and along the cliffside road overlooking the Mediterranean. As if they each knew they were doing something dangerous, unpredictable and out of their everyday routines by taking off with a stranger. He gave her a one-shouldered shrug. "Since you can walk to town from your villa, I thought you might appreciate a change, something different from the usual places that cater to tourists."

"I *am* a tourist."

"Would you prefer to go back?" He hoped not. Though he was generally left alone by locals used to seeing the royal family out and about, he didn't want to deal with any tourists who might identify him, particularly the types who'd whip out their cameras and ask him to pose with them.

"No. Different is good."

They rounded a hairpin curve that afforded a panoramic view of the sea. Kelly spun in her seat to take in the sight. "Speaking of different, this is amazing. You're probably used to it, but I could stare at this view for hours."

"Wait until the sun goes down. The sunset from the top of the hill is spectacular."

"It doesn't get old to you?"

"No." He surprised himself by adding, "I was in the military for the last six years and was out of the country. It's not the same elsewhere."

She absorbed that for a moment before asking, "Where were you?"

"Three months in Antarctica. Here and there in the Middle East. Mostly Central Africa, though." He left it at that. Even mentioning the place left him hollow inside. "What about you? Where are you from?"

"Dallas." Then she clarified, "It's in the United States."

The grin she brought to his face pushed thoughts of jungle heat and famine aside. "I know where Dallas is."

"I didn't want to assume." She shot him a sideways glance. "Though if you're from here, I'll take a wild guess that Italian is your first language. Your English is amazing. Did you study in the U.S.?"

"I was educated here. But I had an American" —he caught himself before saying *nanny*— "teacher when I was younger. My parents insisted I become fluent in at least two other languages and wanted me to learn from native speakers."

"Wow. Parents weren't ambitious for you at all, were they?"

"Not at all." They only wanted him to attend the best schools, then find the best possible wife and have amazingly brilliant, perfect children, all while working to strengthen Sarcaccia's governmental interests. "What about yours?"

"Same, I suppose." He could swear her voice caught, but she covered it by adding, "They weren't as adamant I learn foreign languages, though. Probably would've been better if they were. I only have high school Spanish."

"You speak dog. I've never seen Gaspare like he was with you."

"Lucky for me." She caught Massimo's eye before twisting in her seat to give Gaspare a quick rub under the chin. The flicker of amusement and attraction embodied in that quick look sent another hard jolt of desire through him. He turned his focus to the road, hoping she hadn't noticed how easily she'd captured his attention.

He drove over a high stone bridge, then around one more jaw-dropping turn to enter a small village. Centuries-old tile-roofed houses clung to the steep hill on both sides of the road. Glorious though the setting was, the stone and stucco structures weren't at all glamorous. The buildings showed signs of practical rural living, the type of home- and family-centered existence Sarcaccians outside the bustling capital city of Cateri believed contributed to their long, healthy life spans. Laundry fluttered from lines strung under windows, children's toys and potted plants littered tiny patios, and old men chatted about sports, politics, and the weather while sitting roadside in rickety chairs. The rhythm of life here was as predictable as the sun rising in the east and setting in the west, and it made Massimo's heart glad to see it.

Perched on the cliff side of the road stood the unassuming stone building he'd daydreamed about every time he opened a pack of sun-baked rations during his time in Africa. He slowed the Jeep and eased into its tiny parking area. Simply looking at the place made his mouth water.

"This looks more like someone's home than a restaurant," Kelly observed as he helped her out of the Jeep and they approached the narrow path leading to the front door. She seemed to take it all in at once—the moss peeking through the walkway, the painted tile mailbox attached to the corner of the building, even the scent of garlic and lemon that permeated the air—as her gaze swept the structure and the small roadside sign declaring it to be the location of Trattoria Giulia.

"It's both. The family who owns the place lives downstairs, on a lower level overlooking the water. They run a four-room bed and breakfast on the top floor and the restaurant is here on the main floor."

As they entered with Gaspare at their heels, Kelly paused to finger the pink and purple vinca that spilled from weathered terracotta pots on either side of the iron-hinged wooden door. "I like it already."

"Wait until you try Giulia's food. This is the real deal, not the tourists' Sarcaccia."

The restaurant was empty, which wasn't surprising given the early hour. Most diners didn't make their way here until seven or eight, sometimes later during the summer months, and a quick check of his watch told Massimo it was only five-thirty.

Gaspare plodded to a spot near one of the windows, then lay down on the stone floor and rested his chin on his front paws.

"He looks comfortable," Kelly commented. "Does this mean he's been here before?"

"Giulia allows him so long as he stays under the window. He knows the rules." At least when water wasn't accessible. "Have a seat," he suggested, pulling out a chair at the table nearest Gaspare. "Enjoy the view. I'll let her know we're here."

He crossed the dining room and pushed open the kitchen door even as he heard footsteps approaching from the other side.

"Anyone here who can feed me?" he called out in teasing Italian.

"Prince Massimo!" Giulia brushed her hands against her apron, then pulled him into a hug, stretching on her tiptoes to kiss him on both cheeks before stepping back to give him a top-to-bottom inspection, just as he'd expected she would. The wrinkles at the corners of her eyes deepened as she met his gaze once more. "I heard you were back. I hoped you would find time to visit your old friends."

"How could I not?" He surveyed the familiar kitchen. Freshly made ravioli covered one countertop, while hand-cut noodles hung to dry on a rack above them. A hunk of Romano cheese and a giant bowl of lemons sat nearby. The opposite countertop was stacked with fresh zucchini and tomatoes while the cutting board alongside it held a half-sliced zucchini and a chef's knife. Diced onions and garlic cloves filled bowls near the stove. The scent of warm bread filled the air. "This place is heaven."

And one of the few places he could go to be treated like one of the family. A *real* family.

"You are too thin." She poked his side and frowned. "What did you eat? Why did you not ask me to send you food, eh?"

"It wouldn't taste the same once it sat in a mail room. Besides, the best part of coming here is the company. Speaking of which" —he stepped back and gave her a waggle of his brows— "you look smashing."

"You flatter me because you wish to change the subject. You are too thin."

"I'm perfectly fine. Better shape than ever. But if you're concerned…well, I'm always ready to eat. I even brought a friend if you're able to serve an early meal. But" —he held up a warning finger — "I haven't mentioned who I am and I'm fairly certain she doesn't know. So please, call me Massimo. No titles, no deference. *Capiche?*"

Giulia treated him to an exaggerated eye roll, the head motion causing a few strands of hair to shake loose from her gray bun. "You bad boy. What did you do? Pick up a pretty tourist girl from the beach?" She cupped her hands in front of her chest, fingernails together, then swayed them back and forth. "One with a body made for the men? Like mine, when I was young and wild?"

"As a matter of fact…yes."

Giulia's eyes widened in shock before she shook her head and patted his chest. "Massimo, Massimo, so unlike you! More like your brother Prince Alessandro. Or Prince Stefano, before he found his Megan. The whole country talks about him, you know."

"So I've been told."

There was a spark in Giulia's eyes that indicated she wanted to hear the inside scoop on Stefano's relationship. While a lot had happened with Stefano while Massimo was away, Massimo wasn't in the mood to discuss details he didn't know, anyway. He'd rather get back to the mesmerizing woman waiting in the dining room, who knew nothing of famine, of grief, or of his famous relatives…at least in that they were related to *him*.

Pretending he didn't catch Giulia's hint, he gestured toward her loaded countertops and asked, "I assume this means we can eat, even though it's early?"

"You can always eat at my place. Go." She shooed him out of the kitchen. "Guillermo brought in some beautiful sea bass this afternoon. I'll be out with today's menu in a moment."

"Mind if I raid the wine cellar while we wait? Or grab that bottle of prosecco I saw on the sideboard?"

Her eyes fairly twinkled in merriment. "As long as you don't mind it on your bill, do whatever you like to impress your lady friend. Who am I to say no?"

CHAPTER 3

"WHAT'S THE STORY, Gaspare? Should I be worried?" Kelly reached down to scratch the dog's dark head. She'd probably need to wash her hands again before dinner, but petting Gaspare thrilled the dog at the same time it gave her an outlet for her nerves.

What in the world had she been thinking, going out to dinner with a stranger?

Then again, he'd given her no reason to worry. Yet.

Massimo had waited patiently by his car while she went to the villa to change—she'd peeked out from behind the curtains to see if he was still there while she'd tossed her bikini and towel into the bathroom and selected a clean sundress from her suitcase—and he didn't seem threatening, despite having shoulders and arms that could crush her if he put his mind to it. He'd even taken the time to pull a thermos from his car and pour water for the dog. A man who had no sense of responsibility—or who had no heart—wouldn't have thought to do that. And a man who'd wanted nothing more than sex likely wouldn't have brought her to a place like Giulia's.

She studied the trattoria as she continued to run a hand through Gaspare's coat in lazy strokes. Describing the place as a home hadn't been far off the mark. There were only six tables in the dining room, all of them made of sturdy, timeworn wood. Two of the tables were situated on either side of a stone fireplace that looked as if it enjoyed frequent use while the other four tables—including the one where she now sat—ran along the window. Another two tables, each constructed of metal hefty enough to withstand the elements, occupied a narrow stone patio outside. She stood for a better look and immediately sucked in a deep breath. Good thing she wasn't afraid of heights, given the drop not far from the patio's edge. Construction on the trattoria must have been nerve-wracking, given its position hundreds of feet above the Mediterranean, though with a marvelous visual payoff. The island's capital city of Cateri sprawled in the distance, beyond the crazy curves they'd navigated on the way from the beach. Closer in, trees and brush clung to the hillsides over the water, birds swooped along the coast, and boats of every description passed on the water far below.

"That's a long way down, Gaspare," she told him. "Not sure I'd want to eat out there on a windy day." A misplaced napkin could fly forever.

"We can sit out and enjoy our aperitivo," Massimo's accented voice came from behind her. Before she could turn, he reached around her to offer a narrow flute filled with sparkling wine. "Giulia happened to have a fabulous prosecco ready and waiting, and I do I owe you a drink."

She accepted the glass with a smile, amazed she hadn't heard him approach. Perhaps quiet movement became ingrained during his military training. "Will I be safe out there?"

A wry smile lifted the edge of his mouth, making him seem completely trustworthy, yet utterly dangerous to her self-control at the same time. "Perfectly," he assured her. "As long as one glass of prosecco doesn't turn into four."

"No worries there." It amused her that his answer addressed both of her safety concerns: the astonishing drop to the sea and the company.

He moved to a glass door beyond the row of tables and paused to regard Gaspare, whose eyes were now closed. "We'll let him nap."

They exited to the patio and once again Massimo held out a chair for her. The motion gave her a flashback to Ted doing the same thing when they'd dined at one of Dallas's fancy hotel restaurants. He'd always gone out of his way to impress her, sending oversized bouquets of flowers to her at work, nabbing front-row seats to concerts and sporting events, and—his favorite—taking her to high-profile restaurants.

Well, she'd been impressed. So had all her friends. Now she knew better. He'd done it all for the sake of appearances. He'd won her heart, he'd won over her friends and family, and she'd sworn never again to be swayed by fake chivalry.

Yet when Massimo pulled out the chair for her, it was different. There was no showmanship about it, no apparent attempt to impress her. Rather, the movement seemed habit to him, as unconscious as breathing or walking.

It threw her off balance.

Massimo set his prosecco on the table and turned his gaze toward Cateri. "I love the view from here. You see the city, you feel its energy, but you don't need to be a part of it. You can relax, enjoy a good glass of wine, and breathe the sea air."

She looked past him, toward the city, and nodded her agreement, but found her attention drifting back to Massimo himself. Now that his face was partially turned, she could study him more closely. His white shirt set off his smooth olive skin and brownish-green eyes in a way that had likely driven more than one woman mad with want. The collar was open just enough to give her a glimpse of the base of his throat. Somehow, he seemed sexier now than he had standing before her on the beach in only his swim trunks and the thin white shirt that emphasized his torso more than it hid it. And that view had been plenty sexy.

She was about to comment on a bright blue fishing boat gliding toward Cateri when the patio door opened and a short woman with graying hair piled into a loose bun came out carrying a tray of vegetables, crackers, olives, and cheeses. After she greeted them in Italian and set the appetizers and two small plates before them, she turned to

Kelly and introduced herself as Giulia. "Here are today's menus," she said, pulling two narrow laminated pages from the front pocket of her apron and handing one to each of them. "We also have fresh sea bass served with a light basil cream sauce and grilled tomatoes."

"Caught today," Massimo said with a wink.

"By my husband, Guillermo." Pride filled the older woman's voice. "Our other special today is ravioli stuffed with spinach and goat cheese." To Kelly she added, "All our pasta is made by hand from my great-great-grandmother's recipe. No big machines, no shortcuts. Best pasta on the whole island. And the goat cheese comes from a family farm down the street. All natural."

Kelly's stomach rumbled at the descriptions on the handwritten menu. Each looked divine, like a dish one might be served at a luxury resort's fanciest restaurant, yet the prices were surprisingly reasonable. "I think I want everything."

"Then have what you want today and come back tomorrow for another dish. This one" —she actually pinched Massimo's cheek— "always returns for my food. He knows where to find the best. And sometimes, he prepares it himself."

"No!" Kelly couldn't imagine this man in a kitchen, at least not one the size of the kitchen in her Dallas apartment. He'd barely fit.

"It is true!" Giulia laughed as if expecting Kelly's stunned reaction. "He begged me so many times for the secret to my tiramisu, I finally taught him. Better than listening to a grown man beg, yes?"

"I have never begged," Massimo retorted, and Kelly had to agree. She couldn't picture it.

"Wait until you see what I have for dessert tonight. You will beg."

Massimo shook his head while Giulia turned to Kelly and asked if she had any questions about the menu.

"None at all. The sea bass is very tempting, but after your description, I have to try the homemade ravioli."

"In that case, I'll take the sea bass," Massimo said without bothering to peruse the menu. "We can try each other's dishes that way."

"Wonderful!" Giulia took their menus and urged them to enjoy the patio as long as they liked. "Watch the sunset while you wait and help yourselves to more wine. Massimo knows where to find it. And this"—she pointed to one of the cheeses on the tray— "is Massimo's favorite. So you must try it."

His face lit as he looked at the tray. "The Roncal?"

Her hand flew to her heart. "You think I would forget? I keep it just for you."

"And I'm very grateful."

"She's wonderful," Kelly commented once Giulia departed for the kitchen. She took a long, decadent sip of her prosecco and leaned back in her chair. "This is exactly why I came to Sarcaccia."

"For Giulia?" Massimo raised an eyebrow and shot her a dimple-inducing smile. Man, but she loved dimples, and she hadn't noticed his until just this moment. He was probably so used to being forceful, the way he was on the beach, that it took a while for him to relax enough to let them appear. Sitting this close allowed her to see other details she'd missed before. A tiny white scar ran from the edge of his left eye to his hairline. And his eyes—while she'd certainly noticed the color and shape—she now realized weren't quite identical. The right appeared slightly larger than the left, as if he were deep in thought and about to squint with one eye. Oddly, she found the minor imperfection reassuring. It made him all the more human.

She met his smile with one of her own. "Sort of. I came to experience life in a way I haven't before. Seeing new places, meeting new people...it gives a person perspective."

If there was anything she needed after her Ted fiasco, it was perspective.

"That it does, for better or worse." She thought there was a note of regret in his tone, but it disappeared as he pushed the platter toward her. "The square crackers on this side of the tray are from a local bakery. Can't find them anywhere but Sarcaccia. Try one. They make a great palate cleanser."

She plucked one of the crackers from the tray, then watched as Massimo did the same. As they each bit into the thick, wheaty crackers, an unexpected frisson of heat passed between them, as if the breaking of bread constituted foreplay to a more intimate encounter.

A palate cleanser, as it were.

"So tell me," he said, swishing the last of his prosecco, "how is it that I found a beautiful woman like you alone on the beach? Did your friends abandon you to the surf while they went to party back in your villa? Or had they already been whisked away by strange men and their wandering dogs?"

"All very mysterious, isn't it?" she teased, not quite ready to admit she had no friends in the country, let alone back at her villa. "I mean, how is it that a good-looking man like you came to be alone on the beach?"

"I wasn't alone. I had Gaspare."

"Actually, *I* had Gaspare. So let me rephrase." She cleared her throat, then made a show of leaning across the table to interrogate him. "How is it that a good-looking man like you came to the beach with only your dog? Or had your friends already left with strange women?"

He seemed amused by that. "I see your point. I was out on my boat enjoying the sunshine and fresh air. I had spent the day...gaining perspective."

"And Gaspare?"

"Gaspare could care less about perspective. He only wanted to swim to shore. Though perhaps he thought I could use a dinner companion and decided to find one for me." He gathered their empty prosecco glasses, holding them by the stems in one hand, then stood and rounded the table. "Come on. You said you wanted to see new places. Let's explore Giulia's wine cellar."

Before she could say a word, he grabbed her by the hand and helped her from her chair. Not that it mattered. She suspected Massimo would lead her on an adventure whether she agreed to it or not.

Right now, she was definitely in the mood to agree.

THE WOODEN STAIRS leading from the main dining room to Giulia's wine cellar creaked with age as Kelly descended behind Massimo. Only the tiny antique chandelier hanging near the top kept the narrow space between the stone walls from delving into creepiness.

"This is like a movie set," Kelly told him, straining to see to the bottom. "How old is it?"

"Very." His voice was matter of fact. "The lower level of the house was built beside the entrance to a cave that's been used as cold storage for centuries. Eventually, Giulia's ancestors converted the cave to a wine cellar. They enclosed the area around the entrance and added the staircase to connect it to the main level about two hundred years ago."

She ran a hand along the wooden railing, which was shiny and worn smooth from use. "I suspect these are the original stairs, then. The centers of the treads even dip. I love that she's kept them. They suit the house." If this had been a cellar in the States, the stairs inevitably would've been replaced with something light, bright, and new that would pass safety inspections, but kill the romantic atmosphere.

When they reached the bottom of the stairs, Massimo flipped a switch to illuminate the room. She drew in a sharp breath at the sight. To their right, in the direction of the cliff's edge, stood three rows of wooden shelves containing hundreds of wines. Stone walls extended from the house's lower level to surround the shelves and seal off the room from the elements. To their left was the opening to a shallow cavern. It had been left in its natural state, with freestanding wooden wine racks placed in front of the rough rock walls. She imagined the temperature stayed cool and constant, summer and winter, making it the perfect location for the trattoria's wine collection. Beyond the wines, at the back of the small cavern, a large wooden shelf held several wax-encased wheels of cheese.

The cellar was exactly the type of romantic spot Kelly had hoped to explore when Ted mentioned Sarcaccia as a possible honeymoon location. Granted, as the CEO of a global communications company, Ted had been invited to attend a glitzy charity ball on the island.

While he'd liked the idea of combining business with pleasure, Kelly had wanted to see the island for its history, its cuisine, and its gorgeous beaches and architecture. Having Massimo show her this ancient cellar felt like being given a precious gift.

"If there's ever an apocalypse, this is where I want to be," Kelly said as she admired the unique space.

"As long as it's not today. I want dinner first." Massimo gestured to the bottles filling the shelves. "You have a preference? Whatever you like, Giulia is bound to have it."

Intrigued by the cavern area, she turned to the left and bent to glance at the bottles, being careful not to brush against them.

"Afraid you'll break them?"

"A bit." Cautiously, she used her index finger to wipe a light layer of dust off the nearest bottle. Her eyes widened fractionally as she scanned the label. "I've never heard of this winery, but judging from the date, the bottle's been stored here awhile."

He moved closer to look over her shoulder. "A twenty-year-old Barolo. If you like reds, this is a very good one. It's one of my father's favorites."

"And expensive, if I had to guess." Kelly stepped back, nearly bumping into him. "I hate to admit it, but I'm not enough of a wine connoisseur to tell the difference between a twenty-year-old wine and a five-year-old wine or if it even matters. As tempting as it might be to try, I don't need fancy."

"Perhaps you could try the other side of the cellar?" He angled his chin toward the area opposite the cave. "Those are all good, but not as 'fancy,' as you say."

"You don't mind?"

"Not at all. Everything Giulia stocks is of the best quality, so you can't go wrong."

She scanned the shelves while he waited near the bottom of the staircase and ran a hand along the old wooden railing. Though his stance was casual, there was something almost too casual about it. As if being in the cellar made him nervous. She wondered what brought it on, especially given that selecting a wine was his suggestion. Was it her? The tight space? A fear of offending Giulia if their dinner arrived while they were exploring the cellar?

She put it out of her mind and scanned the shelves, unsure what she sought. She withdrew a bottle at random from hip level, then slowly turned it to show Massimo the beige label with black lettering. "How about this? Would a Spanish wine offend your Sarcaccian sensibilities?"

He approached and wrapped his hands around hers as she cradled the bottle so he could better see the label. "*Torre Muga, La Rioja*," he read aloud as she tried not to think about the feel of his hands on hers. "No, this wouldn't offend my sensibilities at all. It's a great choice."

"Then we're set." Desire ripped through her as she raised her face to his. The man had the most sensuous eyes, even—perhaps especially —in the dim light. Though the flicker of attraction in his gaze was unmistakable, she still sensed he didn't care to linger in the cellar.

Just as he indicated that she should lead the way upstairs, footsteps thudded overhead and the door creaked open. Giulia descended and clapped her hands together and said, "Ah, I thought I might find you here. Tell me, what have you discovered?"

Kelly turned the bottle so that Giulia, who now stood on the bottom step, could read it. "Good, good. Did you make the selection or did Massimo?"

"I did, but he assured me this will be wonderful."

"And he is right. I have no bad wine in my cellar." She beamed at them even as another set of footsteps sounded on the staircase behind her. Without turning she said, "Dinner is ready, but I can serve you only if this man behind me moves out of my way."

A squat man with a close-clipped gray beard, brown slacks and a dark brown vest worn over a long-sleeved cream-colored shirt descended. Clunky leather shoes, the type reserved for those whose gait wasn't entirely stable, encased his feet. He deliberately ignored Giulia—though not without a mischievous lift to his lips meant for her to see—and greeted them. "My dear wife said you were home again, Massimo. Should I be jealous that she is hiding you in our cellar?"

"I asked her to run away with me, but she only has eyes for you." Massimo put one hand on the railing and leaned past Giulia to give the older man a warm hug and slap on the back. "It's good to see you again, Guillermo. I understand you provided tonight's dinner. Brought in some good sea bass today?"

"Don't I always?"

"And he's more than willing to brag about it," Giulia said at the same time.

Massimo smiled at the pair, but his hand gripped the railing tighter. Giulia introduced her husband to Kelly, but while Kelly made the appropriate greetings, Massimo's strained body language distracted her. As Guillermo descended, crowding into the small space to comment on the wine Kelly selected, Massimo moved to the far wall, his spine stiff and smile increasingly forced...at least to her mind.

"Are you all right?" Kelly asked him quietly as Guillermo made a playful comment to his wife in Italian.

"Of course," he replied, but didn't meet her gaze. "Just getting out of the way. Are you all right?"

"Fine." There was a disturbing brusqueness to his tone that made her realize he wasn't all right, despite what he claimed. To Giulia, she said, "I'm dying to try that homemade ravioli. Please tell me you weren't teasing us when you said that it's ready."

"I never tease about my food. Come, come." She waved for everyone to follow her upstairs. "Here, I will take the wine and bring it to the table for you. Do you want one of the window tables, or by the fireplace?"

Without looking to Kelly for her opinion, Massimo said, "We'll stay on the patio. It's warm out and there's a nice sea breeze."

Surprise registered on Giulia's softly lined face at his authoritative tone, but her response was easy. "Then I will bring the dishes outside. I promise, you are in for a treat."

CHAPTER 4

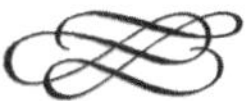

DINNER WAS every bit as decadent as Giulia promised. The sea bass practically melted in Massimo's mouth, the freshly steamed asparagus and mushrooms had been seasoned to perfection, and Kelly's wine choice was superb. Still, it had taken several minutes for his heartbeat to slow enough for him to appreciate the melding of flavors that danced across his tongue.

Much as he'd like to attribute his pounding pulse solely to the voluptuous woman before him, he knew better. He'd experienced the same sense of horror and sickening disorientation once before. He'd brushed off the event as an oddity then, but now...now he was as disturbed by the fact it happened a second time as he was by the event itself.

He blotted his mouth with his napkin and reached for his wine-glass, grateful his hand didn't shake at the same time he thought, *what the hell is wrong with me?*

A fight-or-flight urge had gripped him as he'd neared the bottom of the cellar stairs. He'd flipped on the light, expecting the bizarre sensation to dissipate, but it hadn't. In fact, seeing the thick walls around him while he'd breathed in the deep, earthy scent of the cave increased the disturbing sensation to such an extent he couldn't force it from his mind. And he was very good at forcing things from his mind if he didn't want them there. Years of military training provided him that useful skill. But this…this was different than the mind-over-matter methods he'd used to get through the physical punishment of basic training or sweltering days spent navigating bug-infested African jungles.

In his memory, Giulia's wine cellar was cozy, warm, seductive. A hidden corner of the world he could explore at leisure and the perfect spot to bring a date in hopes of enjoying a romantic first kiss. Tonight, however, the room seemed claustrophobic. Almost as if the ceiling were coming down on top of him and the walls forcing the air from his lungs. It'd taken all his military training to remain calm and remind himself that he was in no danger. He was in the safest of all safe havens.

What in the world caused his body to rebel that way? If there was one thing he prided himself on, it was his control. He resented holding it by such a narrow thread.

"This is phenomenal," Kelly murmured as she savored a bite of her ravioli. "Giulia is incredibly talented."

"Says the woman who hesitated before accepting my invitation." He leaned back in his chair and swirled his wine, then took a long, satisfying sip.

"I've always been told to be careful around strangers," she replied, "but this is exactly what I wanted to see here in Sarcaccia. Not only the touristy stuff. Thank you."

"It's my pleasure." The answer came by rote as he studied the woman across the table. There was something different about Kelly. She might not know his identity as a member of the royal family, but she seemed to know *him*. She'd noticed his discomfort in the wine cellar when even Giulia and Guillermo, who'd known him from birth, had not.

Of course, now he wondered if others noticed the last time he'd experienced that same sensation.

As with the visit to the cellar, the deep-seated feeling of dread had caught him off guard. In fact, he'd been in a fantastic mood when it'd occurred. He'd just deplaned, having arrived home from Africa with his unit, and was waiting in the massive line at immigration, passport in hand. The guys around him were quietly discussing what they planned to do first when they exited the airport. Some only wanted to sleep in their own beds, others waxed poetic about wives and girl-friends, and more than a few wanted to hit up Sarcaccia's bars and nightclubs for a night of celebration. Massimo was explaining to one of his friends that he was obligated to attend a family dinner—and that he'd much prefer meeting the men at a bar—when the line began to move. He bent to shift his duffel bag forward and, predictably, was bumped from behind. Without warning, the overwhelming sensation of being crushed to death made his stomach heave and his lungs squeeze in protest. He'd swallowed hard and looked side to side at the snaking line in an effort to quash the sudden wave of nausea that enveloped him, but that only made the sensation worse.

The line ceased its forward movement, yet the noise around him increased as passengers from another flight crowded into the immi-gration hall. A few rows behind him, a child began whining in Spanish about the wait while an infant started to cry. The sound became palpable, pushing against his temples. He sucked a deep breath through his nostrils, schooling himself to keep his expression as neutral as possible, acutely aware he was the only one experiencing the horror of suffocation.

It's in your imagination, he'd repeated to himself over and over. *It's not real.*

Then, dear God, he felt his breath catch. Once, twice. He knew that within minutes he'd vomit. Between the security threat and the medical threat, there'd be a scene, one likely to be reported once his identity became known to those outside his unit. His breath caught a third time and he swallowed back a wave of nausea even as cold sweat pricked the surface of his skin.

He'd been ready to jump the line and claim a bathroom emergency when a uniformed agent came through the room and called for the military personnel to move to a separate line. Disregarding his friends, he snagged his duffel and bolted after the agent. Once free of the immigration hall's confines, he'd waited on a bench for his buddies while he calmed his breathing. When they emerged into the terminal, he told them to go ahead to baggage claim while he made a restroom stop. After splashing his face with cold water, he'd stared at himself in the mirror, wondering what would've happened if that agent hadn't pulled him from the crowd.

By the time he'd reached baggage claim, he'd felt like himself again. The car ride home relaxed him, leaving him convinced he'd merely eaten something that disagreed with him or needed sleep more desperately than he thought.

He took a long sip of his wine and smiled at Kelly across the table.

More worrisome than the idea that one of his buddies might've taken note of his odd behavior was the thought that what occurred at the airport wasn't a fluke. One occurrence he could explain away. But multiple occurrences…not likely. Especially if the sensation came over him in public, say, at a palace function or media event where there'd be multiple witnesses and cameras.

Such a scenario was too disturbing to contemplate. He could not—would not—allow it to happen.

"I'm glad you decided to trust me," Massimo said, forcing his thoughts in a more pleasant direction. "Otherwise I'd have missed Guillermo's sea bass."

"Oh, I didn't say I trusted you." At his raised eyebrow, she said, "I trusted Gaspare."

"I'll keep that in mind as I'm driving you back down the mountain in the dark and he's snoring in the back."

That drew a refreshing bubble of laughter from her. It gladdened him to see her at ease rather than guarded, as when she'd first climbed into his Jeep. A bit of unspoken tension with a woman was always good for the libido, but laughter was better. Hers could light a room.

He topped off her wine glass, but didn't add any to his own. As he'd said, he eventually needed to drive down the mountain and Kelly could prove enough of a distraction.

"Tell you what," she said as she speared a piece of ravioli on her fork and held it aloft, "as a peace offering, I'll let you try my ravioli. And I'm not sacrificing this bite easily."

She leaned closer, extending the fork in such a way that it'd be equally easy to take it from her or to lower his head and simply allow her to feed him. It was cliché, sharing one's food as flirtation, but effective. He shifted forward in his seat and took the bite into his mouth. The texture was heaven to his taste buds, but not as heavenly as the fire he could see banked in her soft brown eyes. As he slid his lips from the tines of her fork, he knew she was imagining what it'd be like to share a kiss.

Good.

"Fantastic, isn't it?" she asked.

"That's why I love this place." He'd never brought a woman to Giulia's—not one outside his family—but he'd known the atmosphere would work magic. Carefully, he lifted a bite of sea bass toward her. "Care to compare?"

"Thought you'd never ask." She wrapped her long, lean fingers around his hand to keep from spilling the fish onto the table, then murmured in pleasure as she sampled the bite. Once she released his hand and sat back, she said, "I love fish, but I've never tasted one that light and flavorful. I wonder if Giulia would share her secret?"

"Not on her life. Believe me, I've tried to convince her. I've been coming here since I was little and all I've managed to learn is her tiramisu, and then only because she was about to publish the recipe in a local paper as part of an interview."

Kelly's lush mouth perked in amusement. "She said you've cooked in her kitchen."

"She said *preparing*, and believe me, it was a deliberate word choice. Calling what I do anything more than that is an exaggeration. She runs the place like a military commander organizing a top secret mission. Her soldiers are on a need-to-know basis. When I'm in her kitchen, I only do what she tells me. Chop vegetables, slice meats, that type of thing. She guards her recipes and methods as the family treasures that they are. She says they're what keep her in business."

"Between the wine cellar and this view, I imagine Giulia could stay in business even if the whole planet had her recipes." Kelly turned toward the sea, where the sun now dipped low enough to brush the horizon and send bright orange rays skimming across the surface of the water. The breeze caught the loose strands of hair at her temples, lifting them away from her face. "But I understand. I'll consider this special occasion vacation dining, something to reminisce about when I get home."

He watched Kelly's expression as she caught sight of a fisherman coming in to shore far below them. The man waved to a friend fishing from the rocks alongside the tiny harbor and the friend waved back as if they'd done this every night for decades. Massimo smiled to himself, realizing that they probably had.

Life in Sarcaccia didn't change. Only he seemed to have changed in the last six years.

"Is it always this peaceful here?" she asked, her gaze still on the fisherman.

"Most of the time. It gets crowded when there's a large convention in Cateri or during certain festivals, but even those are low key compared to what you see over on the mainland, in Italy or France." He polished off the last of his sea bass and set down his fork. As if on cue, Giulia came bustling through the door at the end of the patio, wiping her hands on her apron.

"How are you two? Need to come inside yet?"

"Not yet, I don't think," Massimo replied, looking to Kelly for confirmation. The overwhelming need for fresh air had passed, but he had no desire to move. "Unless you're cold?"

"Not at all. I don't want to miss a moment of this sunset."

"In that case, you will want dessert. I have chestnut ice cream with homemade toffee sauce. Shall I bring one, or two?"

He was about to say she could bring a dessert for them to share when Kelly said, "Two, please. I'm not letting him have a single bite of mine."

"Wonderful!" Giulia beamed. "Now if only I could enjoy a bowl and stay as lean and beautiful as you, I'd join you."

"You're perfectly beautiful, but we both know you likely have more customers coming," Massimo added, shooting her a discreet look asking for confirmation of how long he could expect to keep his dinner with Kelly private. Once the sun set, Giulia would be compelled to turn on the outdoor lights, highlighting his presence to anyone who entered the main dining room.

"True, true. The first reservation is due to arrive in about twenty minutes."

"Next time, then?"

"Next time."

Giulia took off to fulfill their dessert orders, balancing their dirty plates on her arm as she went. Massimo was surprised to see that Kelly had finished her entire meal. Years of palace life and fancy soirees gave him the impression that women rarely ate much when out to dinner. More than once he'd heard his mother admonish his sister for eating too much, too fast, in public, saying it "wasn't lady-like." It'd galled his sister, who'd complained endlessly about double standards.

Then, of course, his parents had admonished Sophia for complaining.

It'd bothered him enough that once, back when he and his sister were still teenagers, he'd gone to her room after a state dinner where she'd dined in a "ladylike" fashion and handed her a sandwich he'd filched from the palace kitchen. She'd inhaled it, thanking him profusely all the while. Every time he'd taken a woman to dinner after that and watched her take only the daintiest bites of her meal, he'd secretly suspected she'd raided the fridge afterward.

He found it strangely appealing that Kelly wasn't concerned about eating in front of him. He wondered if that'd change if she knew his background. Then again, he didn't know that much about her background, either.

"So tell me, Kelly Chase from Dallas, Texas, in the United States, what do you do when you're not relaxing on the beaches of Sarcaccia?"

She smiled at his teasing, but it didn't quite make its way to her eyes, making him wonder if the question bothered her or merely caught her by surprise. "Well, until two weeks ago, I ran my own business."

Impressive. "What type of business?"

"Closet design and organization." She gave her wine a swirl. "I imagine that sounds frivolous compared to what you've done with the military, but it was a great way to make a living. I made a lot of people's lives easier. I'd help them get rid of belongings they couldn't use and focus on those that improved their productivity. Then I'd install a new system to keep everything organized for the long term. It improved their efficiency and made them happier. Like a weight had been lifted."

"Sounds like hard work," he mused. "Not sure I'd want to spend days on end slogging through other people's closets and cleaning them out."

"See, that's exactly why people put it off. They worry it'll be a huge undertaking. But in most cases, the entire job can be done in a few days. It's only the huge, walk-in closets that are the size of a bedroom and stuffed to the gills that take longer. Even then, the payoff is worth it. My clients are always stunned at the transformation and tell me they wish they'd done it sooner."

Sounded like it made her as happy as her clients. "And you decided to toss it all away for a wild Sarcaccian vacation?"

"You could say that. I sold out to a competitor."

"I hope he—or she—paid you a fortune." It would certainly explain the villa she'd rented. He knew enough about the price of vacationing on Sarcaccia to know her chosen location wasn't cheap. Particularly at this time of year, with balmy weather and the country's Independence Day celebration about to begin.

That brought a droll smile to her face. "Not nearly enough, I'm afraid. I'm using this vacation to plan what I'll do next. My last venture was successful, so I hope to take that experience and use it to launch a new business. An even better one."

"Closet organization again?"

"Can't, at least not in Texas. I signed a noncompete as part of the sale. But I'm sure I'll come up with something I enjoy." She set down her glass and leaned forward. "Why don't you tell me more about you? What do you do when you're not visiting exotic countries as part of your military duties?"

He considered his answer carefully. He refused to lie, but he wasn't ready to reveal his true vocation, either. "Well, for the last few days, I've spent most of my time on my boat. I finished my tour of duty only a few weeks ago. So, like you, I'm considering what I'll do next."

"No plans to re-enlist?"

He shook his head. Much as he'd like to sign up for a three-year extension, his parents expected him to attend to his royal duties sooner rather than later. As they'd told him over and over, there were thousands of Sarcaccians who could serve in the military, but only a few who could enrich the country by wielding the power and resources accorded to those bearing the Barrali name.

"I loved my time in the army—it was fulfilling in a way that few other jobs are—but it's time for me to come home. Explore new options." He forced a grin to his face. "Besides, Gaspare missed me. He's tired of staying with my sister."

"Nice sister. Any ideas about what you'll do?"

"A government job." When she waved her hand for further explanation, he added, "I guess you could say it's in my blood. My parents and siblings are all in public service."

Oh, he was on fire tonight.

"So it's family tradition driving you there?"

"It's a factor." Understatement of the year. "But my ultimate reason isn't so different from yours. I want a job where I can improve people's lives. Working for the government—depending on what I do, of course—means I can finish each day satisfied that I've made the world a better place. It sounds trite to say it aloud, but I don't think I could spend my life pursuing a career that didn't make a difference."

He'd never told anyone his feelings on the subject before, probably because they'd have had preconceived ideas about what he should and shouldn't do. But talking it over with Kelly gave him a sense of relief, like a man who'd been handed a cool drink on a hot day before he'd even realized how much he needed it.

Her face glowed in the reflected light of the sunset as she regarded him. "It's not trite if it's true."

"No, I suppose not."

At that moment, Giulia appeared with Gaspare at her heels. Two dessert bowls and cups of espresso were expertly balanced in her right hand while in her left, she held a foil box with a plastic lid. "Dessert for you, and a serving of ravioli to take to Princess Sophia."

Kelly raised an eyebrow. "Princess Sophia? What, do you have a cat, too?"

"No, never," Massimo gave Giulia a look of mock irritation. "It's her nickname for my sister. That's all."

"Yes, since she was a little girl. She liked to wear pink dresses," Giulia covered as she set the bowls of ice cream and tiny espresso cups before each of them. "Not so much now. But she does love my ravioli, so be sure she gets it."

"I will," he promised.

Kelly closed her eyes and breathed deeply. "This smells absolutely divine."

"I make the best *caffe* you'll have on the island," she bragged. "But don't tell anyone. I want them to come for the food first."

Giulia disappeared through the patio door as quickly as she arrived, clicking on the indoor lights to illuminate the main dining room. A young couple stood near the front door, their expressions lifting when Giulia approached to show them to a table.

"We're losing our exclusive service," Massimo said. Soon Giulia would have to turn on the patio lights.

"It'd be selfish to keep her to ourselves anyway." Kelly glanced down to greet Gaspare, who promptly curled up beside her chair, rather than by Massimo's.

"Speaking of selfish, you've enchanted my dog."

"I'm a novelty. He'll be all yours shortly," she assured him, reminding Massimo that his time with Kelly was coming to an end.

Perhaps she was a novelty for him, too. He hadn't felt so at ease in a woman's presence in…well, ever. Given that he hardly knew her, it didn't seem possible.

Kelly turned to face the last vestiges of the setting sun. "Look at the reds to the north and that stripe of orange just over the purple. Is it always like this here?"

"We have colorful sunsets more often than not, but no," he admitted, "this is one of a kind."

"I think I'm in heaven."

He glanced her way to see her licking the back of her spoon in languid strokes. In other women, he'd think it deliberately erotic, but he doubted Kelly realized what she was doing to him. As she popped the spoon into her mouth then slowly withdrew it, ensuring she'd devoured the entire bite of ice cream, he felt himself growing hard with desire. She let out a low moan of satisfaction that set his body ablaze.

Heaven, indeed.

He ripped his gaze from her before she caught him staring, then took a bite of his own ice cream and nearly moaned in pleasure himself.

"See what I mean? Heaven."

He nodded as he took another bite and tried to focus on the dessert rather than on what Kelly was doing to her spoon. And what it would feel like if she did that to him.

"So tell me," she said as she scraped toffee from the side of her bowl, "what made you think to bring me here? There are dozens if not hundreds of restaurants on the island, and my guess is that you know the owners of several, yet you seemed to know exactly where you wanted to go from the moment we left the beach."

He shrugged. He *had* known where he'd wanted to go the instant the invitation left his mouth. Perhaps it was the food, perhaps it was the romantic atmosphere—if one wanted to put a woman into a passionate frame of mind, Giulia's was certainly the place—or perhaps it was something else entirely. "I suppose I missed it while I was away and assumed you'd enjoy the food as much as I do."

"Good assumption."

Now that he thought about it, he realized Kelly was right. There were dozens of other restaurants in Sarcaccia that served spectacular meals using local ingredients. Restaurants that would've been closer to her villa. Restaurants that wouldn't have felt so personal, given that this was a first—and perhaps only—date, since Kelly was a tourist. But Giulia's felt safe. Secure. *Comfortable.*

That he craved comfort was a thought that left him decidedly *un*comfortable.

Soon, the uppermost rim of the sun's fiery outline met the horizon, replacing the sky's orange hues with purples and grays. They watched the darkening sky in silence as they finished their desserts and sipped their espresso. Much as he wanted to linger over the finished meal, he knew they had to go.

"Ready for the ride down the mountain?" he asked.

"Not really. But it'll get cool soon, so I suppose we should go."

He walked around the table to pull out her chair for her, but she frowned as she stood. "Shouldn't we wait for Giulia to settle the bill?"

"Already settled." Surprise registered on her face, but he explained, "I have an account with her."

Kelly's gratitude for the dinner was evident in her voice as she thanked him. She turned to head through the patio door, but he hooked her elbow first. "There are steps over here, to the side. We can go directly to the parking lot."

"You don't want to say goodbye?"

Typically he would, but doing so wouldn't be simple now that there were diners in the restaurant. Giulia would understand. "She and Guillermo have other customers. I'll give them a call later."

Kelly's expression made it plain she wanted to thank them herself, but she said, "Please let them know how much I enjoyed meeting them," then waited while he corked the leftover wine to bring home. Gaspare, true to form, kept to her heel as she climbed the stairs, though the dog did spare Massimo a brief look. At the end of the day, he knew who filled his bowl.

The ride back to town was quiet as they took in the sights and sounds of the evening: roadside fruit stands closing for the day, lights flickering to life in the town below, church bells ringing to signal the evening service. Even the birds circling the hillsides gave the impression they were on their final patrols before nesting for the night.

Once Massimo made the final turn that brought them to the edge of town, where Kelly's villa occupied a coveted spot between the main road and the beach, she pointed to a narrow driveway under an arched branch of wisteria vines. "It's just there. You can pull in."

He slid her a sideways glance before signaling the turn. "Dare I ask if I'm invited in, or is this goodbye? If it's goodbye, there may be an argument over who gets the leftover wine."

Laughter spilled from her. "You're forward, aren't you?"

"Not usually." Not when it came to women. They were forward enough with him he had no need.

"Well…I don't usually ask men into my home on a first date."

"Usually," he repeated as he guided the Jeep to a stop and put the gearshift into park. "Though you have to admit, this has been an unusual day."

"That it has."

He studied the villa, taking in the whitewashed exterior and tiled steps leading to the front door. It appeared to have been recently renovated, likely due to the income its location generated. The lights were off inside, preventing him from seeing if anyone was about. For all he knew, she had a house full of roommates sitting on the back deck, lingering over drinks while they waited for her to come home.

He wasn't ready to send her in to them and say goodbye. Not yet.

Taking a chance, he turned and looped his arm over the back of Kelly's seat. "What about tonight?"

CHAPTER 5

THE MAN WAS UNBELIEVABLY DIRECT. He also smelled unbelievably good.

The soft fabric of his shirt tickled the bare skin of Kelly's back in the sensitive spot just below the tie of her sundress. As if linked by a direct connection, the skin on her arms pricked to gooseflesh.

She imagined he didn't suffer rejection often.

"I'm not sure it'd be wise," she said, using the excuse in order to gauge his intentions. She had no idea if asking a man into one's home after a date carried the same implication in Sarcaccia it sometimes had in the States. It was obvious he wanted to carry on their flirtation; how much further he wanted to carry it was the question. Let alone how much further *she* wanted to carry it. "Is it safe?"

"Safe as you were on the patio at Giulia's."

"We weren't exactly alone on the patio."

"We won't be alone now, either. Gaspare is here."

"He is a good chaperone." She flicked a look at the dog, whose ears perked up at the mention of his name though he didn't stir from his sprawl across the back seat. "Of course, you realize that I don't know the most basic things about you. For instance, what's your last name?"

His eyes crinkled at the corners, as if the question intrigued him. "Barrali."

"Massimo Barrali. I like it. It's strong." Just like the man. Forceful, yet somehow elegant. Hearing the name from her own lips pricked a memory. "Is Barrali a common name here? Isn't that the name of the royal family?"

"It is, and it's common enough. Lots of Barralis in Sarcaccia. But no one with the last name Chase, I don't believe." When she smiled at that, he continued, "What else do you want to know?"

"Hmmm..." She took a moment, enjoying their banter. "What color would you call your eyes?"

His look of amusement made her stomach do a flip-flop. "My sister calls them mud. But I'd say brown."

"Some sister. There's green there, too. A lot of green."

"If you say so. I don't make it a habit to stare at my own eyes in the mirror." His fingers grazed her shoulder, the touch warming places far more intimate. He appeared ignorant of the chain reaction he set off within her, which made her all the more certain he knew very well what he was doing. "Anything else?"

Oh, how she loved this game. It felt daring. Liberating. "How tall are you?"

"I'm 192 centimeters." At her blink of surprise, he added, "I think that's six-two or six-three."

"Six-three. Almost six-four."

This time, he was the one to look incredulous.

"I do closets, remember? Or at least I did. I'm quick with conversion." She'd guessed him to be well over six feet, but given the assurance with which he carried himself, she was afraid she might be overestimating his height. Apparently not.

"So it's my height that has you worried about your safety?"

"That's exactly it," she teased. She loved that he was able to poke fun at himself. He looked, smelled, and sounded so different from Ted. Ted had always been so serious, so careful about every word he uttered and move he made. Being wealthy and in the public eye did that to a person. She'd sworn the day she left him never to date a rich man again. Money mangled one's sense of self. At least, it had in the case of Ted and his friends.

"Does that mean I've addressed your concerns?"

Oh, he knew he was coming inside. She could see it in his eyes, read it in the relaxed manner in which he lounged against his seat.

"One last question. Do you end all your first dates by asking to be invited inside?"

"No." His lower lip thinned and his eyes widened fractionally before he added, "In fact, I believe this is a first."

The note of realization in his tone made her believe him, which sent another wave of arousal rippling through her.

An unusual night, indeed.

A little over two weeks ago she'd been certain she'd spend the rest of her life with Ted. Now she felt as if she'd tossed off shackles and stepped into the light. The fact she could experience such desire for a man she'd only known for a few hours cemented her confidence in calling off the wedding. Screw what her friends said. Screw what her parents said. The decision was hers and hers alone, just as taking this trip was her decision. Both had been the right call.

"So what do you think, Kelly Chase of Dallas?" He reached into the space between them and raised the corked wine bottle. "If nothing else, it would be a tragedy not to finish this. Giulia would be disappointed if she discovered it went to waste."

"First off, Giulia wouldn't know unless you told her."

"She'll ask—"

"And second, I'm sure it won't go to waste. But there's still half a bottle and eventually you have to drive home, so it might not be wise to drink it—"

One side of his mouth hitched up on the word *eventually*. She knew in that moment she'd been caught. He leaned forward, ever so slightly closing the gap between them. "I'm not in a rush. Are you?"

The wash of his breath against her cheek sent adrenaline pumping through her body. She shook her head just before his lips met hers. His kiss was gentle, soft, testing. He tasted of wine and Mediterranean sunshine. Warmth spread through her as his arm slipped from the back of the seat to her shoulders. Though the easy spread of his fingers over her bare skin and the dim lights of the driveway made the moment romantic, his kiss left no doubt in her mind what would happen if she invited him inside. They'd share far more than a bottle of wine if she decided it was what she wanted.

He tilted his head, deepening their kiss as his hand came up to cradle the back of her head. The rough scrape of his chin against hers sent her reeling. There was no denying the attraction between them. She'd felt it the moment he'd stood at the foot of her lounger inquiring about his dog in that commanding tone, but checking out her bikini-clad body with his eyes.

She could get drunk on this feeling far faster than on the wine.

A sigh bubbled up inside her, threatening to escape and embarrass her to no end, but at that very moment he pulled back. It was all she could do to keep her breathing steady as he captured her chin in his hand.

"I see two options here. First, I kiss you goodnight now and let you go. Second, we go inside, share the wine and kiss goodnight afterward. Either way, it ensures that kiss" —his mouth curved into a devious smile— "wasn't the last."

He eased back a few more inches, his fingers still cradling her chin but giving her the space and ability to call it a night without awkwardness. Yet she sensed he was playing with her, too, enjoying their flirtation as much—maybe more—than she was. He'd ended the kiss deliberately, leaving her wanting more.

She took a slow, deep breath, weighing his words. She hadn't made the best choices lately, not until she'd made the ultimate decision to dump Ted. Those errors in judgment made a mess of both her personal life and her professional life. On the other hand, what harm could come from having a night of adventure with such a devastatingly handsome man? If his kiss was any indication, it'd be mind-blowing enough to wipe away her recent history and give her a mental clean slate.

She pulled away from him and opened the car door, but not before she caught the look of surprise on his face.

"There's always option three, where I simply walk inside," she said as she climbed out of the Jeep. She hesitated, allowing his disappointment to sink in before she turned back. She doubted her smile was as wickedly sensuous as his, but she hoped so. "But I prefer option two, so don't forget the wine."

"YOU HAVE this whole place to yourself?"

He shouldn't have said it. Massimo realized his error immediately from the defensive flash in Kelly's eyes, despite her attempt to cover her initial reaction with a shrug of indifference. But when she flipped the switch inside the villa's front door, illuminating the open living area with its view to the sea, he'd been surprised to see no evidence of other occupants. No shoes near the front door, no other sets of keys on the counter of the small kitchen, no notes from roommates about where they'd gone for the evening. When he'd put his sister's ravioli in the fridge and saw it was empty, he was certain. He'd turned and asked the question without thinking about it first.

Now he'd likely made her feel a pariah. If there was anything he should've learned from years of etiquette training, it was to think before speaking. You never knew when you might hit upon a sensitive topic, as he'd obviously done.

She leaned one shoulder against the wall near the kitchen entry, the action pushing up the bodice of her sundress in a rather tantalizing fashion. "I know Sarcaccia is a rather traditional country, but surely you don't believe it's taboo for a woman to vacation alone?"

He pounced on the opportunity to save himself. "Not at all. If anything, traveling alone is a sign of being comfortable in one's own skin. I'd simply assumed that you'd come with friends." Though most who rented on this strip of beach were lovers, and with good reason. The idyllic surroundings, unobstructed sea views, and the easy access to the cobblestoned section of Cateri's old town made it a wonderful hideaway.

"Nope. This was a reward to myself."

For selling her business, he supposed. Well, Kelly's reward was to his benefit. No roommates who might recognize him, no one to intrude upon their conversation...or anything else, should he get so lucky.

Backing off that kiss in the Jeep was the toughest thing he'd done in a long time. He'd wanted to pull her across the gearshift and into his lap, to taste the salt on her skin and savor the hint of beachiness that clung to her hair. He'd yearned for her as desperately as a child yearned for chocolate chip cookies after watching them bake and inhaling their mouth-watering aroma, but when Kelly's tongue grazed his and she softened in his arms, he feared his intense reaction might send her scurrying into the house alone.

So he'd backed off. And waited. And wondered at the intensity of their connection.

Was his driving need a response to being deprived of female companionship during his time away, or was it a response to this particular woman? He suspected the latter, though he didn't want to contemplate it too much. Better to indulge in the sight of her leaning against the kitchen wall, her gorgeous sundress highlighting her assets while her eyes skimmed over him as if she were deciding what to do with him now that he stood in her kitchen.

"You did say you'd come for perspective," he pointed out. "I couldn't imagine a better location."

"It's as different from my life at home as I can get, and that makes it perfect." She pushed off the wall and set her small handbag on the kitchen counter, then withdrew a heavy-bottomed bowl from the cupboard.

He eyeballed the bowl as he made his way to the other side of the counter that divided the sitting area from the kitchen, affording her space to move. "Odd choice for a wineglass."

"This is for Gaspare." She filled it with water and set it on the tile floor before reaching to the cupboard once more. Holding up two wineglasses, she said, "These are for us."

He uncorked the bottle as she came around the counter to join him. "This place came fully stocked with everything I could want.

Well, except groceries. Those were supposed to be delivered this afternoon after I arrived, but the market called and said there was some problem, so they won't be able to come until tomorrow."

"Yet somehow, you managed to find a meal."

She shot him a mischievous grin. "That I did."

He surveyed the spacious living room. On one wall, a sleek television topped a long console crafted of local wood stained black. Several modern leather chairs on silver legs were arranged on either end of an off-white wool rug fronting the television, while a thick, dark brown sofa faced the television itself. In the center of the room, an oval coffee table straight from an Italian design magazine sported several glass coasters, a series of jade plants in squat terracotta pots, and an empty glass bottle of cola. The giant blue and green abstract painting above the sofa was one he recognized as the work of an artist who lived in Cateri. Sliding glass doors at the end of the room opened onto a balcony that overlooked the beach.

This place couldn't have come cheap. As rewards went, this was a good one. She'd obviously taken great pains in her planning, since the stack of tourist brochures and guidebooks on an end table near the balcony doors were punctuated with bright yellow sticky notes.

He poured a glass of wine for each of them, then held up his glass and gave it a gentle swish. The scent of the dark red liquid teased his nose. "To what should we toast?"

She stood only a step away, close enough for him to wrap his arm around her, pull her body flush with his, and kiss her once more if he desired. Much as he wanted to feel her against him, to show her exactly how pleasurable the night could be given the preview he'd had in the Jeep, he sensed her need to ease into physical intimacy.

He wasn't sure he could remain patient.

She raised her glass. Tipping her head slightly, she met his gaze and said, "To my luck at meeting a polite, funny, ordinary guy on a spectacular beach."

"Ordinary?" Talk about a blow to the ego. "How charming of you."

"Believe me, ordinary is good," she said in dead seriousness. "And remember, I also said polite and funny."

Not hot? Sexy? Doable? Not that he expected her to utter that particular word in a million years, but he'd sure like her to think it. When she'd asked if he was safe, he'd hoped it was a tease…in that she'd like a night that was decidedly *unsafe*. A vacation escapade.

Instead, her toast could have described her postman or bus driver, people whose conversations consisted of a sentence at most when she encountered them over the course of the day. Not a man with whom she might embark on a sizzling affair.

"You're telling me you're the only woman on the planet who doesn't harbor a secret wish to be swept off her feet by a man who's rich and powerful? No fairy tale princess fantasies for you?" He said it in jest, but found himself curious to hear her response now that she'd used *ordinary* as a compliment. Nearly every woman he'd encountered in his life knew his identity and all that came with it from the moment they met. In Sarcaccia, he was well known on the streets. In the military, his unit knew his background cold. And during his travels abroad, his arrangements had been made beforehand by the palace, meaning he had little opportunity to move about anonymously.

"None whatsoever," she insisted. "Rich and powerful are overrated traits as far as relationships go. In fact, I'd say they're a detriment. I'd rather go to dinner with a laid-back guy who owns a simple fishing boat than a luxury yacht. One who has friends like Giulia and Guillermo and takes me to a restaurant for a meal made with love instead of a swanky place with fussy tablecloths and an overblown maître d'. Besides, rich and powerful men are treated differently, so they view the world differently. And that includes how they conduct their relationships."

Apparently she'd had experience with rich and powerful and the experience hadn't gone well. Interesting.

She angled her chin in challenge. "Too much perspective for you?"

"Not at all. I find it fascinating." There was a lot to be said for anonymity if this was what he could discover. She might've asked about his last name, but she still hadn't made the connection, even with Giulia's slip about Sophia. He doubted Kelly would've spoken so candidly if she had.

"In that case" —she raised her glass, and he couldn't help but grin at the irony of what he suspected she was about to say— "here's to an ordinary guy who treated me to an extraordinary dinner. You've made my vacation in Sarcaccia special."

Well. He'd take that. "And to you, for accepting the dinner invitation despite not knowing my last name or exact height."

"Or your eye color." She clinked her glass lightly against his and took a sip. After he took a deep drink from his own glass, she set hers on the countertop and surprised him by taking his and setting it on the counter beside hers, then reaching up to touch a spot at his temple. Slowly, she ran the tip of her finger around the outside of his left eye to his cheekbone, peering at him as a doctor might evaluate a patient but with a feathery touch that nearly made him come out of his skin. It had been a long, long time since a female touched him with such tenderness. "I'm still not sure if they're brown or green."

He managed to find his voice. "Feel free to come closer and take a better look."

A mixture of trepidation and anticipation filled her gaze as her hand drifted back to her side. "If I come any closer, I won't be looking at your eyes."

"Definitely come closer, then."

He'd felt daring in the Jeep, asking Kelly if he'd be invited in, then kissing her the moment he saw an opportunity. That brief taste of her plush lips and sun-warmed skin left him aching for more. But rather than be daring once more and simply take, he wanted her to give. It was all he could do to remain motionless now, waiting for her to close the distance separating them. Or not.

His breath stilled in his lungs as he waited, lusted. Then saw the same burning desire reflected in her gaze.

All his life he'd been the good son, sticking to protocol, taking extreme care not to gift the royal gossips with fodder for their publications. He'd never lived life on the edge in the way his brothers had, risking their family's reputation for a night of partying at a club, carousing with friends, or—as his brother Stefano once did—running barefoot and shirtless past a crowd outside the royal palace so he could see a certain female.

He'd certainly never slept with a woman on a first date, despite numerous opportunities. Then again, he'd never been as intrigued with a woman as quickly as he'd become intrigued with Kelly. There was an open, honest quality about her that held him rapt, that made him want, and it was high time he took pleasure in his life and had a bit of fun. He'd worked his tail off in college, despite the expectation he appear at every social gathering imaginable. After graduation he'd risked his life for his country and his fellow soldiers, not to mention the people they'd been sent to protect. He'd done everything expected of a royal son and then some. He deserved to have a night of wild sex, sex without fear of consequences. Sex with a woman whose sensually curved body would be the ultimate indulgence for any man. A woman on vacation, with no expectations whatsoever beyond tonight.

A woman whose insights penetrated his very soul when they'd been in that dark, enclosed wine cellar, away from the light of day. She'd seen what others had not.

As he drank in the details of her face now, from the turned up eyelashes at the outer edges of her almond eyes to the arches of her dark brows, then to the soft, full lower lip that called to him, he realized that a night with Kelly Chase wouldn't be something he'd classify as *fun*. It would be far more explosive than that.

He craved whatever *it* was more than he craved fun.

But she'd have to come to him, and she needed to come to him not knowing anything of who he was other than what he'd chosen to disclose. She had to view a night spent with a relative stranger as part of her reward to herself, part and parcel of the spectacular beach and villa. Not as a means to the royal family, to wealth, to fame, or to security.

She had to want him for him.

"Are all Sarcaccian men as flirtatious as you are?"

"I don't know. They've never flirted with me."

Her laugh was low and seductive. "Ordinary…but not at all boring. How can I resist?"

The word *don't* never left his mouth. She was on her tiptoes, stretching to kiss him, but her hands remained at her sides. She surprised him once again by shifting just enough to bypass his mouth and brush her lips over his jaw. The short hairs at the back of his neck stood on end as she lingered there, her warm breath stirring him to full arousal. She moved lower, slowly caressing the skin of his neck with her lips, yet touching him nowhere else.

"Now who's the flirt?" he whispered, though the sound was rougher than he'd anticipated. Oh, but this woman knew how to entice.

"I suppose I am." There was a mixture of desire and nervousness in her exhalation as she continued to tease at his now-sensitized skin with her mouth.

"You are" —he struggled to clear his mind enough for the proper phrase that would let her know he wouldn't think less of her for allowing him to make love to her, yet at the same time making it clear she could cry off at any time if that was what she desired— "one of a kind. No wonder Gaspare made a beeline in your direction when he made it to shore. The boy knew exactly what he was doing."

"You saying you trained him to find me?"

"No one can train a dog that well."

As if on cue, or perhaps because he heard his name, a low canine grumble rose from the other side of the kitchen counter.

"Shhhh," he ground out. "There's a beautiful female flirting with me."

Kelly's head lifted, then her lips brushed the outermost corner of his mouth. He fought to keep his breathing even as she rewarded his patience with the softest of kisses. And then he was lost. Unable to remain still any longer, he wrapped his hands around her narrow waist, pulling her to him, lifting her slightly so he could gain better access to her glorious mouth.

Oh, but he'd missed being with a woman. And this woman held more allure than any he could recall meeting. A wave of over-whelming need gripped him, driving him to deepen the kiss. The fingers of her right hand sought the nape of his neck while her left arm snaked around his back, pulling him closer. She moaned into his mouth, as if she experienced the same deep, unrequited primal craving he did and had finally allowed herself to indulge.

He ravished her mouth with his, taking his pleasure as if he might never kiss a woman again. At the same time, he found himself wondering what drove her. He knew why *he* needed this. Why did she? Her passionate response to his kiss wasn't one of mere lust. This was a bone-deep craving borne of loss or of pain or of having gone without. Five years ago, even a year ago, he wouldn't have recognized it. Now he recognized it because he'd experienced it.

Then she surprised him by smiling against his mouth.

"This is no longer safe," she murmured.

"No, it's not." Not at all. Not for either of them. He kept her body pressed to his but eased his face back from hers just enough to take in her glazed expression.

Her gaze narrowed as she whispered, "Good."

CHAPTER 6

Flirtation turned carnal in an instant as she kissed him once more, fitting the soft curves of her breasts against the harder planes of his chest, allowing him to imagine how it would feel if there were no clothing separating them, if they were skin on skin. He stroked her spine, moving upward until his hands reached the soft, bare flesh of her back where it was exposed above her blue sundress. She smelled of the beach, of Giulia's, and of lemon shampoo. Of perfect femininity and beauty. Yet the scent of desire clung to her skin, too, making her irrevocably *human*. Making him want her all the more.

He rasped a command to Gaspare, sending the dog to a corner to sleep as if they were at home. He didn't check to see if the dog obeyed. The padding of paws behind him was enough assurance.

He yanked the knot at the back of Kelly's neck harder than necessary, loosening the ties that held the blue cotton fabric of her sundress between them, then located the elastic that held her hair in its elaborate twist and pulled it free. He buried both his hands in her waves, savoring the rich texture as he continued to plunder her mouth. Tasting, exploring, meeting every touch and caress of her tongue with his own. Nipping at her lower lip, sliding down to sample the divine column of her throat, then moving back again. Wanting to taste her everywhere at once.

Gradually, he became aware of her hands on his chest and pulled back. The wetness of their kiss left a sheen on her bottom lip, but she didn't wipe it away. Instead, she took a step backward, the movement causing the front of her dress to sag. She didn't fix it. Instead, she kept her eyes locked with his. Slowly, deliberately, he slid his hand inside the fabric, lowering it to her waist so he could see her. She wore nothing underneath, rewarding him with the amazing sight of her full breasts. He bent to take one taut nipple into his mouth, but she stopped him with a gentle hand. "No. I want to feel you against me," she murmured, her eyes fixed on the front of his shirt.

Deftly, her fingers worked the buttons free. For a moment, he simply watched in wonder, but as she released the final button and pushed the white fabric from his shoulders, he wrapped his hands around her waist and pulled her to him, letting her feel all she wanted as he kissed her once more. Taking a step backward, he felt one of the kitchen barstools against the back of his thighs and sat, pulling her flowing skirt high before lifting her into his lap to straddle him. He wanted her to feel him, to know what her hands, her mouth, and her body did to his.

He circled one beautiful nipple with his fingertips, then dragged his gaze from her breasts to her face. She'd been watching him. The unconcealed desire and shock in her dark eyes mirrored the chaotic thoughts filling his own mind. She cradled his face in her hands, then dipped her head to kiss him. As she slid her hands to his shoulders, then wrapped them around him, the full weight of her breasts settled against his chest once more. He groaned into her mouth.

There was no doubt from her kiss what she wanted from him.

"I don't sleep with men on the first date. Ever." The words were said even as the soft, wet sound of their kisses filled his senses.

"I have no plans to sleep," he replied, then nipped her lower lip to show her just how awake he was.

"Still...I needed to make the point." He felt her lips curve into a smile against his. "But I suppose if we're not sleeping, we don't have a problem."

Holding her fast, he stood. She started to slide her legs to the ground, but he managed a, "no, don't," and moved his grip to her thighs, encouraging her to wrap her legs around his waist.

He met her gaze, making his intent clear and ensuring she shared the need that thrummed through his veins. Her breathing came in the same staccato rasps as his as she tilted her head to indicate the door behind her.

"Bedroom's that way."

"How very *polite* of you."

"Bedroom too *ordinary?*"

"Tell me later if you think it's ordinary." He strode across the living room and kicked through the partially open door to enter the bedroom. It, too, had windows overlooking the beach, though the thin white curtains were fortuitously drawn, allowing in the light bleeding over from neighboring villas and from the low-slung moon without sacrificing privacy.

As he neared the side of the bed, he allowed her to slide her legs down his until her toes touched the floor. Without words, she moved her hands to the front of his waistband to unbutton his slacks while she kicked out of her sandals and sent them skidding across the room. He followed her example, shedding his shoes while he watched her fingers work the front of his pants open. Patience finally got the better of him and he moved to help her. In seconds, she caressed her way down his thighs to pool his pants and briefs at his feet. As she stood, she ran her palms from the outside of his legs to a more intimate area. An involuntary shiver ripped through his body as her fingers skidded over him, then moved back down, deliberately coaxing him toward ecstasy.

No, they were not safe at all.

With a kick, he sent his slacks sliding across the floor, grabbed her hands and tumbled her backward into the bed, then covered her body with his own. Her dress remained bunched around her waist, but a quick flick of his wrist divested her of her panties.

In the dim light, he caught a glimpse of plain, white cotton before he flung them over her head to the floor on the opposite side of the bed. In the recesses of his mind, it occurred to him it wasn't what a woman wore when she expected to bring a man home with her, and she'd changed into the sundress knowing they were heading out to dinner. She'd meant it when she said she didn't sleep with men on the first date. But if she noticed him noticing her utilitarian undergarments, there was no embarrassment. Instead, she sighed and arched back against the fluffy pillows as he bent to take one nipple in his mouth and caressed the other with his the pad of his thumb.

She wrapped one lean leg around him, then her hands came to his rear, trapping him. As he shifted his attention to her other breast, her hands came up, exploring the bare skin of his back. Realization hit him at the same moment her fingertips encountered the rough, scarred skin on his left side. He'd been so caught up in the moment—the *woman*—he'd forgotten what she'd discover on his naked body.

"Does this hurt?" Her voice came to him in the dark, using the same words the field medic had as he'd explored the deep wounds and charred skin only a few months ago, but with a completely different emotion packed into them.

"No."

He'd unintentionally bitten out the word. No one besides the medic and the French army doctors and nurses who'd treated him had seen the full extent of the damage since the day he'd sustained the injury. It was his to bear. He didn't want it—or the circumstances that led to the slashed, burned flesh—to become the subject of public scrutiny.

Rather than take offense, Kelly seemed to take his gruff response as an indication he wanted to focus on the task at hand. She continued to explore his back, his arms, his shoulders, until she reached his nape. Gentle pressure at the back of his neck signaled him to shift higher to kiss her once more. She moved as if to roll over and pin him beneath her, but he stopped her with a hand to her thigh.

"No." This time the word was said gently. "I have a better idea."

It no longer mattered how deeply he craved the release that came with a night of wild, unbridled sex. It didn't matter that this was nothing more than a one-night stand, a memory he'd tuck away in a corner of his mind to remember with fondness later. More than anything, he wanted to satisfy *her*. To see the look on her face as she came undone, to know that he'd been the cause.

Still cradling her thigh with one hand, he used the other to explore her most sensitive spots, drawing a muffled cry from her as she turned her face toward the bedcovers and lifted her body to meet his hand.

The sight of her drove him harder, first with his fingers, then his mouth, spinning them both out of control. He felt her peak, coil, then let go in a shuddering, all-encompassing release that sent her fists into the bedding.

Unwilling to wait for her to catch her breath, he repositioned himself and entered her with an unabashed groan of sheer pleasure. Her hands went to his back, his shoulders, his hair—she seemed to want to hold him everywhere at once—as she rocked into him and cried out his name.

For the first time in weeks, possibly months, he felt alive. His skin burned to her touch, his blood pumped through his veins as if on fire, and an overwhelming sense of awe and elation filled him. The light streamed through the sheer white curtains to strike her hair as it splayed across the white bedding, making her look ethereal even as they made love with a passion that bordered on violence.

Dear God, but she was beautiful.

She arched against him, then reached to her side, pressing one palm into the padded headboard for leverage as the fingers of her other hand dug into his back, driving him on. He fought for purchase as they moved in rhythm. Sensing his need, Kelly wrapped her legs tighter around his waist, holding him fast, encouraging him to take what he needed. Their movements were old as time, as inherent to their species as breathing. But it had never, ever been quite like this. This was holy grail sex.

One-night stands weren't supposed to be holy grail sex.

Then again, he'd never had a one-night stand.

He drove harder, as if the fire building in his core would slip away. The room shifted below him. Kelly's stunned eyes met his and a surprised squeak escaped her as the mattress slid sideways off the box spring and they careened headfirst over the side of the bed.

They landed atop the mattress with a *whump*.

Somehow, Massimo managed to stay buried within her. After a heartbeat of silence, laughter erupted from deep within her, shaking her entire torso.

"You okay?" she managed. Tears spilled from the corners of her eyes as she gasped for breath. For what she'd paid for the villa, it really should have a better bed.

"Are *you?* I just landed on you."

"I'm perfectly fine. Actually…that felt pretty damned good."

"No."

"Yes." She gifted him with a gentle kiss. "In fact, I might call it out of the ordinary."

He smiled down at her, marveling at how a simple afternoon escape on his fishing boat turned into such a memorable evening. "You" —he traced her cheek, then paused with a finger to her lips— "seem to have a way of pushing a man to do extraordinary things."

Wickedness lit her eyes. She grabbed his finger and moved it aside. "Pushing. Really? *That's* the word you choose?"

He responded by doing exactly that. Within seconds, any hint of humor faded. Her thighs tightened around his waist as he trapped her knee against him with his arm, holding her fast while he moved within her, then bent his head to touch his tongue to the sweet column of her neck. She lifted her hips, encouraging him to resume their rhythm. He heard himself moan, felt Kelly's knuckles grind against his lower back. Urgency drove him harder. He sank into her as she rose to meet him.

In an attempt to slow himself down, he lowered his forehead to hers, then grabbed her hand with his, interlacing their fingers. The motion had the opposite effect. Rather than slowing him down, suddenly, their connection felt more intimate.

They squeezed each other's hands at the same time. His eyes

drifted shut. He pressed his lips to her hair, relished the choked sound of her labored breathing as they both teetered on the edge.

He wanted so much more than a quick release.

"Massimo, please, Massimo," she pleaded, then a moment later she convulsed around him. But he continued to fly, his mind whirling as he approached his own climax. He knew he was out of control. He didn't care. A second wave gripped her and she let out the most carnal, intimate sound he'd ever heard, one that sent him spilling into her and gasping for breath as he responded with a deep moan of his own. Dizzying, explosive pleasure throbbed through him before he finally collapsed on top of her, spent and deeply satisfied. The very surface of his skin seemed to vibrate.

Best. Damned. Sex. Of. My. Life.

His face crushed into the mattress near her shoulder, but no energy remained with which to lift his head. It didn't matter. He had nowhere to go. Kelly's legs remained wrapped around him, holding him in place as her chest rose and fell with the effort to recapture her breath. One of her arms sprawled across his back. His skin was so sensitized he felt everything at once: the scratch of her thin silver bracelet across the skin of his back, her toes resting against his calf, the brush of her taut nipples against his chest. The bunched fabric of her sundress, which remained twisted around her waist despite the physicality of what they'd just done. And still, it wasn't enough. He wanted more.

He could hardly wait to do it again.

This time, they'd make love slowly, passionately, and perhaps without taxing his control or his lung power so thoroughly. How was it that sex with Kelly drew on his aerobic capacity more than a ten-mile jungle hike with a full pack on his back?

Maybe, he mused, because he'd put in more effort given the rewards.

Finally, he turned his head enough to see Kelly's expression. Her eyes were closed, her lips slightly parted, and her hair splayed across the mattress above her head as if she were asleep, yet he sensed her alertness before he shifted to unhook a strand of auburn hair from where it had tangled in one of her silver hoop earrings.

"You Sarcaccian men really know how to flirt," she said without opening her eyes. "I'm impressed."

"Not all Sarcaccian men."

"Thought you didn't know about other Sarcaccian men." Her fingers moved across his back, her nails tracing a line just below where she'd discovered his scars. "But I'll take your word for it. Tourism would go through the roof if all Sarcaccian men were so talented."

Her winded statement made him realize he hadn't moved off her. He pushed to his elbows, separating their bodies as quickly as possible.

"What's wrong?"

"I'm crushing you."

"You're not." She pulled him toward her, but he braced his forearms on either side of her, preventing it. "I like feeling you against me."

"You won't be able to breathe." He had to be nearly double her weight.

She frowned, then opened her eyes and put her hand between them, over her breast. "Feel my heart beat here." She moved her hand higher, to the juncture where her throat met her collarbone. "Feel it here. I'm breathing just fine. Faster than usual, but I suspect there's an explanation for that."

He eased off his forearms, slowly allowing his weight to settle. He put one hand between them, over her heart, where she'd placed her hand a moment before. The beat was rapid, but steady. Instantly, her arms wrapped tight around him. "See? I'm still breathing. You're not as big as you think you are."

He laughed into her hair and moved his lower body against hers. "Want to rethink that statement?"

"Give me a reason."

"Give me a minute."

"All the time you want."

The comment was said with humor, but desire flickered in her eyes. They lay there, holding each other, allowing their breathing to slow and the sheen of perspiration that covered them both to evaporate. She said nothing, but moved the pads of her fingers along his back in a lazy pattern. As if the scars weren't there, or at least weren't consequential. He fought back the sense of awe that filled him. He'd always enjoyed sex, but this…this had been different. Transcending. It wasn't the fact it'd been so long, much as he'd like to attribute it to that. It was the woman.

Even so, she was an American on vacation. He was a local and nothing more in her mind. Someone she'd met on the beach who'd talked her into dinner and wine. A vacation memory, much like sampling Giulia's secret recipes.

And wasn't that what he'd wanted her to think?

"This has been spectacular," he said at last, kissing the top of her head. "And I'm not one to make love and run, but neither will I overstay my welcome if you'd prefer to sleep alone."

She was quiet so long he wondered if his words bothered her. At long last, she said, "You did tell me that you didn't plan on sleeping." At his quiet chuckle, she continued, "So I won't keep you. But you're welcome to stay if you'd like. It's quite comfortable having you here." She rolled just enough to press a kiss to his cheek.

"Comfortable?" He grimaced. "That's worse than ordinary."

Despite the mirth in his answer, her eyes were serious as she twisted to meet his gaze. "I meant it in the best sense. In the sense that —for whatever reason—it feels natural having you here. Like I said, I'm not a first-date-sex kind of person, so—"

"I want to stay." He said it so quietly, so seriously, it surprised even him. But he meant it. He couldn't imagine leaving now, walking out the front door into the cool night air and leaving her behind. "And for the record, I'm not a first-date-sex kind of person, either."

"Well, then—"

"Oh, shit," he muttered as another thought entered his head. "We didn't use any protection."

How could he be so stupid? Condoms weren't exactly on the

packing list for a solo boat excursion, but how could it not have occurred to him once he and Kelly were tearing at each other's clothes? Unplanned sex was one thing, unprotected sex another.

She sucked in her lower lip and squeezed her eyes shut for a moment. "Oh, geez, I can't believe…how did I not—"

"Have you, ah," —how did one word this, precisely?

"I had my yearly physical a couple weeks ago. I'm perfectly healthy. You?"

"Military discharge exam. Last month."

She exhaled. "And I'm covered as far as pregnancy goes. No worries there."

He nodded, unsure of the proper response. *Hallelujah* didn't seem right.

"Still want to stay? Or did that completely kill the mood?" she asked.

He grinned down at her. How did she know the perfect thing to say? He skimmed his hand along her bare shoulder. Kelly was so open, so honest. So unlike any woman he'd met. Every one, even those with wealth and connections of their own, women who could seduce any man they chose, seemed to want something from him. Something more than banter over a romantic dinner on Giulia's patio. More than a night of passion, more than laughter on a mattress on the floor in the moonlight. It was as if they wanted a piece of his soul without sharing theirs in return.

And that was aside from wanting a piece of the Barrali fortune.

A pang of guilt wound its way through his gut at having kept his identity from her. How ironic that now he wondered if she'd have slept with him if she knew he was one of *those* Barralis, given what she said about "rich and powerful guys." Or how she liked ordinary. Comfortable.

He hadn't out and out lied, but he certainly hadn't told the truth, either.

Does it even matter?

Yes…it did. To him. Even if he never saw her again after tonight, he knew how he'd feel if their roles were reversed.

Still, he couldn't bring himself to tell her. Nor could he bring himself to leave. He wanted her for as long as he could have her, and he'd do his damnedest to ensure she enjoyed herself.

He wondered how long she planned to stay on the island.

"I haven't changed my mind if you haven't," he told her.

She eased out from under him and propped herself on an elbow. "Good, because I could use your muscle. Help me fix the bed?"

He planted a lingering kiss square on her mouth. "Consider it done."

CHAPTER 7

Kelly snapped awake to the sound of books slamming to the floor.

Dazed, she put a hand to her chest as if the physical pressure would slow her heartbeat and put the world to rights, inhaled slowly, then rolled to her side and blinked. Though darkness filled the space over her head, sunshine slivered its way through her cracked bedroom door, casting a thin wedge of light on the white-tiled floor beside the bed.

No, not her bedroom door. The door of her vacation rental.

Not books. A bark. Gaspare.

Using her elbows, she pushed to a sitting position and felt movement beside her. Massimo. He'd spent the night. Not that there was much sleeping.

A satisfied smile flitted across her face at the thought. He'd certainly kept his promise in that department.

They'd made leisurely, romantic love after their initial wild coupling. She'd thought nothing could top their first romp. She was wrong. For hours, he'd practically worshipped her body, discovering every inch of her with strong, slow hands while doing downright sinful things to her with his tongue. She'd done the same, indulging every desire as she stroked her fingertips across the ridges and planes of his magnificent body, exploring to her heart's content. Around three in the morning, they'd shared a soapy, warm shower before collapsing naked into bed.

Never in her life had she experienced such unfettered pleasure.

She surveyed the bedroom, her eyes now adjusted to the dim light. The white sheets were askew, half hanging onto the floor. Filtered light came through the curtains, too, but not enough to have awakened her. Clothing littered the floor. Even her sundress, which she'd finally taken off after they'd heaved the mattress back in place, lay in a heap in the corner.

The most notable thing in the room, though, was Massimo.

The man was buck naked and absolutely glorious, despite the fact he bore a dark shadow along his face and jaw. She watched in languid fascination as he rolled to his side with catlike grace and eased his feet to the ground. His hands came over his head as he stretched, then he scrubbed his palms over his hair and yawned. The muscles in his shoulders rolled with the movement, making her want to reach out and touch him all over again.

Instead, she snuggled deeper into the bedding and allowed her gaze to travel his body, noting the tiny mole near his right shoulder blade, then the temporary red marks created by the crumpled sheets.

Finally, she studied the damaged skin she'd sussed out with her fingertips the night before. During their shower, she'd seen his torso from the front as she'd run soap over his arms and shoulders, then teased at the light hair dusting his chest. But she hadn't yet had a good look at his back. The contrast from the front was striking. It looked as though his left side had been scraped away by a giant, fiery claw, leaving behind burned and tattered skin that was hurriedly plastered together without all the pieces necessary to make the repair. Along the edges, the skin puckered, making her wonder how painful his healing process had been. It wasn't an old injury, either. The raised areas were pink and shiny with new skin, not yet faded to the deep purple or white of old scar tissue.

No wonder he'd stilled when she'd discovered it. Injuries like his were life-altering.

Funny...her initial impression of him had been beach bum. A gorgeous beach bum with an extremely likable dog, but not much more. Then they'd engaged in a bit of banter, and she'd been fascinated enough—and heck, deserving enough after all she'd been though—to indulge her curiosity. But the longer she spent in his company, the more she saw a man constructed of complex layers. One who'd traveled the world and had charisma to spare, yet appreciated simple pleasures like fishing, good wine, and good friends. A man of substance.

So unlike Ted, whose substance clung like shiny lacquer to his surface, but went no deeper.

Then again, she'd misjudged Ted badly. Perhaps she was misjudging Massimo and seeing attributes he didn't truly possess. Not that it mattered. He'd likely disappear before she could utter the words, "Want to go for pancakes?" Because suddenly she craved coffee and a hot, sticky, sweet stack of carbs. There had to be a place to get them on Sarcaccia.

If she was hungry, he was likely ravenous. Once his appetite for food was met, then perhaps she could satisfy his other appetites. Again.

She scooted closer to touch the back of his waist. He was still warm with sleep. Instead of speaking, he reached around to put a hand on her forearm and raised the other to signal that he was listening.

She frowned, straining to hear what he heard.

"Gaspare, come." The words were spoken quietly. A subdued, responding *woof* came from the living room.

"He doesn't bark without reason." Massimo's voice was low and firm, just as it was when he called the dog's name. Gaspare's nose, then the rest of his large body pushed through the cracked bedroom door, sending a blast of sunlight spilling across the bed. "What's up, boy? Someone on the beach get too close?"

As he spoke to the dog, Massimo reached down to the floor to retrieve his underwear and slacks, pulling them on with the deftness of a man used to dressing in seconds.

Aware her own nakedness was now on full display, Kelly lifted the top sheet to cover her breasts. "You think there might be a person outside? He's not just asking to be let out?"

"If he needed to go, he'd have nudged me, not barked. Plus, I let him out after our shower, so he shouldn't have to yet. But we'll see." Massimo whipped on his shirt and was midway through buttoning the front when a pounding shook the front door.

"*Signor Robards! Polizia!*"

A second voice, the accent thick, added, "Mr. Robards, this is the Cateri police. Please now to open the door, or we will enter with the manager of this property."

Massimo spun to look at her. "Robards?"

Ted? Her heart thrummed against the walls of her chest in a panic. What in the world was going on? Why would the police be looking for him here?

And geez, she was naked.

"Just a moment! I'm getting dressed!" she called to the door.

"We will give you *one* minute, yes?" came the annoyed reply.

"Thank you, I'll be right there!" She sprang from the bed and raced across the bedroom for her clothes. Her suitcase was perched on a luggage rack beside the bathroom door. Rummaging through, she located a clean bra and underwear, a T-shirt, and a pair of jeans, then began yanking them on. The silence from the opposite side of the room felt like a knife to her back.

"I had this reservation under another name," she explained as she put one foot, then the other into the jeans. "I'm sure there's some confusion is all. Give me a second and I'll straighten it out."

"Of course, *Signor.*"

She whirled around as she pulled the T-shirt over her head. Bemusement lit Massimo's features as he strolled across the bedroom, then took a seat in the armchair beside the window. His eyes never left her body as she pulled her hair out of the neck of the shirt and fluffed it over her shoulders. Did he actually find this funny? Or was his humor sarcastic? Given that she had a more pressing concern at the front door, she wasn't sure it mattered.

"It's a long story." Because what else could she say? That she was supposed to be here on her honeymoon? "I'm shocked the police are here. It makes no sense."

"I'm sure they're more than willing to explain it to you."

Great. She glanced at Gaspare as she crossed to the bedroom door, then said to Massimo, "You want to hang out in here with him so he doesn't freak out the police?"

Massimo leaned back in the chair and made a wide gesture. "Go right ahead. But don't take too long or Gaspare really will need to make use of the outdoors."

When she reached the front hall, Kelly smoothed her hair as best she could before putting her eye to the peephole. Sure enough, two uniformed police officers stood at the door. Just behind them, an agitated-looking man in a pair of black slacks and a light gray shirt paced back and forth in front of the police car that now blocked in Massimo's Jeep.

She closed her eyes, stepped back from the door and exhaled. These gentlemen were serious.

The door shook with another pounding just as she reached for the handle, causing her to gasp. Slowly, she opened it to the officers. "Good morning," she managed. "How can I help you?"

"My name is Officer Scarpa. I am with the Cateri police. Is Mr. Robards here?" This from the shorter of the two officers, the one who must've called out in English.

"No. I'm Kelly Chase. We booked this villa together."

The man in the black slacks had stopped pacing to study her when she opened the door, but now he said something in rapid Italian she didn't understand, though she did catch the words *Signor Robards*, *telefonato*, and *Euros*.

"I'm sorry," she said to the officers, "but my Italian is very limited. What is the problem, exactly?"

"The manager says that this villa was reserved by a Mr. Robards. But yesterday afternoon, a man claiming to be Mr. Robards called and said that he had been unable to make his flight. He said he would forfeit the deposit and cancel the reservation. The manager, he explained to this man that his wife gave the key to a woman claiming to be Mrs. Robards yesterday morning. Mr. Robards assured him that there is no Mrs. Robards and that he is unmarried. He demanded that the manager accept the deposit and cancel the reservation, because this is what is in the contract."

She stared at the officer, becoming more dumbfounded with every word he uttered. She muttered, more to herself than to the officer, "You have got to be kidding me."

"No." Officer Scarpa's voice was level. "There is no kidding. This is why we are here."

"I see." Anger boiled in her gut. *How dare he?*

Ted had to have heard that she decided to take the honeymoon alone. Even if he hadn't, if he'd called to cancel and was told there was a Mrs. Robards who'd checked in to the villa, he should've known that it was her.

And what right did he have to cancel and forfeit the deposit, anyway? *She'd* paid for it. With her own hard-earned money. Money made from selling her business. Her heart and soul. How he had the nerve—

The jaded looks on the officers' faces as they waited for her to speak suddenly horrified her more than the thought of what Ted had done. Without having heard her side of the story, the two men assumed she was the person at fault in this situation. Not Ted. And they had the villa's manager wearing a rift in the gravel driveway behind them as if to confirm it.

Mustering her most businesslike, placid tone, she explained, "As I said, my name is Kelly Chase. Mr. Robards and I booked this villa together for our honeymoon. However—"

The taller officer interrupted in Italian. Officer Scarpa grunted in response without taking his eyes off Kelly. The grunt sounded ominous.

Before Kelly could continue her explanation, Officer Scarpa said, "Please, do you have your passport? And papers proving that you have paid for this? The manager, he says that only Mr. Robards was named on the reservation, though it was made for two persons."

Not true, she wanted to argue. She'd made the reservation herself and had given the manager's wife both names when she booked. As tightly as Sarcaccia clung to its old world traditions, the woman must have only written down Ted's name. But she could show them proof. She angled a thumb behind her. "I have my passport inside. I don't have the confirmation, but if I can access a computer, I can pull up the reservation info and my e-mail communications with the manager's wife. The final payment was set to come automatically from my bank yesterday after I checked in, so I should be able to pull up a record of that, too."

Officer Scarpa gestured past the villa's manager, who was now grumbling at the taller police officer but was being ignored, toward his police cruiser. "Please, then, to come with us to our station and we will use the computer. Bring with you your passport."

Her relief at having identification faded. "To the police station? Surely we can handle this here and now." Especially since she had a recently nude man lounging in her bedroom and there was ample evidence of what had gone on the night before. Evidence that would not ingratiate her with the manager, she suspected, should he decide to inspect the premises while she was out.

The officers looked at each other, but the silent message passed between them was clear to Kelly. Incredulous, she asked, "Wait, am I being arrested?"

The taller officer couldn't hide his annoyance. Officer Scarpa's voice was firm as he said, "This is not your house. The manager, he called yesterday all afternoon. You did not answer the phone. You are not the name of the reservation and you have not paid. He says that your payment did not work from the bank, and—"

"The payment *what*?"

"—you are to stay in our custody until you prove for us who you are and make payment. This villa, it is very expensive and in demand for honeymoon people like you, yes? And so the manager wishes to rent it to someone else for the week. This is a very busy time now on the island."

The manager apparently knew enough English to understand,

because he stopped his pacing and exhaled, as if his problems were about to be solved.

"I spent yesterday afternoon at the beach, which is what anyone who rented this place would do." She fought to hit the right tone, one that would resonate with the officers. "The manager does not need to re-rent it—I truly understand that it would be a great loss of money to him—but the reservation should never have been considered cancelled in the first place, especially given that I picked up the key before Mr. Robards called." The idiot. "This is a simple matter. I can ensure the manager is paid and show you all the paperwork without—"

"Do you have a dog there?" The click of dog paws against tile came to Kelly's ears at the same time the officer asked the question.

Fabulous. There was likely some no-pet policy that would get her in even more trouble. "I have a guest at the moment, yes. He has a dog with him, but the dog is not staying here."

As soon as the words left her mouth, she realized she should have phrased that better. Who had a male guest at this time of the morning? And after admitting that she'd booked the place for her honeymoon?

The cops picked up on that, too.

"Bring out your guest, Ms. Chase. Now."

THIS WOULD NOT END WELL.

Massimo waited until he heard Kelly open the front door, then made quick work of tidying the bedroom. Sheets smoothed into place, bedspread righted. Her clothing—the panties she wore last night had indeed been plain white cotton—shaken out, folded, and placed atop her suitcase. Towels straightened in the bathroom once he'd glanced in the mirror and splashed his face, hoping he appeared well-rested, though he'd be far more confident of pulling off the look if he had a razor.

She might not know Cateri's local police force, but he did. They didn't operate in the same manner as the American police. There would be no warrants, no niceties, not unless she insisted upon it. If this was anything other than a wellness check—which he couldn't imagine, given her rather vigorous state of health and the fact the man hammering on the door asked for a *Signor Robards*—then the police would soon be walking through the villa as if they owned the place.

He wasn't about to let the police see him inside the villa in its present state. He couldn't believe he was going to see police at all. He preferred his police contact to remain limited to the occasional parade or security detail they provided at state functions.

Then again, what did he expect when he picked up a random woman on the beach?

He signaled Gaspare to heel before slipping from the bedroom to the kitchen. The officer was speaking to Kelly. No one could mistake the fact he was losing patience over whatever was being discussed. Massimo swept the wine glasses from the countertop and—opting not to run water and draw attention—hid them under the sink. Kelly would find them later. As he closed the door to the cabinet, Kelly's voice came to him clearly. She was asking if she was about to be arrested.

She sounded stunned. The policeman sounded brusque. Another voice, one coming from somewhere behind the officers, rambled in self-righteous Italian about a phone call from the United States and how he was losing money by the minute.

Massimo leaned against the refrigerator, straining to hear the man in the background. Whoever he was, he'd clearly been the one to bring the police to Kelly's doorstep at this hour.

Then a phrase from the police officer stood out from the Italian chatter. "This villa, it is very expensive and in demand for honeymoon people like you, yes?"

It was the *like you* that sent a chill through him.

She was here on her honeymoon?

He swiped a hand from his forehead to his jaw as if he could wipe away what he'd just heard.

How in the...what the hell had he gotten himself into with her?

Who the hell had a one-night stand—because that was certainly all it was, no matter what delusions gripped him in the middle of the night —on their *honeymoon?*

A low noise came from Gaspare. He'd remained in place beside Massimo, but his hungry gaze was locked on the bowl Kelly had put down the night before. Massimo muttered an oath, then motioned for Gaspare to go ahead and take a drink. Food would be required soon, too, judging from how quickly the dog crossed the tile floor to lap up the water and the sloppy way in which he did it.

Kelly's arguments grew more and more adamant, but Massimo didn't hear any denial about the fact she was on her honeymoon. In fact, it seemed as if she were well acquainted with the mysterious Mr. Robards, because he'd apparently called to cancel the reservation.

Her fiancé ? Or…her husband?

The idea left him nauseous. Never in his life had he flirted with a married woman, let alone bedded one. There were certain lines he would never, ever cross. Even if she'd portrayed herself as single, he'd feel guilty for the rest of his life if she turned out to be a *Mrs.*

If only the police would decide. Make the arrest or leave. At the moment, he didn't care which, as long as they didn't discover him here. He didn't need a scandal on top of the guilt.

Gaspare crossed the kitchen, water dripping from the fur under his jaw, at the same time the police officer asked Kelly, "Do you have a dog there?"

A few heartbeats later came the words Massimo dreaded, a demand for Kelly to bring out her "guest."

Massimo picked up the water bowl and placed it in the sink, then used a paper towel to wipe the floor. With deliberate steps, he headed for the front door. If he was compelled to see the police this morning, he'd do it on his own terms.

This would not end well.

CHAPTER 8

SHE SHOULD BE INTIMIDATED. The police stood in front of her with their feet apart, hands at their belts, as if prepared for a full-on physical assault. As if they did this day in and day out while facing down criminals who should know better.

Well, she wasn't a criminal. She was a twenty-seven-year-old closet organizer from Dallas visiting the island for a little rest and relaxation. The only eyebrow-raising thing she'd done was have a night of phenomenal sex with an incredibly good-looking—and rather well-endowed—man and, well, good for her. If every visitor to Sarcaccia had a night like hers, tourism would explode.

After a deep breath, she crossed her arms in front of her chest. "Again, am I being placed under arrest? If so, what is the charge? I've committed no crime here. I booked this villa months ago, I paid a deposit, I picked up the key. I have access to the confirmations you've requested and I can prove—"

"Excuse me, may I be of assistance?" Massimo's deep voice came from behind her.

She glanced at him over her shoulder as he filled the entry hall. Aside from the day-old scruff on his face, he appeared as put together as when he'd met her at the parking lot last night. His shirt was tucked neatly into his pants, his shoes were on his feet, and his close-cropped hair kept him from having any signs of bedhead. She sent a prayer heavenward for the small favor. The police were far more likely to consider him an early morning guest—one who just happened to stop by with his dog—than if he looked the way he had five minutes earlier, when he'd been naked in her bed.

And maybe, given that he'd offered assistance, he'd be willing to explain in Italian what the police didn't seem to understand in English. Quietly, she said, "I'm sorry, Massimo, but there's been a misunderstanding—"

"Your Highness," the two officers said at the same time, their tone reverent though their eyes were wide with surprise. "We're honored," Officer Scarpa added. "We are sorry if we have disturbed you this morning, but we have police business with Ms. Chase."

Your Highness? Kelly turned back to the officers just in time to see the taller one straighten. Behind them, the manager had clasped his hands together and folded into a placating bow.

"Prince Massimo!" he cried as he raised his head. This was followed by a torrent of Italian and several wide gestures she took as a welcome.

Slowly, she looked back at Massimo and raised an eyebrow. Were the police and manager for real?

He didn't meet her gaze. Instead, he stepped forward and began speaking to the police in such rapid Italian she couldn't pick out any but the most basic words. Officer Scarpa asked him a question—the only word Kelly thought she understood was *cane,* for dog—then nodded understanding as Massimo gave him a relaxed-sounding response. Massimo then said a few words to the manager, who waved his hands in the universal signal for no problem.

Slowly, the knots that wound Kelly's gut eased. Maybe, just maybe, she would be able to deal with the police rationally, rather than having to spend her day sorting out the villa payment at a police station.

Then she could ask Massimo why he was being called Your Highness. And Prince Massimo.

She tried to recall exactly what he'd said in the Jeep last night when he'd told her his name was Barrali. She'd asked if it was common…and whether she was right in thinking that was the name of the royal family.

He'd said it was common. But he hadn't exactly said he wasn't royal. And though she knew the names of King Carlo and Queen Fabrizia, she couldn't remember what all their children were named. She only knew they had a lot of them. She bit the inside of her lip as the men continued talking.

What in the world—*who* in the world—had she done last night?

"Ms. Chase," Massimo said in a courteous but formal tone, "I explained to the police that you found my dog on the beach and were kind enough to call the phone number on his collar so I could retrieve him. I am in your debt. I apologize for putting you in the position of violating the policy against dogs, but the manager assures me that you will not incur any fines."

Playing along, she said, "Oh, I couldn't leave a stray dog on the beach alone. And he's so well-behaved, he wasn't a problem at all."

"Again, I thank you for your assistance." He gave her a polite nod, then whistled for Gaspare. "I'll leave you to sort out your misunderstanding."

She felt her jaw drop open, then snapped it shut before the officers noticed. He wasn't going to help her? Maybe explain her situation to the cops or the awestruck manager? She didn't expect he'd be thrilled to hear she was supposed to have been spending this week with another man—even if that man apparently was so angry with her for canceling the wedding that he canceled the reservation—but she thought that last night was meaningful enough that Massimo might consider spending five minutes translating for her.

Apparently not.

She tried to formulate a proper response, but Massimo was off the porch and climbing into his Jeep without a backward glance. The taller officer hurried to move the cruiser enough to allow Massimo access to the main road.

Anything for a prince, she supposed.

A prince. She'd had sex with a prince. A lot of sex. A lot of *good* sex.

She exhaled and ran her hands over her hair. The roots still held moisture from the shower she and Massimo shared. Even if he didn't look like he'd spent the night rolling in the sheets, she imagined she did.

"Ms. Chase, if you would come with us now?"

Her attention whipped from the driveway, where Massimo was backing his Jeep under the wisteria vines toward the main road, to Officer Scarpa, who remained with his feet firmly planted on the front porch, then back to the Jeep. Massimo's hand gripped the gearshift as he put the Jeep in drive, then took off, out of sight, with Gaspare riding shotgun beside him.

"Ms. Chase."

"What?" Massimo hadn't even looked back. Was he so used to mind-blowing, earth-shattering sex that he didn't think twice about leaving her?

"You must now come to the police station. We will resolve this issue there."

A protest popped into her mouth, but dissolved before she could utter it. There was no give in Officer Scarpa's stance, no sign he'd listen to any further discussion until they reached the station.

"All right." She glanced at the taller officer, who'd returned from moving his car looking as stern as ever. "But I'd like to get my things." No way was she leaving her belongings behind for the manager to peruse...or toss.

"We will escort you inside, yes?" He turned and spoke to the manager in Italian, apparently asking him to wait, then gestured for Kelly to lead the way. She wanted to argue, but his expression made it clear the issue was non-negotiable.

Hopefully they'd stay in the living area while she gathered her clothing and toiletries from the bedroom. If the police went in there, there'd be no mistaking what went on the night before. *All* the night before.

"I'll grab my suitcase from the bedroom. It's nearly packed," she said as she moved from the entry hall to the living area. To her surprise, the kitchen counter was clear. No wine glasses, no wine.

Even the bowl she'd put down for Gaspare had been moved. She turned to the bedroom, hoping like mad the police would stay behind her, and nearly gasped aloud at the sight.

Massimo was a one-man cleaning crew. The bedding looked as if a hotel maid had whipped everything into perfect shape. Perfectly stacked pillows lined the top edge of the fluffed comforter. The bed didn't even look slept in. Even more impressive, not a stitch of clothing remained on the floor. Her wadded dress had vanished from the corner, her underwear were…wait, where did he put everything? Discreetly, she scanned the room as she walked toward the bathroom. If everything had been kicked under the bed, she'd have to fish it out. Worse, she'd probably have to explain it to the cops.

Her suitcase remained on the rack beside the bathroom door. There, folded as neatly as if she'd done it herself, were the clothes she'd worn the previous evening.

Oh, geez. He'd folded her panties.

Her face burned as she entered the bathroom and plucked her bikini from the small towel rack where she'd hung it to dry, then swept her toiletries into her makeup bag. After zipping everything into her suitcase, she rolled it past Officer Scarpa, who stood at the door to her bedroom. "That's all of it. Once I prove that I did rent this villa and made the required payments, I assume you'll give me a ride back here? This is cutting into my vacation time."

She hoped she sounded like a typical vacationer—an innocent vacationer—dealing with a travel snafu. But as irritated as she was by the headache Ted had caused her, her mind remained fixated on Massimo. Though she wanted to believe he'd cleaned the place as a favor to her, she doubted that was the case. He had his own reputation to protect. A *royal* reputation, apparently. He wasn't about to leave behind a mess.

Her stomach twisted with a sick feeling of déjà vu as she crossed the gravel driveway to the police cruiser.

Two short weeks ago, she'd pressed her engagement ring into Ted's palm and insisted he take it back. He'd stared at it for a moment. She'd worried that he'd refuse or that he'd come up with yet another excuse for why he'd acted the way he had. But he'd curled his fingers around the diamond and nodded as if accepting her decision. He'd looked up from his fist with a smile hooking the edges of his mouth. When he spoke, his response was so unexpected it had burned itself into her brain.

This is a mess, Kelly. But I clean up my messes. Before you know it, everything will be put to rights. We'll both be happy again.

At the time, she'd thought he'd meant he'd be able to put his life back together. Nothing in his tone implied a threat. In fact, he'd sounded placid, as if he'd come to a place of acceptance.

Now she wasn't so sure.

The tall officer took her bag and placed it in the trunk of the police cruiser with a thump while Officer Scarpa guided her by the elbow into the back seat. She reached for the door handle just as Officer Scarpa used two hands to push it closed without meeting her gaze. The men climbed into the front and simultaneously shut their doors.

The sound may as well have been a jailhouse door slamming shut.

***

He'd avoided a scandal. So far.

Massimo strode through the long gallery leading to his private apartment, which was located on the ground floor in the rear of the palace. Gaspare kept pace at his side, no doubt salivating over the thought of his waiting food bowl. Hungry as he was himself, all Massimo wanted was to fall face first into bed. Physically and mentally, he was exhausted.

Despite the tiredness that gripped him clear to the bone, sleep wasn't an option. Daytime in the palace meant someone—a sibling, a staff member, or God forbid, one of his parents—would want to see him. If a family member discovered him asleep, they'd either ask questions he didn't care to answer or they'd fret about his health. There'd been enough of that since his return from Africa to last him a lifetime. He hated being grilled about his recovery. Worse than that, though, he hated being fussed over. It made a man feel impotent, and if last night proved anything to him, it was that he wasn't *that*.

He swore under his breath as a new thought occurred to him. At his request, his family had taken steps to ensure the public was unaware he'd been wounded while on duty. He'd explained to his concerned parents that it was a security measure. If the enemy ever learned the details of his injuries, it was possible they'd determine where he'd been stationed. That knowledge could cause irreparable harm to those still operating in the area as well as to the locals his unit had helped. But now someone outside the family knew he'd been hurt.

Kelly knew.

To her credit, she hadn't fussed. Nor had she plied him with questions. She'd merely run her fingers over the burned, scarred area, traced the still-healing ridges with her fingertips, then moved along to caress the rest of his body…exploring, sucking, kissing, tasting. Making him feel more alive, more vital, more *normal* than he'd felt in months.

But apparently he knew nothing about *her*. Her body, yes, a few tidbits about her life, but nothing that was truly important. Yet she knew some rather important things about him.

He desperately needed a nap so he could think about what to do. Or not do.

Gaspare slowed his gait to look behind them. A beat later, the sound of heels clicking against hardwood came to Massimo's ears. He knew without using the towering mirrors lining either side of the long gallery or glancing over his shoulder that it was his mother.

More than once he'd wondered if she'd always sounded royal when she walked or if it was marrying King Carlo that imbued her with that particular trait.

The clicking deadened as she stepped from hardwood onto the carpet that ran the length of the gallery, meaning she was close enough he couldn't ignore her. He stopped walking and slowly turned, a warm smile on his face.

"Good morning, Massimo." She was alone, a rarity at this time of day. If she was in the palace rather than attending a luncheon or political event, she was usually surrounded by staff. He wondered how long she'd been waiting for him.

"I thought that might be you behind me. You look lovely today." And she did. Tasteful beige heels and a form-fitting emerald green wrap dress made her appear both young and stately at the same time. Her blonde hair was arranged in a perfect updo, disguising the wisps of gray she'd allowed to appear in the last few years. A pair of delicate, pear-shaped diamonds graced her ears. Despite being in her early sixties, Queen Fabrizia's face glowed with a radiance usually seen in women half her age.

Of course, it probably helped that she prioritized her exercise time when outlining her schedule each week. The woman could knock out a six-mile run in a better time than most men he knew. Having a personal chef create fresh, vegetable-heavy meals didn't hurt her figure one bit, either.

"Thank you." Her assessing gaze took in his stubble and the wrinkles at the elbows of his shirt before alighting on the duffel bag he'd carried in from his Jeep. "Were you out this morning?"

"Yes." She knew perfectly well he'd been out this morning and all night, too. He suspected that was precisely the reason she'd followed him into the gallery. She'd likely asked the staff to notify her when his Jeep entered the palace's underground garage.

"I assume you're heading to your apartment. May I join you?"

Since saying no to Queen Fabrizia wasn't an option, he gestured down the hall in the direction he was already walking. She fell into step beside him, saying nothing more until they reached the double doors leading to his suite of rooms. One of the housekeeping staff exited just as they arrived. Despite the stack of towels balanced in her arms, the young woman gave the pair a deferential bow. The queen greeted her by name and asked after her brother's health, mentioning his recently broken leg, then offered well wishes for the woman's entire family.

Once the doors were closed behind them, Massimo said, "You have an amazing memory for names, Mother. I didn't think Maria was assigned to any of your rooms."

"She's not, but it's only polite to know the staff. It's our duty, as well."

Ah. So that was where the conversation would go. Duty.

Massimo invited her to take a seat on one of the living room's two large sofas as he set his duffel bag near the door. Gaspare disappeared toward the apartment's kitchenette, where he'd find his food dish. A strip of light below one of the floor-to-ceiling windows that overlooked the palace's rear garden caught Massimo's attention. The heavy curtains had been pulled most of the way shut. Ostensibly it had been done to protect the furnishings and carpets from the sun's bright rays, but it gave the place an abandoned, foreboding feeling.

He walked to the first window and used the hidden pull cord to let in more light. As he moved to the second window, he heard his mother lightly clear her throat. It was her way of letting him know she'd searched him out for a specific reason and that her time was limited.

Much as he loved her, and much as he knew giving her his undivided attention would get her out of his apartment faster, he wasn't in the mood. He grasped the cord to the side of the second window and pulled, allowing sunshine to stream across the room's gleaming hardwood floors, masculine brown sofas, and antique furnishings. Eventually he'd need to redecorate the apartment and replace the palace treasures from generations past with more modern and—frankly— more livable furnishings. His mother had been after him for years to update the rooms, but when he'd been granted the space after returning home from university, he'd known he'd only be in residence temporarily and didn't much care what was in it. He certainly hadn't any urge to hire a decorator or order furniture during his time abroad.

By the time he'd crossed to the third large window, Queen Fabrizia had tired of waiting. "Massimo, dear, take a seat. We need to talk."

"Sounds ominous." The cord on the third window stuck. He reached behind the curtain to locate the source of the snag.

"Let me call someone to fix that. You should sit."

While politely stated, it wasn't a suggestion. Reluctantly, he left the window and moved to the sofa opposite the one where his mother sat. Her back was perfectly straight, legs crossed at the ankles, hands folded in her lap as if she were posing for a portrait.

He didn't flop onto the sofa, exactly, but he didn't lower himself quite as she expected him to, either. "What's on your agenda this morning?" he asked.

Her smile was tolerant. "I'm attending a brunch in the garden with a group from Doctors Without Borders and later this afternoon there's the opening of the new tennis center. But my first priority this morning is my children."

"Alessandro causing trouble again?"

"Always." Amusement flickered in her eyes, then faded. "But at this precise moment I'm worried about *you*, Massimo."

She expected him to ask why or to state that all was well, but he knew better than to give her such an opening. Instead, he remained quiet as she stared at him and waited. And waited. Though she appeared unruffled on the surface at his prolonged silence, he could tell it flustered her. There was a slight flare to her nostrils, the most miniscule of movement in her hands. Tics only he—and perhaps his siblings—would notice.

"You were out overnight," she said at last.

"Yes." He made it a point to frown as if confused. As a royal he didn't have quite the same freedom of movement as most people, but his mother should realize that twenty-eight-year-old men occasionally stayed out all night and didn't check in with their parents.

"Were you on your boat?"

"Not all night, no. Not the most comfortable place to sleep."

This time, it was her turn to play the silence card. Queen Fabrizia was nothing if not a quick study. He knew she wasn't going to speak until he explained himself. As she watched him, a curious twitch made the corner of her mouth jump. He knew then that she knew.

It wasn't that he was out all night, hanging out at a bar or playing cards with friends. It was that he'd mentioned sleep, and comfort, which suggested that he'd been prone in a bed besides his own.

CHAPTER 9

His mind raced for an explanation that would satisfy her curiosity without confirming he'd had female companionship. Queen Fabrizia was worldly enough to know that her sons were no paragons of celibacy, nor did she expect it; however, she didn't want them flaunting their sexual escapades and risking the family's reputation. As each of her sons hit puberty, she'd asked her husband to speak to them about the need for discretion, given their family's high profile position.

King Carlo's stern warning: Unless you're telling us over tea that you've met a woman who is above reproach and that you are a couple, and will be appearing together in public as such, your mother and I should not hear of it.

His sterner warning, given out of his wife's hearing: Keep it in your pants. If you don't, you'd better not get caught. And for God's sake, never, ever do it in public, pay for it, or allow it to be recorded.

At fourteen, Massimo's horror at hearing such frank talk from the king kept him on the straight and narrow, but as Massimo matured he'd watched his older brothers and learned from both their good examples and their mistakes.

Then again, to his knowledge none of them had the police show up at the crack of dawn while they were lying naked in bed, recovering from an all-night marathon of body-wrenching sex.

"Will I be seeing you on tonight's news?" his mother asked, as if reading his mind.

"I can't imagine you would." After all, there hadn't been anyone with a camera at Kelly's this morning and with any luck, his name wouldn't appear in the police report. "I spent the afternoon on the boat, then visited Giulia and Guillermo. Had a lovely dinner and bottle of wine while I watched the sunset from their patio. They asked that I wish you and father well." Let her think he overindulged in the pleasures of Giulia's wine cellar and stayed the night in one of her guest rooms rather than get behind the wheel.

Surprise registered in her soft green eyes, followed by genuine warmth. "I haven't seen them in years. How are they? Healthy? Busy?"

"As ever. Guillermo brought in last night's sea bass himself and Giulia's countertops were covered with homemade pasta when I arrived. I ate like I haven't eaten in months. Even had dessert." Which reminded him that he'd left his sister's ravioli in Kelly's refrigerator. With any luck, Giulia would forget about it by the next time she saw Sophia, or he'd have some explaining to do to his sister as well as his mother.

"That's wonderful. I had no idea you'd planned to see them." She waited a moment, as if contemplating her next words, then stood and walked to the center window. With her back to him, she said, "I know you've only been home a few weeks, and I've been reluctant to push you into your formal duties here. Your father and I made that mistake with Stefano after he was away and regretted it. But have you given thought to what you'll be doing next?"

He'd known this was coming from the moment he arrived home. "Of course. There's not much to do on the boat besides think."

"And?"

"I haven't made any firm decisions yet."

She turned away from the garden and gave Massimo the barest tip of her head, making it clear that the mere fact she felt compelled to raise the topic should light a fire under him. "You've been through a lot, I know. More than anyone outside the family will ever understand —probably more than anyone inside the family can understand—but unless you're willing to publicly acknowledge that you were injured in combat—"

"I'm not."

"—you must act in the manner expected of you as a resident member of the royal household, complete with all the duties that entails. That means making appearances before questions are raised about why you're not."

"I understand that, Mother."

"Have you looked at the calendar lately? Independence Day is this weekend."

He pressed his lips into a tight line and nodded.

"You know as well as I do that you can't be entirely absent. You're expected in the royal box at the parade, at a minimum. Preferably you'll attend more of the festivities. The dinner and the royal ball, especially, would be nice. I hate to compel you to do so before you're ready—"

"I'll come to the parade. And I'll look over the list of events and let you know which others I will attend."

He'd heard it from birth. Being born a Barrali meant one had to put duty first and personal needs second. Most of the time he considered it a privilege. While he owed his country a life of service, his position also offered him access to a vast network of business, political, and social powerhouses, people who could make a difference in the world. People who interested him and who challenged him to be a better man, and who'd shown him how he could use his position to benefit others.

But until he figured out the exact path he wished to take now that he was out of the military, he needed to be alone with his thoughts rather than surrounded by the movers and shakers of the world.

"Thank you." She paused for a moment. "After making your first public appearance, you'll need to take the appropriate steps to fulfill your role here in Sarcaccia, even if it's gradual. Have you considered which charitable causes you'd like to support? Perhaps one of the children's organizations or a health-related cause would suit. Of course, I assume you have economic and political interests...are you considering something similar to Stefano's work on the country's transportation infrastructure?"

He couldn't imagine a more snooze-inducing pursuit. "I've been weighing my options."

Her eyes narrowed fractionally as she assessed him. She was unused to being put off, especially on matters she considered important. "While you make your decision, begin assembling a staff so they'll be in place when you're ready to work."

"I'll begin today." Once he took a nap. Assuming he could stop thinking about Kelly Chase long enough to sleep. How was it that after a few weeks at home, it was an American tourist who made him feel vibrant again? Who made him feel *anything* again?

"Good." She brushed a piece of imaginary lint from her hip. Her nails were painted an understated pink, but the diamond and emerald ring she'd received as a fortieth anniversary gift from her husband last year sparkled in the light from the windows as her hand swept from her dress toward his desk. "I assume you were supplied with paper and a pen when your apartment was prepared for your return?"

He assumed so, too. "You can check. Why?"

"I'll leave notes for you." She moved the antique chair aside and slid open the narrow wooden drawer in the center of the desk, then withdrew a piece of stationery and a pen.

"I know what needs to be done, Mother." He resisted adding a, *for crying out loud, I'm a grown man.* Grown as he might be, a mother-son relationship wasn't the same in a royal family as in a traditional one. A power factor existed that other families didn't have, one built into the legal fabric of the country.

"Yes, but I can make it easier." She seated herself at his desk as if it were her own and began writing. "First, you'll need an assistant to manage your schedule and your correspondence. Since Vittorio recently hired a new assistant, you should speak with him about candidates. Also, we have several events at the palace in the coming weeks. I expect you'll attend at least a few, which means you'll need to update your wardrobe. For that, you need a stylist."

The thought made him want to close his eyes and lean back into the sofa. Meeting with a stylist, especially one who'd want to take his measurements, discuss suit colors and fabrics, or—worst of all—offer suggestions on his personal grooming habits, was akin to opening a vein in his arm with a rusty spoon. Instead of protesting, as he suspected his brother Alessandro would do, he kept his gaze riveted on the queen. When she got into one of her get-everything-done-now modes—a key sign of which was her need to make lists—the only way to end it was to let her think he was grateful for her help and would do everything she asked.

As if she could sense his horror over her use of the word *stylist*, she glanced at him to be sure he was paying attention. "Do you know where to find a good stylist, Massimo?" Without waiting for an answer, she said, "Your sister recently found one for Stefano's fiancée, Megan, so if you're uncertain about whom you wish to hire, ask Sophia."

"I'll do that."

The queen's updo had the audacity to bobble atop her head as she continued writing. "Megan was a hard sell. Didn't want a stylist. Said she'd worked in the hotel business for years and knew how to dress professionally. While she does have good taste, one can always use refinement, especially when it comes to attending events as a member of the royal family."

Since Megan was from Minnesota, which didn't pride itself on stylists or royal soirees, he could see why a suggestion that she could "use refinement" before becoming a member of the Barrali family might've rankled. Megan was used to her independence and to making her own decisions. It was like imagining Kelly with a stylist. A stylist wouldn't have selected the blue sundress she'd worn to dinner last night. They'd have claimed it was too boring, too common. They'd have urged her to choose a more luxurious fabric while overlooking the way the dress hugged her upper body, the way the color contrasted with her brown eyes to make them seem even more deep and soulful. The way the skirt floated around her long, long legs.

The ease with which it could be hitched up over those legs.

He cursed himself for the mental image and shifted forward on the sofa.

"Maybe Megan has a different perspective, given that she and Stefano don't reside in the palace," he suggested. Instead of living with the rest of the royal family, the couple purchased a large apartment a few kilometers away, near the waterfront. The location offered them easy access to the palace and Stefano's staff, yet afforded them a modicum of privacy as they prepared for their upcoming wedding. It was as close to rebellion as any of his siblings dared. Massimo wasn't sure whether it was a brilliant move on Stefano's part or one he'd come to regret.

"I'm hopeful they'll move back," the queen replied, her tone ever-practical. "You'll need to get up to speed on the current economic and political environment so you can speak intelligently on such matters. I'll have the relevant information sent to you, unless you'd prefer to work with an adviser."

She was on a mission now. Apparently, talking about Megan and Stefano made her more determined than ever to keep Massimo on the track she'd set in her mind.

"The information will be fine, Mother. I don't need—"

"And you simply must hire a decorator. These rooms are terribly outdated." She set down her pen and faced him. "Start with your closet. Most of what's in there is from your university years or before. You'll need to clear space for new suits, clothing for casual events, new accessories—"

"I met with a closet organizer yesterday."

Why that came out of his mouth, he didn't know. Perhaps it was to stave off his mother's attempts to organize *him*. Perhaps it was because he hated all discussion of stylists and decorators—two items that he wished to ban from his vocabulary, let alone his apartment. Perhaps it was because he couldn't shake Kelly from his mind.

Perhaps it was guilt at leaving Kelly to fend for herself with the police, though he had no reason to feel guilty. He wasn't the one renting a place under a different name or cheating the landlord out of money for a honeymoon villa. He certainly wasn't sleeping with someone else while *on* his honeymoon.

He let out a long, slow breath. Problem was, despite the police presence or the landlord's red-faced insistence that Kelly was squatting on the property, he didn't believe it. Whatever happened with the honeymoon, there was something...not right. Because what he'd felt about midnight, when he'd laced his fingers through hers and their foreheads were pressed together, stirred his soul. It may have been a one-night stand, but there was more than sex involved.

"Who?" His mother couldn't hide her shock. "When was this meeting?"

He blinked, jerking his attention back to the queen. He intentionally ignored the first question and answered the second. "Yesterday afternoon. Before I went to Giulia and Guillermo's."

He stood and crossed the room. Gently, he put a hand on his mother's shoulder. He could feel her collarbone underneath the soft silk of her dress. Though she looked robust, she seemed thinner than usual, as if worn down by worry.

"I'm fine," he assured her. "I've been away for a long time. I worked long, hard hours for the last few years and I've needed time to get my bearings now that I'm back to civilization. That's all. I've always been responsible. I'll always *be* responsible."

"I know." Her hand came up to cover his. "But I like the reassurance."

He glanced down at the list she'd composed. Immaculate handwriting covered the fine stationery. He wondered if the handwriting, like her walk, was part of her when she was young or had come with time and the impossibly high expectations of becoming the Barrali matriarch. "Consider yourself reassured. No one can miss with a checklist like yours. Too bad I can't hire you as my assistant."

"I'd drive you crazy." She patted his hand, then pushed back from the desk. Gaspare chose that moment to plod in from the kitchen. The dog glanced at them and, satisfied that he wasn't needed, found a square of sunshine in which to lounge. Though he was out of the way, his appearance in the room was enough of a distraction to alter the mood.

"I need to prepare for my brunch," his mother said, "and you need a shave and shower. I'll have budget information sent to you this afternoon from the family accountants so you'll know what you can spend on your staff. But please, follow up with the closet organizer. Today, if you can. It's important you get started. Then you'll feel better hiring everyone else."

He nodded his thanks, then escorted her to the door, folding her list and sliding it into his front pants pocket as he went. Once she was gone, he returned to the windows, still craving the light and fresh air of the outdoors. Despite its soaring ceilings, the apartment felt stuffy, as if the air merely used the extra space it was allotted in order to press down more heavily on the room's occupants.

He couldn't begin to guess what the massive windows weighed, but surely there was a way to open them. He could've sworn he'd seen maintenance workers open the lower sections before. His fingers skimmed the lower perimeter of the glass, feeling for a lever. Gaspare twisted his head to watch, then shifted his body further into the sunshine and let out a low whine, as if annoyed that Massimo dared move close enough to cast a shadow.

"What?" Massimo frowned at the dog. "Am I bothering you?"

Gaspare settled his head on the floor, but didn't close his eyes. He looked forlorn. It wasn't a typical expression for the dog, but now Massimo had seen it twice in twenty-four hours. The last was when a certain woman was scratching Gaspare's rear and the dog knew he was about to be commanded to his owner's side.

"You liked her, didn't you, old boy? Yeah, well, I liked her, too."

When the lower edge of the glass provided no openings, he moved his fingers along the sides. There was a groove indicating that the window could be raised, but no lever was apparent. Stretching as far as he could, he reached to one of the higher panes and caught a whiff of his shirt. It was faint, but enough to cause him to pause, then put his nose to his sleeve and inhale more deeply.

Kelly.

Giving up on the window, Massimo jammed his hands into his front pockets and stared sightlessly at the gardens. After several minutes, he shook his head, knowing there was only one way to dislodge thoughts of the previous night's experience from his brain. After telling Gaspare to be a good boy—easy enough if the dog stayed away from water—Massimo crossed to the apartment door and whipped it open, coming within inches of colliding with his eldest brother, Vittorio. The serious, dark-haired crown prince was walking alongside Queen Fabrizia in the direction of the garden exit, presumably headed to brunch. Staff members followed at a discreet distance, allowing the queen and her son to speak privately. More than one set of eyes widened at the sight of Prince Massimo bursting out of his apartment.

People did not burst out of rooms in the palace.

"Where are you headed in such a hurry?" Vittorio asked.

Beside him, their mother raised an eyebrow as if to add, *and without having yet showered?*, but as her gaze snagged on the folded stationery protruding from his front pocket she said, "Meeting the closet organizer?"

"Dressed like that?" Vittorio gave Massimo's wrinkled clothes a pointed once over. "What you need is a stylist, not a closet organizer."

"No doubt I'll have both soon enough," he grumbled, leaving them staring after him as he strode away.

CHAPTER 10

A ROW of bars stretched from the floor to the ceiling in front of Kelly, separating the small, cinder block room she now occupied from the rest of the police station. Steel, if she had to guess, though someone had taken it upon themselves to paint them a jaunty yellow. Beachy color or not, they weren't the type of bars she'd come to Sarcaccia to enjoy, the ones with ocean views, fruity drinks, and good-looking bartenders catering to her every whim. The type where she could tilt her face into the summer breeze and brainstorm a new business plan, one that she'd reminisce about years later by saying she'd originally scribbled the idea on a cocktail napkin while looking out over the Mediterranean.

On the other hand, the area where she now sat smelled like the bars she remembered from college. Vestiges of cigarette smoke and the occasional hint of vomit and sweat tinged the air, but they were easy to ignore compared to the odor rising from the cement floor. If she had to give it a name, she'd call it Eau d'Spilled Alcohol. It wasn't strong enough to make her ill, but it permeated the space. The jug of bleach and the mop propped next to the desk of the officer on duty didn't seem to have helped matters.

Worse than the smell, however, was the sound. Located somewhere nearby but out of her line of sight, a clock loudly ticked off the seconds. She wondered if it'd been installed specifically to torture those waiting in the cells, reminding them that life went on outside while they remained in limbo.

She rose from the metal bench that was bolted to her cell wall and approached the bars, waiting patiently for the officer to finish his report before she spoke. He tapped away on a computer keyboard that looked at least a decade old. When she was certain he wasn't looking, she discreetly huffed a breath into her palm. As she suspected, she needed out of here soon to brush her teeth, if nothing else. She was beginning to offend herself.

Her gaze swept the walls behind the officer. The room looked like it could belong to a police station in any part of the world. Drywall painted a grayish blue—much nicer than the walls inside the cells—held bulletin boards displaying duty rosters, descriptions of wanted criminals, and the occasional poster warning against the dangers of drug use.

Then her eye caught the framed photos near the main doors, the ones that led to the lobby. Rather than showing the current President and Vice President, as government offices did back in Dallas, they featured King Carlo and Queen Fabrizia.

Massimo's parents.

She'd seen their photos before, of course, but now she studied them in a new light. They made a striking pair, Fabrizia with her golden hair and clear, bright skin worthy of Hollywood, and Carlo, who was the epitome of tall, dark, and handsome. Though his hair was now more salt than pepper and his face had grown slightly wider with age, even his police station photo radiated charm. Massimo looked more like his father, she decided—at least in his coloring and general build—but had his mother's nose and cheekbones. Yet Massimo's eyes and mouth seemed entirely his own. She couldn't imagine either of his parents displaying the sultry smile that had played at Massimo's lips as he'd watched her lick her ice cream spoon.

She hadn't intended the action to be so flirtatious. When she'd offered him a bite of her ravioli, sure. But later, as she'd sucked the ice cream off her spoon…in that moment, she'd been swept away by the sunset, the decadent dessert, and the company. The mere fact she was half a continent and an ocean away from her routine, experiencing life in a country about which she'd only dreamed, left her in a blissful daze. But when she'd glanced at Massimo and caught him staring at her withdrawing the spoon from her mouth, she'd known exactly what he was thinking.

She clamped her teeth into the inside of her lower lip and looked away from the photos.

"Yes, Ms. Chase?" the officer said without looking up or slowing his typing. The man was as gruff as Officer Scarpa's partner, but older. Deep wrinkles radiated from the corners of his eyes and his brawny shoulders drooped slightly, as if years manning the holding area had taken their toll on what she suspected had once been an impressive physique. No doubt he had a lack of sympathy for those who occupied the spot where she now stood. She couldn't imagine sitting at his desk day in and day out and maintaining a cheery disposition.

"I can't see the clock from here. What time is it, please?"

"Almost noon." His tone was akin to that of a parent answering a toddler's twentieth request for a snack. "We'll tell you when it's two o'clock and you may call your bank."

She thanked him in as pleasant a tone as she could muster, hoping he'd realize she was a decent, law-abiding tourist who had no business spending a sunny vacation day in a holding cell. On the inside, she wanted to let loose with every four-letter oath she'd ever heard. The cops should've realized she was no criminal after spending nearly an hour questioning her while they checked her passport, travel documents, and reservation confirmations against information in their computers. But apparently not.

Settling her rear on the bench once more, she leaned back against the wall and lifted her face to the ceiling. A long, gray piece of lint—or was it a thick spiderweb?—hung in one corner near a vent, flitting back and forth with the movement of the air. She suspected it had been there for weeks, if not months. Exhaustion washed through her, making her limbs heavy, and she fought back a sudden urge to explode with laughter at her predicament. The only people who ended up in jail on their honeymoon were those who partied too hard or starred on reality television shows. Not professional women who planned their vacations well in advance, read guidebooks cover to cover before traveling so they'd appreciate a country's history and traditions, and kept their confirmations where they could be accessed online, just in case. Not that confirmations mattered when the bills weren't paid.

It could be worse, she told herself. Most of the police spoke English. The guy manning the holding area spoke it as well as she did. They'd also promised to let her call the bank to see why her payment to the property management company wasn't put through. From what the officers at the station explained, it was refused due to a lack of funds, which she'd insisted was impossible, but time alone in the holding cell gave her the opportunity to think long and hard about what must have happened. The only conclusion she could draw was that Ted had emptied their joint account, the one into which she'd deposited the money from the sale of her business. The account that was meant to be used for honeymoon expenses, then a down payment on a condo. She'd intended to pay for the honeymoon herself as a wedding gift to him.

And that was after she'd paid the deposit on the villa, which in itself was no small chunk of change, especially since she'd done it prior to the sale of the business.

The officer stopped typing long enough to clear his throat, then spit noisily into a tattered paper coffee cup. Two teenage boys—if she had to guess at their age—in the cell adjacent to hers imitated the sound, then fell into choked guffaws. From what she could translate of their conversation throughout the morning, they'd been out drinking the previous night and were waiting for their parents to come fetch them. She imagined the boys' laughter would end at that point.

Then one of them retched. The officer barked at him to use their cell's toilet.

Kelly crossed her arms over her chest, willing herself to temper her fury at Ted and at being stuck in a six-by-eight cell for the last few hours. She hadn't touched the joint bank account before she'd left because she'd already set automatic payments for the honeymoon. The villa, the groceries—groceries that hadn't been delivered, which should have given her a clue—even the tours she'd booked were tied to that account. It'd been the easiest way to pay for everything and avoid having to carry a lot of cash, since several of the mom-and-pop businesses on Sarcaccia didn't take credit cards. Then, once she returned home, she planned to close the account and transfer the portion originally earmarked for a condo down payment to a business account and use it as the seed money for her next business venture.

Never in a million years did she think Ted would close the account before she returned.

Of course, she wouldn't know for certain until the banks opened back home in Dallas and she could speak to an actual human being. Until then, she desperately wanted to believe it was a snag. An easily fixed error. Not that all her hard-earned money—years and years worth of savings—was gone, sitting in the pockets of a man she'd dumped. To contemplate that scenario made her nauseous. She'd been wrong about Ted—wrong enough to know she could never marry him—but she didn't think she'd been that wrong. The last thing Ted needed was her money.

She propped her elbows on her knees and forked her hands through her hair, wishing the action would wipe all desire for the male species from her brain. She'd been sorely mistaken about what she meant to Ted. And apparently she hadn't learned a darned thing from it, because she'd gone right out and expected she meant something to Massimo, too. Not that one night with a man—a man whom she'd told herself would be her vacation indulgence—was the same as being engaged, but after the intensity of the night they spent together, she didn't think she'd mean *nothing* to him.

Well, at least she wouldn't be seeing Massimo again. Too bad, because right up until he walked out on her this morning, she'd been having the time of her life. A smile lifted one corner of her mouth as her mind filled with a vision of their shared shower, his large hands sliding over her back under the hot spray, the pressure from his thumbs easing the tension from her muscles with as much skill as any masseuse and with infinitely more passion. Then his lips landed on the back of her neck, doing wondrous things to her nerve endings as he lathered the area between her shoulder blades. When the soap went flying, they'd had a rather detailed, stimulating debate about who should retrieve it and what else they'd do while down there.

Crazy.

She released her hands from her hair, letting them fall into her lap. She'd only known Massimo a few hours, yet never before had she felt so at ease with a man and at the same time, so sexually charged. Every fiber of her being thrummed at his touch, leaving her at the very edge of her control. When he'd interlaced his fingers with hers as they lay in the moonlight, the look in his eyes sent her pulse into the stratosphere. No man had ever looked at her that way. He made her feel beautiful. Wanted. And oddly enough, though they were in the midst of having sex on a mattress on the floor of all places, respected.

Stupidly, she'd believed it was real. Part of her still wanted to believe it, which was why *not* seeing him again was the best possible thing to happen to her today.

Voices came from the front of the police station. In the cell beside her, the boys quieted, then began urgent back-and-forth whispers, making her suspect one or both sets of their parents had arrived. The officer's fingers paused over his keyboard and he turned his head, his ears tuned to what was happening in the front hall. After a few seconds, he rolled his chair away from the computer and lumbered to the door separating the cell area from the station's lobby and reception desk.

When his shoulders straightened and his hands flew to his waistband to adjust his uniform, the tiny hairs at the back of Kelly's neck flared to life. Whoever stood in the reception area commanded the man's respect. In the cell beside her, the boys' whispers abruptly ceased. She wondered who their parents might be and how severe a punishment they faced at home for their night of carousing. The officer listened for a minute, nodded a few times to the people standing outside, then spun on his heel and walked directly to the cells, removing the keys from his hip as he covered the short distance. Rather than approach the boys' cell, he came to hers.

"You're being freed, Ms. Chase," he said, unlocking the door. The extra keys clanged against the bright yellow bars like in a scene from a movie. He waved for her to accompany him, suddenly in a great hurry to get her out of the small space after hours of telling her to be patient. "Your debts have been paid."

He said it in a manner that insinuated she'd shirked multiple bills for months on end. She bit back her annoyance and asked, "So the payment went through?"

"No. A payment was made on your behalf for the night you spent in the villa."

She froze in place. "A payment was *made*? By whom?"

The officer seemed surprised by the question, as if Kelly should know who bailed her out. "There's a gentleman waiting in the lobby who claimed that the bill was his responsibility. He has offered to give you a ride to wherever you need to go."

She felt her jaw hang open in surprise and quickly pressed her lips together. It had to be Ted.

She shouldn't be surprised to discover he'd come to Sarcaccia. After all, he'd been invited to the charity ball that'd prompted her to look into honeymooning here in the first place. Instead of staying in the villa, he'd likely made a reservation at one of the five-star hotels on the island, which was where he'd wanted to stay in the first place. It would explain why he canceled the villa reservation and why the call she'd placed to him after arriving at the police station—once she'd discovered there was a problem with the joint account—went straight to his voice mail.

Great. Now she'd have to deal with Ted on the honeymoon they weren't enjoying together.

The officer pulled open the door to the reception area and waved for her to go through. "Your belongings are at the front desk. Officer Scarpa will have a few forms for you to sign, then you're free to go."

She took a deep breath, girding herself for whatever might be on the other side of the door. As the scent of old coffee, dust, and ink filled her lungs, the rest of the officer's words sunk in. She glanced sideways at him. "Wait…you said the night was paid for. What about the rest of the week?"

"I believe the landlord planned to rent the villa to another couple." He appeared bewildered, as if Kelly should've expected this. "You'll need to contact him. We don't have anything to do with that. Maybe your, ah, friend knows."

Of course. She wondered what story Ted had fed the police, given the way the officer used the word *friend*. Squaring her shoulders, she passed the officer and sailed through the door to the reception area, ready to face Ted in all his blonde-haired, blue-eyed, polished glory, undoubtedly wearing his usual immaculately pressed clothes and a self-satisfied expression at bailing her out of jail.

Instead of Ted, she found herself face-to-face with a scruffy-faced, broad-shouldered man wearing the same white shirt he'd worn to dinner last night. A man whose intelligent olive eyes seemed to see right through her bravado. A man whom, frankly, she couldn't decide whether she wanted to strangle or take to bed.

That is, assuming she even had a bed.

She managed to contain her astonishment at the sight of her apparent liberator. She couldn't yet call the bank to access her account, meaning that, for the time being, she would have to endure the presence of His Royal Highness, Prince Massimo Barrali.

CHAPTER 11

AWARE that they stood before a rapt audience, Kelly managed to conjure the same courteous smile for Massimo she often used for ticket takers or waiters, despite the fact that looking at the man made her mouth go dry. She should have realized he was more than a random, good-looking beachgoer when he'd approached her lounger yesterday. She definitely should have figured it out by morning. He radiated charisma and sex appeal even when standing in a nondescript police station lobby. When he tipped his head in polite acknowledgement as she entered the lobby, her stomach did a slow, needful flip.

How was it that she could instantly *want* him again? He appeared as disheveled as she did. Perhaps worse given that, though she could hide her morning breath, he couldn't hide his need to shave. Yet he drew her attention as surely as a flower turned toward the rays of the morning sun.

For crying out loud, she should know better. She *did* know better. He let her go to jail.

Yet he appeared to have the same mesmerizing effect on everyone else in the room…and they were all male.

"Hello again, Ms. Chase. I felt terrible about your situation this morning, given that you located my dog for me. I asked the police if I could pay your debt, as I am in yours. And I vouched for your identity, so they now know that you are, indeed, the person who reserved the villa, even if the names are different."

His voice sounded so formal, so...*regal*...that she could swear the officers sucked in their stomachs and puffed their chests as Massimo spoke. No wonder the laughing, barfing boys in the cell beside hers had quieted when they'd heard the commotion in the lobby. They likely recognized the voice as belonging to one of their country's most well-known inhabitants.

In her mind, however, she heard the more casual version of that voice, the voice that had whispered in her ear during the night. The voice that offered her wine, teased her in the shower, groaned as he'd found release. It was the most intimate sound she'd ever heard a man make, and it'd come from *this* man.

This man who said he'd paid her debt.

The dichotomy of it rankled.

"Thank you," she managed. She stood immobilized for fear of putting her foot in her mouth. It wasn't her debt. Well, it *was*, but it should never have been a problem. She hadn't been irresponsible, though everyone in the station treated her that way. And now Massimo wanted to fix things with money and influence.

The creak of a door caught her attention. Officer Scarpa materialized from a room behind the counter, carrying a clipboard with several papers. He extended the clipboard to her and asked that she complete the documentation. Once she finished and handed the papers back to him, he set her purse on the counter and had her check its contents. When she confirmed that everything was in order, he told her she was free to go and that if the police had any further questions for her, they'd be in touch.

He hardly looked at her as he spoke. He—and the rest of the officers—appeared transfixed by Massimo.

Massimo gifted her with a patronizing smile as she turned to look for her bag. "I'm happy to give you a ride, Ms. Chase. It's the least I can do." He pushed open the set of glass doors leading to the street, his behavior reminding her of a five-star hotel's doorman. That's when she noticed that her suitcase was already in his hand. Rather than yanking it from his grasp and creating even more gossip for the police, she kept her head high and exited into the bright sunshine. Massimo's Jeep was at the curb directly in front of the station, in a spot marked for government personnel only.

Well, she supposed he was the epitome of government personnel.

Massimo lifted her suitcase into the back seat as if it weighed nothing, then opened the passenger door for her. She glanced back at the station to ensure they couldn't be heard, then said, "Don't you find this a little bit awkward?"

"Perhaps." His eyes met hers in challenge.

"And you didn't bring Gaspare as a buffer?"

"He's napping at home. The boy had a late night."

She blinked at the casual, almost flirty tone, so different from what he'd used in the station. The change flustered her. "You do own a dog named Gaspare, don't you?"

"I do. And you're asking me…why?"

"To make certain you told me at least one truth last night before I trust you to drive me anywhere." Not that she had a clue where to go whether he gave her a ride or not.

He glanced up and down the street, then returned his attention to her. "Why, do you have other transportation?"

"I might." If her feet counted.

"Glad to know we're being honest with each other." He gestured toward the front seat with a flourish and issued a commanding, "Get in."

"First I'd like to know where we're headed."

The smile he flashed looked exactly like the polite, professional one she'd deigned to give him only a moment before, when she'd exited the holding area to discover him waiting for her. "Away from the cameras across the street. No, don't look. There are two of them.

My guess is that either the property manager or someone in the police station tipped off the local paparazzi, though they did seem surprised when I drove up. More will come if we don't leave soon."

That got her moving. She slid into the Jeep as Massimo rounded the vehicle to the driver's side. He moved at a relaxed pace, as if he were visiting the police station on a routine errand rather than bailing out the woman with whom he'd spent the previous night. The sun-warmed leather sent heat straight through her T-shirt, bringing sweat to the surface of her skin. Or maybe it was the thought that she was sitting beside a man so famous he actually had paparazzi following him that made her sweat.

"As if I don't look bad enough already," she grumbled, pulling her sticky shirt away from her back. Now her clothes would look as nasty as her mouth tasted.

"What's that?" Massimo said as he closed the door.

"Nothing. Talking to myself." She propped her elbow against the door and scrubbed a hand across her forehead. "The last twenty-four hours have been rather unexpected."

His silence drew her gaze. Once he had her attention, he waggled his eyebrows—the goofiest, most un-royal action she could imagine, particularly from a man of his size and imposing demeanor—then quietly said, "Surprise."

He'd done it to make her smile, but she couldn't muster one. Instead, she exhaled and rolled her head back into the palm of her hand. Yes, his appearance at the station was a surprise. But once the officer stood before her cell and told her that her debt was paid, maybe it shouldn't have been.

How stupid was she to think for even a moment that Ted had come to bail her out?

First, he likely hated her for ending the engagement so close to their wedding date. No matter how placid he'd been after accepting the returned diamond ring, Ted wasn't the type who'd deal well with asking family and friends to cancel their travel plans because there wouldn't be a ceremony. She wouldn't be surprised if he'd learned that she'd opted to take the honeymoon trip on her own. If he had lingering anger, canceling the villa and insisting there was no Mrs. Robards would've been sweet revenge for having to make all those embarrassing phone calls about the canceled wedding. He'd probably revel in the thought of her spending their honeymoon time in a cell. He'd only have bailed her out to see the look on her face at having been humiliated.

And second, he couldn't have used his original plane ticket. She'd have seen him on the plane if he had, plus the manager claimed that Mr. Robards had missed his flight. The word *duh* echoed in her head at that thought.

A mortifying yawn escaped her. Her brain and body both craved sleep. Crankiness had set in and she needed her wits about her to deal with Massimo, her inability to access her bank account, and an angry landlord who may or may not have re-rented her dream villa.

As it was, she couldn't even think logically about Ted...and Ted was her past, not her present dilemma.

Massimo's arm brushed against hers as he shifted gears, making her aware she was alone with him for the first time since waking up beside him, when she'd studied the planes of his back in the morning light. She'd wanted to touch him, to share breakfast, to make love to him all over again.

Now she wasn't sure what she wanted. Her gaze lit upon a small blue container of mints propped near the gearshift. Without asking, she reached for them.

"Why'd you do it?" she asked as she popped one. The instant zing was enough to keep her awake at the same time it rectified the cottony taste in her mouth. Before replacing the container, she popped another.

"What, pay for your villa? Bail you out? Politely offer you a breath mint?"

Make love to me like I've never been made love to before. Walk out on me. Conveniently forget to tell me you're a prince. "Yes."

She kept her eyes fixed on the road ahead. The police station was located in the Cateri town center, an area dominated by centuries-old cobblestone streets. Even in her state of exhaustion, she was awed by its beauty. Buildings on either side of the road housed bakeries, cafés, and family businesses such as shoe repair shops and clothing boutiques. On a corner in front of them, a streetside florist busied herself wrapping a bouquet for an older woman, who was making space for the arrangement in her bicycle's straw basket. Over the rumble of the Jeep's engine, she could hear the heavy toll of church bells. Tourists wound their way through the old city, holding up cameras to snap photos of the architecture or consulting maps to see which side streets led to the museums. More than one person walked with an ice cream cone or pastry in hand.

Any other day, Kelly would have enjoyed the scene immensely. At the moment, she almost resented it. It was all so...Massimo. His country. Under his control. Just like she was now under his control.

"The honest answer—" he drew out the word honest "—is that I felt guilty about leaving you there to deal with the police. What I said at the station is true. I do owe you a debt for finding Gaspare."

"You think you owe me money? You don't, not a dime. Or a Euro or whatever." An apology for walking out on her was something else. Her elbow fell from where she'd propped it on the door as she turned to glare at him. "And what the hell, by the way? You're a prince. An honest-to-goodness prince! And you're *rich!*"

He reached to the space between them to snag a pair of aviator-framed sunglasses, then slid them onto his face. "I don't think I've had anyone describe me to myself in quite that way...but yes. To both."

"Why didn't you tell me?" Especially before she'd given him that whole speech about how rich and powerful was overrated and that she didn't harbor any princess fantasies.

Princess fantasies. Of all the things to say.

"Oh, I don't know. Why didn't you tell me you were on your honeymoon?"

"Because without a groom, it's not a honeymoon," she snapped. "It's a vacation."

"Right." There was a minute shake of his head. "You're rather surly for someone who was thoroughly bedded last night on her—" he paused for effect "—vacation."

The words *thoroughly bedded* said in his light accent made her stomach clench, but she forced herself to ignore the sensation. "At least I didn't lie. I asked if you were related to *those* Barralis."

"You did not," he countered, his voice oozing confidence. "You asked if Barrali is a common name on the island, and it is. I may not have told you the whole truth, but I most certainly did not lie."

"Oh, and Princess Sophia is a nickname? Because she wore pink dresses when she was little?" What a crock that had been.

An audible sigh escaped him. "All right, I did lie about that. Not the pink dresses part, but the nickname."

She crossed her arms and tried to revel in the small victory. She couldn't. When his eyes flicked to the rearview mirror several times in quick succession, she frowned. "What is it?"

"Checking to be certain no one's behind us. I think we're clear, but I want to give it a few more minutes." He turned at the next corner, taking a narrow side street that twisted back in the direction from which they'd come. It was a residential area, with close-set buildings that boasted tiny wrought-iron balconies on the upper floors. Flower pots brimming with summer blooms hung over the edges of some, while others had laundry lines strung from end to end with clothes fluttering in the light breeze.

As his gaze went to the mirror again, understanding dawned. "That's why you kept checking the rearview mirror on the way to the restaurant, isn't it? You were worried that we might've been followed from the beach. Does that happen very often?"

One shoulder lifted, then lowered. "If I'm with my parents or my oldest brother, Vittorio. He's the heir, so he draws a lot of attention. Otherwise, I'm mostly left alone. It's primarily tourists who want my picture. But if the local paparazzi think I'm doing something interesting, like seeing someone new—" she could swear his voice hitched as he said it, but his hand remained relaxed on the steering wheel "—they'll try to snap a salacious photo they can sell to gossip magazines or websites. There are several that focus on royalty." He slowed the

Jeep before cornering onto another narrow street. "I've learned to be cautious. If I'm not, my private life won't remain that way."

She turned that over in her head for a moment, thinking back to the previous night. "Giulia knows who you are—"

"Of course."

"—which is why you wanted to know when she was expecting her first reservation. And why she mentioned turning on the patio lights. You didn't want to stay once the sun went down because we would've been visible to anyone dining inside. It's also why you didn't want to go back inside to wish her good night."

"Your powers of observation are astounding."

The wry comment made her reevaluate their date from his point of view. "Apparently not. I didn't realize you're King Carlo and Queen Fabrizia's son, though I've seen pictures of your family several times. There's even one in the front of the guidebook I have in my suitcase." A derisive laugh escaped her. How odd must it have felt for him not to be recognized? "It's not as if you didn't leave me plenty of clues as to your real identity."

"Ever consider that my real identity has less to do with a title foisted on me at birth and more to do with the topics we discussed last night? My likes and dislikes, my military service, or my dog?"

His voice was so even, so calm, it froze the resentment that'd been coursing through her veins at the fact he'd deceived her.

When she said nothing, he continued, "It shaped me, of course. Being raised in a palace with housekeepers, a nanny—she's the American who taught me English, by the way—and with parents who are recognized all over the world, well, it isn't typical. I know that. It changes one's outlook. But so does time abroad at university or serving in a military unit. As does time on a boat, where you're surrounded by an ocean that's much larger and more powerful than you could ever be." The steering wheel spun in his hands as he guided them around a curve. "What I'm trying to say is that while being a prince is part of who I am, it does not define me."

"Nor," she said carefully, "does the fact I originally planned this trip as a honeymoon define me."

Silence reigned after that. He steered the car through a series of impossibly narrow alleys to emerge on the same side of the city center where they'd begun. As they crossed the block with the police station, he shot a quick look down the street. The men holding the cameras were gone. At the traffic circle just below the station, he opted for the lower of Cateri's two main roads, the one that ran along the waterfront rather than the one he'd just taken through the center of town.

He didn't seem to have a destination in mind. Eventually, she'd need to give him one, but she wasn't quite ready. Not only did she have no idea where to direct him, the scenery was a feast for the eyes, one she could appreciate even in her tired, grumpy state. Low bushes covered in pink blooms were interspersed with white and yellow flowers along the median of the divided road. Grass as green as she'd ever seen filled the space between the road and the beach, broken only by a winding path filled with joggers, skaters, and couples walking hand in hand. Palm trees cooled the area, inviting picnickers.

Beyond the grass, the beach beckoned hundreds of locals and vacationers. Unlike the quieter beach near her villa, this was a wide expanse given to more active pursuits. Volleyball nets divided large groups of players. Adults and children alike flew kites high into the cloud-speckled blue sky. Frisbees sailed over the heads of those savoring the midday sun from their positions on oversized towels and the occasional lounge chair.

The entire scene was postcard perfect. Fresh air carried the scent of the flowers and the sea, helping to shake the cobwebs from her mind.

She shifted to look at the side of the street opposite the water, where luxury hotels competed for the best views, and the dashboard clock caught her eye. It was morning in Dallas now. She could call the bank and find out what happened to her money. If the issue couldn't be resolved today, she'd have to figure out another way to pay for the rest of the week in the villa—or a hotel, if she'd truly been booted—and pay back Massimo.

No matter what had happened between them last night, no matter how insignificant the money might be to a man of his resources, she would not allow him to pay her expenses.

Reluctantly, she fished her cell phone from her bag. "I need to call my bank," she explained. "Once I figure out what happened to my villa payment, I can tell you where to take me."

He nodded, but said nothing. A few moments later, as canned music came over the line, she let him know she was on hold. Again, he only nodded. His focus remained locked on the road before them, as if another topic occupied his thoughts.

"So why'd you really keep your identity to yourself?" she asked, since she never did get an answer to that. "You had any number of opportunities to tell me who you are, so you must have had a reason."

A muscle jumped in his jaw as he slowed for a red light. A family of five crossed in front of them, making their way from one of the island's larger hotels to the beach. The parents' attention was on helping the youngest, a boy of about three, toddle across the road. They took no notice of who sat behind the wheel of the Jeep, only that it had stopped well before the crosswalk to allow them space.

"I wasn't ready for you to know. I liked that you treated me the way a normal person is treated. Not the way a prince is treated." The family stepped onto the curb and the light turned green, but Massimo waited until they were several paces from the busy road before stepping on the gas. "As you said, rich people are treated differently. And royals even more so."

"For the record, I don't treat normal people the way I treated you. Last night was unique." She let that sit with him for a heartbeat, then pushed her rear end further back in the seat so she could sit straighter now that the breeze had cooled the leather seat and dried her shirt enough to make her comfortable. "As for my comments about rich people, I can't remember my exact words—"

He made a noise that indicated that he did, even if she didn't.

"—but I've had some rough experience in that area. I let it get to me and I ran my mouth when I shouldn't have. I wasn't talking about you."

"Obviously."

They rounded a bend that brought them alongside Cateri's famous marina. Dozens of luxury yachts lined the docks near the boathouse while others were moored in the bay. Massimo switched lanes, which afforded her a better look at a sleek white vessel as it moved out to sea. An impossibly fit-looking couple stood on the aft deck gazing back at the island. Wind caught the woman's hair, blowing it in her face. She held it back with one hand and knotted a scarf around her head with the other, her motions smooth and elegant, the way one would expect a woman on a yacht to move. It was like watching a scene from a movie with Cary Grant and Grace Kelly, but in real life.

She stole another glance at Massimo. "I said something about yachts, right? That I'd rather go out with a man who owns fishing boat than a man with a yacht. But I bet you own a yacht, don't you?"

"Not personally." His tone sent her brow arching skyward. He grinned and added, "My family owns three. The fishing boat, however, is all mine."

She didn't want to think too deeply about why that reassured her. It wasn't as much about his honesty on that point, but about what it represented. This morning as she'd awakened beside him and studied his back, she'd thought about his scars, his dog, and yes, his fishing boat, and she'd thought him a man of substance. One with complex layers. One who may have been as moved by what transpired between them as she was.

And she'd hoped.

Hope, however, was a dangerous thing. It caused women to make disastrous decisions. Decisions like the one she'd made with Ted.

She sensed he was waiting for a response. "I give you points for being honest about the fishing boat."

"Thank you." His tone, once again, was dry.

"And you were honest about your height. When we left the police station and you held open the door for me, I noticed that according to the measurement on the door frame, you're precisely 192 centimeters tall."

"Does that earn me points, too?"

She opened her mouth to make a wry comment about what he

could do with the points, but at that moment, a cheery male voice came over the line thanking Kelly for her call and asking if he could be of assistance.

Massimo turned back to the road and began humming quietly to himself. It took Kelly a moment to realize that she recognized the tune.

I Saw Three Ships.

CHAPTER 12

WRINKLES FURROWED Kelly's brow as she listened to the voice on the other end of the line. Massimo didn't envy the man at the bank his job. Given Kelly's lack of sleep and the time she'd spent with the police, he doubted she had much patience for dealing with bank bureaucracy.

He doubted she had much patience at the moment, period.

Massimo eased the Jeep into an empty parking spot in a lot located a few blocks past the marina. It afforded them a panoramic view, yet kept the traffic of the main road and pedestrians well behind them for privacy. He cut the engine so Kelly could hear without straining. The conversation did not seem to be going well. To give her the space to speak candidly, Massimo caught her eye and motioned that he was going to one of the benches in front of the Jeep. Once settled, he took a deep breath, savoring the brisk sea air and the warmth of the sunshine on his skin as he stared out across the blue waves. It didn't take long to spot the *Libertà*, the largest of the three yachts belonging to his family, anchored offshore. Its white hull and silver trim gleamed. He hadn't been on board in at least three or four years. Having been built for entertainment rather than for sport, the yacht was more to the twins' taste. Vittorio used it frequently to host business luncheons or entertain foreign dignitaries. Alessandro, who escaped the privileges and duties bestowed upon the crown prince by virtue of being born four minutes after Vittorio, preferred to entertain foreign actresses and models.

The mental image of the twins standing on the deck surrounded by flowing champagne and platters of hors d'oeuvres made his stomach rumble. If he'd had half a brain in his head, he'd have grabbed food on the way out the door. No matter what happened with Kelly and her bank, a meal was his next order of business.

A polite, "Would you please check that? It's very important…yes, of course I'll wait," came from the Jeep, though he suspected the words were said through clenched teeth. He didn't turn around to look, choosing to keep his eyes trained on the distant vessel. He could understand why Kelly had trouble meshing her idea of Massimo, the dog-owning man from the beach, with Massimo, the yacht-owning prince. The two sides of his life were worlds apart both economically and socially. But last night, when he'd made love to her, he'd been completely honest about his emotions. From the first kiss in the driveway until the moment he'd left her bed this morning, he'd been completely focused on her and on what she did to him. While the sex was astounding, it was more than that. He'd never felt more like *himself* than in those hours with her. He might've been dishonest about his identity, but he hadn't been dishonest during those hours in her bed. Or on her floor. Or in her shower.

He swiped a hand over his face. If he didn't purge the image of her naked, perfectly sculpted body from his thoughts, he'd end up primed to go all over again, and now was not an opportune time. He had to figure out what to do with her, and that "do" did not involve sex.

Typically he wasn't the impulsive one in the family. That character trait was more descriptive of Alessandro or Stefano. But in this case, Massimo hadn't thought past getting Kelly out of jail, he'd only known he needed to do it. Tooling around town in his Jeep with her at his side for the rest of the afternoon wasn't an option. Life was complicated enough at the moment as he made the transition from being on his own, answering only to his military commanders, to being back in his formal role as a prince, answerable to his parents and to his country. The last thing he needed was to be entangled in a foreign woman's legal trouble.

He stretched his legs in front of him and eased his arms across the back of the bench. He was kidding himself. He was entangled, whether he wanted to be or not.

When he'd spoken with the officers manning the lobby desk, they'd pulled up Kelly's info on their computer. He'd feigned interest in one of the officer's badges so he could lean across the desk and read the information on screen. Within seconds, he spotted his name in the report as being present at the time of arrest. If any of the press looked at the day's police logs—which they were bound to do, now that he'd been seen leaving the station—they'd start asking questions.

Picking her up at the station had been the right thing to do, regardless of the risk. Hopefully his appearance convinced the police that there was nothing more to his relationship with Kelly than a dog rescue. If they'd dropped that tidbit to the carnivores at the station door, he'd be fine. Kelly would soon be on her way home and he'd be back at the palace, reading his mother's lists and listening to Vittorio's demands that he attend this or that reception.

Problem was, he wasn't ready to let Kelly go just yet. Despite the tension between them on the drive from the police station—no surprise, given that he'd left her in the lurch this morning—he wanted to know more about her. Their discussion over dinner gave him insight into her character, but it wasn't enough. She'd run her own business, she was kind to Giulia, and she appreciated the simple things in life. Her ability to read his mood in the wine cellar and to enchant Gaspare intrigued him. But now he wanted to know what happened to her wedding. What had convinced her to take what was obviously a well-planned honeymoon alone. What really happened with her bank account.

Why their sexual chemistry left him on fire hours later.

Why, for the first time in his life, he'd given precedence to lust over common sense.

His phone vibrated in his back pocket. A glance at the Jeep showed Kelly was still on her call, so he clicked to answer.

"Mother says you need a stylist," his sister said without preamble. "Do you really?"

"She's the boss."

That drew a particularly unladylike snort from Sophia. "I suppose I need to find one for you?"

"I suppose. Someone efficient. Not too chatty. And I only want them long enough to satisfy Mother that I'll have all the appropriate suits." Not that he couldn't pick them himself.

"Anyone specific in mind?"

"You're kidding me, right? I barely know what they do." At her answering laughter, he added, "I still can't fathom why Mother doesn't believe I can dress myself."

"You can," Sophia assured him. "You have surprisingly good taste. But you haven't been to any big public events in years. How many suits do you own now?"

"That fit?" He did a quick mental inventory. His closet primarily held suits from his university years, when he'd attended royal functions during summers and his visits home. The military had changed his physique since then. "Maybe three."

"That's it?" He could envision her look of horror. "You need an entirely new wardrobe."

"*Need* is such an overused word—"

"I can't picture you wanting to shop for clothes. A stylist will meet with you to discuss your preferences and offer suggestions, then do the shopping for you. Once he or she brings you a selection, you can try on everything and choose what you think suits you best—pun completely intended—in the privacy of your apartment."

"Shopping made faster, in other words."

"Precisely."

"Then hire away. And thanks. I owe you one." Perhaps he'd tell Giulia he spilled the ravioli and get another order to go. Sophia would love him for it.

He was about to say goodbye and pocket the phone when his sister asked, "So where are you now?"

"Running errands." Safe an answer as any.

"With the closet person?"

Vittorio and his mother must've talked about him at their luncheon. He twisted on the bench to steal another look at Kelly. She was leaning back in the passenger seat, cell phone pressed to her ear, with her other hand pressed to her forehead and her face turned up to the sky. Her auburn hair gleamed in the sun, but he suspected she wouldn't be appreciative of the effect at the moment. "I haven't hired one yet."

"Do it soon. Mother is on a mission." There was a commotion on the other end of the line, then she said, "I have an appointment, so I need to go. I'll let you know when I find a stylist."

He thanked her again, then hung up. Life in the military was so much easier. As long as he kept his hair buzzed, his boots shined, and his equipment clean, no one nagged him. It was taken for granted that he'd do what needed to be done when it needed to be done, because that's how he'd been trained. To meet real *needs*. Yet for all the training he'd received as a royal, his parents—his mother in particular, lately— seemed more and more concerned he or his siblings would fall down on the job and embarrass the family.

He'd have to ask his mother why she worried so much more than she used to. But it was a question for another day, a day when he didn't have an American tourist sitting in his Jeep. He raised his hip to return the phone to his pocket when it vibrated once more. This time, a text from Vittorio lit the screen.

Who is Kelly Chase?

His throat tightened. How in the world did Vittorio have her name? He pondered his response for a moment, then typed:

A tourist who found Gaspare on the beach. Why?

Maybe he'd seen Giulia or Guillermo. But then he wouldn't know Kelly's last name...he didn't think he'd mentioned it to them, though he might've. His breath stilled as he waited for Vittorio's response.

Bail? Really?

He exhaled. It'd been less than an hour. And if Vittorio knew, likely his parents did, too, or they soon would. He stared at the phone. Refusing to answer would only lead to more questions.

Call it chivalry. She found my dog. I owed her one. See you shortly.

The Jeep door thumped closed behind him. He turned toward the sound and shoved the phone away for good. If Vittorio had more questions, they'd have to wait.

No grown man should have to live under the same roof as his adult siblings, let alone under the same roof as his parents. Even if that roof was the size of the one topping the country's royal palace.

"Get things settled?" he asked as Kelly approached the bench.

"Yes and no. I found out what happened, but it'll take a while to unravel."

He both admired and hated the coolness in her voice. "What can I do to help?"

"You've helped me plenty. I'm not in jail." She waved a hand, as if that would wave off the problem. "It's just one of those things. And I apologize."

"For what?"

"Inconveniencing you. Embarrassing you in front of the police. Being snarky when you offered me a ride." A tinge of pink crept into her cheeks as she took a seat beside him on the bench. Close, but not too close. "Look, I was taken aback when you didn't help me out this morning—"

"You don't say."

"Okay, angry is more like it. I'd hoped that you'd intervene with the police, since they didn't seem to understand what I was saying. But now that I've had time to think, I realize what a bad position you were in."

A smile tugged at the corners of his mouth. The lack of sleep made him punchy, because her use of the phrase *bad position* made him remember what a good position—correction, positions—he'd been in prior to the officers' arrival.

"What's so funny?"

"The entire situation," he said, opting not to share his exact thoughts.

"You've got to be joking."

"Think about it. We're in bed. Fantastic night of incredibly hot sex, if I do say so myself, complete with a flying mattress. Then the police come pounding on the door. You get dressed like lightning, I clean up as fast as I can—"

"Thanks for that, by the way, since they followed me inside while I packed my stuff."

"Then I walk out on you. Comical." He shook his head before tipping his face toward the midafternoon sun. The weather couldn't be more perfect. It was exactly the type of day she should be spending on the beach in that unbelievable pink bikini.

"I suppose, when you think of it that way, it is funny," she conceded.

"But I still owe you an apology." He turned on the bench to look at her. "I'm sorry I walked out on you this morning. And that I kept my title from you. In retrospect, I shouldn't have."

"How about this…I'll forgive you if you'll forgive me for not being clear about why I came to Sarcaccia."

He reached out a hand. "Agreed."

The handshake was quick, as if she feared touching him for too long.

A second later, she added, "I have to say, the jail part and my finances aren't so comical."

"No." Nor was his guilty conscience after returning to the palace. "So what are you going to do now? Need me to take you to the villa?"

"The police seemed to believe the landlord re-rented it. I'll need to call to be sure." She pulled a face. "Even if it's still available, though, I need to find a way to pay for it. My bank account was closed and the money withdrawn. Then when I tried to use my credit card at the police station ATM, it triggered a fraud alert. The credit card company said it'll take twenty-four to forty-eight hours to sort out."

"Someone closed your bank account without you there?" How could that happen?

She took a moment to answer. When she did, the pads of her fingers were pressed hard against her legs, as if she were physically pushing back her temper. "It was a joint account with my fiancé. *Former* fiancé. He closed it yesterday and withdrew all the funds. However, the money was mine from the sale of my business. When I ended our engagement, I thought it best to leave the money where it was until all the payments from the trip cleared. I planned to transfer the balance to a new account and use it to start my next business when I returned home."

Her voice was matter-of-fact, despite the fury she had to feel, which raised his respect for her another notch. At the same time, he hated hearing the word *fiancé* coming from her mouth. He didn't want to imagine Kelly with another man.

Which was insane. He hadn't even known her twenty-four hours.

"I'm sorry. You must be livid."

"Good word for it. And thank you."

"I'm happy to lend you money to pay for the villa if it's still yours." He noticed her stiffen as he made the offer, so he added, "Of course, you could always stay on one of my family's yachts. They're quite well-equipped. And they have the ocean view you came to Sarcaccia to enjoy."

The teasing suggestion served to lighten the moment. She smiled and gave his knee a quick, friendly pat, the contact sending his mind to thoughts far from friendly. "Thank you, but no. It was more than generous of you to come bail me out of jail. I'll pay you back for that, by the way, and—"

"Not necessary."

"Yes, it is. I've worked hard and saved. I have plenty of money. I don't have access to it at the moment, but I will." The way Kelly said it, he wouldn't want to be in her ex-fiancé's shoes when she caught up to the guy.

"If you're certain," he told her. "But it's truly unnecessary."

"I'm certain." She stood and brushed her hands against her thighs. The jeans she'd tossed on this morning before running for the door were likely stifling in the Sarcaccian heat. "But if I could ask you one more favor?"

Take me to bed again. The words popped into his head at the sight of her standing before him, her T-shirt clinging to her curves. It would be stupid beyond belief to make love to her again. She had trouble written all over her. "It depends on the favor."

"Assuming the villa is gone, would you mind driving me to a hotel? I should be able to negotiate a rate I can afford out of my backup account. It's not much, but I do still have access to it." A self-deprecating smile lifted one side of her mouth. "I was smart enough to keep an account in my own name. Just wasn't smart enough to keep more money in it."

He shoved to his feet. Beside him, she seemed small and delicate, yet he knew she wasn't. "I could, but I think it's a bad idea."

"I'm sure I can work out some arrangement. It doesn't have to be fancy. As long as I have a bed, I'll be happy." There was confidence in her words, though tight lines formed around her mouth. "Please, you don't have to worry about me. I'm more resourceful than you think."

"Tell me something. How far ahead did you book your villa?"

She paused. "Almost six months."

Which meant she'd been engaged—and had a wedding date set—for some time. He shoved that disturbing thought aside. "How tough was it to book? Was there a higher deposit than usual?"

"It was the first place I called. I saw it online and thought it was perfect." She shrugged. "I had to book for a two-week minimum stay, which I thought was unusual, but that was how long I planned to visit anyway. Why? You're looking at me as if you think there'll be a problem."

"First, it's high season here. On top of that, our Independence Day celebration begins this weekend and there are tie-in events all next week. Nearly every hotel and villa on the island requires a minimum stay right now because they're in high demand. The odds of you finding a hotel room—particularly one at a decent rate—for the duration of your vacation are slim to none. Not unless you luck into someone else's last-minute cancellation."

She considered that before pulling out her phone once more. "I won't know unless I call. And for all I know, the villa's still mine. It should be."

More likely the landlord banked Kelly's forfeited deposit and immediately filled the vacancy, but Massimo took a seat and waited for her to make the calls. No sense in wasting his breath when she seemed only to trust herself.

Again, not that he could blame her. He kept his eyes on the water while she paced the seaside walkway, making call after call once she'd ascertained that the villa was gone. A short time later, she stood before him with her hands at her hips. "You were right. I was wrong. You win."

"Wasn't a competition to win or lose." He didn't move his gaze from the sea until she shifted and cast a shadow over him.

"We should go."

When he raised his head, he saw what precipitated her statement. A large group of teens was headed in their direction with picnic gear in tow, presumably so they could set up on the shaded table just beyond the parking lot. Once he and Kelly were out of the lot, she said, "Didn't want to put you in another bad position, where we'd be seen together by high schoolers."

He kept his lips firmly pressed together so he wouldn't smile. Once he knew he could maintain a serious demeanor, he asked, "Where to?"

She pointed to an intersection about a hundred meters in front of them, where the stoplight changed from yellow to red. "Drop me off at the corner up there."

"So you can do what?" It came out sounding more astonished than he wanted. The more he thought about it, the more he realized he couldn't let her go anywhere on the island alone. Not until he determined what the press—and his family—did or didn't know about her.

"I'll think of something. There are hostels, bed and breakfasts, any number of places I can try."

He moved the Jeep to the inside lane, away from the curb. "No."

"What do you mean, no?"

"No. You can't just get out of the car and wander."

"I'm not your problem, Massimo, but I could be if I stay in the Jeep. You don't need that." She reached for the door handle as they stopped at the light, but another car pulled to a stop in the lane beside them, blocking her exit. She shot him an exasperated look. "Come on. Pull over at the next intersection. I'll be perfectly fine. Tell you what, I can call you later and let you know where I am, just so you feel you've done your job."

The trees lining the road sent dappled sunlight across Kelly's face, casting shadows in such a way that a tiny brown dot near her mouth caught his attention. Without thinking, he reached out to wipe it away. It didn't move. At her baffled expression, he said, "Sorry. Thought you had chocolate on your face."

"Freckle." Her fingers reached to the spot he'd just touched. "Wish it were chocolate."

The car beside them began to move. He tore his attention from Kelly to drive through the intersection and then the next, ignoring her requests to stop. "I have a better idea."

The image of what he'd been doing the last time he uttered that sentence leaped full-force into his mind's eye. She'd been about to roll on top of him, but he'd wanted desperately to explore her most intimate places, to taste her, to see her come apart at his touch. He'd held her fast, then slowly worked his way down her body—

Stop stop stop stop stop.

"How better?"

He forced his attention to the situation at hand. "We'll both think more clearly on full stomachs. I'm starving, and I bet you haven't eaten since last night, either." At her confirmation, he said, "That settles that. I know a place where we can eat in private."

"Giulia might have questions if we show up twice in a row, and every restaurant we've passed is jam-packed with tourists."

"More private than Giulia's. My apartment."

CHAPTER 13

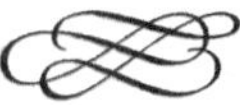

"This is not what we call an apartment in the States."

Kelly froze inside the doorway of Massimo's suite of rooms, unsure where to sit. When he'd turned away from the waterfront and its grand hotels to nose his Jeep through Cateri's twisted streets, she assumed he had a place in the old part of town, near the palace. She hadn't equated the word *apartment* with the palace itself. It wasn't until after he turned the Jeep into a gated alley, past a guardhouse, then down a ramp into an underground garage that she realized she was going underneath the country's most famous residence. And that Massimo lived here.

What in the world was she doing?

Digging yourself a deeper hole, idiot. But there was nothing to do about it now. Massimo had used a pass card to bring them up in a private elevator from the garage, and she doubted she could simply make her apologies and walk out of the palace without running a gauntlet of security.

And frankly, she wanted to eat first.

"It's not a typical apartment for Sarcaccia, either, but it's what I have. Make yourself at home. If you need a restroom, there's one down there, second door, past the library," he said, indicating a wide hallway off to her right. "Assuming Gaspare will let you go. Here he comes."

Sure enough, the dog approached from Kelly's left. He pressed his furry body into the side of her leg, anxious for attention.

She decided her bladder could wait as she scratched the dog's head and took in the main living area of Massimo's so-called apartment. The most notable thing about the room in which she now found herself was its sheer size. Richly papered walls rose at least twenty feet from the floor and decorative squares of carved wood—was it walnut? mahogany?—covered the vast ceiling. Beneath her feet, elegant rugs in shades of red and navy spread out over immaculately polished hardwood floors. Detailed inlays wrapped around the floor's perimeter. She'd thought the marble floors and carpeting in the gallery they'd just walked through were impressive. This was…unbelievable. Museumlike. And dark.

It wasn't the type of place she expected Massimo to live, palace or not. He didn't strike her as the dark type, especially given his affinity for the outdoors. Even the furniture was heavy. Muddy brown sofas devoid of pillows faced each other on either side of a thick coffee table. Beyond that, a stone fireplace almost tall enough for her to stand inside anchored the room. A mahogany bureau topped with an antique clock dominated the wall to her right, opposite a set of drawn curtains in a brocaded navy fabric. A writing desk she guessed to be an expensive antique occupied a corner not far from where she lingered near the door.

The entire place struck her as the type of spot dour, gouty old men came to brood.

"Staff shut the drapes again. They claim it's to protect the furniture and rugs when I'm not here, but it drives me crazy." He strode across the expansive room and reached behind one large panel. Within seconds, the fabric was withdrawn to expose a massive floor to ceiling window and she was gifted with a first-rate view of the palace's famous gardens. As he moved to open the curtains over the second and third windows, Kelly approached the glass for a better look. Now she could understand the appeal of living here. The view was even more breathtaking than that of the flowers fronting the marina road.

"Massimo, this is spectacular."

"The roses are in bloom now. Makes the place less of a villain's lair, more of a residence."

She let her fingers drift along the substantial window frame as she stared outside. A massive fountain surrounded by low, perfectly trimmed hedges and hundreds upon hundreds of flowers filled her sight. Pink, white, red, and yellow roses ran as far as she could see. The grass surrounding the flowerbeds was bright green and thick. She could only imagine how soft it would be under her bare feet. At the edge of her vision, near the wall that marked the end of the gardens, a colossal tent had been erected. A party appeared to be taking place. "Can you get out there from here?"

"There's a back exit from my bedroom. I don't use it during the day unless I need to let Gaspare out for a quick break. Public events are often held in the garden so it's kept locked for security purposes. But at night, when the place is quiet, I've gone to sit on the benches and stargaze." He let out a little laugh and admitted, "Well, I've done it twice since I returned from Africa. But I hope to do it more often."

"The stars must've been brilliant there, where they didn't have to compete with Cateri's city lights." She couldn't imagine having access to such a beautiful place as this garden. At night, when the breezes blew and no one was about, it would be particularly restful. The scent of the flowers then would be heavenly. "Still, if I lived in these rooms, I think I'd be out in the garden all the time. Not that there's anything wrong with the rooms. I mean, they're amazing—"

"No, you can say it. The place resembles Batman's Batcave." He grinned, glad to talk about the rooms instead of what the sky looked like in the jungle, with the smoke of burned-out villages stinging his nostrils. "I've only been in this place a few weeks. The rooms sat empty while I was away at college and in the military. While I was growing up, I lived in my parents' apartment. It's at the opposite end of this wing."

Before she could make another comment about the space not

meeting the definition of an apartment—or the high-tech Batcave—he said, "Their apartment is significantly bigger than this one. A veritable palace."

This time, his attempt at humor did work. She couldn't stop the smile that crept over her face.

"So would you rather stare at the flowers or eat?"

"Oh, food. Definitely." As if on cue, her stomach let out a long, bubbly rumble. "You said you have a kitchen?"

"I do, but it's small."

"Compared to what?" She swung a hand to encompass the massive room. A few minutes later, once he led her through the hall opposite the one where he'd pointed out the bathroom, he proved he was being honest about the kitchen.

"It used to be a storage closet," he explained as she took in the cramped space. Barely big enough for its European-sized fridge, a two-burner cooktop, and a sink, it held only the bare essentials. Even the tiny counter was useless, given that his coffee maker took up much of the real estate. "It was added in the seventies so these rooms could be used as a living space separate from the rest of the palace."

She lingered outside the door, apparently not trusting herself to stand as close to him as necessary to fit inside the room. "Where do you keep the food?"

"Well, there's the refrigerator. And here." He opened the lone cabinet to reveal three boxes of cereal, two boxes of pasta, and a few cans of soup alongside a stack of plates, bowls, and coffee mugs.

"I'm hungry enough to eat anything, so I won't complain."

He pulled a box of cereal from the cabinet and set it in front of the coffee maker. "Help yourself. Or if you can wait another fifteen minutes, we can have sandwiches with all the fixings."

She eyeballed the tiny fridge, not bothering to hide her doubt. "Really?"

A slow smile spread across his face, one he hoped would put her at ease in his presence once more. "I'll call the palace kitchen and have them sent up. Unless you'd rather have breakfast. For some reason, I could really go for pancakes. Haven't had them in ages, but I woke up craving them today."

"Pancakes?"

He shook the cereal box. "Unless you'd rather—"

"No, I'd love pancakes."

"I figured."

Her eyes narrowed in suspicion, so he explained, "You were mumbling about pancakes as you woke up. I've been craving them ever since. They might not be brain food, but I think a full stack each will help us see the situation more clearly, don't you?"

She leaned against the door frame. "Massimo, I was feeling awkward before. First, I discover you're a prince. Then you bail me out of jail and hear my tale of woe about my bank account and how my ex screwed me over—and believe me, that's a subject I prefer not to discuss—and now you're telling me I was talking pancakes. While I remember thinking it, I don't remember saying it. I'm feeling doubly awkward now."

"Do you want pancakes or not?"

"Yes." It came out as a plea. She realized it too, and flushed.

"Then I'll call in an order. Feel free to take your suitcase to the bathroom and freshen up. I'll go to my bedroom and do the same. Meet you in the living room in fifteen. We'll discuss how to un-awkward our relationship then. Deal?"

She didn't hesitate. "Deal."

DESPITE THE GNAWING in her belly, a full twenty minutes elapsed before Kelly exited the bathroom. Once she'd rolled her suitcase into the quiet, cozy powder room and spied the fluffy towels and wash-cloths hanging beside the porcelain sink, the compulsion to put herself completely to rights took hold.

Fresh clothes, a quick scrub, and a thorough toothbrushing went a long way toward making her feel human again. Applying makeup and combing out her hair did the rest. When noises from the main room reached her ears, quickly followed by the scent of fresh pancakes, she abandoned the suitcase and cautiously approached the main room. When she poked her head out of the hall, Massimo was alone—save for Gaspare, who lay beside one of the room's two sofas —and busy removing dishes from a covered trolley and arranging them on the coffee table. He hadn't said as much, but given the speed with which he'd walked her from the Jeep to his suite, she wondered if Massimo wanted her presence at the palace kept quiet for the time being.

"Breakfast is here," he said, waving for her to come out.

The sight of him standing in the center of the room left her speechless. While she'd pulled herself together, so had he, and the difference in his appearance was astounding. The scruff covering his jaw had been shaved away, his hair was damp from a shower, and he'd changed clothes. A pair of well-fitted black slacks highlighted his long legs while an olive green shirt made his eyes pop against his Mediterranean complexion. Unlike the casual shoes he'd worn to dinner, the pair he now sported were made of high-quality leather with exquisite construction. She might not be in the fashion industry, but she knew well-made accessories. Even his belt, simple and clean as it was, made it clear he came from money. A *lot* of money.

It wasn't the clothes that transformed him, though. His demeanor seemed different now that he stood in the royal palace looking as refined and polished as any business mogul or head of state.

I made love to a real prince last night.

Until now, the reality of his identity hadn't sunk in. Seeing him like this left her flailing for words. How did one talk to a prince?

"Unfortunately, I don't have a dining table of any kind," he said. "I'm supposed to hire a decorator, but haven't gotten around to it yet."

As tempting as Massimo himself appeared, her attention drifted to the trolley, which stood a few feet in front of him. Warmed butter, hot syrup, and an assortment of jellies filled its surface. Needing something to do, she carried them to the table, where Massimo had set out two large stacks of pancakes and silverware. A carafe of hot coffee and a selection of creamers and sweeteners were already in place, as were two chilled glasses of orange juice. Her mouth watered at the array. "You don't sound too excited about the prospect of redecorating."

"Even I know this place needs a face lift, but I want it done without having to actually do it."

"You sound like every one of my clients," she said as she read the label on one of the jelly jars. "I tell them that's why they're hiring me. To save themselves headaches."

He waved for her to take a seat on one sofa as he stepped past Gaspare to sit on the other, across the coffee table from her. "This isn't the most comfortable or practical way to eat, but I'm too hungry to care."

"If you don't care, then I don't." Frankly, she'd eat off the floor right now.

With plates in their laps, they dove in. For several minutes, neither said anything, each of them too intent on satisfying their need for sustenance. Once Massimo polished off half his pancakes and was pouring himself a second cup of coffee, he said, "When you wake up thinking about breakfast, you sure do it right. This hits the spot."

His mention of their time spent in her bed sent a flame of embarrassment through her again, though she knew that wasn't what he intended. "I only wish we could've had this six or seven hours ago." She stole a look at him in between sips of her own coffee. Never had coffee tasted so divine as it crossed her palate. "Again, I'm sorry for everything that happened this morning."

"Water under the bridge. The question is what you'll do next."

"I've been thinking about that." She set her coffee cup on the table. "Having coffee and some quality carbs helps."

"Told you we needed to prioritize food," he said before taking another syrup-drenched bite, then murmuring his pleasure as he withdrew the tines of the fork from between his lips.

She tore her gaze from his mouth. "While I no longer have the villa, I do have my plane ticket home. I hadn't thought about it earlier, but I can contact the airline to see if I can switch to one that leaves sooner."

"You'd cut short your vacation?"

She didn't have much choice, did she? "The island isn't going anywhere, so it's not as if I can't return. Maybe even next summer." Forcing a smile, she told him it was all for the best. "I can use the time to find a temporary job in Dallas that'll tide me over until I get my money back and get started on my next business."

After taking a long drink of her orange juice, she cut another triangle of pancake and forked it into her mouth. Whoever cooked for the palace had a way with pancakes. These were phenomenal. "Besides," she said once she swallowed, "if I know I have a future beach vacation lined up, I'll have incentive to eat healthy so I can rock a bikini next year."

"You rocked a bikini plenty this year."

Her face heated. "Well, if I did, it's not because I've been living on pancakes like these. Or on Giulia's food."

Amusement lit his face at that. He watched her over his cup as he took a long, slow sip of his coffee. Only a few bites remained of his pancakes, but she was sure they'd disappear soon. Then *she'd* need to disappear.

Funny, as uncomfortable as it was to tell him about her financial woes—and as embarrassing as it was to admit to being duped by a former flame—she didn't relish the thought of saying goodbye. Even with the headache of the villa and the bank account, this turned out to be the most interesting trip she'd ever taken.

She was in a *palace*, for crying out loud. Eating pancakes. With a man who gave her the most mind-bending, full-body orgasms she'd ever experienced.

His cup clattered when he set it on its saucer. "You've formulated a rather logical, straightforward plan for yourself."

"Thank you," she replied as she stabbed another bite. "Told you I'd be fine. Just needed time to think."

"Oh, I didn't say it as a compliment, though I do give you credit for being resourceful." He straightened, as if gearing up for a momentous announcement. "Unfortunately, your oh-so-logical plan didn't take me into consideration."

She paused with a jelly-smeared wedge of pancake halfway to her mouth.

"You?" Was he about to ask her to stay…for *him*? Uncertain of his point, she simply raised her brows and ate the bite of pancake to buy herself some time.

Massimo moved his plate from his lap to the coffee table and steepled his fingers under his chin. "Here's the thing, Kelly. I have a reputation to protect, too. The fact I was present at the time of your arrest and paid your villa bill to get you out of jail is now public record. So even if you do manage to rebook your flight—which may be a challenge, since it's the busiest time of the year for our airport—it's possible I'll have questions to answer. How do you think it'd look if you took the first available flight back to Texas?"

It'd probably make her look like she'd skipped out on a bill and suckered a prince into paying it for her, Kelly thought. Or worse, that the prince was attempting to cover up a scandal. On the other hand, she had no options if she stayed, not unless she lucked into a hostel or other inexpensive accommodation. "You did tell the police that you were doing me a favor because I returned Gaspare to you. So really, I'm the one who looks bad. Not you."

"That's assuming no one digs deeper and discovers that the three of us—you, me, and Gaspare—were together at Trattoria Giulia the night before. Because then it definitely looks like there's more to the story."

She fumbled for a response. She hadn't considered that angle. "From what I saw of Giulia and Guillermo, they'd keep quiet if you asked. And I doubt anyone would suspect that you spent the night at my villa…except possibly the two officers and the villa manager. But the manager struck me as a dramatist. Not entirely believable."

"My brother Vittorio has already asked me about you."

Shock rippled through her. The *crown prince*? The guy whose face she'd seen on a huge advertisement inside the airport welcoming her to the country? "Does your brother know about…about us? About—"

"No, no." He waved a hand in dismissal. "Not about *that*. But Vittorio somehow knew about my visit to the police station. He texted me while you were on the phone with your bank and asked about you. I told him exactly what I told the police. You found my dog, I wanted to express my gratitude. End of story. But if he's asking questions about why I was at the station, others may be asking, too. It would only take a bit of gossip in the wrong ear to lead to Giulia's. What I'd rather do is guide gossip in a different direction. One that makes both of us look good."

Deliberately, she set her fork to the side of her plate and looked at him. "What do you mean?"

"While you were changing clothes—and that's a fantastic dress, by the way—I did some thinking of my own." To her surprise, a smile lifted one side of his mouth and brought out the dimple in his cheek. "How would you like to stay the full length of your vacation time, take the tours you had planned, and have all the money to pay for it?"

She had one guess where he was heading with this, and she didn't like it. "You know I'd love to. But I'm not going to take a loan from you under any—"

"Not a loan. A job."

CHAPTER 14

KELLY PAUSED, her mouth agape. "A…you want to offer me a *job?*"

He wanted to say, *yes, even though you have red jelly smudged in the same spot where I was certain you had chocolate an hour ago.* Instead, he said, "Yes. Look, I need you. Or someone like you, if I can't have you. So why not?"

Shock registered in her large eyes.

He quickly clarified, "What I mean is, I need a closet organizer. You need to earn money so you can finish your vacation. Win-win."

"That's ridiculous."

The dismissal was immediate, but her use of the word *ridiculous* made him even more convinced this was the right move. His mother's mention of a closet organizer planted the seeds of the plan in his head. At first, he'd told himself the whole idea was ludicrous, that he was grasping at straws in order to spend more time with a voluptuous, fascinating woman, a woman who might shake up the routine of his day to day life in the palace. But as he'd come to understand the gravity of her position—and his own, given the fact his name was in the police report—it started feeling less and less ludicrous and more practical for them both.

"Maybe on first blush," he admitted. "But think about it. The account that was closed can be dealt with from here. I'm sure you can show that you put the deposits in yourself, since, as you said, they were proceeds from the sale of your business. Then you should be able to recover your funds from…." Had she told him the guy's name? Or was he simply Mr. Robards?

"Ted." Her effort to rein in her anger was slipping. "His name was…is…Ted."

"Ted, then." Saying it back to her made his skin crawl. Besides, he hadn't met anyone named Ted in years. Was it a trendy name in Texas? Or was this guy one of a kind? "You can start the process of retrieving that money from here as easily as you could in Dallas. Did you have employees? Is there anyone else who can access the records from the sale of your business and show that you made those deposits?"

She nodded, though she seemed reluctant to do so. "Then there's no need to fly home unless and until you discover you must be there in person to rectify this. With those sale records, you can show your ex that you can prove the money was intended to be yours and that if he tries to keep it, he'll be in for a legal fight. One threatening letter from a lawyer might be all it takes to show him you're serious. In the meantime, you can call your credit card company again and ask them to expedite removing the hold on your card. I can vouch for the fact you're employed here. If you've been a good customer and have good credit, it shouldn't be a problem. Given your obsession with planning—"

"Obsession?"

"Your *talent*, then, for planning, I assume you have good credit?" He let that dangle and waited for her reaction.

Her lower lip puckered. She smoothed the front of her white and yellow dress—one that flattered her body every bit as perfectly as the blue one she'd worn the night before—then nodded.

"Of course, your other problem is that you have nowhere to stay for next two weeks. I can't possibly allow you to sleep on an airport floor while you wait for an open seat on a flight—"

"You can't *allow* me—"

He held up his hands. He suspected Kelly's ex had been controlling, given what little Kelly had said about the guy and the way he'd ruined her vacation. No way would Massimo let Kelly believe he was the same way. "Again, let me rephrase. I'd hate the idea of knowing you're sleeping on an airport floor waiting for a standby seat that may or may not even become available. Your ex has tried to take your money—"

"Oh, he's taken it. At least for now."

"—but you shouldn't let him rob you of your vacation. As you said, you'll get the money back. It may take time, but you will. And you can still have the vacation."

"By working for you?"

"Yes." He exhaled, hoping she could listen to reason. "There are several guest suites at the far end of the long gallery, so you'll have a place to stay until you're ready to go home. You said you'd rented the villa for two weeks. When we were at dinner, you mentioned that most of the closets you do take only a few days, a week at the most. Is two weeks enough time to redesign a closet and take your tours?"

"Depends on the closet."

Hope sprung in his chest. "Does that mean you'll do it?"

"No." She blotted her mouth as she stood—managing to wipe away most of the jelly—then folded her napkin and set it beside her plate. "It's kind of you to offer. But you're perceptive enough to realize that I'm not the type of person who'll accept charity I don't need."

"This isn't charity." He rounded the table to face her. "I'm not giving you the money."

"Nor a loan. Nor a job you've concocted for the sake of making me feel better. Nor a place to stay in the palace." Her smile softened. "And here, after you joked about letting me stay on the yacht. I should've known it was because you had a palace available."

"The suites are empty, so why not?"

"Because I doubt anyone else you hire gets a palace suite thrown into the deal."

"They're also likely coming from the local area and don't need a place to stay. Or they're working on longer-term projects and we provide a housing allowance."

"You have an answer for everything, don't you?" She smoothed the sides of her dress, a habit he noticed popped up whenever she was nervous but had a point to make. "Look, I appreciate the pancakes—I haven't been that hungry in as long as I can remember—and I really appreciate what you've done for me. But it's best I go home."

"I didn't concoct the job, nor do I offer it lightly. Follow me." He crooked his finger and crossed the living area in long strides. She hesitated, then hurried to catch up to him, just as he knew she would when he used what he thought of as his commanding officer's voice. Low, serious, and delivered with the expectation that those to whom he spoke would simply do as he asked. "When we entered the apartment, I mentioned that I'm supposed to hire a decorator. Well, I'm also supposed to hire a closet organizer."

"Supposed to?"

If she didn't like being controlled by men, she should try being controlled by royal parents. "I haven't lived at home since leaving for university, which means I haven't had to engage in many public functions. But now that I'm back, I'll be attending events almost daily. I need an entirely new wardrobe, but I can't do that until I get rid of what's already here and renovate."

He opened the wide door to the left of the fireplace, then ushered her into the master bedroom. As with the main room, the curtains here had been drawn. After flipping on the overhead light, he moved to the windows and pulled the cords to the curtains. Kelly paused in the doorway and waited, as if crossing the threshold to his bedroom meant crossing a line she wasn't sure she wanted to traverse.

Much as he wanted her in his bed—and now that he'd had food, both sleep and another round of sex would be heavenly—he needed to convince her to do what would be best for both of them in the long run.

He'd meant it when he told her this would be a win-win.

And maybe, just maybe, having her take this job would get her out of his system. Let him see her as she really was, an attractive, fascinating, but altogether troubled tourist and closet designer, rather than thinking of her as the best sex of his life.

He lifted the small latch on the door at the far end of his room. "My mother insisted just this morning that I hire a closet organizer. As you can imagine, she's not the type who likes to take no for an answer."

He slid open the pocket door to reveal the walk-in closet. As with the kitchen, this room had been a storage closet once upon a time for palace furniture, art, and holiday decor. However, unlike the kitchen, this space was almost big enough to be a bedroom itself. His father once told him that when this section of the palace was repurposed as living quarters, there'd been quite a debate over whether to convert this closet into the kitchen and make what eventually became the master bedroom into the library. In that case, the current library would have been the suite's master bedroom and closet, while the current kitchen would have remained as it was—a simple storage space.

The architect who favored using the smaller closet as the kitchen won the argument, noting that anyone living in these quarters was unlikely to cook for themselves very often, but highly likely to own a vast wardrobe.

If Kelly truly enjoyed her job, if she loved the challenge of tackling a complicated, disorganized space and turning it into a functioning closet, she should be thrilled with this task.

"You really expect me to believe that the queen wanted me here? That strikes me as quite a coincidence."

"Not you specifically, but a closet organizer, yes." He waved her over from where she lingered in the doorway. "Come look, then tell me I don't need one."

Shoulders squared, she crossed his bedroom—without looking at the bed, he noticed—and stepped past him into the closet. Her look of doubt dissolved as she absorbed the sight with shrewd eyes.

"Well, you're right. This does need work. There's a lot to purge and the design is…let's call it less than ideal."

"Told you." Boxes covered the far wall, stacked until they

blocked the lower half of a high, narrow window that gave the room its only natural light. Wooden clothes rails at various heights covered both the right and left sides of the room. All were empty, save for the one closest to the door on the right side, which held his limited supply of current dress shirts and the three suits he'd told his sister still fit, though now that he looked at them, he doubted that was the case. An old dresser with two broken drawers was jammed under one of the rails on the left. On top of it perched stacks of jeans, slacks, and shirts he hadn't worn in almost a decade. Rugs from other parts of the palace were rolled, then stacked vertically near the boxes opposite the door. A broken clothes rod leaned against the rugs, as if holding them in place.

Kelly took a few steps into the room before placing her palm against one wall. She frowned at the uneven brown paint before inspecting the small overhead bulb. The light fixture itself had been removed years ago, after the glass cracked in several places. "It's a wonder you can find anything in here. It's quite dark."

"You can fix that."

"I'm able to" —she cast a glance in his direction, then quickly looked away— "but I can't. It could cause me real problems to work here."

"I thought you said your noncompete is limited to Texas."

"It is."

"You're concerned about the fact we've slept together."

She didn't meet his eyes. Instead, she moved further into the closet, analyzing the spot where one of the worn rods connected to a support. "I've never had that type of relationship with a client, and frankly, I consider it unprofessional. It's a perfectly good reason to say no."

Massimo took a few steps into the closet, then ran his hand across the top of the bureau. Dust coated his fingers, which he brushed off on his slacks. At his request, the housekeeping staff hadn't entered this room. He'd hardly entered it himself. Since returning home, he'd kept most of his current clothing in the small bureau in the bedroom. On the rare occasions he needed a dress shirt, he could reach in from the doorway and grab one.

"If you plan to start another business, having a recommendation from Sarcaccia's royal family would be icing on the cake. And assuming this doesn't take all your time over the next two weeks, you could go out, tour around, see the island. I'd get you a security pass so you'd be free to come and go as you please."

Her throat muscles worked as she swallowed. "That all sounds very nice."

"And, as I said, you'd have a place to stay."

Her eyes went to the rod once again. Silently, she turned to survey the rest of the closet. Judging from her gaze, she was mentally measuring the space. "You said your mother told you to hire a closet designer just today?"

"She did. And a decorator, a stylist, an assistant...she was quite thorough. In fact" —he pulled the paper from his front pocket and held it out to her— "she even wants me to hire an adviser to ensure I'm updated on the current political and economic issues, given that I've been out of the country so long. I tried to convince her that I'm capable of reading reports."

Kelly frowned and accepted the paper. "My gosh. This was written by your mother? By Queen Fabrizia?"

"She's a list maker."

"She likes to keep things in order. And she has beautiful handwriting." Kelly's fingers ran over the page as if she were stunned to be holding a note written by the queen herself. On an exhale, she handed the page back to him.

"You'd be doing me a big favor, Kelly."

Their eyes met as she contemplated an answer. "But—aside from redirecting gossip—why me? You could hire anyone. I don't believe in mixing business with pleasure."

"So you don't want to tour the island while you work?"

The eye roll she gave him was well-deserved. "You know what I meant."

"I do." He couldn't resist teasing her. Other than for a few minutes while she'd savored the bliss of midday pancakes, she'd been far too serious since arriving in the palace. He craved the relaxed Kelly, the Kelly who'd enjoyed Giulia's patio as she drank her prosecco and told him about her life back home in Dallas. When they'd shared thick wheat crackers and decadent cheeses and stared out at the sunset and local fishermen, or when she'd grinned and rubbed Gaspare's head in the Jeep. Before she knew she had a financial headache awaiting her back at the villa.

Before they'd slept together. Before he knew about Ted. Before she knew he was a member of the royal family.

She had a point. Working for him after what they experienced last night wasn't a typical morning-after arrangement. Then again, the experience might not have affected her the way it affected him.

"Look," he finally said, "given what you've told me about your ex-fiancé, I suspect you agreed to go to dinner with me because you needed a fling. That I was nothing more than your rebound guy. A night of phenomenal sex."

"Says the man who just got back from an Army stint and wanted to get laid?"

Even though she'd delivered the response in a smooth, even voice, her words set him back a step. He deserved the insult—and he did consider it an insult, given the intensity of what they'd shared—considering that he'd just accused her of the same thing.

What he hadn't expected was for her observation to twist his gut so painfully. Because when he'd called himself her rebound guy, it was because a deep, needy part of him wanted her to say, *no, what we had was more special than that* or *no, I could never see you that way.*

Instead, she confirmed his worst fear. He was completely disposable to her. Never in his life had a woman dismissed him so easily and, frankly, it stung.

"Touché." He said it with a grin, because God forbid he let her know that he was foolish enough to believe the Earth moved beneath them last night. "In which case, there's nothing stopping you from taking the job, is there?"

"Maybe. Maybe not." After giving the closet another once-over, she squared her focus on him once more. "You didn't really answer my question. Given that you could hire anyone for this job, why me, Massimo? What's in it for you if you're not getting sex out of the deal?"

<hr>

KELLY KEPT her hands to her sides, hoping to hide the fact she shook.

He really thought he was a rebound guy. Granted, she'd even told herself Massimo was her reward when he'd shown up in front of her on the beach in that ab-tastic thin shirt, but her attitude toward him changed as they'd spent the evening at Giulia's.

Apparently, his attitude toward her had not. He'd all but confirmed that he considered her a one-night stand and nothing more.

She'd be insane to take the job, even if it solved problems for them both. He was too great a temptation.

But if he didn't want to sleep with her, why in the world did he really want her in his apartment? Working all of about twenty feet from his *bed*? It was all she could do to appear cool as she awaited his answer.

He merely shrugged. "It saves me having to hunt for anyone else and deal with interviews. Plus, if the press discovers I came to the jail for you, being able to say that you're working here makes us both look good. I went to help the woman who found my dog, just as I explained to the police, then I ended up hiring her for a position at the palace—at the same time I made several other hires, of course—because, out of sheer luck, she happened to have the perfect qualifications for the job opening. Anyone who researches you will see how successful you were in Dallas. Right?"

"They would." Several Dallas newspapers and the local business journals covered the sale of her company. Prior to that, she'd been profiled in *D Magazine* and interviewed by several Dallas and Fort Worth radio stations about closet organization and design. A quick search would pull up that information, and all of it made her look extremely well-qualified for the job Massimo now offered.

"Good. It makes a much better story for us than if the press runs with the idea I went to bail out a woman with whom I'd enjoyed a fling. It's simple, it all checks out, you look good, I look good. And there's no scandal to give the story legs."

Her throat constricted. Okay. Maybe she'd be insane *not* to take the job.

"What's your usual rate?" he asked. "While we were out in the Jeep, my staff budget was delivered. I'm confident we can come to an arrangement that will enable you to cover the cost of your tours as well as adequately compensate you for your services."

"I usually base it on the number of hours the project will require, plus materials. I don't know what materials might cost here in Sarcaccia, though, or what you might want. We'd need to discuss that. At a minimum, you'd need to replace the hang rods. They're splintered."

"We both know it's a bigger job than that." He named a figure that blew her mind. "Will that cover it, you think? Of course, I would also provide you with the services of a carpenter. Given the age of the building, we keep a few on salary. They do excellent finish work, so you wouldn't need to account for that in your budget."

She couldn't contain her laughter. Could he really be that naive about costs? And to have a carpenter who could do custom work, rather than using premade cabinets and shelving? Unreal.

"What? Am I that far off the mark?"

"Unless shelving and hang rods run triple the price of what the most expensive custom work does in the States, yes. What you're offering is an astronomical budget."

"If I paid you that amount as a flat fee, would it give you enough to cover your tours? And would the time be sufficient for you to both see the island and do the closet?"

"It's enough time and more than enough money. And that's assuming you want a total gut job on the closet. Massimo, if I charged that at home, it'd be highway robbery."

His face split into a wide smile, one that sent her heartbeat into overdrive against her will. "You're saying yes."

"At that fee? Heck yes, I'm saying yes." She could handle being around him for two weeks, she rationalized. If anything, maybe cleaning out the man's closet and refurbishing it would put a damper on the insane attraction she felt for him. Nothing like sorting a bunch of old skivvies to kill a woman's libido.

Except she knew that wouldn't be the case. He was a living, breathing sex god, and she'd find him attractive even if he had a stash of pink- and purple-striped ratty underwear lurking in those boxes, though she knew he wouldn't.

But it beat going back to Dallas with her tail between her legs and having to explain to her family and friends why she'd returned so soon. This way, she could return with a surprise boost to her resume, enough money to live on while she recouped her money from Ted, and the sightseeing experiences she'd dreamed about when she booked the trip in the first place.

"Fantastic. How soon can you start? What do you need from me?"

She blinked, then took another look around the closet. "Well, I can start today. The question is when *you* can start. I can empty this out and get measurements and offer some design suggestions. But I'll need you to either sort through these boxes with me or give me a quick, general list of what needs to go, what can stay, and what can be donated. My rule of thumb is that if you haven't used or worn something in a calendar year, it needs to either go or be donated. For special occasion wear, I'll give you three years. Anything sentimental needs to be marked as such—say you have a hat that you never wear, but that belonged to your favorite uncle—so we can keep them. Oh, and I'll need to set up a meeting with the carpenter. That will give me a better sense of their timeline and what materials and options are available here in Sarcaccia for the actual design."

He looked at her in admiration. "You get right down to business."

"It's how I stayed in business." She couldn't help the pride in her voice. "I'm efficient and I try to make the process as easy and predictable as possible for my clients."

"All right." He let out a breath and backed out of the closet. "Let me arrange for the carpenter and pull together a general list of what's in the closet. There's very little I want to keep, so it won't take me long.

In the meantime, I'll call the head housekeeper for this wing and have her show you to your rooms. You can take a nap and make any calls you need to in order to straighten out your finances. We can meet back here around four-thirty. Sound like a plan?"

"Works for me."

"In that case" —he extended his hand toward her— "Kelly Chase, I'm glad to have you working here at the palace."

His handshake was cool and professional, but she could swear she caught a spark of attraction in his gaze before he broke contact and went to dial the housekeeper.

CHAPTER 15

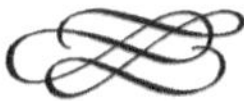

HE NEEDED HIS HEAD EXAMINED.

Massimo stretched his arms overhead and yawned, then reluctantly returned his attention to the thick stack of papers and shiny brochures that had been delivered to his suite over the course of the afternoon. His sister sent over the profiles of three stylists along with her personal comments about who might work best with Massimo given what she knew of them. Briefs on political, economic, and charitable issues involving the royal family arrived from both his father's and his mother's offices. His mother followed up less than an hour later by offering once again to have advisers update him verbally if that would be easier than wading through the briefs. Massimo glanced at the towering pile of documents and weighed reading them against feigning interest while listening to the endless drone of a policy wonk. He doubted there was a right choice. Either would require a fistful of aspirin.

On the bright side, Vittorio had called and offered the services of his own personal assistant until Massimo hired an assistant of his own, saying she'd be happy to arrange Massimo's schedule and set up the interviews for him, a thankless task for which he planned to send her a generous bouquet of flowers. Then, of course, Vittorio asked again about Kelly. Massimo kept his response nonchalant, telling Vittorio he'd fill him in later, in person. By that point, perhaps there'd be progress on the closet and Vittorio would let the issue rest.

While he was on the phone with Vittorio, the queen left a message asking if Massimo wanted suggestions for decorators, saying that when she returned to the palace following the athletic center opening, she'd be happy to share the names and contact information for those who'd previously worked in the palace. She also had recommendations from friends of hers who, in her words, "have aesthetic sensibilities similar to yours."

Did he have aesthetic sensibilities? He supposed he did, if having an I-know-what-I-like-when-I-see-it attitude counted. He wasn't sure how his mother reconciled that with her friends' opinions on home decor.

He shoved aside the stylists' resumes. More coffee was in order if he was going to make sense of them. He walked to his kitchen and filled the chamber of the coffeemaker with water, then clicked it to life. As he located a mug and a packet of sugar, he wondered how Kelly managed to stay awake all afternoon. Or if she had. The head of housekeeping notified him that the guest suites were full for once, given the number of dignitaries visiting Sarcaccia for the upcoming Independence Day celebrations, but she had Prince Stefano's permission to house any additional guests in his suite, which was next door to Massimo's. She offered to put Kelly there, if that was fine with Massimo, pointing out that it would give the new closet organizer easy access to his apartment.

Of course, he'd said yes. And of course, while standing in the closet doorway writing out the promised inventory of its contents for Kelly, he'd allowed his mind to wander to what might be happening on the other side of his apartment wall. When he realized he'd listed his old sports equipment for the donation pile three times, he knew he was in trouble.

He needed to get on with his life. His real life, here in Sarcaccia. The one that demanded he find a cause about which he was passionate, then use his resources to pursue it to the best of his ability. He didn't need to moon over a tourist who'd had a streak of bad luck and would be gone in two weeks. One who would've been gone from his life today, if he'd simply dropped her at the airport.

Instead, he'd created a catch-22 for himself. He could only move forward with his life here by protecting his reputation, which meant covering his tail after his hedonistic night with Kelly. Hiring her lessened potential public relations problems where she was concerned. Nailing down that first hire would also give his mother a sense of relief, knowing that her son was once again focused on his royal duties.

On the other hand, he couldn't move forward as long as he kept Kelly close, either. She'd pointed out that he could've hired anyone for the job. While he doubted that was true—working in the royal palace required a certain level of discretion—he certainly didn't have to hire *her*. He'd done it because it was the path of least resistance.

He'd done it because he couldn't let her go.

He was a five-star idiot. He was attracted, deeply attracted, to the woman.

She saw in him what no one else saw. Laughed at his jokes, took his teasing in the spirit it was intended, then gave as good as she got. Noticed his discomfort in the wine cellar, but didn't embarrass him when ensuring he was all right. Treated his scars as the wounds they were without asking for more detail than he offered. And she understood him well enough from the first few hours they'd spent together to know that's what he wanted. He leaned against the refrigerator and waited for the coffee to finish brewing.

An overwhelming desire to help her had fueled him into keeping her around, a desire to fix her asshole ex's wrongs and show Kelly that she both deserved and expected better. And, frankly, a desire to prove to her that despite having money and connections—and yes, a few yachts—he was nothing like her ex.

But what then? What if he did prove himself to her?

He'd be right back where he started, with a complication. And now he'd put her in the one position that meant that, even if he proved all that and more, they couldn't sleep together again. He'd made her his employee for the duration of her time in the country. Shaking her hand to seal the deal as if she were any other hire and knowing what that meant for their relationship was downright painful.

"Necessary," he muttered to himself.

Beeps finally marked the end of the coffeemaker's brewing cycle. After pouring himself a cup of invigoration, he strode back to the living room and grabbed an economic brief from the top of the pile. It could be worse, he rationalized. Kelly would be gone in two weeks and he'd end up with a killer closet in the deal. Five minutes online finding information on her former company showed him that much. Besides, he had Independence Day activities to think about. Two weeks should go by in a flash, given that he'd hardly be in his apartment for the next few days.

A glance at the garden showed that the section near his rooms was empty, so after whistling for Gaspare and snapping a tie-out rope onto the dog's collar, he let himself out the back door and settled on one of the benches to read. With Gaspare's rope hooked to one end of the bench, the boy had enough room to play without being able to reach the fountain.

An hour later, Massimo was so engrossed in his reading that he wouldn't have heard footsteps approaching behind him if not for a happy yip and tail wag from Gaspare. Two hands came down on the bench beside Massimo just as he turned to see who was behind him.

"Whatcha reading, little brother?" Cheer filled Stefano's familiar voice. "Whatever has you so focused, I want some."

Massimo held the papers aloft as Stefano rounded the bench. "Economic brief? Really?"

"On second thought, keep it to yourself. I've read them all already."

"No doubt." Massimo set the papers to the side. "Looks like you've made a lot of progress on the conference center and on upgrading the transportation system. Well done."

"Thank you." He gave an exaggerated bow before taking a seat beside Massimo. "It's been my passion."

"*That's* your passion? Have you informed Megan?"

"Very funny." He looked sideways at Massimo and flashed a smile that lit his clear green eyes, eyes identical to their mother's. "So much has happened this summer, I can't begin to comprehend it all. Happy as I am that the transportation upgrades and conference center refurbishment are on schedule, I'm far happier about finding Megan."

"I imagine so." He returned Stefano's smile and added, "If you weren't, she might strangle you."

"That she might." Stefano leaned back on the bench, then made a few innocuous observations about the garden as he scratched Gaspare's head. After a few minutes of chatter, he asked, "By the way, who's the woman staying in my old apartment? I didn't recognize her name. She here for the Independence Day celebrations?"

"No, Mother insisted I begin hiring staff. She's in charge of revamping my closet. Since she's only here temporarily and needs access to my rooms, I figured she should stay in the palace."

"That's all?"

Given the teasing tone in his question, Stefano had probably talked to Vittorio. Great. Massimo kept his tone level and asked, "What, you want to hire her to do your closet while she's here?"

"First, my apartment has already been redone, closet and all. And even if it hadn't been, my clothes are all in my new apartment, where my future wife has the closet handled, thank you very much." Stefano gave a half-hearted shrug. "I was simply wondering why you put her up at the palace."

"If you want her out of your rooms—"

"I didn't say that."

"She's from the States. I didn't want to make her stay in a hotel given that they're overrun at the moment."

Stefano contemplated that. "If I were single, I'd put her next to my rooms, too."

"So you saw her?"

His mouth took a devilish hook. "Saw her in the long gallery talking to the housekeeping staff. Hard to miss her with that hair. If the rest of your hires look like she does, you'll have Alessandro stalking your rooms."

"He'd have to be around the palace, first." Massimo noted.

"Speaking of which, I assume you didn't leave your fiancée and daughter because you wanted to hang out with me in the garden."

"My fiancée is at work and Anna is in the palace kitchen. The chef called this morning to say he's preparing appetizers for tomorrow night's dinner and told Megan he desperately needed Anna's help."

Massimo grinned at the thought of his niece's reaction to such an invitation. The dark-haired girl was happiest when wearing a chef's hat and learning her way around the kitchen. "I see. So you brought Anna over?"

"At this very moment, she's using a tube to make stars out of salmon paste." He raised a hand in response to Massimo's quizzical look. "Don't ask me to explain it. All I know is that she's thrilled. Anyway, I saw you out here and I thought I'd say hello. And" —he checked his watch, then pushed to his feet— "I have a meeting with the head of the tourism bureau in the green parlor in ten minutes. He's giving me an update on the events being planned to coincide with the conference center's grand opening."

"You can cut through my apartment. I have a meeting in ten minutes, myself." He unhooked Gaspare's tie-out line and allowed the dog to walk freely as they made their way back indoors.

"So you're getting back into the swing of life here?" Stefano asked. "Believe me, I know how hard it is to adjust after time away."

"Slowly but surely." Which wasn't the pace his parents expected. As he keyed into the rear door, Massimo asked his older brother, "Out of curiosity, what made you choose to pursue all this work on the transportation system and conference center? No offense, but to me it sounds about as exciting as studying dust bunnies."

"To each his own. The idea of bringing more visitors to Sarcaccia gets me excited."

One visitor in particular got Massimo excited, but he was certain that wasn't what Stefano meant.

Stefano gave his brother a hearty clap on the back as they walked through the living room. "Don't worry. You'll find what makes you just as happy. Give yourself some time. It took me a while to figure out what I wanted."

"Remind our parents of that, will you?"

"Like they listen to me." Stefano opened the door to the long gallery and wished Massimo a good day. Before the door closed behind him, he paused and popped his head back inside.

"Yes?" Massimo asked.

"You know, if you really want Mother to ease up on you, why not have dinner with her one of these nights when she's not busy? Ask her about her projects. It'll show her you're interested and it might give you some ideas of your own."

"I can do that." Besides, the queen looked like she could use some attention. "Think the same thing would work with our father?"

"Guess you could try. But I wouldn't." Stefano's laughter echoed through the door after it closed behind him, which made Massimo smile to himself. No, dinner alone with their father wouldn't be the easiest thing in the world. Though King Carlo was popular, he wasn't an easy man to know one on one, even with members of his own family. He did best in a crowd, perhaps because he'd been surrounded by them from birth.

Massimo moved back to the coffee table and dropped the brief he'd been reading on top of the stack. He'd found himself more interested in the economic update than he'd imagined. Learning about the positive changes that had taken place in Sarcaccia during his absence made him remember what the country meant to him. If he read through a few more briefs and started attending state functions as his parents had encouraged him to do, perhaps his purpose would find him.

It certainly wouldn't find him if he hid out in his apartment.

He dialed Vittorio's assistant and asked her to contact Queen Fabrizia's office to arrange dinner at her convenience, and then to schedule interviews with the decorators she'd indicated as her top two choices. After that, he sent a message to Sophia asking her to let him know when she found a stylist so he could get started as soon as possible. It felt like the most roundabout way possible to accomplish his goals, but it was the nature of his family.

Plus, the more items he knocked off his mother's list, the faster he could get on to real business and stop thinking about Kelly.

As if on cue, a knock sounded at his door. When he called out that it was open, Kelly entered. She held a measuring tape and a pen in her hand and cradled a light blue notebook in her arm.

"You ready for me?"

Ready as he'd ever be. "Come on in."

KELLY HAD FULLY INTENDED to make her phone calls upon settling into her suite of rooms. At least, that was the plan until she'd stepped through the door. Soaring white ceilings graced with antique crystal chandeliers drew her eye upward while shining hardwood topped with modern rugs in shades of beige, charcoal, and sage fought to pull her attention to floor level. As in Massimo's apartment, a large fireplace served as a focal point. However, where Massimo's apartment was dark, this room was light and bright. Diaphanous curtains fronted the windows, plush linen-colored sofas invited one to sit and relax, and paintings of water scenes reminiscent of Monet graced the walls. The windows afforded the apartment's occupants a garden view almost as beautiful as the one Massimo enjoyed.

All in all, it was one of the most restful, clean, and inviting rooms Kelly had ever seen, yet the majestic scale of the furnishings and lighting meant its style fit well into the palace as a whole.

And she'd thought her villa was the most beautiful place on the entire island. Even without an ocean view, this apartment made the villa look ordinary.

Adriana, the head housekeeper, showed Kelly around with all the deference one would show to an ambassador or head of state. Finally Kelly pleaded with the woman to call her by her first name, saying she was only an employee, and a temporary one at that as she was here to remodel Massimo's closet.

Adriana's expression resembled what might happen if she'd swallowed a bug, though she quickly masked it.

Kelly couldn't help but grin. "Not what you were expecting?"

In her gentle accent, Adriana said, "I admit, I assumed you were here for the Independence Day events. However, I still prefer to call you Ms. Chase."

A thought occurred to her. "Guests aren't typically in rooms like this, are they? Let alone employees."

"Guests reside in whichever rooms the royal family feels would best suit."

"But not here."

"No," Adriana conceded after a moment's hesitation. "Not here. But Prince Stefano only recently vacated these rooms and all the suites are full with Independence Day guests, so it was a logical spot for you to stay. I do hope this will be fine, regardless? I'm afraid we are rather limited—"

She thought it was a problem? "No, no, it's more than fine. It's amazing. Thank you very much."

Adriana nodded, then proceeded to show Kelly the location of a small but updated kitchen, a phone that would connect her to housekeeping should she need anything, and then to the apartment's spacious bedroom and bathroom. In a layout that was similar to Massimo's bedroom, it boasted a gigantic walk-in closet. On the other side of the bedroom was a door Adriana explained would take Kelly to the garden. "If you do go out, be sure to take the key card with you and lock the door behind you for security," she said, showing her the key's location in the bedside drawer. "If you need anything at all, please feel free to call. Maria is the housekeeper in charge of these rooms and she'll be happy to provide you with any linens, pillows, or other needs. Also, the computer in the main room is free for your use. The login directions are on a card inside the desk."

"That's fantastic." Not only could she use the computer to pull up design photos to show Massimo, she'd be able to confirm her tours and research other spots she might want to visit while in Sarcaccia. "Thank you, again, Adriana. And please thank Maria for me in advance."

Once Adriana had gone, Kelly took a moment to sit on the sofa and breathe. Other than the few minutes she'd had in Massimo's bathroom this morning, it was the first time she'd been alone since she'd met him on the beach yesterday. She sank into the soft, welcoming cushions and wondered at how different this apartment was from Massimo's, despite having a near-identical floor plan and the same basic architecture. Where Massimo's rooms were dark and foreboding, Stefano's were light and welcoming. Next thing she knew, the alarm on her cell phone pinged her from a deep sleep, indicating that she only had fifteen minutes before her appointment with Massimo.

Which meant when she knocked on his door, she'd made no calls. She was no closer to recouping her money from Ted, had no preliminary sketches for Massimo's closet, and hadn't logged on to the computer to pull up any photos to show him. She'd had to race simply to brush her teeth and gather the necessary items to measure out his closet space.

His voice came from the other side of the door, inviting her in as casually as if she walked in and out of palace rooms every day. *His* palace rooms.

Cautiously, she poked her head inside. "You ready for me?"

"Come on in." He waved her over to where he stood near the coffee table. Official-looking documents filled the space where they'd eaten a few hours earlier. "I'm getting caught up on leisure reading."

"I see that." How he'd managed to stay awake after such a long night was beyond her. The drained coffee mug at the corner of the table wouldn't have kept her alert enough to muddle through the volume of paperwork he seemed to be tackling. Yet he looked robust and energetic, as if he'd gotten his second wind, and the skin of his cheeks appeared bronzed with hints of pink. "Were you outside?"

"I was. Have a seat and we'll get down to business." He indicated the sofa opposite the one he chose. More than the physical space he created between them, however, was the distance with which he spoke. If an observer were to see them, they'd think Massimo was an acquaintance meeting her for a specific business purpose. Polite, friendly, but emotionally detached.

For the next half hour, they discussed the details of how she handled a closet redesign from beginning to end. He asked insightful questions, offered a few opinions on materials, and handed her a general list of the closet's contents and what he knew offhand could be donated or thrown away. She wrapped up her introductory questions by asking about his typical day, what types of clothes he'd wear most often, how frequently he traveled and would need access to suitcases or other gear.

"I'll have a better idea of how much hanging space I'll need for suits or slacks once I hire a stylist," he said. "I imagine it'll be significant, though, based on what my brothers have."

"My designs allow for flexibility." She drew him a quick picture as she spoke. "I'm a fan of moveable rods and shelving so as your needs change, you can alter the closet's arrangement without going back to the drawing board. You want it to work for you for the rest of your time in the apartment."

"That makes sense." He gave her sketch a quick once-over. "So what's next?"

"I want to take some measurements so I have a better idea of layout options, then I can get to work." She thought he'd join her as she went to measure the closet, but as she stood and turned in that direction, he remained near the coffee table.

"I'll leave you to it," he said when she looked back. "The carpenter will be here any minute to talk over plans with you."

"You don't want to walk through some ideas?"

He shook his head. "Use your best judgment. Keep a list of questions for me as they arise. If you need access to the apartment and no one answers your knock, feel free to simply enter as if you were a member of the housekeeping staff. You have free rein as far as I'm concerned. I don't have an opinion on things like, say, what color paint you use or what type of flooring is in there. If it fits with the look of the palace as a whole, I'm fine."

"Even if I think that's hot pink?" she teased.

His shrug was practically dismissive. "You wouldn't do that or I wouldn't have hired you."

Disappointment welled in her, but she tamped it back. Keeping a professional distance was for the best, wasn't it? "Thanks for the vote of confidence."

"You've earned it. Speaking of which, before I forget" —he shuffled through the stack of papers on the coffee table and withdrew an envelope— "here's half the payment for your work. If you need a larger portion to cover materials, let me know. If you're agreeable, I can pay the next quarter when you're halfway through, then make the final payment when the project is complete."

His fingers brushed hers as he handed her the envelope, but he showed no more emotion than a child would when handing a paper to a teacher. "I'm sure it's plenty," she assured him. "And the payment schedule is fine."

"Good. Then I think we're set. And please, take your tours or explore the town as you wish. Adriana explained how to go through security so you can get in and out?"

At Kelly's nod of confirmation, he added, "You're not on the clock. As long as the closet is finished before you have to return to the States, I'll be satisfied."

With that, he disappeared out the front door of the apartment, a sheaf of papers in his hand. He didn't look back.

CHAPTER 16

KELLY KNEW she should be grateful.

She knelt on the carpeted floor of Massimo's closet, ran the measuring tape along the baseboard, then scribbled in her notebook, all the while reminding herself that only yesterday she'd been lazing on the beach telling herself that her next job would come along soon enough and that she shouldn't spend her vacation time fretting about it. That her inane decision to sell her business would end up being the closing of a door that resulted in the opening of a window, or whatever the saying was. That in the long run, selling her business would end up being an opportunity.

Well, not many opportunities arose to redo a closet for such a high-profile client, let alone one with a royal pedigree who openly stated that working for him would be good for her resume.

So why'd she have the urge to pout like a toddler being told to finish her veggies?

"Get over yourself, Chase," she grumbled aloud. "It could be worse. You could be in jail instead of a palace. This could be a lot of fun." How many times had she dreamed of a budget like this? Or the ability to design a closet however she wanted?

"I hope it's fun, though I'm not sure what jail has to do with it."

The female voice coming from the direction of the bedroom was lighthearted, but its unexpectedness sent Kelly's measuring tape flying back into its case with an embarrassingly loud snap.

Before Kelly could ask the woman who she was, the tall, striking blonde entered the closet and offered Kelly a hand up from the floor. "I'm April. I'm told you're redesigning Prince Massimo's closet."

"Yes, I—"

"I'm your carpenter. Great to meet you! It's Kelly, right? I heard that you're from the States. Where? I'm a New Yorker, myself." April put her hands on her hips and looked around the closet, assessing its size before she walked to the far wall and ran her hand along it, checking its condition.

"Dallas. And did you say you're the carpenter?" The woman's movements had an easy flow, similar to what Kelly had seen in other craftsmen. In her experience, those who worked with their hands stayed relaxed in every other body part. But she had yet to meet a carpenter who looked like April. Her neat blonde bob, gold hoop earrings, softly faded designer jeans, and closely-fitted black top oozed casual sophistication.

She also sported black Converse sneakers and had more energy in her little finger than Kelly possessed in her entire body at the moment.

"I know, I totally don't look it. But I swear I know a bandsaw from a jigsaw. You can quiz me. My dad rehabbed prewar buildings in Manhattan when I was a kid and I spent as much time as possible tagging along. Those old buildings were glorious. Best hide-and-seek spots ever." She ran a finger along the lower edge of the window frame and shrugged. "Turned out I learned a lot along the way. My brother and I eventually took over my father's business, but Queen Fabrizia lured me away by promising better beaches. How could I say no to that?"

Kelly tried not to laugh at the quick recitation of April's qualifications and life story. The blonde would be a joy to work with, assuming she was as competent as she professed. "Was she right?"

"You've probably seen the beaches," April said with a shrug. "You tell me. What really got me, though, was that the queen sought me out after staying in a building I'd renovated. She noticed details most people don't, then asked the building's owner who'd done the remodel. I was impressed by how much she saw. Well, that and she called back twice after I refused her first offer. So now I make a great income doing what I love and don't have the stress of running a business."

Kelly could understand the appeal in that. While she'd loved running her closet design company, day-to-day management headaches often added to her stress level.

April tucked her hair behind her ear as she gestured to the notebook lying open on the closet floor. "Tell me what we're doing in here. Better be a total remodel, because it's dismal as is."

"I haven't come up with a final plan, but if you have a few minutes, I can pull up some photos on the computer to show you. You can let me know what's possible."

April's blue eyes widened with excitement. "Please tell me you mean the computer in your room. You're staying in Prince Stefano's old place, right?"

"I am." Word traveled fast in the palace, apparently.

"Awesome. I did the cabinetry in his closet and kitchen when it was remodeled five years ago. It was my first project when I came to the palace. Haven't been in there since and I've been dying to see how it's held up. Maria—she's the housekeeper—insists it looks as good as when I did the installation, but I want to see it with my own two eyes."

"Come see for yourself, then." Kelly gathered her belongings and they made their way to Stefano's suite. After April inspected the cabinets—noting a few scratches she wanted to touch up and hinges she felt needed tightening—they spent the rest of the evening brainstorming closet layouts and finishes. It quickly became apparent that their approaches complimented each other, as did their personalities. They tended to like many of the same design elements, finding them both visually appealing and practical. As the dinner hour approached, April picked up the phone and ordered an appetizer tray and a bottle of wine from the kitchen.

"You can do that? I never would've thought to order food as if I were in a hotel." Kelly's jaw dropped as April hung up the phone. Massimo might've done it with pancakes, but he was the prince. Not a guest or an employee.

"I don't do it often, but if we're busy working, then you bet. Prince Stefano even encouraged it when I did these rooms. In my experience, a bottle of Sarcaccian wine is the best thing for the creative juices. I mean, you've seen Prince Stefano's kitchen. How do you think I managed to construct such spectacular cabinetry in such a tiny space? There were at least two or three bottles of wine along the way."

Kelly pushed away from the table where she and April had spread out several sketches and photos. Her legs ached from hours of sitting, but until she stood and moved to the windows, she hadn't noticed the tightness in her muscles. She'd been so caught up in her discussion with April she'd lost track of time. As she looked out at the gardens, lit only from the glow of the palace windows above, the lack of sleep finally hit her.

"I'm not sure how much creativity I have left in me, wine or not," she admitted. "I was up pretty late last night."

"Beats jail, though, doesn't it?"

How much gossip went through the palace, exactly? "Um, sure."

"You were talking to yourself when I met you, remember? The word 'jail' tends to stand out when anyone's talking."

"I suppose it does." She'd momentarily forgotten what April had overheard. She leaned against the wide window frame and turned to face her new friend. Explaining the statement felt like it would be a violation of Massimo's privacy, so she kept to what he'd said earlier. "I actually got this job after Prince Massimo helped me get out of jail this morning."

"No way." April's mouth wrenched into a wicked grin. "I wouldn't have pegged you as the type to live a life of crime. You strike me as pretty straight-edged."

For the moment, she'd take it as a compliment. "I was here on vacation and found his dog on the beach. Unfortunately, at the same time he was claiming his dog, I was trying to talk sense into the landlord of the villa I was renting. There was a bank snafu with my payment and since I couldn't fix it until the banks opened back home, the landlord wanted me arrested. Prince Massimo was kind enough to pay the landlord for me. We got to talking after that. Turns out he needed a closet designer and I just happen to be one. So he hired me."

April let out a low whistle. "Wow. And I thought I had a great getting-hired-by-the-Barralis story. Yours is much better. It's like the beginning of a fairy tale."

"Other than the jail part," Kelly laughed.

"I'll grant you that. No glass slippers there."

"Or evil witches, unless you have something to tell me."

April faked throwing a notebook at Kelly's head before they went back to work. As they scribbled out plans, Kelly realized that Massimo's point had just been proven. Give people an interesting enough story, one that's believable, and they'd be entranced. It wouldn't occur to them to think anything more salacious took place. Judging from April's tone, it certainly hadn't occurred to her.

A short time later a knock sounded at the door, announcing the arrival of their food. They wrapped up work for the evening as they savored cut veggies and an assortment of small sandwiches and drank their wine.

"What made you decide to take on work in the middle of a vacation?" April asked between bites of a cucumber and salmon sandwich. "Either you really love what you do or you couldn't say no to Prince Massimo."

Kelly managed not to choke on her own sandwich at the second part of April's observation. "I imagine anyone would have trouble saying no to the Barralis, but even if Massimo wasn't a prince, I figured it's a once in a lifetime opportunity. Who gets a budget like this one and carte blanche for the design?"

"Massimo's good that way," she replied as she popped a piece of crust into her mouth. "But Stefano had definite opinions on his closet. He wanted everything to be just so. All the plans were done ahead of time and my job was simply to build it."

"Was it a bad thing?"

"No, not at all," she insisted. "Stefano could've been an architect. He sees everything at a glance when it comes to functionality. But with Massimo, you can use your imagination. It adds an element of fun to the project."

"That it does." Kelly picked up a photo of a clean-lined closet with masculine gray shelves and an industrial-style silver carpet that had caught her eye a few years before. There were a few elements she planned to incorporate into Massimo's closet, though she'd change the color scheme, given the lighting challenges she faced. "I'm looking forward to seeing this finished. I never in a million years thought I'd work on vacation, but having so much latitude makes me realize how much I love what I do."

Or *did*, at least until her noncompete expired. Much as her job had eaten all her free time over the last few years, she already missed it. Whatever new business she started needed to give her the same creative fix or she'd be miserable.

"I hope you haven't given up your whole vacation for this," April said. "There's so much to see. And the weather's been spectacular lately."

"I have a tour booked tomorrow morning. I'll be back by two, though."

When April asked for more details, Kelly explained her itinerary. A bus tour of the city that included a stop at two museums and the cathedral were on tomorrow's schedule, then later in the week she'd scheduled a tour to the center of the island, where she'd visit a winery and have lunch.

"Sounds like you're hitting some of the highlights. Good." April poured more wine for Kelly, then tipped the remainder of the bottle into her own glass. "If you don't have plans Saturday night after the parade, how about if I take you out in Cateri? We'll catch the fireworks over the marina, then you can see the nightlife the tourists miss. It'll be a great time. The whole country's in a partying mood after the Independence Day parade. You can soak it up like a local."

Nightlife and parties weren't exactly what she'd envisioned when she'd booked the trip. "I'm not much of a club person."

"Then how about we go to the parade itself? If you want to go out afterward, great. We can keep it tame. If not, no big deal."

April's openness won her over. "In that case, sure. Let's plan on it."

"Just remember that I said tame. Not boring."

"There's a lot more to you than jigsaws and bandsaws, isn't there?"

The spark of mischief in April's eyes as she cleared the plates made Kelly wonder just how April defined *tame*.

MASSIMO HAD NEVER BEEN the type to avoid people. Situations, yes, when avoidance kept conflict from escalating and allowed tempers time to diffuse. His parents had always encouraged waiting out anger and saving certain conversations for times when all parties could speak reasonably. More than once his mother said that it saved friendships, marriages, and even lives. But Massimo never avoided people. Especially when he wasn't even angry.

With Kelly, the opposite was true. He was becoming more and more attracted to the woman with each passing hour as he listened to her banter with April.

Despite Kelly's tempting, near-constant presence in his apartment the last week, he had yet to spend a moment alone with her. She'd floated in and out of his bedroom sorting through boxes, carrying shelving samples, and arranging the shirts from his closet on a rolling rack in his bedroom so he'd have access to them during the renovation, but others were always there. Workmen removed the carpeting, April tore out the old hang rods, and painters arrived to smooth the walls and repaint them. Even when Kelly asked him the occasional question about whether a particular object stowed in one of the boxes should stay or go, his responses were limited to the expected yes and no answers.

All the while, Massimo busied himself knocking off items on his mother's checklist. He'd met with the stylist his sister hired, using the time to talk over preferences and have his measurements taken. After that, two decorators his mother recommended and three possible personal assistants met with him in his library for interviews. Though the decorators were way off the mark—the portfolios of designs they'd shown him didn't come close to his taste—two of the three assistants held promise and he'd arranged second interviews with each of them. When he wasn't occupied with interview preparation, he'd spent time in the garden reading more of the briefs. Slowly but surely, he was reacclimating to life in the palace, making it his new normal. Though he still craved time alone, he hadn't felt the urge to take Gaspare on any long drives or boat excursions.

Much as he knew no one would mind if he took an hour here or there, he found Kelly's presence invigorating. Even if he wasn't alone with her, he couldn't bring himself to leave.

"I have another for you, sir. This is Armani." The stylist, a British man in his late sixties or early seventies who looked as if he'd walked right off London's Jermyn Street or Savile Row, shifted clothing along a rack in the main room of Massimo's apartment as Kelly's laughter reverberated from the direction of the closet. He raised a well-groomed gray eyebrow in the direction of the sound as he presented a midnight blue pinstriped suit for Massimo's approval. To the older man, the laughter was inappropriate for the setting. No doubt he found it took away from the solemnity of a royal household. But to Massimo, it was as if Kelly stood before him in the shower all over again, massaging shampoo through his hair while teasing him about his water-loving dog. The echo chamber quality of the closet wasn't far from that of her villa's bathroom.

Her laughter—along with that of April, the workmen, and everyone else who met with Kelly during the last few days—brought energy to what could have been a rather dull few days.

He inspected the suit and nodded. "Thank you, Robert, I'll try that one."

"A solid choice, sir. Now, if you will, I have a selection of shirts and ties to show you that work well with either this or the two Tom Ford suits."

Massimo gestured to the sofas, where the suits he'd selected earlier were on display. As stern and proper as Robert might be, Massimo liked the man. Sophia had chosen well. Robert was efficient and had excellent taste. Nothing he chose was too staid—despite the appearance of Robert himself—nor was it too edgy to be worn by a royal on public occasions. And everything he'd presented so far fit Massimo like a dream.

As Robert laid out the shirts alongside the suits so Massimo could inspect the various combinations, he said, "If you don't mind, I took the liberty of selecting an outfit for you to wear to this afternoon's parade. Queen Fabrizia indicated that you plan to attend. However, she was not certain whether you were attending tonight's banquet. If so, I'd be happy to suggest clothing appropriate for that event, as well."

"I'm not certain I'm attending yet, myself." He'd planned to decide once he'd made it through the parade. "But I'd appreciate having something ready, just in case."

"Of course, sir." Robert returned to the rack and selected an elegant black suit with a barely-there jacquard print. "This should work well for evening."

"Excuse me?" Kelly rounded the corner from the bedroom into the main room, her gaze sweeping over Robert and the vast selection of clothing. "I'm sorry to interrupt, but I have a question for Prince Massimo, if he's available for a moment."

Massimo took in the surprising sight of her curve-hugging white top, beige linen skirt, and chocolate-colored sandals. The outfit wasn't as formal as what one usually wore when in the palace. Neither was the top cut for climbing closet ladders or sorting through boxes, given that if she leaned too far forward, he'd have an excellent view of her cleavage. He imagined she'd chosen it because she'd limited her packing to vacation wear, rather than work wear. Lucky for him.

He doubted Robert approved, though if the man had an ounce of testosterone in his body, he should.

"Did you need me to look at something?" Massimo asked once he'd gained his tongue.

"Not yet. The closet's a disaster at the moment." She moved close enough for him to notice the tendrils of hair falling from her casual ponytail, no doubt the result of a work-filled morning. "I was wondering if you'd hired a decorator yet?"

He frowned at the unexpected question. "No. Did you need an opinion on some aspect of the closet?"

"Not an opinion so much as permission." Her gaze slid across the room to the massive mahogany bureau on the far wall. "I noticed that the first day I was here. Are you using it for storage? Is it a piece you plan on keeping in this room?"

"I have no plans and have nothing in it. Why?"

"If the decorator didn't want to use it here, I thought it could work in the closet. But I'll wait until you hire someone. I don't want to step on toes."

He couldn't imagine the gigantic piece in his closet. It didn't seem close to the streamlined cabinets Kelly had briefly described as a possibility for the design. On the other hand, he couldn't imagine a decorator wanting to keep any of the furniture currently in the living room. "Since there's no decorator yet you get first dibs. Have at it."

Her eyes lit as she strode to the bureau and ran her hands over it, feeling the surface before opening the drawers and inspecting them one by one. She pulled out her measuring tape and ran it along the top, then checked its height. "I think this could work."

"Glad it can be of use." He had zero attachment to the piece, but hated to see an antique being relegated to storage.

"Thanks." As she turned back toward the closet, he realized it was the longest conversation they'd had since he'd hired her. Unable to leave it at that, he said, "You know that the Independence Day parade is this afternoon, right? Are you planning to go?"

She stopped near the fireplace and tilted a look at the windows. "With weather like this, you bet. April says she knows a spot near the review stand where we can watch."

She wouldn't be far from where he and his family would be watching the festivities. "Perhaps I'll see you there."

After she'd gone, Robert asked, "I assume that is the source of the, ah, giggles, sir?"

Robert's delicate phrasing made Massimo grin. "It is."

"I can understand why she is in your employ, sir. She has beautiful" —he took a long breath and glanced at the bureau, then in the direction she'd gone— "taste."

So the man had a good supply of testosterone after all.

"As do you, Robert," Massimo replied as he was handed a white button-down shirt, a green and yellow patterned tie, and a pair of finely tailored, yet comfortable light gray slacks to wear to the parade. "As do you."

CHAPTER 17

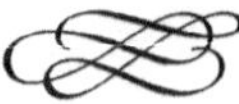

A CHEER ROSE as the wrought iron gates fronting Cateri's royal palace swung open, the raucous sound moving through the palace courtyard like a series of ocean waves cresting, then crashing to shore.

At a signal from the head of the ceremonial guard, Massimo joined his sister, parents, and older brother Vittorio and exited through the gates for their annual walk to the reviewing stand where they'd watch the Independence Day parade. A tradition started by King Carlo's grandfather, the two kilometer walk generated almost as much excitement as the parade itself. Members of the royal family took the opportunity to greet their countrymen in person and wish them well. As always, the Barrali family sported the national colors of green, yellow, and white.

The anticipation for the crowd lay in which royals would make the walk in any given year. Either the king or queen, usually both, made appearances, but their offspring were always a question mark. In order to keep the mystery, only the security detail was told ahead of time who would participate.

Once through the gates, Massimo shielded his eyes to take in the incredible sight. Low barricades lined either side of the cobblestone street with police posted every few meters along the way. Behind the barricades onlookers stood two to three rows deep as far as the eye could see. Children in strollers commanded the area in the front, many grasping ice cream cones or cotton candy. A few of the strollers even had Sarcaccian flags mounted to the handles. From the upper floors of the buildings on either side of the road, residents waved and cheered. His heart swelled with the sound. Near the parade route itself, he suspected the crowds would be larger and even more boisterous.

Yesterday, when he'd told his mother he'd join the group walking to the parade, he wasn't certain it was the right thing to do. Now he knew. This was where he belonged, showing his pride for his home country and assuring its citizens that his entire family treasured and appreciated both the country's rich history and its people. Soaking in the uplifting, festive atmosphere.

"Big turnout this year," his sister Sophia murmured beside him. "Guess because the sun's out. No rain until tonight."

"Or because they haven't seen Massimo in a while." Vittorio nodded to one of the guards standing at attention beside the gate, then smiled and waved to the crowd. Speaking just loud enough for his siblings to hear, he added, "You'll have to make up for the fact that Bruno's out of the country and Stefano and Megan decided to meet us at the reviewing stand rather than walk so they could spend the morning with Anna."

"You saying they'd rather see Stefano than me?" Massimo retorted. "I'm hurt."

"I'm saying they were hoping to see Stefano and Megan. All that starstruck love makes for great photo ops. You, dear brother, have no beautiful woman to escort you. No tale of love and loss and redemption to set the tabloids ablaze. Instead, they have to settle for you, a boring military guy with a buzz cut. And I suppose for Sophia."

"Thanks for the lovely compliment," Sophia deadpanned. "By the way, what were the bookmakers' odds on Alessandro joining the walk this year? Three to one? Four to one?"

"Funny," Vittorio answered. They all knew full well the odds were ten to one with an hour to go before the start of the walk, since they'd each sneaked peeks online. And, of course, Alessandro had begged off at the last minute, which surprised none of his siblings.

"More walking, less talking," came a low, commanding voice from behind them, to which Massimo, Sophia, and Vittorio instantly replied, "Yes, sir."

Queen Fabrizia glided ahead of them, pausing a few meters past the front gates to shake hands with a young family who'd likely been waiting for hours to catch a glimpse of the Barralis, before she moved on to say a few words to a soldier who'd worn his dress uniform for the occasion. King Carlo, satisfied his adult children would now act as he expected, made his way to the opposite side of the street, shaking hands and making small talk as he went.

"I'm with Mother," Vittorio hissed, sending Sophia and Massimo to follow King Carlo. For the next hour, the family slowly made their way along the route, talking to as many people as possible and posing for photos. Many bunches of flowers were handed their way. By the time they reached the reviewing stand, the entire family and the escorts walking behind them had armloads, all of which were set into strategically placed containers lining the front of the royal box.

Massimo clapped along with the rest of the crowd as King Carlo took his usual position in the center of the box. Queen Fabrizia, radiant from the walk, joined him and received equally rambunctious applause from the crowd. At the same time, uniformed solders raised flags on either end of the stand and drumbeats sounded in the distance as the first group of marchers began the parade a little over a kilometer away, near a waterfront statue commemorating the signing of the treaty with Italy that granted Sarcaccia its independence.

"Pomp and circumstance done right," Massimo commented to Sophia, who stood beside him. "I've missed this."

"And we've missed you." She gave his arm a quick squeeze before turning to face the direction from which the marchers would approach. Massimo put a hand on her shoulder as he surveyed the scene. Since returning home, he'd felt uncomfortable in his own skin.

The only exceptions were when he was out on the water with Gaspare or when he'd been with Kelly. But now, with the sun shining and his family around him, he felt at peace once more. A sense of command and surety filled him as he looked beyond the crowd, toward the marina and the water. Stefano had been right. It might take time, but Massimo would find his role and his purpose here.

The first group of marchers came into view, a school band who'd won a competition for the honor to lead the parade. The sound of trumpets, flutes, and trombones carried along the main avenue preceding them. Onlookers craned their necks for a better look. As Massimo leaned forward, his gaze snagged on a woman on the opposite side of the street.

The sight caused his heart to rise into his throat.

Kelly's head was thrown back as she laughed. Her hand was on April's forearm, and April had a hand over her own mouth as if to smother a bout of out-of-control laughter. The pair were at the front of the crowd, at the barricade. Kelly wore the same outfit she'd had on in his apartment earlier, but a pair of sunglasses now covered her eyes. She brought her laughter under control, though it was clear the task wasn't an easy one. He wondered what April had said to draw such a reaction.

He wanted to see it again. Hell, he wanted to be the cause of that abandon himself.

"Is that April?" Sophia asked, following his gaze. "She looks happy. Glad to see she took the afternoon away from work. Hasn't she been working on your new closet?"

"She has. Should be done next week."

"Mother will be thrilled." A moment later, Sophia asked, "Who's with her?"

He feigned a second look, as if he hadn't noticed. Kelly was craning her neck to see the approaching parade, a look of anticipation on her face. "Oh, that's Kelly Chase. She's the closet designer." He managed to sound nonchalant, even though the simple act of saying her name sent tension coiling through his chest.

"She's gorgeous."

When he didn't respond, Sophia whispered, "Oh, Massimo. Please don't tell me you like her."

"Of course I like her. I wouldn't hire someone I disliked." He cheered as the band reached the reviewing stand, with the marchers in front holding their school banner and waving Sarcaccian flags. "On that subject, I like Robert a lot. He can be a bit crusty sometimes, but he's straightforward and knows what looks good on me. Thanks for finding him."

"You're welcome, though Robert wasn't the subject. Don't think I didn't notice you change the topic."

"We were discussing recent hires, weren't we?"

"I didn't think so."

"Oh." He paused, then frowned. "Sorry if I confused you."

"You're impossible." She swatted at his arm. At the same time, he noticed a flare in her eyes and followed her line of vision to the bleachers adjacent to the reviewing stand. A lean, elegant blonde stood in the second row.

"That's Madeline Lockwood," Sophia whispered. "Scottish. She's a guest of Father's. Her mother's company owns several casinos."

"I've heard of the Lockwoods." They were wealthy, as one expected the owners of a casino business to be, but they hadn't been born to it. They'd worked their way up, Madeline's mother in the casino and hotel businesses, and her father in aviation.

"I believe they're interested in expanding to Sarcaccia. Father said he'd meet with the family, but informally. Hence the invite." Sophia turned her attention back to the parade and clapped as a large float went by. "Don't look now, but if you check the row behind Madeline Lockwood, there are the Thyssen sisters from Denmark. The younger one is—"

"Stop."

"Stop what?"

"You're matchmaking. Stop."

A heavy sigh escaped her, though her public smile remained fixed. "All right. But I thought you should know who's who before tonight's banquet."

"Not necessary." He smiled down at his sister. "But I appreciate the thought."

When she grinned back, he couldn't help but think how much lovelier she'd grown during his years away. "Anytime."

The rest of the parade passed as it did every year. Flowers in every imaginable hue decorated giant floats, dancers in both traditional and modern costumes kicked and spun their way down the boulevard, and bands played patriotic songs as they marched past the royal box. Amongst the crowd, the occasional balloon came loose from a stroller or a child's fist and drifted skyward. Ice cream, candy sticks, and oversize pretzels were consumed by the cartload as vendors wended their way along the area behind the barricades. Happy banter filled the air. When a group of disabled veterans made their way past the royal family—some on foot, others with canes or in wheelchairs—Massimo saluted them. Though most were close to his father's age, he picked out a few he knew were his peers, making him wonder where and how they'd sustained their injuries.

I understand.

The words ricocheted through his brain. If he could push the thought to the men and women on the parade route, he would, simply to reassure them that they weren't alone in their suffering and that their sacrifice wasn't forgotten or in vain.

When a young soldier saluted back from his wheelchair, a sense of gratification filled Massimo's chest. Even across the distance between them, Massimo could see the spark of pride in the man's face. It was no different than the pride displayed on the faces of the baton twirlers who came afterward or the equestrians whose horses pranced expertly along the route.

Through it all, Massimo kept watch over Kelly without allowing his gaze to linger. As Sophia had pointed out, there were any number of beautiful women lining the parade route. Those near the reviewing stand, in particular, had taken care with their appearance, as many were invitees to tonight's royal banquet and hoped to catch the ear— or the eye—of one of the Barrali family. Men, too, were hoping to make inroads with the powerful family. In years past, before he'd been abroad with the military, Massimo used his perch on the review stand to scan the immediate crowd and make his plans for the evening.

But this year, though he managed to look interested in those nearby, his heart wasn't in it. Even when a friend of Vittorio's—a gregarious, statuesque brunette from a wealthy, well-connected family—flirted with him, he found it an effort to match her witty repartee. Try as he might, he couldn't tear his thoughts from Kelly. When Kelly and April disappeared into the crowd, he felt as though a part of him were missing.

Absurd, he told himself. Perhaps as the days wore on, his fascination would fade and he'd rediscover the bounty of Sarcaccia...namely, its astonishing women. Kelly had been the first after a long dry spell while he was on deployment. He'd get over it. He'd have to. She had her life—a mixed-up one, at that—and he had his. They weren't suited in the long term. Sophia's disapproving *please don't tell me you like her* comment made her opinion on any match clear.

After the last float went by, one filled with schoolchildren singing the national anthem, Queen Fabrizia materialized at Massimo's side. "Ride back to the palace with me? I'd like a moment to chat before we're swept up in the banquet preparation."

"Of course." It wasn't as if he had a choice. Taking her elbow, he escorted her down the stairs.

He looked to the secured area behind the reviewing stand to see his father and Vittorio entering a limousine with Sophia. Stefano, Megan, and their daughter Anna stood at the curb waiting for the driver of a second car to open the doors for them. A policeman waved to his mother's driver, urging him to park behind Stefano's car. The lineup made it plain that she'd sought out Massimo for a confidential conversation. Whatever it was, she apparently didn't want to wait for their private dinner tomorrow night.

He wondered what she knew that he didn't.

Queen Fabrizia beamed as she waved out the car window. She had the ability to look as if she were greeting a group of dear friends, rather than giving the same dispassionate wave displayed by other celebrities when faced with fans. Her voice, however, was subdued when she finally spoke.

"You seemed at ease this afternoon, Massimo."

"I was. I'm glad I went."

She absorbed that. "Does this mean you'll attend the banquet tonight?"

"For you? Of course." Now that he'd made it through the parade—had actually *enjoyed* the parade—he had no reservations about attending.

"I want you to attend for *you*. Because you want to be there, to be part of the family and the celebration."

"I do." He smiled out his window and waved to an excited young boy while using his other hand to pat the queen's forearm. "You need to stop worrying."

"Never. It's a mother's job." A moment later, once they'd passed through the gates into the palace courtyard, she turned to face him. "If there's nothing for me to worry about, then why did you want to have dinner with me? My assistant scheduled it for tomorrow night."

"Because I've been away and we need some time together. That's all."

"You've never booked a dinner with me before."

"So?"

Her look was knowing, in the way mothers had wordlessly communicated with their children since the beginning of time.

"I've never been home before. Not like this, when I wasn't about to leave for school or an assignment. And frankly, I want to hear about you. Your projects. Your interests. Anything wrong with that?"

"You're saying that you're worried about *me*?"

"Let's call it curiosity."

Her lips took on a droll curve, one he'd seen captured by photographers and plastered on magazine covers, much to his mother's chagrin. She felt it unroyal—the expression gave her a mischievous bent—but often couldn't help herself. "All right. I'll see you tomorrow night. You can tell me about the closet designer you've hired. And I haven't heard...did either of the decorators I recommended work out?"

"There's another reason we need to talk. You clearly have no idea of my taste."

Her humorous expression morphed into an affronted pout. "What do you mean?"

"I believe the most apt word for those two decorators is *somber*. If I wanted to decorate a mausoleum, they'd be my go-to people. But my living space? No. They missed the 'living' part."

"I see." She glanced ahead of them, toward where they'd exit the car at the palace's rear door, then flashed her famous cat-that-ate-the-canary grin. "And I'm very glad to hear it."

Come again?

She took in his look of bewilderment and said, "Oh, Massimo, you're my son. I know your taste better than anyone. I wanted to be sure you were making decisions for yourself and not for anyone else, including me. Hire whomever you wish. So long as they don't have anything in their background that might tarnish our family's reputation, you're fine."

The car rolled to a stop, but he waved off the guard who'd approached. He needed to finish this conversation. "Don't you think that was cruel to do to the designers? They sent portfolios and sat through interviews with me. They even drew up designs for my rooms. *Detailed* designs. Do you realize the time commitment that took?" And not simply for the designers. It took his time, as well. And extreme amounts of his patience. If he'd had to endure another description of toile wallpaper or crystal sconces, he'd have gone mad.

"Of course I do. And now I know they'll go the extra mile." She shrugged. "I'm hiring them for some of the unfinished rooms in the east wing. Prepping a few extra designs for you was not a hardship. Believe me, they're being well paid."

Massimo reached for the door handle. "You are a crafty woman sometimes, Mother. I never would've suspected. "

"When it comes to my family? You have no idea. Now, get some rest this afternoon. I'll see you tonight at the banquet." She nodded to the guard, who opened her door and escorted her from the car with all the reverence she deserved, leaving Massimo to wonder what else he didn't know about his mother.

CHAPTER 18

APRIL PEERED at herself in a handheld mirror as Kelly relaxed beside her on the covered deck of a seaside bar not far from the parade route. They'd been fortunate enough to nab a free table and quickly order drinks and appetizers, but the crush of revelers who'd entered a minute behind them meant they'd likely be waiting a while. All around them, people who'd lined the city's walkways for hours clamored for cool, liquid relief.

"I think my nose is sunburned," April declared. "I don't get it. I even wore sunscreen!"

"You look fine to me." Kelly squinted at April before inspecting her own arms. "I don't think I burned, but if I'm not more careful while I'm here, I'll start to freckle. Downside of being fair. And no, don't be fooled by the hair on my head. My skin lacks enough melanin to handle the sun, no matter how much sunscreen I slather on."

She'd gotten more than enough sun when she'd arrived and fallen asleep on the beach, but jet lag and the need for tranquility won out, keeping her on her lounger long after most other beachgoers departed. In the short run, it was lucky in that she'd met Massimo. In the long run, it wasn't so lucky for her complexion.

"Guess you'd know, being from Texas. In New York it's steamy in the summer, but days like this, with blue skies and the kind of warmth that actually make you want to be outside, are few and far between." She sighed, then tipped her face upward and closed her eyes for a moment. "I think that's part of why I love living here so much. I'm making up for lost sunshine. The Independence Day celebrations aren't bad, either."

"I admit that was a ton of fun."

"Admit?" April intentionally bugged her eyes. "What do you mean, *admit*? You thought it wouldn't be?"

"Well…you're about to hear my deep, dark confession." Kelly allowed her gaze to dart around the bar, mimicking a Cold War movie spy afraid of being overheard. She dropped her voice to a mock whisper. "I've never understood parades. All the organization it requires for clowns and marching bands and horses to walk down the street strikes me as a tremendous waste of effort, both to those parading and to those watching. So there. I admit it. I didn't think I'd like the parade."

April rolled her eyes as if to say, *what's wrong with you?* "So why'd you say yes?"

Kelly lifted a shoulder. "It's my vacation and I'm getting to know the country. Plus, it was a chance to hang out with you. And you're always fun."

That brought a smirk to April's face. "Don't you forget it."

A waitress sidled through the crowd to deposit their drinks on the table and promised to be back in a few minutes with appetizers. After Kelly took a much-needed sip, she told April, "The parade itself was better than I expected. It was more like a festival with all the activity."

"It was, wasn't it?" April leaned back in her chair and sighed. "Still is a festival, judging from the crowd here in the bar. They've barely gotten started. Fireworks aren't for hours, and you know none of these people are going home between now and then."

Kelly murmured her agreement. There was a charge to the atmosphere she hadn't felt during her previous days in Sarcaccia. At first, she couldn't pinpoint why, or if others detected the same buzz, but from the time she and April arrived at the barricade across from the royal box, she'd been on an emotional high. It differed from the thrill she'd experienced during her tour of Cateri's famous cathedral or while ogling the masterpieces in its museums.

Within minutes, she'd realized the sense of excitement ran deeper inside her than in those around her. Their pulses quickened in anticipation of the parade and the arrival of the royal family; hers had quickened in anticipation of seeing Massimo. While she'd seen him moving about his apartment during the last few days, this was different. She'd see Massimo the way his country saw him, during a public event in his role as their prince. She suspected it'd differ from the way he'd entered the police station or the manner in which he interacted with his stylist or other palace employees. He'd be in the spotlight.

Inexplicably, she was nervous for him.

In the end, there'd been no need. Despite the increasing roar of the crowd, the entire royal family appeared at ease as they approached the reviewing stand from the road that led downhill from the palace. Massimo appeared larger than life as he stood alongside his parents and siblings and cheered the marchers. His white shirt and gray slacks fit to perfection, emphasizing his fit frame and daunting size. His movements were graceful and sure, as if he attended events like this and enjoyed the adoration of thousands on a daily basis.

She bit back a sigh, unable to reconcile that Massimo—the prince who commanded the attention of thousands and stood confidently above her, both literally and figuratively—with the man who'd flirted with her on the beach, treated her to an intimate sunset dinner, then made love to her with a single-minded passion she'd never before experienced.

She knew why she wanted to sleep with him. But why in the world had a man like him made love to her? It might've been a one-night stand, but it wasn't a case of a celebrity wanting to get laid and get out. She'd felt, deep in her bones, that there'd been more to it than that. It was in the way he'd lingered in her bed, the twinkle in his eyes as he'd shampooed her hair, the tenderness with which he'd spooned her body to his as they fell asleep and ran his hand along her hip as if she were precious to him.

He looked nothing like that man now. He seemed distant. Powerful. From another world.

When the first marchers approached the reviewing stand, he casually put a hand on his sister's shoulder and gave her a warm, protective smile. Even from her vantage point across the street, Kelly could see the dimple in his cheek, the one that only seemed to appear when he completely relaxed.

Just the way he had on the patio at Guilia's.

After that, the rest of the parade passed quickly. Kelly tried to focus on the floats, but occasionally sneaked peeks at the reviewing stand, unwilling to be caught staring, but unable to look away. She'd struggled to find the balance between a normal level of curiosity—because the Barralis were, after all, the main attraction—and a level of intensity April would suss out as romantic interest.

April was too perceptive by half, and the last thing Kelly needed was for April to detect the waves of lust coursing through Kelly simply by looking at Massimo.

But then, near the midpoint of the parade, she'd seen Massimo scan the crowd. Noticed his gaze light on her. Had shivered under his watch, but knew he couldn't possibly see her watching him back, since her head was turned to the side and she'd been studying him from behind her sunglasses.

Nevertheless, his scrutiny unsettled her. Thankfully, April had grabbed her arm just before the final marchers approached, pulling her toward the bar in hopes they could nab a seat before the crowd dispersed.

"You look far away. What's on your mind?" April asked, snapping Kelly's mind back to the bar.

"Prince Massimo, I suppose. We still have a lot of work to do." Both true statements, even if the man's closet wasn't the specific direction her thoughts had taken. "Though now that the floor is done, I feel like we're making progress."

Kelly had been thrilled to discover the original hardwood remained underneath the ugly carpet. The intricate details matched those of the apartment's main rooms, making the closet feel more spacious since it now flowed from the rest of the suite. Best of all, it was in such good shape it didn't need refinishing. A good scrub followed by a light polish restored it to its original glory.

"I never thought it'd turn out so beautifully. That nasty carpet protected it. Go figure."

April glanced over her shoulder, looking for the waitress, then turned back to the table and smacked her palm to her forehead. "I can't believe I forgot to tell you! The head of maintenance called me. The extra carpenter is available to help me install the shelves tomorrow, otherwise he can't come until next week because he's working on a project in the royal kennels. I went ahead and told him to come tomorrow. Are you ready?"

"Tomorrow should be fine." Though it was a day earlier than she'd expected. After doing a quick mental inventory of the tasks remaining, she said, "I haven't decided yet whether we should use that dresser from the main room. If so, it would need to be moved into the closet first. It'll be easier to get it in there without having to navigate around the new shelving. I can call maintenance and get it moved tonight."

"We don't need maintenance. I'll help you move it after we eat."

"I thought you wanted to go to the fireworks?" April couldn't be serious about the offer. "Besides, it must weigh a ton."

"It's hours before the fireworks and I'm stronger than I look. So are you." April raised her drink in a toast, so Kelly did the same. "Here's to us."

"And here's to you reconsidering your offer to help. Unless you have a few tricks up your sleeve."

At that moment, a man with dark, glossy hair and clear, light olive-toned skin walked by, beer in hand. His soft yellow shirt and white shorts set off his complexion to perfection. He gave April a subtle wink.

April tucked a lock of her blonde hair behind her ear and gave the man a sultry smile. To Kelly, she softly replied, "Oh, I do."

"WHAT DID we toast at the bar? Here's to two stupid women?" Kelly muttered two hours later as she and April struggled to lift one corner of the bureau high enough off the ground for April to toe a sliding disk underneath. "We may kill ourselves doing this."

"No one's allowed to die when there are so many guests in the palace. Bad form," April huffed. When they'd approached the palace, they'd had to avoid a long line of limousines depositing well-dressed guests at the front stairs for the banquet. "But let's hope this fits in the closet the way you think, otherwise we'll be moving it back."

"No kidding. I'm glad you had sliders to protect the floors. If we had to carry this, could you imagine what might happen to—"

"Ahem!" April paused and bugged her eyes at Kelly over the top of the bureau. "One, we couldn't move it without the sliders, and two, thou shalt not speak of the floors or anything that may or may not happen to them. Bad juju."

"All right." Kelly exhaled, then put her hands on top of the massive piece of furniture. "No more talking. Let's get this thing in place."

"Then I'm going in search of the fireworks."

"The fireworks, or the guy from the bar?"

"Both. And the sooner, the better."

On that note, the women put their weight behind the bureau. Fortunately, with sliders under each of the thick legs, it glided across the hardwood floor with less effort than Kelly anticipated. No evidence of its transit was left behind as they rounded the corner from the living room into the bedroom, though it took several minutes to maneuver the huge piece through the closet door and into the spot Kelly indicated underneath the window. After a few adjustments, Kelly stood back to take a look. "You know, I think it's going to work."

April flexed her hands to loosen the kinks as she walked to the door and turned to inspect the closet. "Not just *work*. It *wows*. It was lost in the living room, but in here…well, you can really appreciate the thing."

Satisfaction filled Kelly's being. A blend of classic and modern design was exactly what she'd hoped to accomplish in the space, and the bureau satisfied the classic component.

"It'll look even better once the shelves are installed. And wait until you see the chandelier I found for the center of the room. It's a clean design that'll work well with the shelving, and it has cut crystal accents that will help it feel true to the era of the rest of the palace. Then I'll put a couple of matching crystal lamps on top of the bureau, at the edges." She talked with her hands, demonstrating exactly where she wanted to position the lighting for maximum effect. "Prince Massimo can use the space between the lamps to set out small items like ties or cufflinks as he's getting dressed."

"So we're all set?"

"Yep. But let's leave the sliders underneath until tomorrow, just in case it needs to be moved while the shelving and hang rods go in."

"Agreed." As April continued to study the space, she added, "From what I know of Prince Massimo, he rarely lets anyone do anything for him. Nothing personal, like designing a closet, at least. But I can see why you've earned his trust. You've thought of all the little details, like giving him a place to lay out his ties."

"Thank you. I hope he's happy. He's certainly paying me enough."

That brought a grin to April's face. "Did you negotiate up his original offer?"

Kelly looked at her askance as she bent to wipe some dust from the front of the bureau. "No."

"You should've. You'd be getting more. Trust me."

"More isn't necessary. Besides," she said with a dismissive wave, "it would feel as if I'm ripping off the people of Sarcaccia. I do already."

"It doesn't come from taxpayer money. The palace is privately owned and maintained."

"Really?" Most European palaces were owned by the government since the funds to build them originally came from state coffers. "I had no idea."

"The Barralis have been very financially savvy over the years," April explained. "They bankrolled the construction of this place with proceeds from their own shipping company centuries ago. These days they have investments all over Europe and the U.S. Here in Sarcaccia, they own wineries. They also make money from the royal kennels and I'm pretty sure they own the polo grounds down on the southern end of the island."

Kelly must've looked incredulous, because April elbowed her and said, "Trust me, they won't feel ripped off if you do a good job for them. But if they hire you again, haggle for more money. You're the one who got ripped off this time."

"Not at all," she insisted. "Prince Massimo's been extremely generous."

April exhaled, as if exasperated with trying to teach a stubborn student, then let her gaze sweep the closet.

"I have to say, I'm glad you're going to be able to use this," April said, approaching the bureau once more. She studied the front, then pulled open one of the lower drawers and ran her hands around the interior. "I couldn't imagine it going into storage down in the depths of the palace. It must be several hundred years old. The workmanship is astounding. Did you get a look at the drawers?"

"I did. They're smooth as can be. Even the bottoms are finished."

"Keeps delicate clothes from being snagged." April commented. "If a king wanted to store his valuable silks, he'd have commissioned a piece specifically designed to protect them. My guess is that's what this was for. It'd be interesting to find out who ordered it and who built it."

"I have a request in to the royal historian. It's unbelievable how much history is under this roof."

"No kidding. Speaking of which, I'm outta here. Time to celebrate all this Sarcaccian history with some fireworks." April closed the drawer and straightened. "You sure I can't talk you into joining me? I'm meeting some friends near the marina. That way, if it actually does rain, we can duck into one of the bars and keep the party going."

The expectant tilt to April's brows nearly made Kelly say yes. Nearly. "I'm wiped out from being in the sun all day. And with the shelves going in tomorrow, I should mark out the spots for the electrical outlets and the chandelier. It won't take me long, then I can get a good night's sleep before we start tomorrow."

"Nikolai from the bar will be there. He's bringing his hot friends, too."

"No doubt." When they'd made their way to the parade route and then to the bar, she'd noticed April's knack for attracting male attention. "But believe me when I say that meeting a cute guy is the last thing I need at the moment. I really appreciate the invitation, though."

April shrugged. "Your loss. See you tomorrow, then."

Once Kelly had the closet to herself, she grabbed a pencil to mark out spots on the walls where she wanted two new electrical outlets. Wiring in the palace was tricky, given its age, but she'd done a walk-through with an electrician the day before to see what was feasible. She then pulled a ladder from where she'd stowed it in the corner, taking care not to tangle the work light she'd hung from the side, then climbed to the ceiling to mark the circumference of the new chandelier's canopy around the old fixture.

She paused while atop the ladder, taking in the unique view of the closet. Once again, her gaze fell to the bureau. Years of careful polishing made its top shine despite its age, while the curved front of the piece gave it unique charm. When viewed from this angle, the bureau seemed deeper, as if the top extended further to the back than the drawer April had inspected earlier. The contrast piqued her curiosity. Kelly climbed down from the ladder and pulled out the top drawer, but nothing struck her as out of the ordinary. Frowning, she tested the lower drawers. When she reached the one April checked earlier, she noticed that, sure enough, it wasn't as deep as the others.

On a ripple of excitement, she eased her fingers along the sides of the drawer, releasing the mechanism that kept it in place, then withdrew it all the way from the case. After setting the heavy drawer to the side, she felt along the back of the bureau. She sussed out a small wooden piece that didn't seem to have a function. She pushed on it, but nothing happened. A wiggle to the left and right, however, and the piece gave way, revealing a narrow hidden compartment behind it.

She lowered the false back and was rewarded with a *thunk* as something small and weighty fell into the bottom drawer.

She opened the bottom drawer and withdrew a bag crafted of plush cornflower blue velvet and slightly larger than a deck of cards. A white silk drawstring held the top, but Kelly didn't need to open it to know it contained jewelry. The weight of the bag alone told her it must be a significant piece. Gently, she pushed the drawer shut and stood. As she placed the bag on top of the bureau, something slithered out a hole in the bottom. Instinct made her reach for it, catching it in her palm before it hit the floor.

A gasp escaped her lips as she looked at the necklace in her hand. Laden with brilliant diamonds and sapphires, and boasting a massive sapphire as its centerpiece, it was fit for a queen.

CHAPTER 19

A GASP, then a wave of applause went through those gathered on the long patio outside the palace's main ballroom as blasts of green and yellow lit the night sky. As the colors faded, gold streaks crossed through the smoky air and erupted into a shower of glitter, which was followed by more large green and yellow starbursts. The breeze, which blew inland from the direction of the marina, carried the scent of exploded fireworks and the damp chill that prefaced a rainstorm. Still, the rain had stayed offshore, allowing the fireworks to begin on schedule.

In the distance, Massimo could hear the roar of the thousands of people gathered near the marina as the display reached its crescendo.

He wondered how many of those revelers would end up drenched, or if the downpour that'd been forecast would hold off until they could make their way home. The well-heeled crowd on the palace patio had it easy. They could duck inside the ballroom within seconds to escape a storm if necessary.

"I see you met with the stylist."

Massimo turned his attention from the fireworks to the source of the droll comment. Vittorio stood just behind his right shoulder. Massimo raised his brow marginally, but kept his sarcastic response to himself. They watched the fireworks in silence for a few moments as the crowd around them chattered away, with couples pointing out different colors to each other and commenting on which types of fireworks were their favorites.

"It's good to have you back," Vittorio said just loud enough for Massimo to hear. "Not just back to attending events—which I think you've needed—but back to the family."

The seriousness of Vittorio's tone made Massimo glance at his older brother, but the crown prince's gaze remained fixed on the skies, his eyes reflecting only the blues and reds of the fireworks blossoming overhead.

"You remember the text message you sent me asking about a particular tourist? What prompted it?"

Vittorio shielded his eyes as if to better view the fireworks, with the positioning of his forearm blocking others from seeing him speak. "A rumor floating amongst the paparazzi that morning claimed that a well-known palace insider was about to be arrested for defrauding the family. That's why they were at the station."

The information surprised Massimo. "Was there a story?"

"About you? All that was reported—since *you* apparently haven't checked—is that the police chief stated you were at the station in regard to Gaspare, who'd wandered off that morning but was located on the beach. The tourist's name was never mentioned. The reporters thought they had their fraud story when you walked out, but when the police chief stated that it wasn't related and that he knew nothing of a palace insider committing fraud, they left."

That was a relief where Kelly was concerned, but didn't explain why Vittorio had been paying such close attention. "So what of the original rumor?"

"Let's just say that I'm monitoring the situation." A smile lifted one side of the older prince's mouth as he dropped his hand from his forehead and turned to Massimo. "Of course, I hadn't anticipated discovering your information along the way. That was a nice bonus."

"Anything to make fun of me?"

Vittorio's eyes lit, but he said nothing.

"On a more interesting topic, where's Carmella tonight? I'd hoped to get to know her better." Vittorio's girlfriend was nowhere to be seen during the cocktail hour that preceded the fireworks, nor had she joined them in the royal box at the parade. Massimo had only met the woman in passing during a leave of absence two years ago. He'd thought her a passing fancy, as the part-time actress didn't seem Vittorio's type, and hadn't paid her much attention. However, from what Massimo had heard and read, the two had been inseparable for the past year. An engagement announcement was rumored in every other issue of the tabloid press. Bookmakers across Europe were waiting with bated breath to see when, and how, Vittorio would propose. If the crown prince weren't his brother, Massimo might be tempted to place a bet himself, just for fun.

"She has the flu."

Though Vittorio's face remained neutral as he looked skyward, Massimo knew it was a lie. "I see. I hadn't heard."

"It's unfortunate," Vittorio continued, his tone conveying far more than his words, "as the timing couldn't be worse, given how much the family is in the public eye this week. But these things can't be scheduled. They happen when they have to happen."

In other words, the relationship was over and Vittorio had been the one to end it. Whatever had happened between them, Vittorio must have felt it necessary to call it quits before the Independence Day festivities.

"I'm sorry to hear it."

"I'm sorry, as well. Naturally, there have already been questions, so the press had to be informed about her sudden illness." Vittorio finally met Massimo's inquisitive look. "I suspect she'll be on the mend very soon. She's rather resilient. She also has someone taking care of her."

Massimo gripped his brother's shoulder. Anyone who observed them would've seen a quick show of lighthearted camaraderie and not thought twice about it, given the upbeat spirit of the evening. Between the brothers, however, a sense of deep mutual support was shared, one that said, *I have your back.* As the next round of fireworks lit the sky, both men clapped and cheered with the rest of the crowd.

"We'll talk soon," Vittorio said as the Italian ambassador caught his eye and began to approach through the crowd. "In the meantime, enjoy yourself."

Massimo nodded, then resumed watching the fireworks as his brother went to speak to the ambassador. When the display ended, he made his way through the crowd, greeting local socialites, politicians, and foreign dignitaries he hadn't seen in years. When he finished speaking to a French financier, he turned in search of a glass of water, only to have a drink dumped on his arm.

"I'm so sorry, Your Highness." The voice was soft and feminine, as was the hand brushing liquid off the sleeve of his jacket. "I'm afraid this isn't the safest place to carry one's champagne."

"Yours isn't the first drink spilled on this patio, nor will it be the last," he said to the striking blonde. He studied her for a moment before placing her. "It's Madeline Lockwood, isn't it? I hope you're enjoying yourself?"

"Of course. Your family has been exceptionally welcoming. Thank you." She glanced over her shoulder, then looked at him conspiratorially. "I trust my parents haven't hit you up for business purposes tonight? They mean well, but often don't know when to quit and simply enjoy themselves."

Her candor surprised him, though he realized it was calculated to put him at ease. He got the sense Madeline moved through parties like this one on a regular basis and knew how to work them. "They've done no such thing. In fact, I believe I saw your mother and mine discussing the royal gardens earlier."

"Perfect." The young woman's smile was earnest without seeming over the top. "My mother has a spectacular garden at home in Scotland and has talked for years about wanting to see the gardens here. You grow flowers we couldn't dream of at home."

"I'm sure the reverse is true, as well." He hesitated for a moment before asking, "Have you had a tour of the gardens?"

The flash in her eyes let him know she'd hoped for the question. "I haven't. Are you offering one?"

"If you'd like." Suddenly, he felt like an actor in a play, going through expected, well-rehearsed motions as he responded to her easy flirtation. As if attempting to convince an audience of his feelings, but without really *feeling* them.

"I'd appreciate that, if it's not too much trouble. I wouldn't want to take you away from your guests."

"Aren't you a guest?" He gestured toward the staircase that led from the patio to the nearest garden, a smaller one that fronted the patio, rather than the larger ones that occupied the area behind his palace apartment.

She thanked him, taking his arm as they walked down the stairs. No one seemed to pay any attention. He knew that chatting with beautiful women at parties was what everyone expected of him.

So why did it feel…off?

Once they reached the bottom of the stairs, he carefully kept to the well-lit areas, pointing out the various trees and flowers. Madeline answered politely, making a few observations of her own as they went. He had to admit, she was perfectly lovely. Her skin radiated health, she held herself with confidence without coming off as egotistical, and she struck him as intelligent and witty. And yet…

She's not Kelly.

He swatted back the thought as Madeline pressed a hand to her bosom, careful to keep the front of her gown discreetly in place, so she could sniff a large red rose at the side of the path. When she straightened, she lightly placed her fingertips on his arm again. There was nothing overtly flirtatious about it. He'd do the same for any of the women at the party were he walking them through the front garden, with its uneven stone path. Yet he knew she hoped for more. And against all logic, his mind—and his body—rebelled.

He flashed a smile as they walked. She really was the perfect woman for a prince. She didn't need his money or his connections. She was educated and felt at home in luxe surroundings. Her family was humble, yet successful. And there were no scandals in her past… not that he'd heard of, and he was certain Sophia wouldn't have pointed her out at the parade if there were. When she returned his smile, though, there was no adrenaline rush as there'd been when

Kelly approached the Jeep and asked if her dress was appropriate for dinner. He wasn't tempted to check out Madeline's assets or the way her dress skimmed her hips. There was simply…nothing.

For the next few minutes he circled her through the garden, gradually making his way back toward the patio, and kept the conversation light despite subtle attempts on Madeline's part to get to know him. Once they reached the stairs, the rain began to fall in slow, large droplets. He hurried her inside, along with the rest of the crowd, as it picked up, threatening to soak them all.

Once inside, she ran a hand over her hair and grinned. "Good timing, Your Highness."

"And see, a little champagne on my sleeve didn't hurt a thing. I was going to get wet, anyway." He shot a pointed look at the tables, which were set for the banquet. "I apologize, but I need to circulate a bit before dinner is served. It was lovely meeting you. I enjoyed our walk."

"As did I. I look forward to seeing you again." She didn't allude to the dancing which would take place later, as women often did when introduced to Massimo or his brothers at these functions, hoping they might be remembered when it came time to find partners.

She had class, Massimo decided as he took his leave. But his lack of attraction to her was…disturbing. And illuminating.

On the bright side, walking with her hadn't bothered him in the slightest, nor had the crush of the people on the patio watching the fireworks. Now that he was inside the ballroom, moving through the masses surrounding the elegantly set tables, greeting guests as he went, he actually felt comfortable.

Controlled.

It was the word his father once used to describe Massimo to a friend when he thought Massimo was elsewhere. It gave Massimo more satisfaction than any other label his father could have used. Mostly because he'd known it to be the truth. From birth, he'd had a formidable amount of control, but he'd honed it through endless mental and physical challenges. During his school years, he'd driven himself hard, both in the classroom and on the athletic fields. Once in the military, he'd led his unit, and not because he was a prince. He'd led them because he'd earned it. His men trusted him because he was predictable, demonstrated good judgment, and because he trusted them in return. He'd kept his orders precise, his emotions in check, and his men alive.

And now, for the first time since his injury, he truly felt in control again.

He stood to his full height, then made his way through the ballroom, shaking hands and exchanging pleasantries as he went. As if he'd never been away.

His attention lit upon a group of soldiers clothed in sharp gray dress uniforms. Sophia had mentioned during the parade that they were home on leave from assignments around the world and had been invited to enjoy the banquet as special guests of the king in honor of their service. The group stood near the windows, taking in the massive room with its the glittering chandeliers, dozens of tables, and the string quartet playing opposite them. Though the soldiers stood with confidence, he sensed they were uncomfortable with the formality of the event. He could relate. Watching waiters circulate with dainty appetizers on silver trays was as far from passing around field rations as a soldier could get.

He approached them, escorted them to their table, then ended up sitting down and spending so much time chatting about their service —their specialties, where they'd been stationed, personnel they knew in common—that he nearly missed the call to his own seat at the head table. As he stood to take his leave, one of the soldiers, a sharp-eyed, raven-haired woman wearing ribbons indicating she'd served in Africa, circled the table and asked for a moment of his time.

She turned her face away from the group and spoke to him in low tones. "Your Highness, you might be interested to know that I'm currently serving in the Central African Republic. My unit is part of an international force tracking down warlords in that area. I'm sure you're aware what a problem they've been to the stability of the region."

He tried to hide his surprise at her words. The woman's voice was as familiar as that of his own troops. He'd heard it in his earpiece on numerous occasions and could tell from her expression that she recognized his. During his time in the field, she'd kept him informed about the movements of other units in the region and provided key intelligence reports.

"I happen to know a few soldiers in that area," he said. "How's progress on your mission?"

A flash of pride crossed her face. "Our primary objective was met three days ago. The news will make it to the mainstream media in the next few weeks."

Meaning Matambe, the worst of the African warlords, a violent man responsible for hundreds of deaths as well as for Massimo's own injuries, was either captured or killed. He couldn't help but reach out and shake her hand with both of his. "That's the best news I've heard in a long time. When you return, please congratulate your unit for me."

"They'll be honored to hear from you and to know you're faring well."

He gave her a heartfelt thanks for the information before she returned to her table. He could hardly believe it. He never thought he'd live to see the day.

A short time later, as the waitstaff cleared away Massimo's salad plate, Sophia turned to him. With a pointed look toward the soldiers' table, she said, "Found your crowd, did you? You looked happy there."

"We speak the same language." The six men and two women were all smiles now, enjoying themselves as their drinks were refreshed by the palace waitstaff. "We were in the middle of talking about one of the men who'd served in my unit in Antarctica when the dinner call came. Hopefully I'll be able to track them down later to finish the conversation."

All of which was true, though it was the news from Africa that made him most satisfied. Knowing that bastard warlord would never starve, kill, or torture innocent people again meant Massimo's sacrifice hadn't been in vain. It meant thousands of people would live freer, more peaceful lives...the lives they were meant to live.

"And Madeline Lockwood? I saw you walking in from the patio with her."

"I like her. She's easy to talk to." At his sister's smirk, he said, "Forget it."

"I didn't say anything!"

"You didn't have to." He schooled his features to remain polite, as expected, but his tone was low. "I told you. No matchmaking."

"I didn't say you had to marry her. On the other hand, dating a woman like Madeline might get you out of your funk."

"There's no *funk*, Sophia."

At that moment, the waitstaff materialized at their elbows, whisking the covers from plates of freshly grilled zucchini, Moroccan couscous, and glorious-smelling rosemary chicken. "In fact," he added once the waiter behind him left, "I can tell you that even if there were a funk, I could be cured by the kitchen's rosemary chicken. It's one of my favorites."

"Now I know you're in a funk. I don't know a single male who values food over females, let alone females who look like Madeline."

He paused with his knife above his chicken. "Sophia, is there something you wish to tell me about the men in your life? Because I'm all ears."

She popped a tiny bite of the chicken into her mouth, then gave him an innocent look. They spent the rest of the meal bantering about the parade, Stefano's work on transportation issues, and on Alessandro's brief appearance during the fireworks. He'd apparently chatted with Vittorio and their parents, but hadn't found Sophia or Massimo. Finally, when dessert was over, King Carlo spoke briefly about the importance of maintaining Sarcaccia's independence and its unique traditions. Then he introduced a dance performance. Twenty men, each carrying massive wooden torches, filled the floor in the center of the ballroom. The chandeliers overhead dimmed as drumbeats echoed through the hall. The well-choreographed dance told the story of a series of battles early in Sarcaccia's history, when the island stood fast against seafaring invaders while being denied help by the city-states on the Italian peninsula. Those battles—and Sarcaccia's eventual triumph, despite the island's small population and lack of assistance—sowed the seeds of its independence movement.

The drumbeats grew faster and faster, rising to a crescendo as the dancers twirled, moved to form a circle in the middle of the floor, then lit their torches in a massive flash of light. One by one, the dancers peeled off from the circle and moved about the floor, spinning their torches end-over-end to the delight of the crowd. Some of the dancers threw their torches in the air, nearly to the ceiling, then caught those thrown by other dancers before wielding them like swords, swooping dangerously close to each other's heads. The effect in the semidarkened room was extraordinary. They wove their way through the tables, tossing the fiery would-be weapons over the heads of the guests. Two of the dancers moved beside the royal table to the applause of King Carlo and Queen Fabrizia. One lit torch, then another, flew the length of the table, each passing in front of Massimo and Sophia, to be caught by the dancer at the opposite end. The entire room broke into rowdy cheers as the lead dancers proceeded to juggle the torches in front of the Barrali family.

Massimo clapped just as he had all day long, during the parade, the fireworks, and the speeches, though now he had to force himself to keep his expression appreciative as his throat grew tighter and tighter. The pungent scent of chemical torch fuel singed his nostrils and the heat, though mild, made his flesh crawl, as if a thousand white-hot ants raced along his back.

Breathe.

Under the table, he ground his toes down in his shoes, rooting himself to the floor. He would not get up. He would not leave. He would not let anyone see that while they enjoyed themselves, the mere act of taking in and expelling air became more and more difficult.

Then it was over.

The dancers formed a circle in the center of the floor, made a grand display of snuffing the flames, then held the still-smoking torches high before bowing to thunderous applause. Massimo smiled, mirroring those around him, though his back teeth clenched so firmly he doubted a crowbar could separate them. The dancers raced off the floor and out a side door, their footsteps light in contrast to the physical weight that seemed to be pressing down on Massimo's body as the crowd clapped and sound filled the room. The orchestra began to play and the king urged everyone to dance. Within seconds, the clapping died down and guests crowded the space occupied by the torch dancers to spin to the lively music.

The pressure in Massimo's chest eased, yet he couldn't shake the odor of the torch fuel from his sinuses. It seemed to fester there, wending its way to his brain.

"Are you planning to dance?"

Massimo forced a cheerful tone for his sister. "Not yet. I was about to take a few minutes to visit the men's lounge. You?"

"Perhaps. Thought I'd call it an early night if I can get away with it. It's been a long day."

He leaned over and gave her a quick kiss on the cheek. As he gripped the arm of his chair to do so, he realized his fingers trembled. "If I don't get a chance to speak to you again, have a good night."

Her look was quizzical, but she was quickly distracted by the approach of a guest. Massimo nodded to his parents, then slipped into the large hallway adjacent to the ballroom. Throngs of guests filled the space. Some were heading for the restrooms, others lingered in the hall in hopes of conducting conversations away from the swell of the orchestra music. Massimo found himself engulfed in a mass of warm bodies.

There is no fire. No danger. You're in the safest place in the world.

He spoke briefly with a friend of his father's, then with one of his mother's distant cousins, continuing to tell himself that his sense of unease was all in his head as he made his way down the hall. But cold logic didn't knock back the feeling. When a strong hand came down on his tattered shoulder and upper back, it was a miracle Massimo stayed rooted to the floor and didn't either jump in pain or turn and flatten the guy.

"Prince Massimo," the burly man boomed. A former American football player, he'd recently purchased a vacation home in Sarcaccia and was in the process of establishing a sports club for Sarcaccian teenagers. "Good to see you. Loved the fire dancers. Haven't seen a performance like that before."

"Nor have I." A beat, then two, passed. "What do you think they use for fuel in those? Butane? Kerosene?"

"Hell if I know. Sure worked to keep 'em lit while they flew through the air, though. Not one of 'em went out. Why?"

"Just curious. I swear I can still smell them."

That brought forth a bellow of laughter. "Eh, likely you're smellin' some woman's perfume. Or the alcohol on everyone's breath, 'cause Lord knows there's been a lot of it tonight. I don't smell anything." The man continued to talk, but Massimo felt his smile hardening into place. The chemical scent seemed more intense now, but no one around him sniffed the air or commented on it. And this was a crowd who loved to comment on such things.

Massimo drew in a breath, but the stench of fuel burned through to his lungs.

Retreat. Regroup.

With effort, he extracted himself from the football player and the surrounding knot of guests, keeping his pace unhurried as he made his way past the men's lounge to the very end of the hall, where a pair of royal guards kept watch over the door leading to the family's private wing. A minute of quiet, maybe two, and he'd be good as new, ready to socialize again.

Once through the door, he turned into an empty parlor and leaned against the wall. Still, the scent lingered.

He knew what this was. His mind was playing tricks, an aftereffect of the events leading to his injury.

You've recovered.

Inhale. Exhale.

You were fine at the parade. You're fine now. It's in your head. Breathe.

Inhale. Exhale. Inhale...and then he couldn't.

His throat clogged as if filled with smoke, and again he experienced the horrifying sensation of hot flames crawling down his back, decimating the surface of his skin. Instinct sent him to the far end of the parlor, where a small door led to a back hallway used primarily by the staff. He passed two men carrying cleaning supplies, wished them a polite good night, then cut through another room to access the rear garden. The night air hit him full force as he forced his key card into the appropriate slot, then yanked the door.

Better.

He stood on the threshold, eyes closed, allowing the cool air to purge his lungs. Gradually, he registered the chill and damp before him and the contrasting warm palace air behind him. Soon security would note the door hadn't shut, as each exterior door was wired to a central command center, and someone would be down to check on it. He withdrew his card from the slot and stepped out, letting the door close behind him. Much as common sense dictated he remain inside, his body seemed intent on maintaining a fight-or-flight response.

Massimo forced one foot in front of the other, slowly making his way along the garden's gravel path, then sank to a bench and dropped his head to his hands. Rain soaked through his slacks and the shoulders of his dinner jacket. He threaded his hands through his hair, surprised to find it'd grown long enough to hold water. Despite the deluge, he wasn't cold. Rather, the rain created a gratifying dissipation of heat from his back, his nostrils, and finally his lungs. Slowly, he took a deep, full breath of the moist air, then another, and exhaled in relief.

All was well. Equilibrium was restored between his mind and his body. His heart beat at a normal pace and the sense of urgency that pushed him out the palace doors was gone.

It galled him that his mind-over-matter methods weren't effective tonight. Then again, he hadn't expected to discuss warlords and have fire thrown in his face.

Gradually, he became aware of the rain pinging against the leaves on the boxwood and rosebushes around the bench. Massimo turned his eyes skyward, taking in the softly falling sheets of rain, which glittered in the light streaming from the palace's large windows. In the distance, he could hear the hum of happy conversation and the strains of the orchestra, though he couldn't identify the piece.

Much as he needed to return before he was missed, he couldn't do so in his current condition. He wracked his brain, trying to remember whether Robert had selected any formalwear similar enough to what he currently wore that he could make it through the rest of the event without raising questions.

Then another sound came to him from the direction of the ballroom, one closer than the orchestra swell or the crowd noise. A door creaked open, then thumped shut, followed by the snick of a lighter.

Rather than risk being seen, Massimo decided to head for his apartment, which lay in the opposite direction. Before he could rise from the bench, he heard a scuff behind him.

Then a hand came down on his bad shoulder.

CHAPTER 20

KELLY STARED at the necklace in her hand, gobsmacked by her discovery. She wasn't an expert, but the weight of the piece alone was enough to convince her it was the real deal. Even with nothing more than the closet's temporary work light to illuminate it, the diamonds sparkled and the dark hue of the sapphires tempted one to peer into their depths.

She carefully laid the necklace and bag on top of the dresser, then checked the rest of the hidden compartment before replacing the false back and sliding the drawer into place.

Gingerly, she carried the necklace and bag to the living room, clicked the lamp to the side of the sofa, then held the jewels under the light for a closer look. What looked extraordinary in the closet took her breath away now that it was fully illuminated. Diamonds ran the entire circumference of the piece, punctuated along the way with small sapphires. Dangling at the throat and surrounded by diamonds, a stunning dark sapphire with a whitish mark in the shape of a star commanded attention.

Whoever designed this necklace must've spent a fortune on it. It could be displayed at the Tower of London with Britain's crown jewels or in the Museum of Natural History's gem exhibit in New

York and draw long lines to ooh and aah over its splendor. But what was it doing hidden away in a drawer, in a piece of furniture that very nearly ended up relegated to storage? How long had it been there?

She'd let Massimo know about the necklace first thing in the morning—she doubted he was aware of its existence in the dresser—but wasn't sure what to do in the meantime. Taking it to her room for the night seemed wrong, as did leaving it for him with a note. And safe as it had been in the dresser, she hesitated to return it to its original hiding place. She didn't want to have to retrieve it for Massimo tomorrow in the midst of construction.

She returned the necklace to the velvet bag and carried it toward the desk, taking care to hold it flat to keep the piece from falling out the small hole near the bottom. If she tucked it in the top drawer for safekeeping, it shouldn't be disturbed and Massimo would be able to retrieve it tomorrow in private. Halfway to the desk, she was surprised by the sound of footpads on the hardwood, then the appearance of a wet nose followed by a big body.

"Hello, Gaspare." She set the necklace on the low windowsill before bending to scratch the boy's ears. "What are you doing up so late? I thought you were sleeping in the kitchen."

He'd come to greet her and April when they'd arrived to move the bureau, but after assuring all was well he'd retreated to his favorite spot. Now, as he rubbed against her legs and looked up at her with big blue eyes, so vivid against his dark fur, she realized he likely hadn't been out in hours. Talking to him as she went, she slid the necklace into the top desk drawer, located her key card and a leash, then took him to the garden exit. The rain fell in sheets now. Much as Gaspare was excited by the puddles, she wasn't willing to linger to let him play. She remained just inside the door, letting him out to the length of the leash so he could relieve himself, then patted her thigh to urge him back inside. When the dog's paws hit the exterior step, he paused, then turned and looked over his shoulder. Kelly followed the direction of the dog's determined gaze.

"What is it, boy?" she whispered, squinting into the rain. At first, she saw nothing but the glittering lights cast by the chandeliers on the opposite side of the palace, where the banquet was in full swing. Then, on a bench not far away, she saw the outline of a man leaning back, his face turned up to the falling rain.

Even in the dark, there was no mistaking the strong profile or the positioning of the arms draped across the back of the bench. The same man sat like that only a few days ago, waiting by the marina while she made frantic phone calls to her bank and local hotels. But while he'd been the epitome of casualness then, with his face turned toward the sunshine and his open-top Jeep parked behind him, his pose tonight bothered her. It was as if he held the weight of the world on his shoulders and was attempting to shrug it off, only to find the weight more and more burdensome.

Perhaps her news would prove a distraction from whatever troubled him.

She hustled Gaspare inside, pocketed her key card, then dodged across the rain-soaked grass. In the distance, she heard another door open and close. An orange-red light flickered, then disappeared, the sign of a person covering their cigarette in an attempt to protect it from the rain.

Unwilling to draw the guest's attention to Massimo by calling out his name, she padded quietly through the grass and touched his shoulder.

In a flash, he was on his feet and facing her, his massive body half over the bench, grabbing her throat with one large hand while cocking back the other for a punch.

"It's me." Even as she hissed the words and tried to duck, he froze in mid-attack, the brunt of the force he was about to unleash still coiled. His eyes were hard and flat, his grip on her throat firm. As realization dawned, confusion, then horror flashed across his face. Somewhere in the distance, Kelly thought she heard a door open and close, but her gaze was riveted on the face before her.

"Dear God." His fingers released their death grip on the front of her neck and he eased back to his side of the bench. Rain dripped from his eyelashes as he blinked at her, while his chest rose and fell like a man who'd run for miles. "Kelly."

"I'm sorry. I didn't mean to startle you." She managed to keep her voice down, despite the horror welling inside her. Another second and he'd have decked her. With his size and power, he'd have caused her serious injury. But as afraid as she should be for herself, she was far more afraid for him. The expression on his face as he'd leapt from the bench was that of a man fighting for his life, devoid of anything but the single-minded mission to kill or be killed.

He apparently understood the gravity of the situation, too, because he seemed more taken aback by the second. His eyes drifted closed and he swiped both hands over the top of his head, sending a spray of water flying into the night.

"I didn't think you'd want anyone to see you here." She forced a quiet, steady tone, hoping a display of calm would transfer to him, easing the tension that visibly gripped his body.

"I am so sorry, Kelly. I can't believe I did that." He extended a hand toward her, then yanked it back, as if afraid she'd break were he to touch her now. "Are you hurt?"

"I'm perfectly fine."

"I don't know how you can be. I nearly took your head off. I…I didn't hear you." The last was said more to himself than to her. "I can't believe I didn't hear you."

"You were looking in the other direction. I think someone came outside to smoke, because I heard a door close and thought I saw the flash of a lighter. And I was walking on the grass to avoid the puddles."

He wiped the water from his face once more, then glanced at the path, as if checking for the actual presence of puddles. "I should be at the banquet."

"Not like that. Why don't you come inside and dry off first? Sit down. Have a drink if you need one."

"Christ." He looked at her as if truly seeing her for the first time since she walked up behind him. "That's what I was about to do. When you showed up, that is. I heard the other door bang shut and thought I should get inside to dry off."

Their gazes simultaneously went in the direction where the

smoker had exited earlier, but no one was visible, nor was there the telltale scent of cigarettes. In the downpour, Kelly doubted the person would've had much luck. He'd probably gone inside before Kelly'd even reached Massimo.

"I'm sure he's long gone. Come on." She turned and picked her way between the puddles toward the back door of Massimo's apartment. A heartbeat later, she was gratified to hear his steps on the gravel behind her. She keyed them in to see Gaspare waiting just inside the door, as if it'd been his place all along to ensure his master made it home.

Massimo stepped inside behind her and frowned down at the dog. "He's wet."

"He needed a bathroom break. I only saw you because he did first."

Massimo processed that as they entered the bedroom. She crossed to his en suite bathroom and grabbed two large, white towels from the shelf beside the shower enclosure.

"Were you working?" he asked when she reentered the bedroom. Standing in his room in a formal suit and jacket, dripping water onto the floor, he appeared an entirely different man than the one who'd commanded everyone's attention at the parade this afternoon. He had the same strong, debonair look as James Bond might if he'd pursued a villain through the rain, but there was a vulnerability, too, as if he'd faced a life and death battle and had doubted his ability to survive it. She forced her gaze away, knowing he'd never want her to notice.

"I had a couple things I wanted to do after the parade, but I'm finished for the night." She handed him a towel, then unfolded the other and started rubbing her head. Gaspare watched from the corner of the room, fascinated, but Massimo made no move to dry himself. It was as if his thoughts were stuck on whatever occupied him while he'd been sitting on the bench staring into the rain. She paused, draping her towel around her shoulders. "And you?"

"And…me? Me what?"

Now she knew he was preoccupied. "Were you finished for the night? I assume whatever you were doing in the garden wasn't part of your meet-and-greet duties at the banquet."

That brought life back into his expression. Not a smile, exactly, but a crack in the tension that enveloped him. "I was about to go back, but I'm not in any condition at the moment. And by the time I find the right clothing amongst all these racks and change, I suspect the celebration will be winding down."

"I'm happy to help with the clothing part. Your suits and formalwear are mostly on that rack over there if you decide to return to the banquet" —she indicated the far corner of the room— "and the casual clothing is in this dresser and stacked over here. I think Robert was hoping that the closet would be finished before he brought in his first round of purchases, but I did the best I could in the meantime."

"I didn't mean to insinuate that you weren't doing a good job."

"I know." She bit the inside of her lip. "Well, whatever you decide to change into, I recommend you dry off first."

"At this point, I'm going casual." Before she could excuse herself, he stripped off his jacket and dropped it to the hardwood floor, then began mopping his face and hair with the towel. The last time she'd seen him swiping a towel over his head, he'd been stepping out of the shower in her villa and gloriously naked. He'd caught her admiring him, flipped the towel over his head and wrapped it around her, using it to pull her body fast to his. He'd given her a soul-searing kiss, one that drove them right back to bed.

She shoved back the mental image and forced a neutral expression. How was it her mind instantly went to sex with the man when his mind was assuredly on anything *but* sex?

"Would you like me to find something for you to wear?" she managed.

"That'd be great, thanks. T-shirt is fine. Whatever color. And I saw some khaki pants earlier. I think I can find those."

Kelly turned toward the dresser where she had stored the prince's few T-shirts until Robert filled out the collection. She took her time picking through them, allowing him privacy as he dried off while giving herself a break from temptation. She shouldn't have noticed the way his formal shirt clung to his chest after he'd removed the suit jacket, but how could she not? The man was ripped. And a man built like Massimo in a wet, white shirt demanded one's attention. She located a light blue T-shirt Robert had selected, then turned and handed it to Massimo.

Only to discover that now he wasn't wearing a shirt at all. Both the white formal shirt and the undershirt lay on the floor in a soggy pile beside the suit jacket.

She handed him the T-shirt, careful to keep a polite distance between them. She needed to find a way to extricate herself from the room before his trousers joined the pile. If she didn't, she'd be blushing so furiously he'd know the direction of her thoughts. As he looped the towel over a nearby clothing rack so he could pull the shirt over his head, she began gathering his clothes from the floor, then used her own towel to sop up the mess left behind.

"You don't have to do that."

"Better not to ruin the hardwood, don't you think? Where should I put all this?"

He frowned at the sodden clothing as he eased the shirt over his abs. "I have a laundry bin in the bathroom that housekeeping checks daily, but I'd rather not put those in there."

"I'll just hang them in the bathroom."

"I'm perfectly capable." He scooped the dripping pile from her arms. His warm skin, the wet garments, and the faint hint of his cologne combined to render her temporarily speechless. What man with his wealth, his looks, his engaging personality, and a house full of staff would do what amounted to housework as if it were his normal routine?

She gazed up at him as he captured a sleeve that escaped from the bundle, preventing it from leaving a water trail on the floor.

I could fall in love with a man like Massimo.

The thought frightened her as soon as it entered her mind. It'd taken her months to commit to Ted. And now she was looking at a man she'd only known a few days and considering…what?

Massimo paused and met her gaze, then held it, as if the contact affected him, too. "I'm so sorry about the garden, Kelly. I never should have—"

"You've already apologized. It's all right."

She needed to get out of the room before words like *love* stuck in her brain rather than flitting through with all the staying power of a floating soap bubble.

"No, it's not." He looked at her for another heartbeat, his eyes searching hers before he broke contact and strode to the bathroom to set the wet clothing on the counter. He reached back into the bedroom to snare a pair of folded khakis from a stack of clothing near the dresser.

She was about to excuse herself when he said, "Hang on. I'll be right back."

Damn.

The word echoed in Massimo's head as he wrung out his shirt and flopped it over the door to the shower, adjusting the fabric so it would drip dry into the shower rather than onto the tile floor. His undershirt and jacket followed before he stripped off his slacks, wrung them out, then spread them over the towel rack.

Unfortunately, in taking off his slacks, Massimo discovered his underwear soaked through from sitting on the wet bench. He was forced to lean out the door and ask Kelly to hand him a new pair.

It was that, walk out there in drenched shorts, or struggle back into the wet pants so he could fetch the underwear himself, none of which were good options. Ditching them entirely and walking out nude was out of the question.

When she handed them to him from the top dresser drawer, she acted no differently than if she'd handed him a pen. But even in that quick motion, he knew better. He'd seen the tamped-down flare of attraction in her gaze when she'd handed him the towel. And when he'd taken the clothes from her arms, she'd inhaled sharply and he could've sworn her eyes began to flutter closed before she caught herself.

Why the hell would she feel that way when he could have killed her? Didn't she realize what he'd been about to do? If he'd hit her in the face, at the very least, he'd have broken her nose or her jaw. But if he'd caught her in the temple or side of the head as she'd ducked... dear God, he'd have put her in the hospital. It was a miracle he'd been able to hold back his fist. He never could've lived with himself if he'd harmed her.

It was bad enough thinking about what *might* have happened.

And here, only an hour ago, he was congratulating himself on feeling in control, knowing that all was well, that he would be just fine handling his life as a royal. What a crock. Who in the world did he think was going to attack him outside the palace? This wasn't central Africa, there wasn't a well-armed jungle warlord lurking in the rose-bushes to torture or beat or shoot him.

He stared at himself in the mirror, wondering what Kelly had seen in his expression as he'd come over the bench. He could've *killed* her.

He finished dressing, swiped his hands over his face, which was reddened from the chill of the rain, then walked out to the bedroom. It was then he noticed that she was still soaked, despite toweling off. He could see the outline of her beige bra beneath her white shirt, the same top she'd been wearing when she interrupted his meeting with Robert this morning to ask about the bureau in the living room. Her skirt was streaked with rain and her sandals looked like they'd squish if she walked in them.

He forced his eyes to her face, but something about her wet clothing and still-dripping hair nagged at his brain.

"You said Gaspare needed out?" At her nod, he continued, "But when you came to the bench, you'd put him in. What made you come back outside?"

"Maybe I like the rain."

He skewered her with a look of skepticism.

"I wanted to check on you."

Check on him? "Why?"

"Why does anyone check on another person? I wanted to see if you were all right. You were sitting by yourself in a downpour, for crying out loud. You looked" —her brows scrunched— "bothered, like you'd just been given terrible news."

"Funny, because I actually heard some good news tonight. I went out because I needed a moment away from the party."

He should offer her a fresh towel or allow her to head back to her apartment for a change of clothes, but knowing she'd witnessed him in a moment of weakness left him off balance. Worse, her deepening frown indicated she didn't buy his explanation for a second.

"There was more to it than that. You could've gone to another room or excused yourself and claimed a headache." Gooseflesh rose on her arms and she crossed them in front of her, unconsciously warding off the cold. "You needed air, and you needed it badly enough to go out in a storm. Something or someone bothered you at that banquet, whether you want to admit it or not."

He moved toward the bathroom for another towel.

"You asked me why I came out to check on you. Don't ignore this, Massimo."

The insistence in her voice made him stop and look back. "I'm not ignoring anything."

"You're not a violent person. Don't ask me how I know that, I just do. You'd never strike out at someone without reason. It wasn't simply that I surprised you. Anyone could've walked up behind you. There must be dozens of staff and family members with key cards who could've gone out to the garden, just like the person who ducked out to try and grab a smoke. With the banquet going on, everyone in the building is up late."

She took a step toward him. He wanted to move away, but he'd never backed away from anyone. "I'm fine, Kelly."

"Are you? I don't think so." Caring hands cradled his face. Her fingertips were cold, but firm. "I don't expect you to tell me what's wrong. But you scared yourself when you came at me over the bench."

He covered her small hands with his own and stared into her expressive, chestnut-brown eyes. "Do I look like anything's wrong?"

"Not now, no. You don't *look* like it. Other than the fact your hair is wet."

"It's the first time in a long time I've actually had enough hair to get wet."

"But we're not talking about your hair, are we?" Her fingers twitched under his. "I think you need to admit to yourself that something's amiss. Whatever drove you outdoors in the rain, whatever drove you to defend yourself from an attacker who wasn't real, you're more than strong enough to deal with it. But not if you ignore it."

Or fight it off, he thought. Because that's exactly what he'd been doing. Fighting the twinges in his gut and trying to reason his way through the sensations of choking, of being crushed, of being burned.

What was it about this woman that allowed her to see in him what no one else could? What even he himself didn't want to see?

"Thank you." The words were said softly and came out before he could consider them. It was tantamount to admitting she was right. He leaned forward, pressed his forehead to hers, then allowed his eyes to close.

Her fingers relaxed and she started to pull away, to transition back to formality. But he held her in place, dipped his head and brushed her lips with his.

She didn't kiss him back. He felt her intake of breath, sensed her internal struggle. He knew, deep in his soul, that she wanted him. And that made him want her all the more.

"Massimo." Her forehead still rested against his, their breath mingling between their rain-dampened faces. "I'm working for you now. Wasn't part of the point of employing me to—"

"Shhh. For just one minute. *One.*"

CHAPTER 21

THIS TIME, when he caught her mouth with his, she returned the kiss.

There was a pause at first, then a capitulation as she tilted her head to allow him better access before she melted against him. Her fingers remained pressed to his face, his fingers woven through hers, as their tongues made a slow, hot exploration of each other. The emotion of it washed through his soul, cleansing him more thoroughly than any rainstorm.

In another week, she'd go home. On top of that, the woman clearly had her own issues. But for now, he couldn't think about practicalities. He wanted only to make love to her, to slake the bone-deep thirst she'd created within him.

He let go of her fingers to sink his hands into her wet hair. With a shift of his leg, he trapped her body flush with his. God, but she fit against him as if they were made for each other. Even her head fit perfectly into his hands.

Still, he knew he had to stop. Had to give her space to choose what she'd give, though his body ached for one more moment, one more taste. A sigh escaped he as she shifted, stretching to her toes. The friction of her body moving against his nearly sent him out of his mind.

It would be so easy to turn her toward the bed.

With Herculean effort, he broke the kiss and met her hooded gaze. He let his hands drift down to her shoulders, then to her arms. "Do I look better now? Because I feel better."

She was quiet for a moment. At long last, in a tone that made it clear he wasn't going to get another kiss, let alone a night in bed, she said, "You'll do. Robert would tell you that your hair needs work, but the rest is good." Gently, she stroked her thumbs over his cheekbones. "In fact, there are women who would die for skin like yours."

Her declaration brought a booming laugh from him. While she'd said it to break the sexual tension thrumming between them, the puzzled line of her mouth showed she had no clue why it amused him as much as it did.

"They wouldn't if they saw the skin on my back," he explained. "But thank you for the compliment."

Understanding dawned in her eyes and her hands fell to her sides. "Ah. Now it's my turn to apologize. I hadn't considered that. I suspect that *you* almost died for that skin."

"No idea if I did or didn't. No one would tell me. But the recovery hurt like hell."

"I imagine." Her voice turned serious. "Was it an army injury?"

Now he definitely wasn't getting laid. Not that he had a realistic chance in the first place. He should consider himself lucky he managed a kiss, given Kelly's initial resistance. "Yes."

"That's the kind of trauma that changes a person."

"Yes, it does." Saying it aloud made him realize the truth in the statement. Years in the military honed him into the man he was now. He'd known with each day of training and each new assignment that his duties were making him tougher, more resilient. But he'd never thought of it as *changing* him…only as making him a stronger version of the man he'd always been.

The burns, though, those changed him.

A shiver ran through Kelly. Without speaking, he spun and went into the bathroom, intent on getting a towel.

Her voice came to him from the bedroom. "I didn't mean to pry. You don't have to talk about it. I'm sure it's a private matter."

He was back before she finished. Offering her an oversized towel, he said, "I left because you're freezing. The last towel wasn't enough to get your hair dry and then you used it to clean my floor."

"Oh."

"And you're right. It's a private matter. For a number of reasons, I haven't talked about it to anyone." She dried her face and hair as he spoke. The towel prevented him from gauging her expression when he added, "I appreciate that you didn't ask me about it when we were at your villa."

"It didn't seem appropriate." Slowly, she moved the towel to her shoulders and wrapped it around herself. Mascara ringed her eyes, smudged by her efforts to dry off. Less than an hour ago, he'd been surrounded by high-class, cultured women, all dressed to the nines and with their faces made up to perfection. Yet he found the woman before him far more alluring.

She made him want to talk. That made her dangerous.

Gaspare, who'd been watching them from the corner of the room, stood and plodded toward the kitchen, rubbing his big body against Kelly's legs as he went. It was enough to break the spell between them.

"It's late. I should go."

"You don't have to."

"You've changed out of your wet clothes, I haven't. Plus I have an early morning tomorrow. I've scheduled a shelving installation for an important client and he won't like it if I'm late. I've told him multiple times that I pride myself on my professionalism."

Once again, he was awed by Kelly's ability to make him smile. "I'm sure he finds you every bit the professional. Nevertheless, I wouldn't want to jeopardize your reputation. I'll walk you out."

Even if all he wanted to do was kiss her again and again and again, both of their reputations be damned.

He strode to the entrance of his apartment without allowing himself to meet her eyes or let his gaze fall to her luscious mouth. Because if he did, he'd use every means at his disposal to convince her to stay.

"Wait. Before I go, there's something else."

Massimo's hand froze on the door handle when Kelly said it. For a heady moment, he thought she couldn't leave without kissing him again. That one kiss would turn into more, then they'd end up making mad, passionate love the way they had in the villa, though hopefully without knocking the mattress off the bed this time.

Instead, she spun on her heel and strode to the antique writing desk in the corner of the room without looking at him.

"I completely forgot, but when I went outside to check on you, I also meant to show you something back here in the apartment."

Given that she had the desk drawer open, it apparently wasn't the bed. "What?"

"This." She closed the drawer, crossed the distance between them, and pressed a soft fabric bag with lumpy contents into his palm. "Have you seen it before?"

He immediately recognized the brilliant blue velvet as the type used by Conti & Fancetti, a jewelry company patronized by the royal family for generations. It was the same jeweler who'd designed his parents' wedding rings and his mother's emerald anniversary ring. The white silk tie at the bag's neck was crimped, as if it had been knotted for a long time, and a few stray threads drew his attention to a hole in the bag's bottom seam. Slowly, he undid the top. What he'd expected to see inside, he didn't know, but it wasn't the piece he withdrew.

"Stunning, isn't it? I've never seen anything like it." Kelly's words were whispered, as if they stood in a museum ogling a one-of-a-kind painting or sculpture under the watchful eye of an armed guard. The diamond and sapphire creation he held merited that kind of reverence.

"Nor have I." He turned the necklace over, studied the setting, then spread it between his fingers for a better look. It was one of the most breathtaking he'd seen, and he'd seen plenty. "Where in the world did you find this?"

"Your bureau. April and I moved it into the closet earlier this evening. After she left, I discovered a hidden compartment behind one of the drawers." She gestured toward the bedroom. "Here, let me show you."

He followed her through the bedroom, giving only a passing thought to the fact he'd kissed her here moments earlier, then to the closet. When Kelly entered in front of him and flicked the button on a work light hanging from the side of a ladder, he realized that he hadn't seen the room since work began. The old curtain rods and dresser were gone, the boxes sorted through and removed. The high window, which had been partially blocked by stacked boxes, was now fully visible and clean, and its trim had been repaired and painted. A gray drop cloth protected the floor and a coat of primer covered the walls, which had been carefully smoothed to eliminate age-old holes and imperfections. Pencil marks indicated planned locations for electrical outlets and shelving. Above him, the old ceiling light was gone and the plaster repaired, leaving only a small hole from which updated wiring now protruded. As with the walls, a pencil outline indicated the positioning for a new light. The most eye-catching part of the room, however, was the massive bureau, which dominated the wall opposite the door.

"The room's not in a state to be seen," she warned him. "In a few days, though, prepare to be wowed."

"I'm wowed already."

With her back to him, she knelt in front of the bureau and pulled on the next-to-bottom drawer. "Come on in. I want to show you this panel."

He started at her words. One by one, he unloosed his fingers from where he'd unknowingly wrapped them around the frame to the closet's pocket door, then took two steps into the room.

"Massimo?" She was squinting at him now. "Is there a problem?"

Hell yes. Two more steps, then another two, and he was at her side. His pulse quickened, but the suffocating sensation wasn't as intense as in the wine cellar or as when he'd left the banquet. He managed an offhanded, "Don't want to step on anything I shouldn't."

"Grab that end of the drawer, then. Press the mechanism to the side and it'll come all the way out."

He crouched and did as she asked, then helped her lower the drawer to the floor. She gestured to indicate the bureau's exposed interior. "Reach in there. At the back, you'll feel a wooden rectangle that seems out of place. Wiggle it side to side."

It took a few seconds, but he found the protruding spot at the back of the case. When he pushed it to one side, then the other, the back panel fell into his hands. He knelt further to look into the dark space, but quickly righted himself as a wave of nausea caught him by surprise. He swallowed it back, determined not to let Kelly see.

"That's unreal," he managed at the same time her hand wrapped around his forearm.

"You're not okay. Come on. Let's go back to the living room."

"I'm fine." At her resolute look, he sat down on the floor and forced a smile. "*Now* I'm fine."

"Are you claustrophobic?" The question wasn't accusing or pitying, but matter-of-fact.

"No." He ran his tongue over his teeth, wanting to explain, yet knowing it would forever change the dynamic between them. When Kelly remained quiet, he conceded, "Not officially."

One of her dark eyebrows arched. "Wasn't aware one could be officially claustrophobic. Is there a certificate involved? Or a secret government stamp?"

That eased the wrenching of his gut. "No, I don't think so."

"In that case, your unofficial secret is safe with me." She gave his arm a quick squeeze, then withdrew her hand. "Does your family know?"

"Nothing *to* know. It doesn't serve a purpose."

Kelly sat beside him on the floor. She crossed her legs in front of her, taking care to tuck her skirt around her knees. With that easy motion, she made the closet feel intimate rather than oppressive. It reminded him of the nights he spent chatting or playing cards with fellow soldiers when they'd shared a small tent in Africa. Then, he'd never felt imprisoned. On the contrary, he'd felt free.

"Maybe the purpose is to make you feel better," she said. "To know you're not alone, that another human being is taking note of what you're experiencing."

"Now you're a closet designer *and* a therapist?"

Amusement caused her to roll her eyes. "Not in my wildest dreams. If I were, I wouldn't have to explain to my former assistant that I need her to go through my financial paperwork so I can recoup money lost to a former fiancé."

"How's that going?" He should've asked her days ago, but never found the right opening. When he'd been alone in bed at night, in those last moments before falling asleep, he'd wondered if the strain was keeping her awake or if the problem was being settled.

"It's progressing. She found all the documents I need to prove the money in the account came directly from the sale of my business, and I hired a lawyer to contact Ted and explain ever-so-firmly that the money is rightfully mine, that we had an understanding to that effect, and that he needs to return it or face legal action. Now I'm just waiting for Ted's response. I'm hopeful he'll return the money and leave it at that."

"Good for you, especially on hiring a lawyer to rattle his cage."

"You're the one who gave me the idea." Her upper body tilted toward his, then she bumped his shoulder and grinned. "It helped me to talk through the issue with you. Even if it was embarrassing. So maybe *you* were *my* therapist."

"A prince and a therapist? I don't think so."

He slid a sideways glance at her only to discover she was doing the same. Their eyes held and an understanding passed between them. They'd each been hurt. They each prized their independence. They each found their ways to cope and move forward.

"The injury to my back and shoulder occurred when I was in a small space," he admitted, keeping his voice low and even. "I assume that's why the closet makes me uncomfortable. It'll fade in time."

"That explains a bit." When he didn't elaborate, she asked, "It's new, isn't it? The discomfort. You felt it in Giulia's wine cellar and it surprised you."

"Yes." The woman was astute. "But now I know what to expect. I think that's half the battle."

"What's the other half?"

He shrugged. "Like I said, time. I'm expected to be around crowds and that often involves tight spaces. But the more I do it, the faster I'll adapt." He hadn't thought of it in those terms until he said it aloud to Kelly, but as the words left his mouth, he knew them to be true.

"Somewhat like a kid eating broccoli," she said. "On the first bite, it's bitter. They reject it. But the more they're exposed to it, the sooner their taste buds adapt."

If broccoli burned and choked, he supposed. But the comparison was apt. The experience at the airport caught him off guard, when he'd had the overwhelming urge to burst through security. At Giulia's, he'd again been caught off guard, but he'd managed to rationalize his way through it, get out of the cellar, and beat his overactive senses into submission.

He'd been fine at the parade. He'd even been fine at the banquet until faced with an unexpected fire practically in his face, and that a short time after discussing the very warlord responsible for his injuries.

"Please tell me that's a look of amusement on your face, and not offense at the broccoli analogy. What you're experiencing is much more…that is, I didn't intend to minimize—"

He cut off Kelly's apology with a shake of his head. "Definitely amusement. I meant 'adapt' in the sense of gaining the experience necessary to fight the sensation, but I'll keep the broccoli analogy in mind if there's a next time." Who knew…it might work. It was certainly a more pacifist approach.

He reached for Kelly's hand and held it. The contact brought a sexual charge that reverberated to his core. Oddly, it also brought him a deep sense of contentment. Despite the way it affected him, he expected her to pull away and claim the need to maintain a sense of professionalism.

She didn't.

CHAPTER 22

Kelly's fingers flexed in Massimo's. "Tell me what happened."

The small muscles of his jaw jumped as he considered her request. She'd stated it as calmly as possible, giving Massimo the ability to beg off if he wanted, but she knew he wouldn't. He'd likely needed to talk from the moment he'd suffered the horrible injury, yet was too proud, too strong, and too stubborn a man to admit it. Even so, she sensed he had other reasons he'd kept the details to himself, reasons that went beyond his own needs. It would help him to let another human being share his burden.

Yet she wasn't certain she had the inner strength to hear it. Discussing an event so personal while in the confines of the man's walk-in closet would draw her deeper into his life than she wanted to go. Given that her confidence was still healing from the slicing and dicing she'd endured with Ted, the last thing she needed was another reason to care for Massimo and another opportunity for her emotional wounds to bleed anew.

Massimo may have kissed her tonight—and oh, how it nearly brought her to her knees—and he may be holding her hand now in the quiet of the night, but those actions were born from primal need, not love or affection. He'd made that crystal clear when he'd hired her.

"Have you heard of Matambe?"

She thought for a moment. "That sounds familiar, but I don't know why. Is it a place you were stationed?"

"Matambe is a man…if one can call him that. There were a lot of other names my unit and I used for him. None of them suitable for use outside of combat."

"I can imagine." Her uncle, a former Marine, was constantly chastised by his parents for using salty language when he'd returned home.

"Actually, I hope you can't." His wry expression indicated her imagination wasn't nearly depraved enough. "Matambe is an African warlord. There are some who believe he's a god. Others believe he's a demon, come from the mouth of hell to visit devastation on those who are less than honorable. He plays up both those local beliefs to his own advantage."

Massimo glanced at the ceiling, but didn't seem to see it as he spoke. "To most of the world, Matambe is a power-hungry monster with no conscience when it comes to getting what he wants. Theft, torture, rape, blackmail, murder. It's all in his repertoire."

"I saw a documentary about warlords who prey upon isolated or poor villages a few years ago. Probably why Matambe sounds familiar to me. They're definitely not the good guys."

"No. And Matambe is one of the most powerful and violent."

His hand tightened fractionally over hers. She sensed he was building toward the difficult part of his story and choosing his words with care.

"On my last assignment, I was part of a multinational force charged with hunting down Matambe. It was a challenging task. He knows the territory like the back of his hand and can move quickly, day or night. He and his army travel across borders and through rough terrain as if it's nothing. His deputies act as lookouts to keep pursuers off their track. He raids the villages for supplies and forces the inhabitants to reveal the whereabouts of any forces who are hunting for him. He's out before an alarm can be raised."

Massimo released her hand with a quick pat and stood. The necklace slid from his knee, landing with a dull thud on the floor, but he didn't appear to notice.

"At times, my unit provided security for food and medical supplies being sent to villages in Matambe's known territory. One afternoon, twelve of us helped a village hide a shipment of donated food and medical supplies in an underground bunker they'd built to conceal their necessities from warlords or other vagrants. Some of the supplies we left out in the village so anyone who might've seen the supply trucks and conducted a raid would think they'd gotten it. Unfortunately, Matambe's men learned about the shipment and alerted him. At sunset, he came."

"You were still there?"

Massimo paced the closet. It wasn't a panicked or nervous walk. Rather, he seemed to think better while in motion. "Nine of my men had already left. I was there with two others finishing up. We never expected an attack so soon. Frankly, we were hoping there wouldn't be an attack at all, since we'd been careful to keep the supply truck on as discreet a route as possible. We were vastly outmanned and outgunned. We had no choice but to retreat. If we were seen helping out in the village—particularly helping hide supplies—it would've been devastating for the residents. Matambe's men would have tortured and killed them to the last man, woman, and child make a statement about what happens to those who consort with their enemies. The villagers were expected to get supplies from whatever charitable organizations they could and immediately turn them over to Matambe. Of course, if they'd done that, they'd have eventually starved to death. Keeping them fed and safe was what made them loyal to *us*."

The image he painted of the villagers' dilemma horrified her. "Were you captured?"

"No, or I wouldn't be here now." Massimo stilled, as if having decided exactly what to tell her. "When Matambe arrived, my two men were in the bunker. They happened to be with a group of teenage boys sorting the last of the supplies when we heard the attackers coming from the jungle. They secured the door and hid inside. It was lucky they were positioned where they were. The boys were fit and at an age where Matambe would want to conscript them. Forcing children into his army helps him control the villages. No one wants to risk firing on their own children or those of relatives."

"That's sickening." A lump formed in her throat at the idea of losing a child that way, never knowing if they were dead or alive, what atrocities they were forced to witness, or what brainwashing they'd endure. "Effective, I'm sure, but sickening."

He huffed an acknowledgement. "The village leaders handed over all the supplies that we'd unloaded in the village itself and even some they'd squirreled away in the woods, hoping to convince the raiders of their loyalty to Matambe by giving up what they claimed was their emergency stash. Some of the women prayed, saying they were making the sacrifice of food to Matambe for his divine protection, acting as if the sun rose and set only at his bidding. I heard every word. Those women were very convincing."

"But not convincing enough?"

"No. Matambe's men refused to leave. They stayed for nearly thirty-six hours, searching the huts and accusing the villagers of withholding information."

"If you could hear all this, where were you?" It was the question she most dreaded asking.

His pacing started again. "The bunker had a smart design. A false front door was installed so that if it was discovered, anyone opening it would see only a five-foot square hole used for storage. The real door was in the floor of the hole, so it'd be covered by anything kept inside. I managed to crawl into the space between the two doors and hide with my weapon drawn. It allowed me to protect the bunker while appearing to be an AWOL soldier foraging for food. At least, that was what I was counting on if Matambe or his men found me. I was good and filthy, and I smelled none too pleasant, so I hoped I could convince them."

Her eyes widened. "You were in a *hole*? The entire time? You couldn't get down into the bunker itself?"

"Once I closed the outside door, the space was too tight to maneuver without making noise."

"And risking the lives of your two men and the teenagers."

"The whole village's lives. But it worked. In the end, Matambe's men left without injuring a soul." He grinned, though the twist of his mouth and crinkles at the corner of his eyes reeked of irony. "At least, not to their knowledge. My injury was nothing more than a run of the mill accident."

Kelly made no effort to hide her confusion. "Barricading yourself in a hole for a day and a half and emerging with that kind of injury hardly constitutes 'a run of the mill accident.' Your back looks as if someone attacked you with a blowtorch and then hacked away with a machete for good measure."

"No, an attack I could've fought off." Massimo crossed the closet to resume his seat beside her, propping his back against the wall and stretching his long legs in front of him on the drop cloth.

Once settled, he explained, "As they were leaving, one of Matambe's men flicked a cigarette butt near the bunker. At least, that's what the villagers told the medic who treated me. The butt apparently caught the dry grass nearby. I couldn't see out, but I heard the stomping of boots as Matambe's men passed over my head on their way to the jungle. A moment later there was smoke and a lot of shouting, but I couldn't risk climbing out before I knew the coast was clear."

Packed into a dark, tight space, with the chaos of fire and enemy fighters above his head, he must have been afraid, though he'd be the last man on Earth to admit it. But he'd rather burn to death than endanger others. Her admiration for him jumped a few notches.

"That's unbelievably brave. You were a hero to those people, putting their lives before yours."

"It was for my own good," he said, waving off the compliment. "The men in the bunker could only be guaranteed their safety if I stayed put. It was built with a small tunnel leading into the jungle they could use to escape. I knew they'd rescue me if the villagers didn't or couldn't. And they did."

"Yet you ended up burned," she pointed out.

"Well, yes, but that doesn't make me heroic. I was unconscious from the smoke when my men forced the door and pulled me out. The villagers were busy fighting the fire. This happened" —he jerked a thumb over his left shoulder— "because a burning tree fell on my back and shoulder after they yanked me out. So no, no glamorous heroics. Just a tree I never saw and don't remember, and a fire I didn't do a thing to help fight. My men and a few of the teenagers ended up having to drag the tree off of me."

A tree explained the gashes amongst the burned skin. And even if he didn't believe he'd been a hero, there was no doubt in her mind.

"It happens a lot in combat situations," he added. "Soldiers are injured through random accidents as easily as by an enemy. I was one of the lucky ones who managed to stay alive. A few centimeters higher and the tree would've hit my head instead of my back and shoulder."

"I'm glad you survived." And glad he'd told her, too, though it wasn't what she'd expected to hear.

Frankly, she didn't know *what* she'd expected. Maybe that he'd been injured in hand to hand combat. Or that he'd been in the wrong place at the wrong time, passing by a roadside bomb as it exploded or a weapon that misfired, causing ugly burns. Not that he'd spent a day and two nights inside what could've become his own tomb, all in an effort to protect people he didn't know in a country far from his home.

"Why haven't you told anyone about this?" She understood if he didn't want to be labeled a hero, but if he'd been able to discuss the incident, even with someone like his sister, to whom he claimed to be quite close, his psyche might heal faster.

"I don't want pity and I don't want reporters asking personal questions about my health. But on a larger scale, it would hurt the villagers if it became public knowledge. It wouldn't take long for Matambe to figure out when and where I sustained my injury. His men saw the fire as they left. On top of that, it'd be a public relations coup for the man."

She stared at him in disbelief. "How? I'd think the world would become enraged."

"First, the world would be focused on me, not Matambe. It's the nature of celebrity gossip." His gaze lit upon the necklace that had fallen to the floor. He stretched to retrieve it, then laid the piece across his knee, where it sparkled with a radiance that contrasted sharply with his dark story. "Second, many in Africa would see Matambe as even more powerful if they learned he'd injured a prince. He'd be feared even more than he is now."

She hadn't considered that. "It makes sense, I suppose. Still, even if you've said nothing, it's amazing it never leaked from the village."

"They didn't know my identity. Only the men in my unit knew, and they're smart enough to keep quiet to avoid making us targets."

A lengthy sigh escaped her. It had been a long day and long night. The world Massimo described filled her mind with images she didn't have the energy to confront anymore.

"Now aren't you glad you asked?"

His wry tone made her smile. "You know, I am. I understand you a little better now...or at least that part of you." After a beat, she added, "My guess is that your family or others who love you would like to know, too."

"No." The word was crisp and immediate.

"What about a professional?"

This time, he hesitated before answering. "I've considered it. But— as with broccoli—I'm adapting."

Skepticism clouded her face. "It didn't seem that way tonight when I saw you on the bench."

He acknowledged the point with a nod and lift of his brow. "Believe it or not, tonight was fantastic right up until dinner. I was feeling quite comfortable with the crowd, and even heard positive news about the hunt for Matambe, which put me in a very good mood. But while I had Matambe on my mind, a group of torch dancers began to perform. Next thing I knew, I had a blazing fire in front of my face, then I was caught in a crush of people." Again, he shrugged as if it were no big deal. "Even so, it took time before the need to escape set in, and when it did, I couldn't leave for a while."

"Then I surprised you by touching your bad shoulder."

"Which shouldn't have been a problem. Again, I'm very sorry."

"Don't. It's over." She put a hand on his knee, but didn't linger. She suspected that he wanted—needed—to move forward without using physical reassurance from her as a quick fix.

"In any case, the odds of having fire flung in my face in the midst of a crowd are rather low. Having faced it once, so to speak, I suspect I'll handle it better if it ever happens again. If not, privately consulting a professional may be the next step." The set of his jaw made it clear he hoped he'd never have to, but if it was necessary to ensure the safety of those around him, he would.

It was an admission that took an incredible amount of fortitude.

She pushed to stand, then offered him her hand. "Come on. Let's get out of here. You weren't supposed to see this place until my big reveal, anyway. Just remember when you see the finished room that I want you to be wowed."

"I promise, I'll express appropriate awe." He palmed the necklace and rose in one smooth motion, shooting a quick look at her hand that said, *you're kidding, right?*

"Only if that awe is earned."

That prompted him to grin. "Understood."

When they reached the living room, he placed the necklace on the coffee table. After giving it a long look, he raised his head. "Thank you, Kelly. I really appreciate this. And I value your discretion."

"It's a gorgeous piece. And it was yours in the first place, not mine."

Intense emotion filled his eyes, making them appear an even darker green than usual. "You know what I mean."

If she hadn't told anyone about their one-night stand, he should realize she wouldn't blab about his injury or the circumstances surrounding it. But some secrets were so intense, so deeply personal, worry was natural no matter the character of those who kept them. She chose not to take offense.

"I do."

He nodded his thanks, then with an amused lift of his mouth he said, "You know, you aren't at all what I expected when I met you on the beach."

"I could say the same about you, Your Highness." At his nod of acknowledgement, she added, "In fact, I could say it about my whole experience here. When I came to Sarcaccia, I imagined I'd spend most of my time sitting on the beach with a daiquiri in my hand, brainstorming ways to restart my career. Maybe visit your museums, see the art and architecture, learn about the local culture. Never in a million years could I have predicted the last week and a half."

"Sorry," he teased. "I'm about as far from sunshine and umbrella drinks as you can get."

"And I'm glad. Truly. You've opened my eyes to the wider world, one outside what I'm used to in Texas. That's what I wanted more than anything when I came."

"So why'd you choose Sarcaccia, when you could've visited anywhere?"

"While I was researching potential honeymoon spots, my ex mentioned receiving an invitation to a charity ball here," she admitted. "Once I looked into it, I decided it'd be fun to honeymoon on Sarcaccia and attend the ball at the end of our stay. But as fun as the idea of dressing up and going out for a night on the town might be, I was far more intrigued by the charity itself. Sun-something. They distribute communications equipment to poor and rural areas where it's desperately needed. It's amazing what can be done with—"

"Wait a minute." Incredulousness laced his voice. "Do you happen to remember where this charity ball is being held?"

She frowned, curious where he was going with the question. "I didn't see the actual invitation. Ted only said that it would be grand and to dress as if I were going to the Academy Awards. Why?"

"Well, assuming there aren't two charity balls this week raising funds for the distribution of communications equipment, it's a group called SunTalk. And it's being hosted by my father's cousin right here in the palace."

"You're kidding. I had no idea. I was really impressed with what I read about the charity."

"But you weren't planning to attend?"

She shook her head. "The invitation was Ted's, not mine. Once the engagement ended, needless to say, it fell off my travel agenda."

He crossed his arms over his chest and regarded her. "Would you like to go anyway? With me?"

CHAPTER 23

Massimo thought he'd shocked Kelly with the details of his injury. Yet it was a simple invitation to a ball that widened her chestnut-brown eyes and left her mouth agape.

He bent forward, lifting his injured shoulder and pulling a face. "I've cast myself as Quasimodo now, haven't I? Too ugly and frightening for a woman like you?"

"Of course not." Pucker lines crisscrossed her forehead. "I'm…I'm just not sure what to say. Why would you want me to attend such a formal event with you?"

"Broccoli goes down easier when you have a dining companion," he said. "And it'll be fun. My father's cousin, Alberto Zacchi, knows how to throw a party. He's been working with the palace staff on this event for months. And as you said, SunTalk is an intriguing charity."

Her stance was wary. "Are you asking me…is this a date?"

"If so, it wouldn't be our first."

"No, but our first date was…unusual. And things have changed since then." In other words, the romantic date and hot sex occurred before he'd revealed his identity or discovered she'd come to Sarcaccia for another man. Before he'd employed her. Before he'd admitted she was nothing more than a one-night stand to him.

"Maybe. But you've earned a night out and I'd like you there. It's that simple."

She regarded him for a moment before saying, "It's a lovely invitation, and I'm honored, but I couldn't. My suitcase consists of beach gear and casual clothes. I feel underdressed around this place as it is. I'm not the least bit ready for an event like that."

"Appropriate clothing isn't a problem. Your build is similar to Sophia's. She'd be happy to send a few choices to your suite. I'll ensure you get shoes or anything else you need. *If* you want to come. That's the question."

"I can't wear a gown that belongs to Princess Sophia," she protested.

"Kelly, forget clothing concerns. Yes or no?"

She wanted to say no. He could read it in her expression, a battle between common sense and temptation where common sense would eventually triumph. But when she opened her mouth, she said, "Yes."

THE NEXT EVENING, Massimo took the stairs leading to his parents' apartment in twos. Upon reaching the landing, he nodded to the familiar security guard who monitored the comings and goings in the palace's most private section.

"How are you tonight, Umberto?"

"Quite well, Your Highness," the lean, extremely fit man said with a respectful dip of his head. "Queen Fabrizia mentioned that you would arrive at eight p.m. for dinner."

"And it's" —Massimo consulted his watch— "two minutes to eight. Am I permitted to knock, or should I wait?"

"I leave that to your discretion, sir."

"Wise man."

"Enjoy your meal, sir." The words were said with the usual palace formality, but a twinkle of humor lit the guard's eyes.

Massimo took his leave, then traversed the long, windowed hallway at the top of the stairs, pausing to look across the garden toward his own apartment. From this vantage point, he could see the overhead lights glowing in his bedroom, but not the activity within.

When Kelly mentioned that she had a long day planned with the shelving installation, she wasn't kidding. She arrived moments after he'd showered this morning and warned him she'd be working until at least sunset. Her appearance was quickly followed by that of an electrician and the carpenters. Before long, workmen carrying shelving components entered, toolboxes at the ready. He'd avoided the apartment the rest of the day, but was curious to see the result of Kelly's hard work.

Hell. He was dying to see *her*.

He'd lain awake most of the night, his brain jumping from one thought to another, but all having to do with Kelly. How she smelled. How her hair danced around her shoulders. How she bewitched his dog. How she knew exactly what to say and when to make him feel at ease. How her dark eyes sparkled when she spoke of things that mattered to her. How she'd melted into him during last night's all-too-brief kiss.

How stunningly beautiful she was, even when rain-drenched and freezing.

It wasn't the focused path his mind was accustomed to following. Nor was his body used to the powerful stirrings he experienced in her presence.

He leaned one hip against the high windowsill and squinted at his apartment.

Before the fire, the army owned his mind and his body. There'd been room for nothing else. The challenge of daily life had kept him fully and happily occupied.

Before the fire, he'd known a return to Sarcaccia would mean a return to a different life, and to different women…women unlike the one he'd met during a study abroad program in France who'd shown him the joys of making love in her tiny attic apartment overlooking the Montmartre while the sounds of street vendors carried up to them. Or the one he'd met while on a trip to Istanbul who'd introduced him to the rejuvenating pleasures of a hammam, then the pleasures of her bed.

He'd figured there was a time and season for everything. A time for study, a time for work, and a time for play. A time to leave soldiering and perform his royal duties, a time to marry and have children and represent his countrymen. He'd liked the way his life was unfolding. It was a path that kept him fully engaged and challenged.

But the fire burned that away.

The rush of accomplishment, the rush of desire, all of it left him, charred away with the layers of his skin. That is, until Kelly brought it back. The night spent with her in the villa was as if waking from a long, dreamless sleep.

But why *her*? He interacted with dozens of beautiful, intelligent, witty women each day. Women with pedigrees traceable as far back as his own, in some cases further. Women who'd entertain him both mentally and physically. Women like Madeline Lockwood, who had beauty, intelligence, and charm to spare. Women who fit the life plan he'd always envisioned.

But it was Kelly Chase who'd captured his attention that evening on the beach. Kelly who'd listened to him describe the most transformative event of his life without pity, without judgment.

Hell, she'd even called him a hero. It was a word he'd grown to despise over the years, given that the media liked to slap the label on anyone with a compelling survival story. But Kelly hadn't used it wantonly. From her lips, it had emerged as a well-considered compliment.

Much as he hated the word, deep down, he found that hearing it from her mattered.

He could no longer deny how much he wanted her. Wanted to know her mind. Her body. Her deepest desires. Her secrets.

He pushed away from the windowsill. Kelly certainly had secrets. A recently broken engagement, for starters. He wondered if she harbored other secrets and what it might take to discover them.

Before he could take their relationship any further, he had know his decision to trust her was the right one. She hadn't told anyone about their encounter at the villa. He had to believe she'd keep the information about his injury to herself, too. All it would take was for Kelly to tell one person and it'd spread through the palace like wildfire.

So to speak.

Trusting her meant everything. Because if he was honest with himself, what he really wanted was to love her. To sweep her off her feet at a ball and convince her to extend her stay, and not as his employee.

In the meantime, he had another secret on his hands. Literally, in the form of the fabulously valuable necklace curled in his palm.

He'd borrowed his younger brother Bruno's black Audi from the palace garage, knowing it wouldn't be recognized, and made an unannounced trip to Conti & Fancetti to learn about the necklace's origins. He hadn't been surprised to see Selena Conti herself emerge from the back to assist him. However, the conversation they'd had in the confines of her private office when he told her he had questions about a sapphire necklace stunned him. Now he had no other option but to ask his mother about the piece tonight.

"As you know, we keep records of all our creations for the royal family and hold copies of the documentation concerning its value in case of theft or loss," Selena had said once she'd disengaged the security camera in her office, ensuring nothing of their conversation was seen or recorded. "But this is a unique case, Your Highness. At the request of the person who commissioned this piece, no records of its design or purchase were kept here in the shop."

He'd eyed the necklace, which she'd spread out across a soft velvet cloth on her desktop after personally inspecting and cleaning it, then gestured to the large, deep blue star sapphire at its center. "Come on, Selena. How can there be no record of *that*?"

The jeweler's smile had rivaled that of the Mona Lisa for ambiguity. "We acquired the gem from Sri Lanka and can access records to show its origins if necessary."

"All right, then. When was it acquired?"

"When the client requested it."

He'd sat back in his chair and regarded her, but the jeweler remained impassive. "You're being deliberately obtuse."

"I'm doing what the client requested we do. As we would do for you, were you to ask it of us."

"In other words, I should ask within the family if I have questions."

She didn't respond. Instead, she'd gazed at the necklace with pride. "It's an extremely valuable piece, Prince Massimo. It belongs in a proper box, not one of our bags. I don't have an appropriate one here in the shop, but I can deliver one to you in the next few days. It will protect the stones."

He'd thanked her, then returned to the palace with more questions than ever.

Massimo slid the necklace into his blazer's inside pocket, then rapped on the door of his parents' private apartment. To his surprise, Queen Fabrizia answered the door herself, standing back to give him room to pass before quietly closing the door. She wore a red dress with a subtle white and gold Asian floral pattern. It nipped in at the waist and highlighted her lithe form. Her feet, on the other hand, were bare, a rarity even in her private space.

"Dinner will be here in a half hour," she said as she made her way to the apartment's dining room. "I've opened a bottle of my favorite Cabernet. Join me?"

For the next few minutes, they went through their usual repertoire of small talk, encompassing the weather, their respective schedules, and discussion of the recent banquet. Thankfully, the queen hadn't noticed Massimo's early departure. Her focus was on the success of the event.

"At the moment, your father is working with his speechwriters on the address he'll give to the European Union next week," she said, giving her wine a lazy swirl. "I don't expect him back to the apartment until late. You mentioned in the limousine that you wanted to talk about my projects and interests. What, exactly, do you want to know?"

Massimo swallowed a bite of cracker topped with cheese and cucumber before answering. "I've wondered what led you to the various charities and causes you've chosen to support. You came to the palace from the private sector and had to make decisions, as I am now, about where you'd focus your energies. I'm curious about your process."

She angled her head. "When I married your father, there weren't as many choices as there are now. So perhaps it was easier."

"Perhaps." As he reached for his wineglass the necklace inside his blazer shifted, giving him pause. "Do you mind if I change the topic for a moment? Kelly found something in my apartment that I'd like to show you."

At her frown, he clarified, "Kelly's the closet designer."

"I know who Kelly is. You forget, I make it a point to know everyone under my roof." She raised her glass to her lips as Massimo withdrew the velvet bag from his inside pocket. Over the rim, she said, "I also know that you bailed her out of jail before hiring her."

"How do you know about that?"

She took a long sip and savored it. "Word travels. I suspect there's more to the story than the fact she found your dog on the beach and you just happened to need a closet designer, but we'll save it for another day, shall we?" Her lips parted slightly as she spied the distinctive blue fabric. "I'm more interested in what you're holding."

"You should be." He placed the bag between them on the table, but kept his fingers tented over it. "But first, tell me how you knew about Kelly."

She eyed him cannily. "Very well, then. A staffer happened to enter the station by the back door as you were going out the front."

"Let me guess...a member of Vittorio's staff?" The slight lift of his mother's brow provided his answer. "So there *is* something to the fraud rumor. Vittorio told me he was monitoring the situation."

"What else did your brother tell you?"

"We were in public, so he had to leave it at that." Though now Massimo's curiosity was piqued. A person so bold as to steal from the Barrali family defied logic. "But we're alone. What can *you* tell me?" Another thought occurred to him. "Does it have anything to do with his breakup with Carmella?"

The flash of surprise in her eyes, and her quick attempt to cover it, told Massimo he wasn't far from the mark. *Damn.* He hurt for his brother.

The queen's gaze fell to the table, where Massimo's hand still partially covered the jewelry bag. "For the moment, there's nothing more to report than what Vittorio already told you. But if you show me what's in the Conti & Fancetti bag, I promise to tell you when there is."

"Recognized it, did you?"

"Of course." She held her hand aloft, displaying her emerald ring. "Those bags don't just lie around waiting to be found by the staff. I'm intrigued."

He slid the blue velvet bag toward his mother. Eagle-eyed as always, her attention immediately went to the hole in the bottom. He could swear her jaw tightened at the sight, but she recovered so quickly he couldn't be certain.

Slowly, she loosened the white tie that secured the neck and reached inside. As she withdrew the necklace, revealing it jewel by jewel, her hand shook. She spread it between the two of them, fashioning it in a circle as if it were in a luxury display case rather than surrounded by wine, cheese, and crudités.

"Where did she find this? Was it in your closet?"

"Kelly asked me before the parade if she could use the antique mahogany bureau from my living room as part of the new closet design. I told her to go ahead," he explained. "When she moved it, she discovered a hidden panel behind one of the lower drawers. That was inside."

The queen reached for her wineglass. Her gaze, however, remained fixed on the necklace. After a lengthy sip of her Cabernet, she asked, "Was anyone else present when Kelly discovered this?"

"Everyone was at the banquet. She brought it to my attention immediately afterward. No one else knows about it. Needless to say, I was blown away."

Queen Fabrizia released a long breath as her gaze travelled to the hole in the bottom of the bag, then back to the necklace itself. "That was incredibly honest of her. You'd be surprised how often people aren't when faced with a temptation such as this."

Her comment made him wonder once more about the fraud rumors. Rather than needle her about a topic she either wouldn't or couldn't discuss, he said, "You've seen this necklace before, haven't you? You seem to recognize it."

"Oh, yes." Her eyes were bright as she ran her fingertip around the edge of the central sapphire, the one that must have cost a fortune, even by Barrali standards. She picked it up and tilted it in the light, which made the striations in the sapphire appear to move, like a star winking in the night. "In fact, your father bought this stone and had the necklace made."

Massimo sat back in his chair, stunned. Despite the brilliance of the stones and settings, he'd assumed it to be older, perhaps from his grandparents' or great-grandparents' generation. It was hard to imagine the straitlaced, practical King Carlo having such an extravagant piece secretly designed. "That is an unreal gesture of love."

The edge of his mother's mouth twisted into her infamous half smile. "It was."

"But I've never even heard of this necklace, let alone seen it. Why haven't you worn it?"

"Oh, it wasn't made for me. I imagine that's why it was placed in the bureau."

A knock sounded at the door as the sentence hung between them. Massimo stood to answer it as Fabrizia swept the necklace back into the bag, then set the bag in her lap. Once dinner was served and the waitstaff gone, she withdrew the necklace and returned it to the tabletop.

"Whose is it, then?" Massimo asked, ignoring the salmon, strawberry, and pecan salad his mother had ordered for him. "Did he commission it for Grandmother?"

It would explain a lot. The king's mother—a woman known for her flamboyant personality—would've loved such a necklace. However, she'd died only two years after her eldest son ascended the throne. Perhaps he'd ordered it, but never had the opportunity to give it to her.

Still, that didn't explain the secrecy the king had insisted upon at Conti & Fancetti or how the necklace came to be in a hidden panel in the bureau.

"Those are all questions to ask your father." With one last look at the necklace, Queen Fabrizia gently tucked it back in its bag. "Though if you must, I'd appreciate it if you'd wait until after the European Union meeting. He's extremely busy and doesn't need any distractions."

Massimo couldn't imagine how the necklace might constitute a distraction—for all its glory, it was a *necklace*, after all. A thing. Not life or death. But he wasn't going to argue with his mother.

"For now, why don't you keep it," she said, handing him the bag. "It was safe in that bureau for a long time. I imagine it'll be safe for a while longer, and I suspect your father will want it in the hands of you or one of your siblings at some point, anyway. But do watch that hole in the bottom. If the bag were tipped to the right angle, I'm afraid the necklace could fall out."

"I'll take the proper care of it," he promised. "But speaking of care, is all well with you? You don't seem yourself lately."

She didn't seem surprised by the question. "Your father and I are… well, suffice it to say we're facing some challenges. We've overcome worse, though, and we love each other deeply. So there's no need to worry. Even the best marriages have ups and downs, and on the whole, I'm very pleased with my life."

"But—"

She cut him off with tilt of her head that left no doubt in Massimo's mind that she considered the discussion closed.

The rest of the evening was spent savoring their dinner, which was both flavorful and filling, and discussing the queen's current projects. None were pursuits Massimo cared to join, but he enjoyed hearing the excitement in his mother's voice. Though his mother claimed it was King Carlo who was busy, Massimo was quite certain it was the queen who'd been burning the candle at both ends recently.

"It's good to see you so happy," he told her as he polished off a chocolate cinnamon mousse that had been sent up for dessert. His mother only picked at hers, but that was typical.

"Once Bruno's done with school, I'll have all my children back in the country. Knowing you're safe now and that Stefano is getting married…well, it's all wonderful."

She set her napkin to the side, indicating the end of the meal. "I'm glad we did this, Massimo. Let's do it again soon."

Out of habit, he skirted the table to help her from her seat. Her fingers wrapped around his forearm as they strolled toward the door. When they were partway through the grand living room, with its ornate Persian rugs and richly upholstered furniture, she stopped and gave him a meaningful look. "I know you arranged this dinner to brainstorm ideas about what to do with your future, and I know I've hounded you about it. We owe the people of Sarcaccia our service. We're expected to perform—at times like circus animals—in a manner that does the most good for the most people."

She let go of his arm and placed her hands over her heart as she spoke, something he'd never before seen her do. "Massimo, what I want most is to see you happy. Over the years I've learned that choosing the option that made *me* happiest—no matter the consequences or risks, no matter the opinions of others—ended up being the right choice in the long run. Whether it's in your royal duties, your romantic relationships, or in both, your countrymen will respect your decision if you're true to yourself. I said the exact same thing to Vittorio just last week, and I meant it."

"He's had a rough go recently, hasn't he?"

"Vittorio likes to live life according to plan, but love isn't one of those things that can be scripted like a coronation ceremony. It involves a lot of unknowns. A lot of trust. Over the course of a relationship, you discover that trust is either there or it's not. In his case, it wasn't."

Massimo paused. "The fraud allegations *do* involve Carmella, don't they?"

"Let's just say that Vittorio did what he needed to do, both to be true to himself and to protect our family." She shrugged, then strode to the door to let him out. "I'm confident he'll be fine in the long run. As will all of my children, I'm sure."

Her words resonated in his brain as he reentered his own apartment a few minutes later. How was it that a mother—even a mother like his, who was a maternal figure to an entire country and had little private time with him during his formative years—knew exactly which issues her children faced? Because as much as Queen Fabrizia had talked about trust in relation to Vittorio, Massimo knew his mother's words were meant for him.

A snort of laughter echoed from somewhere in the back of Massimo's brightly lit apartment, followed by gales of laughter—presumably aimed at the snorter—and a feminine voice exclaiming, "I can't believe you just did that, Robert!"

The feminine voice he recognized as April's. But surely the Robert to whom she referred wasn't—

"Madam, I have no idea what you mean."

Massimo paused in the living room, a wide grin splitting his face. His *stylist?* Buttoned up, stoic Robert, was laughing with the women in the closet.

CHAPTER 24

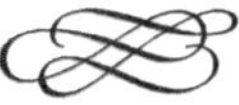

"I HEARD A DISTINCT SNORT," came Kelly's voice, followed by enthusiastic agreement from two male voices whom he assumed to be the second carpenter and the electrician. "But maybe it wasn't coming from you, Robert. It did sound more like Gaspare."

That brought another round of laughter. There was a scuffle of footsteps and a few taps of a hammer before one of the men said, "That's the last of the hang rods. Robert, I assume you'd also like us to wipe everything down and vacuum before you bring in the clothing?"

"Thank you, that would be helpful."

Massimo peeked around the corner to his bedroom only to see a large plastic sheet covering the closet doorway, presumably to stop dust from entering his bedroom. Unwilling to disturb the group, he dropped onto one of the living room sofas and listened as they continued laughing and teasing each other. Apparently, April met a man the afternoon of the parade—one who'd shown her a fabulous night on the town after the fireworks—which resulted in another round of playful chitchat. Before long, the hum of a vacuum filled the air. April and the other carpenter walked through the living room and left without noticing Massimo, but a moment later, when Robert emerged, he instantly tipped his head in Massimo's direction.

"Your Highness, I hope we aren't keeping you awake? I wasn't aware you'd returned."

And no wonder, Massimo thought. Though sporting a well-tailored suit and shoes polished to an impeccable shine, as always, Robert strolled from the back room with color high in his cheeks and a toothy grin spread across the lower half of his face. At least until the older man spied the prince, when his usual serious visage snapped back into place.

"Not at all, Robert." Massimo kept his voice down so those in the back room wouldn't hear. "It sounds like the closet is nearly finished."

"Yes, sir. The shelves are complete and the lighting all installed. I just went through the space with Ms. Chase to confirm the arrangement of your clothing. Now we only need wait for a few spots of wood varnish to dry before your belongings can be put in order." The older gentleman folded his hands in front of him. "I should warn you that your bedroom does smell of the varnish. The closet window was left open, but I'm afraid it wasn't sufficient."

"I'll sleep elsewhere if it bothers me." Massimo raised an eyebrow. "So tell me, what do you think of the closet?"

"I think you'll love it, and that's not a word I use often." Robert's face softened. He glanced toward the bedroom to ensure he wasn't being overheard, then said, "If I may be so bold, you hired the right person for the job, sir. Ms. Chase is one of a kind. In all my years, I have never seen a room more tailored to its owner."

Massimo leaned forward and folded his hands in front of him. "In what way?"

"She plans to show it to you in a few days, once we have your clothing and accessories in place. I wouldn't want to spoil the surprise."

"I see. Thank you, Robert." The British gentleman nodded, but before he took his leave, Massimo said, "I imagine you'll be quite busy with the closet and final clothing purchases this week, but I'm hoping you'll have time for one more task. A favor for Ms. Chase."

When Massimo explained the idea that'd suddenly formed in his mind, Robert's rather ungentlemanly grin made another appearance. "Sir, nothing would give me more pleasure. Consider it done."

AT PRECISELY THREE o'clock Friday afternoon, Kelly hung the last of the black leather belts Robert had purchased on the closet's newly installed retractable belt rack before sliding it into place at the end of the shelf nearest the full-length mirror.

"All we have left are the suits on the rack beside Massimo's nightstand," she told Robert, who was arranging the prince's cufflinks and watches in a velvet-lined tray that fit neatly into the bureau's top drawer. "Then you can go home and enjoy the weekend. I can't believe we're going to pull this off before the prince's charity ball."

The design elements that had concerned her most—the imported area rug, the custom-designed display cases, even the specialty racks —were complete. Everything had fallen into place, exactly as she'd hoped, and with two hours to spare.

"I would say that it's a testament to your efficiency," Robert commented, his voice droll. "However, I suspect it's because you're an invited guest and want time to find something suitable to wear."

Kelly turned from the belt rack to face Robert. "I'd be insulted if I wasn't distracted by the fact you know I'm going. Who told you?"

"No insult meant, Ms. Chase."

"I told you, please call me Kelly. Ms. Chase is my mother."

One of his eyebrows raised slightly, but he kept his focus on the cufflinks, ensuring each pair matched as he moved them from the last of Massimo's old boxes to the new tray. "In that case, Kelly, I can tell you that Prince Massimo himself informed me several days ago. I believe he wanted to thank you for all you've done here. You've left quite an impression on him."

Heat rushed to her cheeks. She wondered exactly what Massimo had said to the older gentleman. Was Massimo's gratitude solely for her professional role, or did it extend to the personal?

He'd kissed her a few nights ago, true. But when she'd asked if tonight was a date, he'd said *you've earned a night out and I'd like you there*. That sounded more like a reward for a job well done.

On the other hand, in just over twenty-four hours she'd be heading back to the States, so there was no point in labeling the event a date or not-a-date. In the end, she'd have a good time and she'd go home to Dallas. Alone.

"The prince is very kind," she finally said.

"That he is," Robert replied. "While I finish this, would you mind fetching that last rack? If you roll it in here, I can help you remove the protective wrap and get the prince's suits arranged on the appropriate hang bars."

She did as he asked, rolling the long rack to the center of the closet, near the section set aside for Massimo's suits. One by one, she began uncovering them, wrapping the plastic used to keep dust off the suits into bundles and tossing them into the bedroom to recycle later. Robert pitched in to help, making the work quick. When they reached the last suit, Robert put his hand over it and said, "Why don't we save this one? Put the others up first, then we'll celebrate putting away the very last item."

"All right." Odd, but why not?

They arranged the suits by color so Massimo could quickly find what he needed. Once finished, Robert gestured to the last suit with a swoop of his hand. "I'll let you do the honors."

She shook her head, then lifted the opaque, off-white plastic covering from the suit. Except it wasn't a suit.

Instead, a stunning light blue ball gown shimmered under the closet's new overhead lights.

"Well, so much for a celebration," she said with an exaggerated grimace. "This must've been delivered to the wrong apartment by the palace dry cleaners. I wonder if it belongs to Princess Sophia or Queen Fabrizia?"

"Neither." With movements honed long ago in London's most exclusive shops, Robert lifted the garment from the rack and laid it across his arm in front of Kelly, drawing it out so she could see its full length. Meeting her gaze, he said, "It was selected just for you for tonight's ball. If my guess is correct, it should fit perfectly."

Shock left her speechless. Robert had selected a gown for her?

"If you wish to try it on, I'll wait in the living room. I have a tailor available to make any necessary adjustments, then I'll have it steamed and delivered to your suite. It should be ready in plenty of time."

Her hand went to her mouth. It was the most amazing creation she'd ever seen, one truly fit for royalty. At the same time, it was very *her*, with a clean, classic cut. "Thank you, Robert. I don't know what to say."

"Just let me see you in it, dear." He placed it in her arms and left for the living room. A few minutes later, she tiptoed in after him.

"It's beautiful, Robert. More exquisite than anything I've ever worn." One look in the closet's mirror had confirmed her initial impression of the gown. The inner label noted that the gossamer-light creation was from one of the most exclusive fashion houses in Italy. And, true to Robert's guess, it fit her perfectly. "I'm touched that you took the time to find it for me."

"It was my pleasure." He swirled his index finger to indicate that she should turn for him. "I don't believe it needs a single alteration. Wonderful!"

She stopped spinning and exhaled, smoothing her hands over the fitted waist. "I feel like Cinderella. But on that note, as much as I love it, I can't possibly afford it. It would be—"

"It's a gift."

"Robert!"

"No, not from me. Though I wish it were." To Kelly's astonishment, color appeared in the man's cheeks. "Prince Massimo ordered it for you. Now go put it back on the hanger so I can have it steamed. You'll find there are a half-dozen pairs of shoes inside your suite waiting for you to try on. Any of them will work with the gown, but if it were my choice, I'd lean toward the silver pair with the round-cut crystals across the toes. They're not as high as some of the others, so they'll make for easier dancing while still catching the light from the ballroom chandeliers."

Proper, prim Robert. He'd become her fairy godmother...of a sort. Though she knew it wasn't at all his manner, she closed the space between them and gave him a hug. After a moment, he hugged her back. First, it was a mere pat on the back, but then he held her close as a father would a beloved daughter and wished her a wonderful evening.

When she left the room to change, she could swear she heard him sigh.

KELLY RAPPED on Massimo's door just as she had every day for nearly two weeks. But for the first time, she carried no design plans. No notebooks. Not even her cell phone. All she carried was her pride, and even that depended on maintaining her balance in the striking silver heels Robert selected for her.

She didn't think she could count the tiny purse looped over her shoulder by a whisper-thin silver chain. The jewel-encrusted number Robert left in her suite with the shoes barely fit her lipstick and powder.

"Come in," Massimo's rich voice came from the other side. He turned as she entered and promptly dropped the cufflink he'd been in the midst of attaching to his sleeve.

"Kelly."

The sound of her name on his lips was all it took to bring her nerve endings sizzling to life. And if his voice hadn't done it, his appearance would have. He wore a crisp white dress shirt, open at the neck, over a pair of jet black bespoke tuxedo pants. A black bow tie hung loose about his neck. Beside him, over the back of the sofa, lay the matching black tuxedo jacket.

A billboard model hawking the latest designer men's cologne couldn't hold a candle to a tuxedoed Prince Massimo Barrali. He was all tight lines, firm jaw, and charisma.

She swallowed back the lump that had formed in her throat. "I wasn't clear on whether I should find you here or meet you at the ball."

"I was about to come to your suite. I believe it's traditional for the man to fetch the woman before a fancy soiree, though I admit I'm sorely out of practice." He gave her a slow, deliberate perusal from head to toe. "On the other hand, I'm perfectly capable of recognizing perfection when I see it. I suspect every man at the ball will have his eyes on you tonight."

"Thank you." When she'd put on the gown and stood before the mirror in her suite, she'd been astounded. Never in her life had she felt more beautiful. "And thank you for the gown and shoes. Robert told me they're from you."

"Don't thank me. It's entirely to my benefit." His devilish grin said everything she'd wanted to hear from his lips when he'd asked her to the ball.

He viewed this as a date. He *wanted* it to be a date.

Or…perhaps…he wanted it to be like their first date. A romantic evening followed by a no-commitment night of spectacular sex. And who could blame him for wanting that?

I want a future with this man.

The thought popped into her head unbidden. There was no possibility of a future beyond tonight and she knew it. They had vastly different lives on different continents. But for tonight, she could dream. And enjoy. As long as she didn't allow her heart to be broken.

When he bent to retrieve the cufflink, she stepped forward and said, "Here. Let me."

He extended his wrist and allowed her to attach the cufflink for him. Having him so close constituted an all-out assault on her senses. Mingled with the scent of his soap was a faint hint of masculine aftershave and a smell she'd come to identify as unique to him. The combination made her want to press her mouth to his throat, to taste and to savor, but instead she straightened his collar, buttoned the top button without allowing her fingers to linger against his skin, then reached for his bow tie.

"So you know how to tie a tie, too?"

"My mother used to do it for my father. When I got older, she showed me how. I admit I'm not as good with bow ties as the regular type, though."

Her focus was on the fabric as she made the appropriate folds and loops, but she could feel his heated gaze on her. Once she'd finished, she stepped back to check her work.

"You might want to look in the mirror and see if it's okay. There's a full-length mirror in the closet. I assume you've seen the new design?" She'd hoped to show him herself so she could gauge his reaction to her work, but given that Massimo wore one of the tuxedos Robert had placed on the appropriate hang rod yesterday, the prince had apparently taken his first look in private.

"I was waiting for the big reveal from you personally. After all your hard work, I want you to see me wowed with your own two eyes."

Her gaze went to his clothing. "But—"

"I asked Robert to select my outfit for the night and leave it in my bedroom, then shut the door to the closet so I wouldn't be tempted."

His thoughtfulness warmed her. Gesturing toward his room, she said, "Well then, shall we?"

Instead of walking that direction, he caught her hand and tucked it in his arm. "I'm expected in the ballroom, so let's save it for later tonight. After the ball. I prefer not to be rushed."

His sensuous tone left no doubt in her mind that he hoped to have her in his bedroom tonight, and not simply as they passed through en route to the closet.

I want him, I want him, I want him.

Side by side, they walked through the long gallery, with Massimo keeping Kelly's hand firmly on his forearm. Security guards near the ballroom nodded as the pair approached, and greeted them with a brief, "Your Highness, Ms. Chase," and a smile.

Rich, happy music and the pattering of hundreds of animated voices filled the hallway leading to the reception area outside the palace's main ballroom. The open double doors gave her a glimpse of the crowd, where gowns of every color and description lent a celebratory air to the affair.

Before they stepped through the doors to join those milling about the reception area, Massimo stopped short.

"I almost forgot," he said. "There was something I wanted to do, but didn't want Robert to handle."

"Do we need to go back?"

He shook his head and opened his tuxedo jacket, then reached to the slim inner pocket and withdrew the velvet bag she'd discovered in the bureau.

"I want you to wear this."

"Oh, Massimo, I couldn't."

But even as she uttered the protest, he took the necklace from the soft bag. It glittered even more brilliantly than before. "I had it cleaned at the jeweler's. When I saw it under those lights, I thought it'd be a waste to let it sit in a drawer during an event like this. Besides" —he reached around her neck, his fingers grazing the sensitive spot just under her nape— "it looks as if it were designed to be worn with this gown."

His warm breath danced across her cheek as he leaned in to secure the necklace, and for a brief moment, she allowed her eyes to flutter closed at his touch.

"There," he said.

Slowly, he moved his hands from the back of her neck to her bare shoulders, ran a finger over her collarbone to where the necklace now rested, heavy with stones, then stepped back. She opened her eyes to see him looking at her with the same lust-filled expression he'd had the night they sat in his Jeep in the driveway of her villa, when he'd asked to be invited inside.

She reached up to touch the stones at her throat. "This is unbelievably generous, Massimo. I don't know how to thank you."

"You're accompanying me into a crowded room, where dozens of people are likely to be hugging me, grabbing me by the shoulder, or doing any number of things that might make me uncomfortable. Knowing you're there is an invaluable gift."

Once more, he extended his arm for her. She felt like royalty herself as they entered the reception area. Within seconds, they were swallowed by the crowd, yet Massimo appeared as relaxed and confident as he had when he stood high above the parade, watching from the grandstand. With his good looks and charisma, no one could mistake him for anything other than what he was: A prince. A soldier. A hero.

For her part, Kelly smiled through introductions to dozens of impeccably dressed dignitaries, including Alberto Zacchi, the man hosting the event.

"My cousin, King Carlo, tells me that you have redesigned Prince Massimo's closet," he said in a booming voice that caught the attention of several other guests. "Tell me, do you have a business here in Sarcaccia? My wife has been begging me to convert our extra bedroom into a walk-in closet and dressing room. I'd like to consult with you on the project as an anniversary gift to her."

"I'm afraid I'm not established here in Sarcaccia," she replied. "But Prince Massimo has my contact information. I'm sure we could arrange something." What, she wasn't sure, but knowing she'd have another source of income should her finances take longer to fix than she anticipated would be nice.

And frankly, she'd had a blast working on Massimo's closet. She'd discovered just how much her job meant to her. No matter what it took, when she returned to Texas she'd find a way around her noncompete. It was what she was born to do.

The rest of the cocktail hour passed in a blur. Kelly was complimented on her gown so many times she lost count and she caught more than one guest ogling her necklace. And no wonder...she felt like a walking museum display. Whenever she passed a reflective surface, such as a window or any of the small mirrors lining the edges of the reception area, the brilliance of the stones captured her attention. Through it all, Massimo remained within a few feet of her, giving her space to meet people, yet making it clear to everyone present that they were together.

She was about to ask Massimo when they should enter the ballroom when she overheard a member of the palace waitstaff asking guests to sign the book near the door, then find their seats for dinner.

"Why don't you sign us in?" Massimo's hand came to the back of her waist, guiding her through the eddies of the crowd as people moved toward the ballroom door. "We're seated at the same table. It should be easy to find once we're inside."

A podium near the ballroom entry held the guestbook. She picked up the fancy pen resting beside it and began to write…then froze.

"What's wrong?" Massimo asked quietly, near her ear.

She finished signing the page and set down the pen, trying to hide the fact her hand shook as she did so.

"Five names above mine," she whispered.

There, in bold black ink, a familiar, swooping signature stood out from the rest.

Edward A. Robards.

CHAPTER 25

KELLY'S WORLD spun off its axis. Numbly, she put one foot in front of the other as she and Massimo left the podium so others could sign the register.

"Edward Robards is the CEO of a large telecommunications conglomerate," Massimo explained as he led her into the ballroom. "His company has offered telecommunications equipment at cost to the charity, and he's personally contributed a great deal of money to ensure it's distributed to those rural areas that need it most. He's quite generous and very well-respected. I'm sure we'll have the chance to meet him at some point. I've wanted to make his acquaintance for some time."

"I'm aware of the man's reputation," Kelly ground out. The ballroom music came to her ears as clatter. Somewhere under the brilliant chandeliers and Renaissance-painted ceiling of the palace's ballroom, disaster waited to crush her under its wingtip-encased foot, ending her fairy tale night as surely as the clanging of a clock ended Cinderella's fantasy.

"Oh, I forgot. He's from Texas. Of course you've heard of—" Massimo stopped walking as realization dawned. He turned to face her, a mix of doubt and incredulousness etched in his features. In a voice barely above a whisper, he said, "Wait a minute. Edward Robards—"

"Is Ted," she finished. The jerk who'd taken everything from her, including her friends. The man responsible for her stint in a foreign jail. The man with the sterling reputation.

The two words silenced Massimo.

"I'm terribly sorry," she said, corralling all her energy and directing it toward appearing collected. "I had no idea he'd be here. He didn't use his airline ticket and as far as I knew he hadn't RSVP'ed for the ball."

She stole a backward glance at the reception hall, which was rapidly emptying as guests entered the ballroom and searched the silver-and-crystal-topped tables scattered around the periphery of the dance floor for those bearing their names on place cards. There was no sign of her ex, which meant he had to have entered the ballroom after signing the book.

"You were engaged to Edward Robards?"

"Yes."

"I imagine he can afford the change ticket fee and fly whenever he wants."

"Yes." Though she never thought he would. She took a step back and offered Massimo a polite, encouraging smile. "Why don't you find the dinner table and chat with the other guests? I think it's best for everyone if I head back to my suite."

"No."

Massimo's face was inscrutable as he slid an arm around her lower back and turned her to face the ballroom. As he did whenever he was in public, Massimo commanded attention, but now she felt the eyes of the crowd on her as he guided her through the tables to one near the dance floor. There was no way Ted wouldn't see her here. And then what?

"Massimo," she hissed. "I never would've come if I'd known. I don't want to embarrass you."

"I'm standing up to my fears by attending this ball. You should do the same." He stopped beside a table topped with crystal glasses and a lush yellow and green floral centerpiece. Silver polished to a high shine was laid out at each place, the pieces bordering an ivory cloth napkin folded into a perfect upright twist. As he pulled out her seat, he moved behind her and breathed into her ear, "Like broccoli."

A moment later, he took his place on the opposite side of the large, round table, introduced himself to those he didn't already know, and warmly greeted those he did. Kelly managed a smile as he introduced her around the table. Relaxed as Massimo seemed on the surface, Kelly wondered what thoughts must be going through his head, both about navigating a tightly packed room and about the fact she'd been engaged to one of the most powerful men in Texas, if not the entire United States.

Dinner went smoothly, filled with laughter and small talk, though she felt ill at ease throughout. Nothing tasted right; her stomach felt encased in lead. It wasn't until Alberto Zacchi took a microphone to the middle of the ballroom floor and everyone turned in their seats to listen to him speak about his cause that she faced her deepest fear: Ted sat two tables away. Before now, she hadn't been at an angle to see him, though she should've felt his presence. He looked impeccable. In fact, more than one set of female eyes rested on him, assessing his short, thick blonde hair, the width and solidity of his shoulders, the distinct angles of his cheekbones and jaw, and his bright, intelligent blue eyes.

She couldn't blame them. Wealth was the last reason she'd been attracted to him. He'd introduced himself to her at a Dallas restaurant one afternoon as she was finishing up a business lunch and she'd been riveted by his easy demeanor, his self-assured laugh, and those captivating eyes.

He caught her staring at him across the ballroom. One of his dark blonde brows arched in greeting before he slid an appreciative gaze over her—taking in her carefully arranged hairstyle, the designer gown and heels, the stunning necklace—nodded his approval, then turned his attention to Alberto.

Kelly's insides went ice cold.

For the rest of Alberto's speech, Kelly could hardly breathe. She didn't dare look in Ted's direction. From that one quick look, he'd told her all she needed to know. He wasn't going to leave her alone tonight. He was going to ruin her evening, just as he'd ruined her business, her friendships, and her solo honeymoon.

Applause thundered throughout the room as Alberto finished his description of SunTalk's successes and the charity's future plans. The older man swooped one arm toward the orchestra, which began to play as Alberto asked King Carlo and Queen Fabrizia to take the floor for the first dance. The royal couple sashayed onto the floor, bringing cheers from all in the room. The monarch smiled down at his wife as they danced, their steps in perfect sync. Then, as the familiar tune reached its crescendo, he surprised everyone by dipping her, planting a rather un-royal kiss on her mouth, then twirling her back across the floor in time with the music. The unabashed look of love between the two warmed Kelly's heart.

A wolf-whistle from a table at the opposite side of the dance floor surprised everyone. Kelly looked in time to see Princess Sophia elbow a man next to her. The room erupted in laughter at the sight.

"Is that Prince Vittorio?" the man beside Kelly whispered to his wife.

"I can't tell the difference between Vittorio and Alessandro," she replied. "I suspect it's Alessandro."

The prince stood and clapped for his parents. Sophia joined him. Within seconds, the rest of the room stood to cheer on the popular couple.

It was the most romantic scene Kelly ever witnessed when King Carlo smiled down at his wife as if they were the only two people in the room.

When the song neared its end, Alberto urged the rest of the guests to take to the floor. He didn't need to ask a second time. Dozens of couples followed the lead of the monarch, turning the room into a feast for the eyes as women in gowns of every color and description spun beneath the ballroom's glowing crystal chandeliers.

A large hand cupped her elbow, startling her. Rather than Prince

Massimo, it was Ted who looked down at her with an appreciative smile on his face.

"You look astonishing, Kelly. I'm surprised to see you here, though I can't say I'm disappointed."

"Ted." It was all she could manage. The flirtatious look on the man's face belied everything he'd done behind the scenes since she'd ended their relationship. She shifted her focus from him to the dancers, not deigning to respond to his compliment.

"You heard Alberto Zacchi. It'd be rude to disappoint our host, wouldn't it? Dance with me. It'll give us time to make amends."

"I don't need to make any amends." She needed her money, and nothing else, from this man.

"Ah, but I do." A warm possessiveness edged his words, but she refused to tear her gaze from the couples dancing in front of her. "I received your letter."

"My attorney's letter," she corrected.

"Yes. I'm so sorry about the misunderstanding."

Now she spun on him. "That's what you call it? I call it theft."

"Oh, Kelly. What use would I have for your money? It was all yours. Always was. My name was only on the account at your insistence. Remember, after the honeymoon you wanted to use those funds for our condo down payment as a gift to me. I was willing to let you, just so you'd feel independent."

"I see. That explains why you closed the account and took every last dime." How could he look at her so innocently, yet at the same time insult her to her face? It was a wonder she kept her cool.

Then again, yelling at this man would accomplish nothing. It would only embarrass her and embarrass Massimo.

"The money has all been returned. I called the bank president personally to reestablish the account, this time solely in your name." He ran his hand up her arm, then let it rest on her shoulder. Slowly, he allowed his gaze to follow the movement, settling on the jewels at her throat. His touch made her skin crawl, but she didn't want to slap his hand away and make a scene.

"I closed it with the intent of returning the money to you right away, of course, but when I stopped by your apartment to give you a certified check, you were gone. Your friends told me you'd decided to travel to Sarcaccia alone." He shrugged. "I thought I was doing you a favor by wrapping up the loose ends of our relationship."

"I see." Liar, liar, pants on fire. "So when I check the account later tonight, the funds will be there?"

"Yes. Your old ATM cards and passwords should all work. If I caused you any inconvenience, again, I must apologize. Though" — once again, his blue eyes lit on her throat, as if assessing the authenticity of the jewels encircling it— "you don't seem to have been inconvenienced. That is quite a necklace. It suits you."

"Thank you." She wasn't about to explain.

"So," he said with a tilt of his head toward the dance floor. "Shall we? For old times' sake?"

Edward Robards.

Massimo watched as the wealthy CEO approached Kelly, all polite smiles and wandering hands. The man had the audacity to look her up and down as if she were his possession.

Despite the temptation to step in and rescue her, Massimo held back, feigning interest in a conversation between the two French businessmen who'd been seated beside him and who were now waiting for their wives to return from the restroom so they could escort the women to the dance floor.

He wanted to see how Kelly handled the man.

He wanted to see how Robards handled Kelly.

One of the Frenchmen clapped Massimo on the shoulder and laughed. Massimo joined in, though he'd missed the joke. And he still didn't like having his shoulder touched.

He couldn't reconcile everything Kelly had told him about her former fiancé with what he knew of Edward Robards. The man was a self-made legend in his industry. Young, astute, generous...they were all words associated with his name. Yet they were the opposite of the way Kelly'd described her ex, Ted.

He'd always thought of Ted as a nickname for Theodore, not Edward. Still, he should have made the connection before now. How many men named Robards from Texas were scheduled to be in Sarcaccia this week? Even if he hadn't figured it out initially, when she'd told him she'd selected Sarcaccia for her honeymoon because Ted had been invited to tonight's event, he should've connected the dots.

One of the Frenchmen straightened, his gaze lighting on his wife, who followed her friend through the mass of people moving toward the dance floor as they zigzagged their way to the table.

"Ah, here comes my beloved," the other Frenchman said. "If you'll excuse me, Your Highness, I've promised my wife that I'll pay attention to her tonight."

"So she'll pay attention to you later?" the other teased.

"Precisely." The two men shared knowing looks, and Massimo sent them both on their way. For his part, enough time had elapsed to give him a good view of the relationship between Kelly and Robards. The blond man still held a torch for Kelly—though why he behaved so abominably, Massimo couldn't fathom—but Kelly's body language revealed the opposite. Though she appeared to be carrying on a polite conversation, it was blatantly obvious to him that she did not want the man's hand on her arm. Or moving up her shoulder, as it was now.

Slowly, Massimo moved around the table. He approached from behind Kelly just as Robards asked her to dance.

"Excuse me. Sorry to interrupt, but I believe Kelly's first dance is mine."

Recognition and a hint of respect lit Robards' expression. He graciously extended his hand. "Your Highness. Edward Robards. It's a pleasure to meet you and to be invited into your home. Your family is very generous to offer it for this event."

"We're happy to do so." Despite Massimo's predisposition to disliking the man, he returned the Texan's handshake and smile. "I'd love to chat with you further—I've wanted to make your acquaintance for some time—but I should escort Kelly to the dance floor before the song is over."

Robards looked from Massimo to Kelly, then back to Massimo. "Of course. I hope to see you later this evening."

"That was easy enough," Massimo said to Kelly once Robards turned away and was out of earshot.

"It's over, and that's what matters," she replied.

He located an open spot amongst the swirling couples and wound an arm around her waist to guide her there. The contact with Robards had shaken her, he could tell, but she seemed resolved to have a good time.

"Then I'm glad I encouraged you to stay. Besides," —he spread his fingers across her back and captured her hand in his free one, pulling her into his embrace— "I don't care to dance with anyone else tonight."

No matter what she might've had with Robards, or with any other man, having her in his arms felt right.

"That might cause a scandal," she noted, though the soft pressure of her hand against his shoulder made it clear she didn't care, that she wanted this moment as much as he did. Very quietly, she added, "Remember, when you hired me, it was to throw reporters off the idea that we might've spent the night together in the villa."

"Funny you should mention that. I spoke with my brother Vittorio about it. Turns out that those paparazzi weren't at the jail because of me. They were pursuing leads on a different scandal."

Her head jerked back in surprise. "Really?"

"Apparently they bought the story that I lost my dog and bailed you out as a way of thanking you. There was a short mention of it in the Cateri paper, but that's it. End of story."

She considered his words. "So...you're saying that I did all that work for you for nothing?"

"Nothing?" He feigned shock. "I seem to recall paying you quite generously."

"That you did." Her fingertip grazed his bare neck, just above the top of his collar. "And I had the best time designing it. April couldn't have been more fun to work with, and Robert was incredibly patient. I think it nearly killed him waiting to see all those clothes put in their proper place."

"He likes you," Massimo said. "In fact, I believe I heard you make him snort."

Lines of confusion formed between her eyes. "Wait…you were there?"

"I walked in just in time to hear it. And I wouldn't have believed it if I hadn't heard it myself." On a serious note, he added, "Everyone enjoyed working with you. They've loved having you here."

I've loved having you here. Her warm spirit seemed to brighten everyone with whom she came in contact, making his dark apartment feel lively. A place he wanted to be.

But only with her in it.

Suddenly, the idea of a life without Kelly horrified him more than the deepest, darkest hole.

"Kelly, I—"

Applause cut him off as the orchestra finished their song. Kelly released his hand and faced the orchestra, politely clapping with the rest of the dancers. Nearby, his parents surprised him by sharing a second kiss. Whatever had gotten into them tonight, they'd engaged in more public displays of affection than he could remember in years.

"They seem very happy," Kelly said, following his gaze.

"They do." Whatever strife they might've had in the marriage appeared resolved. For both their sakes, he was glad.

As if knowing they were being discussed, King Carlo and Queen Fabrizia moved toward their son. His mother's expression was one of surprise at seeing him on the dance floor with Kelly. His father, on the other hand, paled as his attention went from Kelly's face to her necklace.

"You looked as if you were having a good time," Massimo said to his parents as he moved to the edge of the floor to allow other dancers to take their place now that the orchestra began a new song.

"It's nice not to be responsible for the planning," his mother said. "And when Alberto does it, I know the night will be perfect. I can relax." She turned to Kelly. "I take it you're Kelly Chase. It's a pleasure to meet you. Thank you for helping my son get back on his feet now that he's home."

Massimo's father wasn't so mannerly. His tone blunt, he said, "Your necklace is stunning. May I ask where you acquired it?"

"I offered it to her for the night," Massimo replied, saving Kelly the explanation.

Queen Fabrizia put a hand on her husband's arm. Her voice was soft, comforting, and so low Massimo knew she didn't want it to be heard beyond their small circle. "Ms. Chase found the necklace in a hidden compartment in the mahogany bureau in Massimo's apartment. The large one that used to be in your study."

"Why didn't you inform me?" This he directed to Massimo.

"He informed *me*. I told him to keep it for the time being," his wife said. A kind, almost motherly smile lit her face, which she aimed at Kelly. "I hadn't thought he'd give it to you to wear, but it looks absolutely perfect with your gown. I'm delighted it occurred to him. I can't imagine a better pairing."

Without missing a beat, she looked up at her husband. Her fingers flexed slightly on his forearm. "I can only guess what might've happened if someone less honest found the necklace. It was so good of her to notify Massimo of its discovery. Such a piece should be worn, rather than stuffed to the back of a drawer as if it doesn't exist, don't you think? And by the woman who was meant to find it?"

A cryptic look passed between his parents. After the barest of nods to his wife, King Carlo bestowed a brilliant, genuine smile on Kelly. "My wife is quite correct. A necklace like that should be worn. I'm pleased it found such a beautiful neck upon which to rest."

After the pair returned to their table, Kelly said, "I still get the impression your father wasn't so happy to see me wearing this."

"I think he was just surprised. My mother clearly liked seeing you wear it. And so do I." He eased her a few steps further from the dance floor so they could speak privately. "If I haven't told you yet tonight, you look absolutely phenomenal. You're what makes that necklace look good. Although" —he touched a dark spot just below her eye with his index finger— "you must've overexerted yourself dancing, because your mascara seems to have drifted."

Her hand flew to her face.

"It's not obvious," he said on a laugh, then moved his finger against her skin. "I think I can wipe it away."

"Thank you, but it's supposedly waterproof. It's not supposed to wipe away. Or end up under my eyes, for that matter. I was about to run to the restroom anyway, so I'll clean it myself."

"Dance with me when you return?"

"If you're not already dancing."

"I won't be," he promised.

She snaked her way through the crowd, finally disappearing behind a knot of his brother Alessandro's friends.

Massimo turned the opposite direction, threading his way back to the dinner table so Kelly would be able to find him. He'd nearly reached his seat when a man stepped in front of him.

"Prince Massimo," Edward Robards said. "Do you have a moment?"

"Of course."

"In private. I need to speak with you about Kelly Chase."

CHAPTER 26

IF THERE WAS one thing Massimo didn't like, it was following another man. Particularly a man who hadn't earned his respect. While the Edward Robards he knew by reputation deserved respect, the Edward Robards who'd treated Kelly so poorly didn't. So when Robards spun on his heel and strode through the crowd toward the reception hall, Massimo fell in behind him only for as long as it took to grab the man's elbow and stop him.

If a heart-to-heart with the ex would help Kelly close the book on the guy, fine. But Massimo would do it on his own terms.

"We can speak through here," Massimo said, indicating a door just behind the dining tables.

Robards expression made no secret of his desire to leave the room entirely, but he was left with no choice but to follow Massimo. Once he'd pushed through the door, Robards paused at the top of the stairs.

"It's the passage to the kitchens," Massimo explained. "We'll have privacy here on the landing. The waitstaff don't need to bring up dessert for another ten minutes." There. He'd put a ticking clock on the conversation. "Now, what is it you wish to tell me?"

The American hesitated. When he spoke, his voice was cautious, as if imparting a secret. "I'm afraid I find myself in an awkward situation, Your Highness."

Facing a woman from whom you stole, Massimo thought with an inner snarl, and referring to it as "awkward" seemed a bit of an understatement. "How so?"

"I was recently engaged to Ms. Chase. We had planned to attend this event together."

"So she told me."

Robards didn't bother to hide his surprise at the statement. "Well, then perhaps you already know what else I plan to say. When I sent back my RSVP last week, I did not include Ms. Chase. I didn't know she planned to attend despite our falling out. I hope it doesn't cause an inconvenience for Alberto. I know he runs these affairs with the precision of a Swiss timepiece."

The man was smooth. Massimo would give him that. "It's entirely all right, Edward. I brought Kelly as my guest."

"I see." The Texan leaned against the wall. If anyone opened the door, it'd smack him in the face. "I know this isn't the most opportune time or place, Your Highness, but…may I speak freely?"

This would be interesting. Massimo crossed his arms over his chest. "Be my guest."

"I realize that you don't know me personally, but I hope you know something about me. I've worked very hard to build my business and my reputation. I like to think I've surrounded myself with people of integrity. It's absolutely crucial to the success of my business, and I demand honesty in my personal dealings, as well."

"Go on," Massimo urged, wondering how the man planned to disparage Kelly. Despite the CEO's reputation for fairness and generosity, Massimo suspected that was Robards' ultimate goal.

"I must warn you about Ms. Chase. You can take what I say with a grain of salt—after all, she is my ex—but I have no reason to badmouth her. It would only reflect on me and my choices." Robards sucked in a deep breath, as if daring himself to utter his next sentence. "She cannot be trusted."

"How so?"

"Did she tell you that she's a successful closet designer?" At Massimo's curt nod, Robards said, "That much is true. She's excellent, in fact. So excellent that a friend of mine offered to buy her business for a decent amount of money. I actually counseled him against it—as great as Kelly is at designing, she's terrible at accounting, and her business was well in the red—but my friend insisted. He thought he could turn around the finances and make it a success."

"And?"

"She accepted the offer. Best financial decision she's ever made. But a few weeks later, she had seller's remorse. She had told me she planned to spend our marriage working for the philanthropical arm of my business—and I think it would have suited her—but she changed her mind. Of course, by then the ink was dry on all the documents."

On a roll now, Robards continued, "When I told her it was too late, she became irrational. Started telling our friends that I'd manipulated her into selling, when the opposite was true. It was hurtful, to say the least, both personally and to my business reputation."

Massimo shifted as the clatter of dishes rose from below them. He doubted they'd have privacy for long. "You could've supported her in starting a new business."

"I tried, but she was fixated on her closet design business. I explained to her that when she sold, she'd signed a noncompete agreement—my friend needed to know she wouldn't set up a competing operation if he wanted to make her old business thrive—and she was quite upset. Apparently, she hadn't read the paperwork even though I hired a lawyer for her. I wanted her to be clear about what she was doing."

Much as Massimo wanted to doubt the man, he knew Robards' tale was all too common. Newspapers were filled with stories of smart executives who'd made colossal, career-ending mistakes by signing papers they hadn't thoroughly vetted. If Kelly thought a friend was offering her a good deal, she might've been careless.

"What does this have to do with me?"

"You told me you brought Kelly here tonight. Is it a date?"

"That's not your concern."

Robards ran a hand over his jaw and nodded. He was a man's man. Massimo would give him that. "Understood. But let me give you some food for thought. I'm fortunate in that I've been successful. However, success means I can be a target for unscrupulous people. I'm sure you've dealt with a few of those yourself."

When Massimo didn't respond, Robards continued, "When Kelly ended our relationship, I thought it was over our disagreement regarding the sale of her business. But what I've come to suspect since then is that, while discussing the finances of her business, she realized that she'll never have access to the bulk of my cash. It's tied up in my companies and in my charitable works. I've come to believe my money was her goal in the first place. She targeted me. I thought we'd met by chance, but now I'm not so sure."

Robards glanced through the crack in the door, ensuring no one was coming, then turned back to Massimo.

"One afternoon I met a friend at a Dallas restaurant for lunch. Kelly was at the next table, going over designs with a client. The weather was terrible that day. It'd been raining all morning. I inadvertently left my umbrella on the bench...or so I thought. When I went back for it, Kelly was holding it. She'd picked it up, she claims by accident. We got to talking, and that was the beginning. But now...I just don't know that it was random. If she'd truly picked it up by mistake, she could've turned it in to the hostess. But she waited for me to return. She wanted to meet me. I'm positive now she knew who I am and what I'm worth. In your case, I *know* she knows. You can't hide your wealth or your family's influence."

"Well," Massimo said, his words deliberate as he looked the man square in the eye, "that gives me tremendous insight."

He could see why Kelly was attracted to a man like Robards. The man carried himself with dignity, had charm to spare, and was good looking enough that Massimo had noticed women's gazes following the tall blond as he'd walked through the ballroom. But Massimo didn't believe for a second that Kelly would deliberately target the man for his money. It didn't fit with her independent personality or the sincerity with which she'd conducted herself since they'd met.

"Thank you. I felt I had to speak up."

"You should have stopped when you told me Kelly lacked financial savvy. I might—*might*—have bought that. But I don't believe a word of the rest." Massimo gave Robards a smile he knew would leave the man no doubt he was being dismissed. "Enjoy the rest of your evening. I plan to enjoy mine."

He pushed through the door to see the dance floor packed and Kelly sitting at their table alone. As if drawn by Massimo's presence, she raised her head, met his eyes, and smiled…then her gaze traveled beyond him, to Robards.

Her smile fell.

In that moment, doubt forced its ugly fingers into Massimo's mind.

TWO MEN WERE MISSING from the ballroom. One she cared about. One she didn't.

It was the one she didn't care about who worried her.

She hadn't been gone more than five minutes when she returned to find Massimo gone. He wasn't on the dance floor, nor was he talking to his parents or siblings. Perhaps, she thought, he'd taken advantage of her absence to make his own trip to the restroom.

Then she saw that Ted was gone, too. Knowing Ted, who calculated each move he made with the precision of a general mapping out battlefield tactics, it wasn't a coincidence.

Trust Massimo more than you distrust Ted.

She smiled to herself, resolved, and took a seat at the table. Then, without knowing why, she looked up at the very moment Massimo emerged from a door at the rear of the ballroom. Her heart leapt at the sight of him making a beeline toward her.

Then movement behind Massimo caught her eye, knocking back

her anticipation. She felt her smile falter at the same time Ted shot her a self-satisfied look and mouthed, *It's over, Kelly.*

What little she'd eaten turned to a rock in her stomach as the men approached. Ted peeled off in the direction of his own table while Massimo yanked out the chair beside her.

"You've been talking to Ted," she said. The words sounded accusatory, even to her own ears, though of course Massimo had every right to speak privately with his guests.

His response held even more snap than hers. "I have."

She reached for her water glass, but it was empty, so she settled for toying with its stem. "I'm sure he had plenty to say."

"He did." Massimo's voice demanded her attention. She inhaled and tilted her head to face him as he asked, "Tell me why it ended."

She should've known.

She wasn't about to relive the humiliation again for Massimo. Not if he was about to accuse her of what she thought…of what Ted convinced all her friends to believe. "I'm sure he told you. And if you feel you have to ask me, then you don't have to ask."

"Humor me."

Fine. "It was simple. I believed everything he told me. Until I didn't."

A pause. "Did he cheat on you?"

"To his credit, no. I don't believe he did." Cheating her, though, that was another story.

"Then you're saying he lied."

"Yes." She pushed back from the table. "Massimo, either you trust me or you don't. I'm not going to stay here and answer your questions. I won't pit my reputation against Ted's. I'll lose every time."

"Did he cheat you out of your business?"

"No, but he lied to me about it." She frowned at him. "He told you that?"

"He told me that's what you believe."

Infuriating. She'd spent the last few weeks proving to herself that she was worthwhile. That she was good at her job and a professional.

In doing so, she'd hoped she'd proved herself to Massimo. But to have Ted ruin that in the amount of time it took her to blot her mascara….

"Good night, Massimo."

He stood and reached for her. "Kelly, wait. I don't believe everything Robards told me. I'm not that gullible. But I need to know—"

"I'll see you in the morning to say my goodbyes," she said, stepping back from his touch. "My flight home is rather long and I'd like a good night's sleep. Thank you for this evening. The gown and the necklace are lovely. I'll make sure they're returned."

"You don't have to go."

"I most certainly do."

She left the ballroom before he could touch her again. Tears stung her eyes, but she fought them back.

Massimo thought her biggest fear was staying at the ball and facing Ted. Oh, how wrong he was. She'd proven to herself that she could face Ted. She'd done it by leaving him when all her friends urged her to work it out. She'd done it by hiring a lawyer when he'd taken her money, despite the fact the man had every resource at his disposal and might fight her forever over what amounted to a measly sum…to him.

On the contrary, her biggest fear was falling for Massimo and discovering her Cinderella night with him would end just as it had in the fairy tale…with her leaving the party alone, a vast hole in her heart.

Now she was forced to face that fear head on.

It was her own damned fault for allowing herself to believe in a princess fantasy when she knew better.

CHAPTER 27

Massimo took a wickedly long, deep drink from his wineglass.

He *wanted* to believe Kelly. He wanted to believe that Robards, for all his charm, was nothing more than a snake.

On the other hand, if Kelly had nothing to hide, why walk out on him? The excuse about her flight was just that, an excuse. If she was so intent on getting a good night's sleep, she'd have mentioned it earlier. As it was, she'd flirted right back with him when he'd mentioned wanting to see the closet later tonight, after they left the ball.

She'd left him wanting. When he'd slipped his arm around her tonight and led her onto the dance floor, he'd allowed his mind to wander to what might happen later, when they returned to his apartment. When he peeled off her gown. Watched it slip to the floor. Savored the expression on her face as he made love to her in his bed, as they were meant to, by the light of the moon. All night.

But then she'd seen him with Robards and her heart had closed to him. He'd recognized it as surely as a door slamming in his face.

He was about to find a waiter to refresh his wine when a feminine body slipped into the seat Kelly just vacated.

"Once again, Robert did an excellent job," his sister said. "You look positively debonair. I assume that tuxedo was one of Robert's selections?"

"It was."

Sophia's dark hair draped loosely around her shoulders and she wore a form-fitting, deep red strapless gown that suited her complexion and showed off more cleavage than he cared to see on his own sister. She'd likely spent the evening beating off men with a stick. He looked around to see if her choice of seat was a means to dodge the hopeful, but no one appeared to be looking their direction.

"So how are you, Sophia?"

"Fine. Bored. Hungry."

He wasn't in the mood. "You shouldn't be bored, you should be dancing. And we just ate."

"You ate. I only had the soup and salad."

"That's your fault."

"My, are we cranky tonight." She glanced over her shoulder to where couples packed the dance floor, then scrutinized Massimo. "So where did your closet designer go? You're not making her work late, are you?"

"No. In fact, the closet is done."

Sophia's eyes lit with interest. "Really? How'd it turn out?"

"I assume well. I haven't seen it yet."

"Why in the world are you still here?" She gave him a playful smack on the arm. "I'd much rather be ogling a new closet than hanging out at yet another dinner-and-dance."

"Shhh. You're going to insult Alberto."

She waved off his concern. "Alberto loves me. Besides, there's no one to dance with but a bunch of stodgy old men and my brothers, and I'd rather not. No offense."

"Offense taken."

"I meant because you have someone to dance with already. She's beautiful, by the way. Usually a gown as gorgeous as that one makes the woman inside it disappear. But she can carry it off."

Yes, he thought, she can. The men in the room had been staring at

Kelly, not at her gown or even her necklace. They were captivated by the woman.

"She left, didn't she?"

"Sophia, go be bored somewhere else."

His sister sighed. Her voice low and surprisingly serious, she said, "Oh, lose the ego, Massimo. Go see where she went."

"Sophia—"

"I saw how you looked at her. You're asking for trouble wanting to date an employee, but…well, let's just say I hope a man looks at me like that someday." After a moment's hesitation, she said, "By the way, I forgot to tell you that I visited Giulia and Guillermo yesterday. They're wonderful, as always. Of course, you already knew that, since you and Kelly went there for dinner right before you hired her. Funny, Giulia mentioned that she sent you home with a container of ravioli—"

Massimo groaned. His sister, for all her wisdom, was a pest. But she was a pest who loved him. "All right."

"And tomorrow, I want to see that closet. Maybe I'll hire her to redo mine."

KELLY NEARLY PULLED the zipper out of its track as she closed her suitcase. Everything was ready. Her clothes for the flight home were laid out on the chair beside her bed. All she'd need to do in the morning after her shower was toss her makeup bag and nightgown into the outside pocket of her suitcase and she'd be ready to go.

She was more than ready to go.

She picked up the phone to order a taxi for the ride to the airport, only to be surprised by a knock at her door. For a second, she wondered if Massimo followed her. But it was a feminine voice on the other side that called out, "Ms. Chase? It's Adriana from housekeeping. I have a delivery for you. Are you in?"

"I'm here. Come on in, Adriana." She approached the door just as

Adriana popped in carrying a dark blue paper bag with bright gold script that indicated it was from Conti & Fancetti.

"Good evening, Ms. Chase. I wasn't expecting you back from the ball."

"Did *everyone* know I was going?"

"Not everyone." Her ample cheeks and kind mouth lifted into a smile. "I hope I'm not interrupting, but this was just delivered for Prince Massimo. Selena Conti sent it over. Apparently he requested a box for a piece he owns? In any case, since you're organizing his closet this week, I thought you'd know what to do with it."

Kelly suspected the housekeeper also wanted to know if Massimo was somewhere inside her suite. She accepted the bag and said, "Thank you. I'll ensure it's put in the proper place."

Once Adriana left, Kelly reached into the bag. The box was large, and when she opened it, she saw it'd been designed to hold a necklace. A handwritten note on stationery emblazoned with the Conti & Fancetti logo accompanied the box. Though Kelly couldn't read the Italian, she could figure out a few key words. *Protezione. Zaffiro.* Protection. Sapphire. It was signed by Selena Conti.

Kelly set the empty paper bag near the phone before walking to the coffee table, where she'd left the necklace after returning to her suite. Carefully, she set it inside the box and used the enclosed polishing cloth on the jewels before closing the top. After looping her camera over her neck, she caught the sparkling silver heels by their straps and gathered up the gown from where she'd carefully laid it over the sofa. With her free hand, she picked up the jewelry box and her design notebook before exiting her suite and made her way down the hall.

She could face this. All she needed was her camera and her self-worth. She'd leave the borrowed items for Massimo, photograph the closet, then use the photos to update her design portfolio and relaunch her business. Where, she wasn't sure. But she'd find a good market. Maybe L.A. Or Denver. She'd always heard Denver was a great town and there were plenty of quick flights if she wanted to visit family in Dallas.

The long gallery was softly lit, the tall mirrors on either side giving it a romantic glow. She could just pick out the strains of the orchestra echoing from the ballroom. Walking through the gallery alone at night was surreal. It was a world away from the first time she'd entered it, trailing Massimo with her suitcase, wondering how in the world she'd ended up inside the country's famous palace when she'd been invited back to his apartment for breakfast.

Some apartment.

Some man.

She looked down at the gown in her arms. For all her disappointment tonight, she had to admit he'd given her a great deal. Never had a client been so generous. Never had she been given carte blanche to design a space, let alone with the astronomical budget Massimo provided. The photos she snapped tonight would pay off in her portfolio for years to come. On top of that, while she'd foolishly indulged in a ballroom fantasy tonight—complete with a gorgeous gown, stunning jewels, and the most handsome man she could envision at her side—she'd also been approached by more than one potential big-name client.

She really couldn't complain. From the moment she'd invited Massimo into her villa, she suspected their time together would come to an end sooner rather than later. Then, when she'd found out his identity—that he wasn't just rich and powerful, like Ted, but a *prince*—she knew it would.

Yet you fell in love.

She knew it, clear to her bones. She loved him.

Her arm tightened around the gown.

She loved his bravery. His wit. The way he ate pancakes with gusto. The enthusiasm with which he'd clapped for the soldiers and kids who'd marched before the grandstand on Independence Day. Hell, she loved the dimple that oh-so-rarely appeared in his cheek and even the way he'd fumbled with his cufflink. She loved how he treated those around him, no matter their station.

She loved the way he'd made love to her. For the rest of her life, she'd hold the memory of that night deep within her heart.

She exhaled before using her toe to tap on Massimo's door, since her arms were full. As expected, no sound came from within.

With any luck, she'd be in and out before any of the other party-goers called it a night. Tomorrow she'd say her goodbyes, thank Massimo for the opportunity he'd given her—and it was truly an opportunity, no matter how she felt about the man personally—then she'd get the hell out.

"Kelly?"

The lights were on but dimmed when Massimo entered his apartment. Likely Adriana or Maria left them set that way. As usual, the curtains were closed, though he'd told Maria more than once in the last few weeks that he enjoyed looking out onto the garden at night and was perfectly capable of closing them on his own if he wanted them closed.

He reached for the pull cords to adjust the heavy fabric and let in the moonlight. He really would need to hire a decorator soon. But in the days since his mother sat at the desk and wrote out her list, he'd become less and less interested in having another stranger enter his space. He only wanted Kelly. She brought out the best in everyone—April, Robert, Adriana, Maria—even him.

Perhaps subconsciously he'd wished Kelly could be the one to redecorate the apartment.

He strode from the living room toward his bedroom, hoping she'd come here to wait for him even as he realized she hadn't. He tried once more. "Kelly? You here?"

Nothing. Meaning she'd likely retired for the night. Well, she'd damned well better be ready to wake up. She shouldn't have walked away from him. Not until he'd had a chance to tell her why he had to ask the questions he did. Why he had to know if Robards was lying, or if they'd simply viewed the end of their relationship in different ways.

Had she really been confused about money? Had she mistakenly thought her business was in better financial straits and blamed

Robards for the loss? Had she made an error with the bank account meant to pay for the villa?

She wouldn't be the first person to be perplexed by the subtleties of business finances. On the other hand…Robards' words didn't pass Massimo's sniff test, and not only the part about Kelly plotting to meet the CEO. The more Massimo thought about it, the more he couldn't imagine Kelly signing papers and not understanding them. She'd analyzed every aspect of his closet, cataloguing his belongings, organizing the labor, placing dozens of orders for materials, and even coordinating with Robert. He'd seen her lists. They were even more detailed than his mother's. And she'd arranged it all on short notice.

He also couldn't imagine Kelly dumping a fiancé over a mistake *she* made.

And as similar as his first meeting with Kelly was to Ted's first meeting with her—by chance, over a lost item—he couldn't in a million years envision her being so conniving as to target a wealthy man. If she'd really known Massimo's identity when they'd met on the beach, she'd have to be the actress of the century.

He didn't buy it, even if Robards was as well known for his philanthropic pursuits as for his business acumen.

But he wanted to hear Kelly's side of the story. He wanted no more secrets between them. *Nothing* between them. And frankly, she should want that, too.

He glanced into his bedroom. As with the living room, the lights were left dimmed, but the room was empty, save for Gaspare, who'd curled into a corner beside the bed. The dog's watchful eyes closed when he saw his master. Massimo told him he was a good dog before turning to head for the long gallery to knock on Kelly's door, but his mind's eye saw the closed sliding door inside his bedroom.

He paused. Retraced his steps. Entered the bedroom. Slowly, he pushed the sliding door open and reached for the switch.

CHAPTER 28

IN HIS TWENTY-EIGHT YEARS, Massimo had the great fortune to see hundreds of custom-designed rooms. Some he'd hated, particularly when he was still in grade school and his parents dragged him to fancy events at the homes of other European aristocrats, where he'd been expected to smile and act as if he were entranced by their new dining rooms or libraries. Others he'd loved. When he'd spent time in Paris, in particular, and found himself fascinated by the Musée de l'Orangerie, which boasted large oval rooms designed specifically to house Monet's famous water lilies.

In all that time, no room affected him quite like his new closet. In just under two weeks, Kelly had created a work of art uniquely suited to his needs and personality.

Beneath his feet, a stunning natural wool rug in shades of beiges, browns, and ivory invited one to walk barefoot while overhead, a chandelier with modern lines and a hint of crystal cast the room in clear white light. The high window was left unadorned to let in the maximum amount of natural light during the day. Below it, twin lamps topped the antique bureau. The walls, too, were painted a glossy white in order to maximize the amount of light and create a sense of spaciousness. A full-length mirror filled a three-foot wide space on one wall, its position selected, he was sure, to make the room seem larger while providing him with an easy place to make a last minute check of his clothing before heading out to his engagements. In the center of the closet, two modestly-sized square ottomans in a masculine brown leather offered a place to sit so he could put on his shoes and socks without having to bend. He ran a hand over the top of one, testing it. Firm to the touch, it was sturdy enough to hold his weight, yet soft enough to be comfortable.

Despite the addition of the ottomans, the room felt double the size it had previously. It also contained far more storage than before. Clean-lined wood shelves, stained to a deep shade of coffee, covered the walls on either side of the mirror. Cut to the perfect depth to store his sweaters at eye level and his shoes below, they were backed in the same glossy white as the walls in order to make it easier to see the items he sought and add to the airiness of the room. On the opposite wall, sleek rods in polished nickel offered a variety of options for hanging suits, shirts, and slacks. In each section, clothing was organized by color from light to dark, making selections simple. As Kelly had proposed in their first discussion about the design, every rod was adjustable, giving him a variety of options for storage as his wardrobe changed.

Below each hang rod, space had been left to store luggage for quick accessibility, while above each hang rod, a shelf had been installed to hold photographs. A large, goofy, framed photo of Gaspare splashing in the garden fountain occupied the center section. On the shelves to the side were photos of his parents, siblings, and both sets of grandparents. He took each down, admired them, then replaced them. The photos of his family were some of his all-time favorites, casual shots that had never made their way into newspapers or magazines, that'd been stashed in the old dresser drawer. The shot of Gaspare, on the other hand, was one he'd never seen. Kelly must've taken the dog outside and allowed him to jump in the water, then snapped a picture. The sheer joy on the dog's face was beyond compare, an expression Massimo suspected only play time in the water—and perhaps a recent butt scratch—could accomplish.

The attention to detail left him flabbergasted. He moved to the bureau, noting the discreet music player set between the lamps. The rest of the bureau top was left empty, and when he opened the top drawer, he realized why. Organized on velvet-lined trays were his watches, cufflinks, and collar stays. A battered pocket watch he'd inherited from his great-grandfather lay in the center in a place of honor.

He'd marked it as an item to keep, but how had she known its sentimental value?

Carefully, he slid the drawer closed and examined the other drawers. Socks, undershirts, athletic wear, T-shirts, and shorts were perfectly folded and sorted by color.

He kicked off his shoes and instantly felt the softness of the wool rug beneath his feet. The thing was positively plush. He turned slowly, noting the shining hardwood exposed at the area rug's edges, then took in the view of the closet looking toward the door. It was then that he noticed something he hadn't seen upon entering. His breath stilled as he studied the elegant display boxes discreetly mounted on either side of the sliding door. Meant to be seen only by the closet's owner, they contained his military medals, which he'd tossed into the bottom of one of the closet boxes after he'd returned home.

He hadn't mentioned them on the inventory list. But she'd understood their value to him.

Massimo allowed his eyes to drift closed. After only a short time with him, Kelly knew him better than he knew himself. She'd asked the right questions to determine what mattered most to him and incorporated it all into the final design. The room was light, bright, modern, and masculine. It contained everything dear to his heart, yet was so functional he could locate any item he wanted in seconds.

She'd put her heart and soul into it. It wasn't about payment for a job. It wasn't about building her portfolio. It was about *him*.

Since he'd told her about his injury, he'd worried about trusting her. Turned out, she was the one who should've been worried about trusting him.

"I am such an ass," he said aloud. How had he even thought to question her?

"No kidding." The voice coming from the door startled him, but Kelly barreled on, "I thought you were going to wait for me to wow you with a grand presentation. Now you've ruined everything."

It was a fine bit of bravado. She hoped he couldn't see through it.

"I didn't mean to surprise you, but I wanted to snap a few photos before anything got moved. I also wanted to leave you this" —she held up the notebook that was in her left hand— "which contains all the budget details. I told you the budget you gave me was more than enough, and I was right. There's a great deal of money left over."

He blinked. "You kept a budget?"

"Of course. I do for every job." Did his other employees not keep track of expenditures? Or was he surprised she felt the need, given the sum? "There's also a copy of the materials list, should you ever need to repair or replace the knobs, hang rods, belt rack, you name it."

"I should've known." He met her gaze, then frowned in curiosity. "Wait, did you say belt rack?"

She strode to the end of the closet, to the set of shelves beyond the mirror, and pulled out the sliding belt rack on the side hidden from the door. "They're sorted by color."

"I see that."

She crossed to the opposite side of the closet and showed him the second set of hidden racks. "And this is where you'll find your ties. Since you have so many, it's automated. The button up here spins the rack. They should be easier to locate now, since they're—"

"Sorted by color."

"Yes."

"Kelly, I've been an ass."

She forced a smile to her face and waved him off. She needed to get this over with, then get out. "When I said you ruined everything, I was kidding. You could've explored all this on your own. You didn't really need me for a tour."

"That's not what I meant." He closed the space between them and reached for her. Protective hands ran over her upper arms, then he raised her chin, compelling her to see the seriousness in his gaze. "I shouldn't have questioned you about what happened with Robards. It was wrong of me, and I apologize."

"It's not a big deal," she protested. Did he really need to hold her like this?

"I consider it a very big deal. For a brief time tonight, I wasn't sure I could trust you. I let Robards get into my head. And for that, I apologize. I never should've doubted you, even for a second."

No, you shouldn't have. Gently, she pulled back from his touch. "I appreciate that."

"He spun a rather compelling tale—one I know is not true—and I made that my excuse."

She considered showing him the luggage so she could finish the tour and leave, but that last word stopped her. "I don't understand. Excuse for what?"

Massimo huffed out a breath before taking a seat on one of the leather ottomans in the center of the closet.

"It was an excuse not to face my biggest fear...which has nothing to do with crowds or fire." He stretched to grab her free hand, wrapping his fingers around hers and squeezing. "Kelly, I realized tonight that my biggest fear is the possibility I could lose you. I've never seen you look as disappointed as you did when I walked out of that stairway with Robards behind me. The expression on your face terrified me. So I questioned whether you're the person he claimed you to be. But deep down, in here" —he tapped his chest— "I already knew. I've known who you are from the moment we shared that dessert at Giulia's and you waxed poetic about the sunset. I probably knew from the moment I saw Gaspare sharing your chair on the beach. You're honest. You're pure of spirit. And even if you didn't tell me you were on your honeymoon, you never lied about who you are. I never, even for a second, should have questioned that."

The enormity of his words brought her close to tears. "So why'd you do it?"

"I realized at that moment that I could lose you forever." His words were slow, filled with raw emotion. "I think I did it because if I could convince myself *not* to trust you, it'd make it easier to watch you go home without having my heart broken."

His heart *broken*? Emotion clogged her throat at the idea. "So, um, you're saying that tonight really was a date?"

"Hell, yes, it was a date!"

"Even though I'm working for you?"

"*Were* working for me." He swung his arm wide, the gesture encompassing the closet. "It was a fabulous way to keep you around, wasn't it? And it made my mother happy at the same time. But I don't want you working for me anymore. And I don't want you to go back to Dallas. Or at least, if you go back, I want it to be temporary. I want you here all the time. By my side. As my friend, as my partner, as my lover."

Hearing this large, powerful, sexy man—this man who'd been through so much—say those words left her stunned.

"Wow." It was the only response she could manage.

"I'm the one who's wowed." He squeezed her hand again as he looked up at her, his olive green eyes searching hers. "I'm sorry I let Robards throw me. If you could find it in your heart to forgive me, I'd like to take you back to the ball for a proper dance. You deserve to be wined and dined. In front of all those people."

"You've got to be kidding." Laughter broke through the tears that threatened to spill down her cheeks. "Haven't you noticed what I'm wearing?"

"Where's the rule that says Cinderella needs a gown? She can be in...wait, are those your pajamas?" For the first time, he seemed to realize she'd come to his room without expecting anyone to see her.

"They are." She'd packed plain gray pajama pants and a matching top when she'd decided to take her honeymoon solo. She certainly hadn't planned on a honeymoon with a prince.

"So I see." He also finally took note of what she held in her left hand with the design book. "But you seem to have a necklace suitable for a palace ball."

She held out the box. "Conti & Fancetti dropped this by earlier. I was planning to leave it here after I took pictures."

"With the necklace inside?"

"What, you don't trust me?" she teased. "I left the gown and shoes in your bedroom. I swear."

She set the design notebook and the jeweler's box on a nearby shelf, but left the necklace inside the box. Later, she'd suggest he return it to his parents. Or perhaps give it to Sophia for safekeeping. Kelly had an idea the dark-haired beauty would find plenty of occasions to wear such a necklace.

He stood, encircling her waist with one arm, and reached for the top of the bureau. "We'll dance here, then. Given how thorough you were with the rest of the details in your design, I assume you've preloaded this player with music?"

"Oh, about that—"

A wide grin brought out his elusive dimple as he pulled up the lone playlist. "Boat Songs?"

"I've learned a lot about you the last couple of weeks, but other than hearing you hum *I Saw Three Ships*, I know nothing about your taste in music."

He punched the button, then laughed aloud as the first strains of *Banana Boat* floated through the room. He spun her away from the bureau, his feet light on the floor as he eased her into a slow, sultry dance. "This isn't quite what I envisioned," he said, "but it'll do."

"I told you, I'd rather be with a laid-back, fishing boat kind of guy than the yachting type."

"It doesn't get more laid-back than *Banana Boat*. But I can't change the fact I own a yacht, even if I'm not on it very often."

"Three yachts," she corrected.

"All right. Three." His fingers spread across her back as Harry Belafonte's lively voice filled the room. Being in his arms, under the chandelier...even in her pajamas, it was a fantasy come to life.

She sighed. "Regarding that fairy tale princess fantasy you asked me about at the villa—"

"You don't have to explain."

"I do. The thing is, it doesn't have to do with money or position. Or yachts. It has to do with the man." And Ted was *so* not the right man. "On paper, Ted's a great catch for any woman. But once we got engaged, he urged me to sell my business and spend my time pursuing philanthropical activities. He was after me all the time—politely, but persistently—and insinuated that if I didn't sell, perhaps I wasn't truly committed to our relationship."

"I can't fault the man for wanting to spend more time with you." Massimo's arms tightened around her. His lips glided over her hair, tempting her to kiss him. But she couldn't, not yet.

"If that was all it was…but it wasn't. By coincidence, I received a buyout offer from my biggest competitor. He'd approached me once before, but I didn't want to sell. I accepted then because I thought I was making the right decision for us as a couple. Ted was thrilled."

Massimo continued to sway to the music, turning her in slow circles, giving her the time to speak.

"There was a lot of paperwork involved and a lot of legal back and forth. But when it was done, it was done. I knew I would miss it, but I thought it was the right sacrifice to make. After the sale was finalized, I discovered that my competitor—the man who bought the business— was a close childhood friend of Ted's. Ted introduced himself to me at a Dallas restaurant after overhearing a business conversation and figuring out my identity. He knew his friend had tried to buy me out."

"Robards was working both sides of the deal." The words were said gently.

She nodded. "When I confronted him, he claimed that he'd fallen in love with me, and that in pressuring me to sell he was doing what was best for everyone involved. But it didn't matter. He'd lied. Or kept the truth from me…however you want to define it. Not only that, I realized then I'd never be sure if he loved me for *me*. So much of what went into that business is who I am. Can you imagine what that's like?"

"I might have a clue." He dropped a soft kiss on her temple. "Try living a life where everyone you meet knows your life history before you've even been introduced. They know your parents, your grandparents. They've heard all the good and bad. What they don't know, they can find online in minutes. They know if they marry you, that they gain a title, access, and wealth."

She leaned back and studied his face. It hadn't occurred to her that being a royal might be a detriment to one's love life, especially for a man as wonderful, as protective, and as dynamic as Massimo, who had so much to offer without regard to his family tree or financial resources.

"You know," he continued, "when I met you on the beach that afternoon, I was stunned that you had no idea who I was. You flirted, you were charming, and you didn't care about my title in the least because you didn't know I have one. That meeting was the first time anyone has acted that way with me without an ulterior motive."

"Oh, I don't know about that."

His brows knit.

"I wanted you for this." She placed a hand on his chest, then slid it lower, until it rested flat just above his slacks. The feel of the hard planes of his stomach under her palm nearly did her in, but she kept still, wanting to draw out the moment.

"My beer gut?"

"Ha. Your abs. They are truly glorious. If you recall, you were wearing a rather thin T-shirt when you approached me. It was hard to see the details of your face in the sunlight, but boy, did I notice how your shirt clung to your abs. And I was smitten."

"You wanted me—"

"For your body. I'll admit it." Massimo stilled as Harry Belafonte drew out his last line. "When we met, it took me only a few seconds to develop an ulterior motive where you were concerned. I decided right then and there that I wanted an adventure with a gorgeous man. Then we had that wonderful night at Giulia's. I realized how much I enjoyed being with you and I decided that if I got laid on my honeymoon, hey, good for me. Given all I'd been through to get myself to that beach, I decided I'd earned a night of phenomenal one-night-stand sex. Which is exactly what you accused me of when you hired me to revamp your closet and explained that our relationship wouldn't get in the way...because there was no relationship."

"Did you really believe that?"

"Until you, I'd never had first-date sex and would've put money on the fact I never would. Like I told you then, I'm not the one-night stand type."

"I never want you to have a one-night stand again. With anyone."

The first notes of The Honeydrippers' *Sea of Love* brought a seductive smile to Massimo's face she wanted to remember for the rest of her life. She couldn't help but beam in return. "Even though I only wanted you for your abs?"

"Even though. More so because once you got past my front and saw the back, you didn't flinch."

Slowly, deliberately, with her gaze locked on his, she slid hands under his tuxedo jacket, then shucked it onto the closet floor. Her fingers explored the ragged edge of his largest scar through his shirt as they continued to dance. "They do give you texture."

Amusement and desire lit his eyes. "You did *not* just say that."

"I did." Warmth rushed to her face. "They also give you texture as a human being. They've made you into who you are, for better or worse. And when you told me how you got them...well, I wanted you more that night than I did on the beach."

"I tried to kill you that night."

"You tried to kill an imaginary warlord, not me, and you stopped yourself. But seeing you that way made me want you all the more." At his look of doubt, she explained, "I knew from the look of horror on your face when you attacked me and the way you helped me clean up the wet laundry afterward that you have a beautiful heart. Despite your wealth and status, you don't consider yourself above others. You want to make yourself better. And you're honest."

Though he continued to sway in time to the romantic music, he spoke with a hitch in his voice. "Now I understand why you were angry that I didn't tell you about my title right off the bat. You felt you were revisiting the mistake you made with Ted."

"While I was sitting in jail, you bet. But I was dishonest with you, too."

"It's not the same, though. Neither of us was out to deceive the other. We'd both been burned…well, in my case, I really shouldn't use the word *burned*—"

"Oooh, that's as bad as texture."

"—and neither of us wanted a repeat. We were trying protect ourselves, not to hurt the other person." He reached for her face, cradling her head in both his hands. "But you've missed the biggest difference between me and Ted. I love you. I know with every fiber of my being that I always will."

Her throat constricted, leaving her unable to speak. As tears started to spill down her cheeks, he said, "I always thought my life would go according to a certain, preordained plan. But accidents happen. Plans change. Being injured in Africa was an accident. But I think it's led me to my passion." He spun her back toward the bureau. "I've decided I want to help veterans who've suffered accidental injuries. I think it's what I was meant to do, even if it wasn't what I planned."

Given the emotion she'd seen on his face during the Independence Day parade as the veterans marched past the review stand, it seemed the perfect fit. "I think so, too."

"Finding you was an accident, too. I think I was meant to marry you. No…I *know* I was meant to marry you." To her shock, he dropped to one knee in front of her. "Kelly, will you marry me? Trust me with your heart for the rest of your life?"

Through choked laughter, she said, "You just proposed to me in my pajamas. In a *closet*. After we've known each other for two weeks."

"Are those disqualifiers?"

She shook her head. "My friends and family thought I was rash, choosing to take my honeymoon alone. Turns out, I was meant to come here alone." Leaning forward, she touched her forehead to Massimo's and closed her eyes, much as they'd done in the moonlight the night they met. He was everything she ever could want and more. "Massimo, I was meant to find you."

"Then be rash again. Say you'll marry me. It doesn't have to be right away, but someday. I want us to be together."

"It's not rash if it's right. I'd love to marry you."

The kiss that followed was the sweetest, most passionate Kelly had ever experienced. As he pulled her to the soft rug, a low, deep sound startled them both.

Woof.

"Gaspare, go away," Massimo groaned.

"No, wait. The closet has one more surprise." Kelly reached for one of the ottomans, pushed a small button, then lifted the lid on its hidden compartment. "Feel inside."

Massimo did so, his frown turning to a look of wonder, then to a broad grin as he recognized the familiar shape and texture of the item inside. Turning, he threw the massive dog bone Kelly'd stashed there. Gaspare bounded after it in unabashed joy.

"Good dog," they said together, then Kelly laughed as Massimo closed the closet door.

Thank you for reading *Honeymoon With a Prince*. If you enjoyed this book, please consider leaving a review at your favorite bookseller or book club website.

Read on for an excerpt of the next Royal Scandals novel, *Slow Tango With a Prince*.

SLOW TANGO WITH A PRINCE

Prologue

TODAY'S ROYALS: THE LATEST
  By V. Dempsey, December 1

SARCACCIA'S ROYALS COME CLEAN
  Barrali Family Hosts Press, Addresses Recent Scandals

Cateri, SARCACCIA - In a first-of-its-kind event for the Barrali royal family, *Today's Royals* and other select media representatives were invited to what was termed an "informal press reception" in the palace's famed green parlor. While being served traditional Sarcaccian appetizers and wine from the Famiglia Barrali vineyards, the reporters were told they'd be given a half hour to ask questions about both matters of state and the rampant rumors that have plagued the monarch and his family over the past few months. As expected, when the family entered the parlor, media attention zeroed in on the flurry of reports regarding the family's romantic relationships and the apparent disappearance of Prince Alessandro, who is second in line to the throne after his twin brother, Prince Vittorio.

To the surprise of those gathered, it was Prince Stefano rather than King Carlo who raised his hand to quiet the room, declaring that he had an announcement to make before the family answered any questions.

He asked his rumored fiancée, Megan Hallberg, to join him in the center of the parlor before stating that the two are indeed planning to marry. Amid congratulations from those assembled, the prince explained that he proposed on a beach near Cateri in late July, but that the couple wished to have time for Ms. Hallberg to begin her new position managing Sarcaccia's conference center and to become better acquainted with the royal family before making a formal engagement announcement. Though the news was not a surprise, given that Ms. Hallberg has been attending family functions and appeared with the Barrali family at Independence Day festivities in September, the prince then stunned the crowd to silence by further announcing that Ms. Hallberg's ten-year-old daughter, Anna, is his biological child.

"Megan and I met in our early twenties, during my time working in Venezuela," the prince explained. "While I'm sure you have a number of questions about our relationship and what I knew of Anna's existence, what Megan and I believe is most important is that we found each other after many years of separation. We are very much in love and excited to be a family. On that note, our daughter is a wonderful girl, very bright and well-adjusted. She has lived out of the spotlight for her entire life. As her parents, we wish for it to remain that way. Therefore, we kindly ask all of you to give her space to enjoy her childhood." The prince went on to explain that he'd purchased his waterfront apartment and moved out of the royal palace in July in order to provide Anna as normal an upbringing as possible, not due to a rift with his parents as has been rumored.

Ms. Hallberg then showed off her diamond and sapphire engagement ring at a reporter's request. While the sapphire has been in Queen Fabrizia's family for over a hundred years, Prince Stefano designed its diamond setting with the assistance of longtime royal jewelers Conti & Fancetti.

A wedding date has not yet been set, but the couple say they will wed in Cateri's cathedral and are considering dates during which Anna will be out of school.

Following Prince Stefano's announcement, King Carlo reminded those present of Sarcaccia's strict laws concerning paparazzi coverage of minors, then took a question about the recent five-day trip he and Prince Vittorio took to the Middle East, where the king was involved in peace negotiations and the crown prince visited several schools funded by the Barrali Trust. However, the line of questioning quickly turned to Prince Vittorio's twin, Alessandro, who hasn't been seen in public since the early October funeral of Prince Vittorio's former girlfriend, Spanish actress Carmella Rivas, and was rarely seen during the two-week period preceding it.

Prince Vittorio told the media that there is nothing suspicious about his twin's absence. However, he admitted, "At the moment we're unaware of his location, though this isn't unusual. As you've reported on many occasions, Alessandro is an adventurer at heart and often travels to areas where communication is limited." When pressed, Vittorio did acknowledge that Alessandro has never been away for such an extended period. Asked point-blank if Alessandro was missing, the crown prince laughed and responded, "No. As I said, we are simply unaware of his exact location. If there is any cause for concern, we will of course discuss that with the Royal Police. However, I must reiterate that this is simply not the case."

A follow-up question noted unsubstantiated reports that Prince Alessandro was photographed in Croatia, but Vittorio stated that the family had no such information.

The crown prince then accepted a question about his former girlfriend and took the opportunity to once again extend his sympathies to the Rivas family on Carmella Rivas's tragic suicide. "It came as a horrible shock to us all and I hurt for her family. Unfortunately, there is no explaining it. We may never know what drove her to that place," he said. "However, it is my hope that the Carmella Rivas Memorial Fund will help others who are contemplating suicide by offering them free professional counseling. No family should be torn apart by the loss of a loved one this way."

The event ended on an upbeat note when Prince Massimo was asked about his relationship with Kelly Chase, the American he employed as a closet designer in September, but who has not yet left the country...and whether Sarcaccia should prepare for a second royal wedding.

The question drew a burst of laughter from the entire Barrali family and a comment from Queen Fabrizia that, "One royal wedding is plenty to plan. Imagine the hours all of you in the media would have to work if there were a second. Impossible!"

Queen Fabrizia slid the emeralds from her ears and deposited them on a glass end table in the private palace apartment she and King Carlo shared. She hadn't wanted to wear them to the press event, as heavy earrings tended to exacerbate her headaches, but they photographed well and brought out the green in her eyes.

All the better to counteract the red.

Fabrizia prided herself on her steel spine and her ability to keep her large, powerful family together, but recent events tested her resiliency. Learning over the summer that she had a ten-year-old granddaughter—one who was her spitting image—and hearing Stefano declare he intended to break tradition and live outside the royal palace broke her heart.

Worse, though, was having to endure these weeks following Carmella Rivas's funeral. Carmella's deception and her subsequent suicide wreaked havoc within the family. It had taken every bit of Fabrizia's resourcefulness to keep the Barralis on an even keel, at least to the public eye. But if she continued to let it keep her awake at night, a sharp photographer would soon notice the evidence and the tabloids would pounce like buzzards on carrion.

"I certainly hope we never have to do that again. I abhor discussing personal affairs in a public forum," King Carlo said as he sank onto the sofa beside Fabrizia and put a comforting hand on her knee. Across from them, Megan and Stefano occupied a matching sofa while Massimo and his still-secret fiancée, Kelly, adjourned to the kitchen so Massimo could update Kelly on the afternoon's events.

Sprawled in a chair to the side, Alessandro held up his left hand, as if weighing an invisible object. "Hmmm...Mideast peace, or" —he raised his other hand, palm up— "rumors about the love lives of the royal family. Which did you think they'd want to address? I thought that was the point, anyway."

"Sit up," the queen hissed. "What if someone were to walk in?"

Physically, the twins were indistinguishable aside from the tiny white scar beneath Alessandro's left eye—now carefully concealed with makeup—and the location of their ears, with Vittorio's slightly higher and further back than his twin's. Even family members confused them from time to time. But once they opened their mouths, the differences were clear. Though the timbre of their voices was remarkably similar, Alessandro's relaxed, devil-may-care attitude and Vittorio's perpetually formal one gave away their identities as surely as if they'd been born with different hair or eye colors. While all the world thought it was Alessandro, rather than Vittorio, who'd disappeared, Alessandro needed to keep that fact in mind.

"No one will come in, Mother," Alessandro replied, though he straightened in his chair to mimic the carriage of his absent twin. "Umberto knows to keep the staff away for the rest of the evening. Besides, the press conference went exactly as planned. No one thought for a moment that I was anyone other than who I claimed. They were far more interested in Stefano's big news than in yet another Alessandro-has-taken-off story."

"I certainly hope so." Fabrizia sent an apologetic look across the coffee table to Stefano and Megan. "Thank you for being the sacrificial lambs. I know you were planning to make an announcement soon, but not in that manner."

"If it takes their attention off my delinquent brother" —Stefano flashed a look at Alessandro— "then it's worthwhile. Megan and I couldn't keep quiet much longer, anyway. The staff have been suspicious about an engagement for months. Besides—" an embarrassed smile lit his face— "Anna's started calling me Dad when we're at home. It'd only take one person to overhear her for that particular cat to be out of the bag."

"Oh, Stefano, I'm so glad." Tears pricked Fabrizia's eyes, though she blinked them back. How long had she wanted to be a grandmother? To see the joy Stefano took in Megan and Anna now that they were becoming a real family, one built on love and trust...it was everything she desired for her children. Yet, due to the public nature of their lives, such happiness was as often as elusive as a butterfly in winter.

Megan shifted closer to Stefano at the same time he reached for her hand. "It's been a long haul, but Anna's transitioning well. She adores Stefano. You'd never know he hasn't been with her from birth."

Stefano and Megan made a handsome pair, Fabrizia decided. If only she could convince them to move back to the palace, the situation would be perfect. At the moment, however, pressuring the couple held a low spot on her priority list, given what was happening with Vittorio. And perhaps Stefano was right: the paparazzi were less likely to sneak photographs of Anna if she lived in a private home than if she stayed at the palace, which served as both a residence and government office.

"Let me know if the media becomes a problem now that they know Anna is your daughter," King Carlo told the couple, his thoughts apparently mirroring Fabrizia's. "I'll personally ensure that anyone who breaks the law is prosecuted."

After Megan thanked the king, Alessandro asked, "So what's next? Has anyone heard from Vittorio?"

"Not since he arrived in Argentina two weeks ago and called you," the queen said. Why Vittorio picked Buenos Aires as his escape, she couldn't fathom, but at least he was safe there for the time being. He could battle his demons far from the spotlight of Sarcaccia.

Sophia, the king and queen's only daughter, emerged from the kitchen in time to overhear Alessandro's question. "So what were the reporters saying about Croatia? I looked online and saw a photo of a man boarding a luxury yacht near Dubrovnik. It was taken from a distance, but it looked a lot like Vittorio to me."

"He's in Argentina," Alessandro assured her. "He gave me the name he's using at his current hotel in case of an emergency."

"Did you check to see if he was telling you the truth?" Sophia's forehead creased into a frown. "The way the man in the photo tilted his head to the side was just like—"

"Vittorio is not in Croatia." King Carlo's tone was meant to close discussion.

At the same time, Alessandro replied, "Of course I checked."

"Let's forget Croatia," Fabrizia said, rising from the sofa and smoothing the front of her dress. "The press is focused on Stefano and Megan for now. And Alessandro, you did a wonderful job both at the press conference and in the Middle East. I have every confidence Vittorio will return shortly, then we can all get back to business as usual with no one the wiser."

Then *she* could forget Croatia.

Chapter One

Three Months Later

Nearly fifty people depended on Emily Sinclair for their livelihood. Given that pressure, she needed to focus on the shooting schedule and pages of red-inked notes spread across the breakfast table in front of her rather than allow her mind to wander. But the contrast between the serene scene surrounding her and the intense pressure of her job made concentration difficult.

Across the narrow street, in the outdoor seating area of a restaurant similar to the one in which she worked, a dark-haired man in crisp jeans and a white Oxford-cloth shirt sat alone, his face hidden behind the pages of the *Buenos Aires Herald*, a steaming espresso on the table in front of him. The smell of freshly ground coffee beans and warm pastry drifted through the air, mixing with the exhaust fumes of an early-morning city bus as it made its way up Avenue Quintana, which bordered the other side of the restaurant. A mother knelt to zip her son's backpack, then wave him off from his corner bus stop before picking up her own briefcase and heading in the opposite direction. Kiosk owners set out stacks of magazines, shop owners unlocked doors, and a lone black and yellow taxi idled at the corner, the yawning driver awaiting his next fare.

The residents of Buenos Aires' trendy Recoleta neighborhood were ready to start another workweek while Emily feared it could be her last. However, if there was any hope of *At Home Abroad* being renewed for a fourth season, it rested with her as the television show's host and executive producer. Because the program melded house-hunting with travel information and it focused on a different country each season, a bevy of local researchers, travel specialists, and real estate consultants drew a portion of their income from *At Home Abroad*. That was in addition to the usual salaried camera crew, film editors, and sound and lighting experts. She couldn't bear to let them down. The season finale had to be extraordinary and she had only a week left before the wrap deadline.

She stifled a sigh, forcing her attention back to the proposed shooting schedule. Somehow, some way, she had to make this work.

"You don't want to stop staring at him, either?" the show's director and co-executive producer, Rita Bragna, asked while she haphazardly spread fresh marmalade on her morning croissant, her eyes locked on the table across the street. She waved her knife in the man's direction. "I've seen plenty of hot guys since we arrived in Buenos Aires, but he wins the prize. Too bad we picked this place for breakfast instead of Café Luchana."

"Huh? Him?" Emily flicked her gaze toward the man, whose face remained hidden behind his newspaper, then turned back to Rita. Rita had been happily married for nearly twenty-five years, but she liked to look. Even more, she liked to point out good-looking men to Emily in the hope Emily would find the same happiness. But as Emily told Rita time and again, the lifestyle of a television host made it impossible, and she'd fought too long and too hard for her job to quit. She'd learned the hard way that it wasn't worth it to risk her career in order to pursue a relationship. Especially when her health history made a solid relationship a long shot at best.

"Yes, *him*. Didn't you notice when he lowered the paper to turn the page? I'd swear you were staring. The man is gorgeous."

Emily shook her head. "I wasn't staring at him so much as staring into space. I've been wracking my brain, trying to come up with a better hook for our final episode. What we have planned isn't going to generate the buzz we need to guarantee our renewal."

"Hate to say it, but I agree." Rita shrugged, giving up her match-making scheme for the moment. "The Winstons are a nice couple, but boring. We should've arranged for someone with his looks and an outrageous bank account as our finale's house-hunting ex-pat. Problem is, anyone who looks that good can't possibly have a budget to match. It'd go against the laws of nature."

"I'd settle for the budget alone." Unfortunately, every lead their network of real estate agents offered was for buyers seeking midrange properties. Leave it to Emily to select Argentina for season three just as the housing market took off and most foreigners moving to Buenos Aires were unable to afford anything luxe. Featuring midrange properties yet again in the finale would be a Yawn, with a capital Y.

Rita indicated the calendar on their breakfast table. "Whatever we decide, this schedule has to be finalized by tonight. We have the camera crew at six a.m. Unless your real estate contacts come through today with a spectacular apartment that's going cheap, we should try to make the most of our other material."

In other words, cut the finale's real estate footage to its bare minimum and pad the show with the most interesting travel information they could muster. She bit back a sigh. "Are any of the places on the current schedule near tango? Perhaps we can work that angle. Show how deeply ingrained dance is in the local culture?"

"No way the Winstons are up to a tango, but maybe we can send them to a show." Rita tapped a few keys on her phone to pull up a map of the area. "Two of the three apartments on the current schedule are within a mile of tango bars. I'll make a few calls, see if we can get tickets for the Winstons, then get inside to film."

Emily scratched a few notes on paper, then said, "I was also hoping we could get some nighttime outdoor shots. Show the architecture of the buildings when they're lit, capture the music echoing up and down the streets in the evening outside the bars in San Telmo. Maybe show the way residents hold hands and smile while they watch the street buskers. If we can't show sexy real estate—or clients—we can certainly show some sexy street scenes."

"Street scenes. Atmosphere. Sexy. I'm on it." Rita waggled her eyebrows. "But it'd be so much better if I could get you to tango on camera with someone like him."

"You're hopeless," Emily said on a laugh as she reached for her coffee. She glanced across the street, then did a double take. The *Herald* now rested on the man's table, neatly folded beside a plate filled to toppling with French bread and an assortment of jam, leaving his face and upper body fully visible as he wrote on the page.

What a face and body they were. The man looked as if he should be gazing out from a billboard, wearing a custom-tailored suit in an advertisement for a sumptuous cologne or extravagant brand of Scotch, rather than sitting in an Argentine coffee shop in a white shirt and jeans. She was surprised to see he had a beard, but it did little to hide his sculpted cheekbones or the olive skin that set off his light-colored eyes to perfection. From this distance, she wasn't sure of their exact color, but the contrast with his jet-black hair and eyebrows was unexpected and sexy. Yet there was something oddly flawed about his face that made Emily want to study him from a closer vantage point, to determine just what it was that seemed out of place.

Perhaps it was the pen he held in his hand. A man who did the crossword over breakfast inevitably had brains, a trait Emily found even more appealing than his looks. Hell, a man who read an actual newspaper rather than spend his morning meal tethered to his electronic devices did it for her. Not that any man should be doing it for her when she had a season finale to produce.

"See what I mean?" Rita sighed. "Tell me you wouldn't want a guy who fills out a shirt the way he does to sweep you into his arms for a slow tango."

The mental image warmed Emily's cheeks. He was the embodiment of the word sultry. No doubt when he danced with a woman, he made her feel as if she were the only female in the world he'd ever held so close or gazed at with such intensity. And what woman wouldn't want to feel that way?

His hand moved across the newspaper page, making quick circles with his pen. As Emily watched the smooth movement, she drew in a quick breath.

"What?" Rita asked, instantly on alert.

"He's *exactly* the man I want. I'm going over there."

Emily set down her coffee, pushed back from the table, and strode across the street, leaving Rita in stunned silence.

ROYAL SCANDALS

Christmas With a Prince (prequel novella)

Scandal With a Prince

Honeymoon With a Prince

Christmas on the Royal Yacht (novella)

Slow Tango With a Prince

The Royal Bastard

Christmas With a Palace Thief (novella)

The Wicked Prince

One Man's Princess

ROYAL SCANDALS: SAN RIMINI

Fit for a Queen

Going to the Castle

The Prince's Tutor

The Knight's Kiss

Falling for Prince Federico

To Kiss a King

BOWEN, NEBRASKA

The Bowen Bride

A ROYAL SCANDALS WEDDING

More Royal Scandals titles will be available soon. For updates, please visit nicoleburnham.com, where you can subscribe to Nicole's Newsletter.

Subscribers receive exclusive content, including the short story *A Royal Scandals Wedding*, an inside look at the wedding of Megan Hallberg and Prince Stefano Barrali from the novel Scandal With a Prince.

ABOUT THE AUTHOR

Nicole Burnham is the RITA award-winning author of over twenty novels, including the popular Royal Scandals series.

For more information or to join Nicole's newsletter for reader exclusives, visit nicoleburnham.com.

facebook.com/NicoleBurnhamBooks
twitter.com/NicoleBurnham
instagram.com/nicole.burnham